Praise for *Smoke*

'Astonishing . . . It's filling in that gaping hole left by both **Harry Potter** and **Philip Pullman's** *Northern Lights*'

Francesca Brown, *Stylist*

'**Mesmerising and imaginative** . . . Smoke is an evocative and effective metaphor: it is "like a drug, injected into your blood" and "its smell is in your nose. There is no more hateful smell in the world than the smell of Smoke". Vyleta skilfully exploits its visceral potential: the reader sees, feels, smells and tastes Smoke. And there is a cinematic quality to Vyleta's writing: this is **a novel crying out for a screen adaptation**. *Smoke* is at once **profound, moving and timely**: a novel that tackles the most fundamental question of good versus evil'

Hannah Beckerman, *Observer*

'Potter-esque historical fantasy set in a parallel Victorian society where every sin – from wicked thoughts to actual crimes – shows itself on your body. **Original and enthralling**'   *Good Housekeeping*

'**JK Rowling meets Charles Dickens** in this Victorian era-set story of two schoolboys living in a strongly hierarchical world where individual sin manifests itself in the form of visible black smoke'   *Metro*

'A great work of imagination'   Cathy Rentzenbrink, *Stylist*

'Like an adult version of the **Harry Potter** books with a touch of **Dickensian dystopia** . . . a sheer delight'

Maxim Jakubowski, *Lovereading*

'Dan Vyleta has conjured a rich and surprising counter-history, an England saturated with a substance so potent and evocative it vaults instantly into the pantheon that includes the Dust of Philip Pullman, the soma of Aldous Huxley, and the opium of Amitavh Ghosh. *Smoke* is enthralling'

Robin Sloan, author of *Mr Penumbra's 24-Hour Bookstore*

'An intriguing fantasy set in an alternate 19th-century Britain . . . *Smoke* is being marketed as a commercially canny hybrid of Harry Potter and Philip Pullman's *Northern Lights*, and for once both comparisons are apt . . . This is **a novel that stays in the imagination long after it is read**'   Adam Roberts, *Guardian*

'Potter-esque comparisons will be made (with some Dickensian England thrown in) of the richness and intricacy of Vyleta's world'   Susan Riley, *Stylist*

'Comparisons to Philip Pullman are justified, with a complex and rich alternate history combined with challenging philosophical concepts and a strong sense of place, and there's definitely a bit of China Miéville in there too . . . **A vivid, imaginative and gripping thriller**'   Jonathan Hatfull, *SciFiNow*

'It's detailed, multi-layered and feels authentic – and might just win over historical fiction fans too'   *The Pool*

'Vice is made visual in Vyleta's sprawling, ambitious novel, **a Dickensian tale tinged with fantasy** . . . lovely, visceral prose and expert pacing'   *Entertainment Weekly*

'Its subtle touches mean the story takes on a world of its own . . . you'll wonder why no one has seen smoke this way before'   *Emerald Street*

'A supernatural take on a Victorian novel . . . **Vyleta writes with intricacy and imagination** and skilful pacing; never once would I have considered putting his book down . . . In the manner of both a Dickens novel and the best young adult adventure stories (the Harry Potter series among them), the children run away together to uncover the dark secrets of the grown-up world . . . **his ending is a real firecracker**'   *New York Times*

Dan Vyleta is the son of Czech refugees who emigrated to Germany in the late 1960s. After growing up in Germany, he left to attend university in the UK where he completed a PhD in History at King's College, Cambridge. His debut novel, *Pavel & I*, gathered immediate international acclaim and was translated into eight languages. His second novel, *The Quiet Twin*, was shortlisted for the Rogers Writers' Trust Fiction Prize, and his third, *The Crooked Maid*, was a finalist for the Scotiabank Giller Prize and won the J.I Segal Award. When not reading or writing novels, Dan Vyleta watches cop shows, or listens to CDs from his embarrassingly large collection of jazz albums. He lives in Stratford-upon-Avon.

Smoke

DAN VYLETA

WEIDENFELD & NICOLSON

A W&N PAPERBACK

First published in Great Britain in 2016
by Weidenfeld & Nicolson
This paperback edition first published in 2017
by Weidenfeld & Nicolson
An imprint of the Orion Publishing Group Ltd
Carmelite House, 50 Victoria Embankment
London EC4Y 0DZ

An Hachette UK Company

1 3 5 7 9 10 8 6 4 2

A CIP catalogue record for this book is
available from the British Library.

ISBN (Mass Market Paperback) 978 1 474 60095 8
ISBN (eBook) 978 0 297 60994 0

Typeset by Input Data Services Ltd, Somerset

Printed in Great Britain by Clays Ltd, St Ives plc

www.orionbooks.co.uk

For Chantal, my love. In lieu of flowers.
For Mom. You showed me courage.
For Hanna, who lost her Big Man. I mourn with you.

Contents

Part Four: Angel

Part Five: Above and Below

Part Six: Cloud

Part One

School

Those who study the physical sciences, and bring them to bear upon the health of Man, tell us that if the noxious particles that rise from vitiated air were palpable to the sight, we should see them lowering in a dense black cloud above such haunts, and rolling slowly on to corrupt the better portion of a town. But if the moral pestilence that rises with them . . . could be made discernible too, how terrible the revelation!

Charles Dickens, *Dombey and Son* (1848)

Examination

'Thomas, Thomas! Wake up!'

The first thing he does upon waking is to search his nightshirt, his bedding for soiling. He does so quickly, mechanically, still more than half asleep: runs a palm over his skin feeling for the telltale grit of Soot.

Only then does he wonder what time it is, and who it is that has woken him.

It is Charlie, of course. His face keeps changing in the light of the candle he is holding. One moment it is steady, carved into plains of white and shadow. Then it buckles: eyes, nose, lips go roaming, re-arrange themselves; and the light of the flame leaps into his reddish hair.

'Charlie? What time?'

'Late. Well, early. I heard a boy say it was two. Though the devil knows how he'd know.'

Charlie leans down to whisper. The candle swoops down with him, chasing shadows across the bed.

'It's Julius. He says everyone is to assemble. In the toilets. Now.'

There is movement all around the dormitory. Pale figures stretching, rising, whispering in groups. Haste wrestles with reluctance. There are only a handful of candles; moonlight on the snow outside the windows, their panes milky with its ghostly glow. Soon the boys move in procession, out the twin doors. Nobody wants to be first, or last: not Charlie, not Thomas, not even the handful of boys who hold special favour. Best to be lost in the crowd.

Φ

The bathroom tiles are cold under their feet. It's a large room flanked by sinks, square white porcelain sinks, their surfaces crisscrossed by a spider's web of fissures, too fine to be traced by your fingers and as though drawn with a fine pencil. Toilet stalls line the far end; beyond them, in a long, narrow annexe, hulks a row of bathtubs,

3

square and tiled with pale green tiles. The bathroom floor slopes, very slightly so, towards the middle. It's something you learn when you spill water there. It forms rivulets, heads for the low ground. At the lowest point, the room's centre, there is a drain, not large, scum-covered, its square metal grille half clogged with hair and lint.

This is where he has placed the chair. Julius. The boys of the lower school call him 'Caesar', pronouncing the *C* as a *K* like the Latin teacher taught them: *Key-sar*. It means emperor-designate. The one who will rule next. He alone is dressed in all the room: wears pressed trousers, his half boots polished to a shine. A waistcoat, but no jacket, to draw attention to the shirt: the sleeves so lily-white it startles the eye. When he moves his arms, the starched linen makes a sound, something between a rustle and a sort of clapping, depending on how quickly he moves. You can even *hear* how clean it is. And, by extension, he. No evil has touched him. Julius is the closest the school has to a saint.

He places both hands on the back of the chair and watches the ripple of fear spread through the boys. Thomas feels it, too. It's not a matter of courage, he thinks, but a physical force. Like feeling the wind on your face on a stormy day. You cannot opt out.

'We shall have a lottery,' says Julius, not loudly, dispensing with a greeting, and one of his cronies, eighteen and bulky in the shoulders, steps forward with pencil stubs, a stack of paper squares and a large gunny sack. The type you might use to carry potatoes in; to fashion a scarecrow's face. The kind you slip over someone's head when you lead them to their hanging. But that's just being fanciful, Thomas tells himself, as he accepts a piece of paper and a pencil, and marks down his name. Thomas Argyle. He omits his title. The papers go back in the sack.

Thomas does not know how Julius cheats, but cheat he must. Perhaps he has marked the papers somehow, or perhaps he simply pretends to read off the name he has picked out of the sack and sub-stitutes it for one of his choice. The only person to vouch for the proceedings is that same loyal crony who passed out the papers. Julius has turned up his shirt sleeve to rummage in the sack, as though he were digging for sin at the bottom of a murky pond. As though it were important not to get soiled.

The first name is a surprise. Collingwood. One of his own, a 'guardian', as they like to call themselves, a fellow prefect, who holds

4

the keys to the dorm and the trust of the teachers. For a moment his choice confuses Thomas. Then he understands. It demonstrates justice, brings home the fact that nobody is above the rules. That there is no one who has nothing to fear.

'Collingwood,' Julius calls a second time, just that, no first name. That's what they are to one another here. Your first name is for friends, to be used only in private. And for Julius, who is everybody's friend.

He has to call a third time before Collingwood moves. It's not that he's planning to resist. He simply cannot believe his ears, looks about himself for explanation. But the boys around him have long peeled away; avoid his eyes as though even his gaze carries some disease. So he steps out at last, hugging himself around the chest: a tall, gawky lad, his breath always sour from catarrh.

Seated on the chair, his nightshirt hikes up to about mid-thigh. He tries a smile. Julius returns it easily, not showing any teeth, then turns away and walks the length of the room, boys parting for him like the Red Sea. There, perching on one of the bathtubs like some cast-iron crow, is a heavy trainman's lantern, the hooded kind that shines only to one side. He opens it, lights a match, reaches inside to put its flame to the wick. A turn of a valve, the hiss of match meeting oil, and a focused beam of rich, yellow light shoots forth, rectangular, like a window to another world.

When Julius takes the handle and walks it across, the swing of the lamp catches bodies, tense little faces, pulling them out of the gloom and isolating them from their peers. Thomas, too, feels the beam of the lamp on him and shrinks before it; sees his shadow dart from out his boots as though looking for a place to hide. It comes to him that Julius had no need to deposit the lamp so far from the chair, that everything – his walk across to it, the act of lighting, the stately return – is part of a performance planned well in advance. As is his drawing himself up to his full height to hang the lamp from a metal hook that just happens to be hammered into the ceiling there, two steps from the chair. Julius leaves a hand on it, angles it, so that Collingwood sits in a parallelogram of light, its edges drawn as though with a ruler. The light nearly strips him, seems to flood through the cotton of his nightshirt: one can make out the dark of his nipples and the bent struts of his narrow rib cage. Collingwood's face is tense but calm. For a moment Thomas admires him, at whose hand he has so often been punished. It must take tremendous self-possession to bear the glare of that lamp. It is so bright, it seems to separate Collingwood's skin from his freckles: they hover a quarter inch above his cheeks.

'Shall we begin, then?'

It takes Collingwood a moment to collect his voice. He answers with the ritual phrase.

'Please, sir. Examine me.'

'You submit willingly?'

'I do. May my sins be revealed.'

'That they will and that they must. We thank the Smoke.'

'We thank the Smoke.'

And then, in chorus: 'We thank the Smoke.'

Even Thomas mouths it, that hateful little phrase. He only learned it upon coming to the school, not six weeks ago, but already it has found time to grow into him, taken a leasehold on his tongue. It may be it can only be excised with a knife.

The interrogation begins. Julius's voice rings clear in the large room. His is a pleasant voice, precise, rhythmic, sonorous. When he wants to, he can sound like your favourite uncle. Like your brother. Like a friend.

'You're a prefect, Collingwood,' he begins. It is like Julius to begin there. Somewhere harmless. It makes you lower your guard. 'How long has it been now since you earned the badge?'

'A year and a term, sir.'

'A year and a term. And you are pleased with the position?'

'I am pleased to serve.'

'You are pleased to serve. An excellent answer. You discharge your duties faithfully, I take it?'

'I endeavour to, sir.'

'And how do you think of those boys of whom you have been put in charge?'

'Think of them. Sir? With . . . with fondness. With affection.'

'Yes, very good. Though they are perfect little brutes sometimes, are they not?'

'I trust, sir, they are as good as they can be, sir.'

'One "sir" will do, Collingwood.'

Julius waits out the momentary titter that races through the room. His face, standing to the side of the lamp, is in darkness. All the

6

world is reduced to one boy, one chair. When Collingwood fidgets, his nightshirt rides up higher on his legs and he has to pull it down with his hands. He does so clumsily. His hands have formed fists he has difficulty unclenching.

'But you like to punish them, don't you, your little charges who are as good as they can be? Sometimes, you punish them quite severely, I believe. Just yesterday, many a boy here saw you administer a caning. Twenty-one strokes. Good ones, too. The school nurse had to treat the welts.'

Collingwood is sweating, but he is equal to this line of questioning.

'What I do,' he says, 'I do only to improve them.' And adds, with a touch of boldness: 'The punishment hurts me more than them.'

'You love them then, these boys.'

Collingwood hesitates. It is a strong word, love. Then settles on: 'I love them like a father.'

'Very good.'

There has, thus far, been not so much as a wisp of Smoke. Collingwood's shirt remains clean, his collar pristine, his armpits sweat-soaked but unsoiled. And yet there is not one amongst the boys simple enough to conclude that Collingwood has spoken the exact truth. The laws of Smoke are complex. Not every lie will trigger it. A fleeting thought of evil may pass unseen; a fib, an excuse, a piece of flattery. Sometimes you can lie quite outrageously and find yourself spared. Everyone knows the feeling, knows it from childhood: of being questioned by your mother, or your governess, by the house tutor; of articulating a lie, pushing it carefully past the threshold of your lips, your palms sweaty, your guts coiled into knots, your chin raised in false confidence; and then, the sweet balm of relief when the Smoke does not come. At other times, the Smoke is conjured by transgressions so trifling you are hardly aware of them at all: you reach for the biscuits before they've been offered; you smirk as a footman slips on the freshly polished stairs. Next thing you know its smell is in your nose. There is no more hateful smell in the world than the smell of Smoke.

But for now Collingwood remains free of it. He has passed his examination with flying colours. Only, he isn't finished yet: Julius. Still he stands, angling the lamp. It is as though his voice pours out along with the light.

'Your brother died not long ago, did he not?'

7

The question takes Collingwood by surprise. For the first time he appears hurt rather than afraid. He answers quietly.

'Yes.'

'What was he called, your brother?'

'Luke.'

'Luke. Yes. I remember your telling me about him. How you played as little boys.' Julius watches Collingwood squirm. 'Remind me. How did Luke die?'

There is no mistaking the resentment in the answer. Still it comes.

'He drowned. He fell out of a boat.'

'I see. A tragedy. How old was he?'

'Ten.'

'Ten? So young. How long to his eleventh birthday?'

'Three and a half weeks.'

'That is unfortunate.'

Collingwood nods and begins to cry.

Thomas understands the tears. Children are born in sin. Most babies turn black with Smoke and Soot within minutes of being born, and every birthing bed and every infant crib is surrounded by the dark plume of shame. The gentlefolk and all commoners who can afford it employ nurses and attendants to look after the child until Good begins to ripen in it, at age three or four. Sometimes they make a point of barring the child from all family intercourse until it is six or seven: from love, and so they will not grow to despise it. Smoke is tolerated to the eleventh year: the Holy Book itself suggests the threshold before which grace is only achieved by saints. If you die before eleven, you die in sin and go to hell. But (thank the Virgin) it is a lesser hell than those reserved for adults: a children's hell. In picture books it is often depicted as a kind of hospital or school, with long, long corridors and endless rows of prim, white beds. Thomas owned such a book when he was growing up and drew in it: drew colour, people, strange walking birds that trailed long feathers like bridal trains. It is the tradition in many of the older families to hire a bond servant when a child turns ten whose only task is to guard the young one's life. If the bond servant fails, he is put to death. One calls them rooks, these bond servants, for they dress all in black and often trail their own Smoke like a curse.

Julius has given the boys time to digest all this, the weight of little

8

Luke's death. That lamp whose beam he is steadying must be heavy in his hand, and hot. But he is patient.

'Was Luke alone? In the boat, I mean.'

Collingwood speaks but his answer is inaudible. His tears have ceased now. Even though he still wears his nightshirt, he has been stripped of something these last few minutes, some protective layer that we carry on our skins.

'Come, come, man. Out with it. Who was it? Who was in the boat with your ten-year-old brother when he drowned?'

But Collingwood has clamped up and no word will pass his trembling lips.

'It appears you have forgotten. I shall help you, then. Is it not true that it was your father who was in the boat? And is it not also true that he was drunk and slept through the drowning, and only woke when the servants found the boat stuck amongst reeds in a riverbank three miles down the stream?'

'Yes,' says Collingwood, having refound his tongue. He almost shouts it, in fact, his voice an octave higher than it was but a minute ago.

'And,' asks Julius, matching the shout with a whisper, 'do you love your father as the Holy Book instructs us to?'

Collingwood need not answer. The Smoke does it for him. One notices it at the shoulders first, and where the sweat has plastered the nightshirt to his skin: a black, viscous blot, no bigger than a penny. It's like he's bleeding ink. Then the first wisps of Smoke appear, stream from these dark little spots, leaving gritty Soot behind.

Collingwood hangs his head, and trembles.

'You must learn to master yourself,' says Julius, says it very gently, angling away the light. 'You may go now. It is well.'

Φ

There is no punishment, or rather none that Julius need administer. The stains on Collingwood's shirt can be washed out only by soaking them for hours in concentrated lye. The only lye in the whole school is held by the school laundry and is tightly guarded. When he hands over his linen the next morning, as he must, the shirt will be identified by his monogram; his name taken down. The Master of Smoke and Ethics will have a conversation with Collingwood, not entirely dissimilar in nature to the proceedings of this late-night court. A report will be written and sent to his parents, and sanctions imposed upon him. Perhaps he will lose his badge and the privileges of a prefect; perhaps he will be sent to scrub the teachers' lavatory, or spend his free time in the library cataloguing books. Perhaps he won't be allowed to join the other schoolboys on the Trip. He shows no anger as he stands up trembling from the chair, and his look at Julius is like a dog's that has been beaten. It wants to know if it's still loved.

Thomas gazes after him longer than most as Collingwood slinks from the room. If he was free to go he would go after him; would sit with him, though not speak. He wouldn't find the words. Charlie might: he's good with words, and more than that. He has a special talent, a gentleness of the heart. It allows him to feel what others feel and speak to them frankly, as an equal. Thomas turns to his friend, but Charlie's eyes are on Julius. More boys are to be examined to-night. A second piece of paper is about to be picked from the sack; a second name about to be read.

Φ

They call him Hum-Slow, though his real name is Hounslow, the ninth Viscount of. He can't be twelve yet if he's a day. One of the youngest boarders, thin but chubby-faced, the way the young ones sometimes are. As he arrives at the chair and turns to sit down on it, his fear wrests wind from his bowels, long and protracted, like it will never stop. Imagine it: the endless growl of a fart, in a room full of schoolboys. There are some giggles yet hardly a jeer. One does not need Charlie's talent to feel sorry for Hounslow. His body shakes so, he can barely manage his opening line.

'Please, sir. Examine me.'

His voice, not yet broken, tends towards a squeal. When he tries to 'thank the Smoke', he mangles it so badly that tears of frustration roll down his plump cheeks. Thomas starts forward, but Charlie stops him, gently, unobtrusively, takes hold of him by the arm. They exchange looks. Charlie has a peculiar way of looking: so simple, so honest, you forget to hide behind your own little lies. For what would Thomas do, if Charlie let him go? To interfere with the exam-ination would be tantamount to rebelling against the Smoke itself. But Smoke is real: you can see and smell it every day, if you like. How do you rebel against a fact? And so Thomas must stay and watch

Hounslow be thrown to the wolves. Though this wolf wears white and angles a lamp into which the child blinks blindly.

'Tell me,' Julius begins, 'have you been a good boy?'

Hounslow shakes his head in terror, and a sound runs through the room very close to a moan.

But, strange to say, the little boy survives the procedure without a single wisp. He answers all questions, answers them slowly, though his tongue seems to have gone thick with fear, and sticks out of his mouth in between answers.

Does he love his teachers?

Yes, he does.

Love his peers, his books, his dormitory bed?

Oh yes, he does, he does, and school most of all.

What sins, then, weigh on his conscience?

Sins too great and numerous to name.

But name them he does, taking upon himself all the weight of guilt he can conceive of, until he is quite flattened. If he has failed his Latin test this Monday past, it is because he is 'indolent' and 'stupid'. If he has fought in the school yard with a classmate called Watson, it is because he, Hounslow, is 'vicious' and a 'little brute'. If he has wet his bed, it is because he is 'vile' and has been so from birth, his mother says so herself. He is a criminal, a retrograde, a beast. 'I am dirt,' Hounslow shouts, near-hysterical, 'dirt', and all the while his nightshirt stays clean, its little lace ruffles free of all Soot.

It's done in under ten minutes. Julius lowers the lamp and kisses the boy's head, right on the crown, like they have seen the bishop do with the school chaplain. And when he gets up, there is something more that shows in Hounslow's face other than relief. A note of triumph. Today, this night, he has become one of the elect. He has abased himself, admitted to all he's ever hidden in his conscience (and some more besides), and the Smoke has judged him pure. If he gives Watson a bloody nose on the morrow, it will be with the sense of administering justice. Julius looks after him with proud amusement. Then he digs within the sack. And reads a third name, the last one. It won't be Cooper, Charlie's last name. Charlie is a future earl, one of the highest in the land. The powerful, Thomas has been given to understand, are rarely chosen for examination.

'Argyle,' Julius reads, slowly and diligently, not without pleasure.

Argyle.

Thomas's name.

It would be false to say he did not expect it.

As though split by an oar, the sea of boys now parts for him. Charlie's hand squeezes his arm, then he's walking. He'll wonder at it later, this undue haste, the absence of any real will to resist, and will berate himself for cowardice. But it isn't cowardice that shows on his face but the opposite: he's itching to do battle. From the way he raises his chin into the light, you would have thought he was climbing into a boxing ring. Julius notices it too.

And smiles.

Φ

The light is blinding. Behind it, the room ceases to exist. He cannot look to Charlie for guidance or assurance, for Charlie is lost in the darkness while he, Thomas, is bathed in yellow light. Even Julius, who stands not two steps away, is but a shadow from the world beyond.

There is something else Thomas realises. The light makes him feel naked. Not exposed, or vulnerable, but quite literally parted from his clothing, every stitch so flimsy it has turned into thin air. In itself it might not have meant that much to him. At home, he stripped many times to swim the river with his friends, and when he changes every night into his nightshirt, he does so with little thought to modesty. This is different though. The light singles him out. He is naked in a room full of people who are not. He is not prepared for how angry it makes him.

'Start,' he growls, because Julius doesn't, he just stands there, waiting, steadying the lamp. 'Go on. I submit to the exam. And thank the Smoke. Now: ask me a question.' The chair, Thomas realises, slopes under his bottom. His feet have to push into the ground to keep himself stable.

Julius greets his outburst calmly.

'Impatient, are we? Though you were tardy enough about coming to school. And are slow enough about learning your lessons.'

He unhooks the lamp and carries it closer, stands over him, bathing him in the beam.

'You know,' Julius mouths, so quietly only Thomas can hear, 'I think I can see your Smoke even now. Steaming out of every little pore. It's disgusting.

'But if you are so very impatient,' he goes on, louder again, his orator's voice self-possessed and supple, 'very well. I will make it easy for you. Your examination will be a single question. Does that suit you?'

Thomas nods, bracing himself, like you do when you expect to be punched. It is Charlie who later explains to him that it is better to unclench, absorb the hit like water.

'Go ahead, then. Ask.'

'Well, well.'

Julius makes to speak, stops, interrupts himself; turns the lamp around for a brief moment and lets its beam dance over the faces of the boys. Thomas sees Charlie for half a second; not long enough to read his expression. Then the beam is back in his eyes.

'You see,' Julius resumes, 'the question I want to ask is not mine. It belongs to everyone. The whole school is asking it. Every boy who is in this room. Even the teachers have been asking it. Even your friend over there, though he mightn't admit it. It is this: What is it that is so filthy about you, so unspeakably foul, that it made your parents ignore all custom and common sense and hide you away until your sixteenth year?

'Or,' he adds, more slowly yet, articulating every syllable, 'is it that there is something vile, disgusting about *them* that they were afraid you'd disclose and spread?'

The question hits its mark: as an insult (to him, his family, the things he holds sacred) but more so as a truth, a spectre that has haunted half his life. It punctures his defences and goes to his core; wakes fear and anger and shame. The Smoke is there long before he can account for it. It is as though he is burning, burning alive without reason. Then he knows what it marks: he has hatred, murder in his heart.

Another boy would crumple with shame. Thomas leaps. Hits Julius, headfirst, sends the lamp crashing to the floor. Its flame, un-extinguished, lights their struggle from one side. To the boys who are watching they are a single shadow projected ceiling-high against the wall, two-headed and monstrous. But to them, close to the lamp, everything is crystal clear. Thomas is smoking like a wet ember. His hands are fists, raining down on Julius. Insults stream from his mouth.

'You are nothing,' he keeps on saying, 'nothing. A dog, a filthy dog, nothing.'

His fist hits Julius in the chin and something comes loose from his mouth, a tooth, apparently, a black, rotten molar that jumps from his lips like a coughed-up sweet. There is blood, too, and more Smoke, Smoke that pours from Julius's skin, so black and pure it stoppers Thomas's anger.

Immediately, Julius gains the upper hand. More than two years older, stronger, he flips the shorter boy. But rather than hitting him, he bears down with his whole body, embraces him, clings to him, rolls him into the lamp until it tips and smothers its own light. All at once Thomas realises what Julius is doing. He is rubbing his Smoke into Thomas, and Thomas's into himself. Later, he will claim he was sullied by his attacker; that he himself remained pristine all through their fight. Now, in the darkness, he takes Thomas's throat and squeezes it until Thomas thinks that surely he must die.

Julius lets go, judiciously, the moment the other boys have stepped close enough to get a better picture. He gets up, wipes at his shirt, and makes a show of his composure. Thomas, crumpled, remains on the floor. Only Charlie bends down to him, soothes him, and helps him back to the dorm.

Charlie

There is just one thing you can do against Soot if you don't have any lye and that's to soak it in urine. It's disgusting, I know, but there's something in piss that makes it fade. And so Thomas and I sneak back into the bathroom later that night when everybody is gone, put Thomas's shirt into one of the bathtubs (the one used by Julius when he deigns to bathe), drink pints upon pints of water from the tap, and take turns peeing on it. Destroying the shirt is out of the question. They'd know at once: all items of clothing are carefully catalogued. It'd get Thomas expelled without appeal.

I wish I could describe Thomas, capture him. He is neither tall nor short, neither stocky nor slight; his hair is neither curly nor entirely straight. But I am making him sound like a nonperson, when he is everything but. Thomas is someone you notice when he comes through the door. It's a kind of intensity. Like he is walking around with a keg of gunpowder strapped to his chest. It's in his face, partially. He *looks* at things, really looks. At people, too. Evaluates them. Not judging them exactly but rather taking them in for what they are; trying to see the truth of them. It is not something most people like. I think I may be his only friend here, and there are close to two hundred boys all told, though some live in a separate building across the yard and a handful are day students who come in from the village; rich burghers' sons who are here for the schooling and not for the other stuff. The 'moral education'. Burghers may smoke, once in a while. One does not expect better of them.

You'd think I'd hold it against Thomas. That his soul is bad. That, unless he reforms, he is bound for hell. It is true, after all. The Smoke does not lie. There is evil in him the way there are maggots in a cut of rotten meat. But you see, all that exists on one level somewhere, the level of adult reason and truths, where science lives, and theology and the laws of the courts. But there is another level, one I have no name for, and on this other level, I am his friend. It's as simple as that.

15

As for myself, when I look in a mirror I see someone tall and sort of angular; bony, my sister calls it. Red hair. Not ginger but a deep shade of copper, cropped very short. My skin is quite dark too. Some say I must have foreign blood, that hair and skin like that come from east of the Black Sea, where there are still tribes riding the endless steppe. It's nonsense though, because my family is as English as they come. We're an old family, actually, and rather grand. I mean very grand. There are pictures of Father going hunting with the Queen's sons. But enough of this. Whether girls find me handsome or ugly you will have to ask them. I know I don't like my nose very much – too big – and cannot get fat even if I eat nothing but pudding. I am hopeless at rugby but can run cross-country all day. Thomas says I am more than half deer. If so, he must be a badger. When the dogs come for him, he turns and shows his teeth. Unlike me, he does not know when to take to his heels.

We became friends very simply. He arrived in the last week of October. That's unusual, of course. He was five weeks late for term. And then his age. Sixteen. There are transfers sometime, boys sent up from lesser schools who come here for 'finishing' and to rub shoulders with the future leaders of the realm. But Thomas had not been to any other school. He was 'home taught'. Nobody knew what to make of it. There was even some talk that it was illegal. Rumour had it, his parents fought his going off to school; resisted ever since he'd turned eleven. They're poor folk, I think, though noble enough, and live in the far north of the dominion; an unruly land. The Crown's arm reaches that far, but it does not have the same weight. And now he is here, this wild boy. Like something that's been raised by foxes.

But he does not like to talk about himself. Even to me.

He arrived by himself: no parent to see him off, no sibling, not even a servant to help him carry his things. Climbed off the mail coach that had picked him up at the train station, in Oxford. A knapsack on his shoulders and a valise in each hand. That's how I ran across him, in my free hour after lunch: him standing at the inner gate, chin raised, tired, listening to the porter who was talking at him in his coarse country tongue, shouting practically, asking him who he was.

'It's the new boy,' I said. 'They brought up a bed for him just yesterday. To the dormitory. I'll take him, if you like.'

Thomas did not speak, not until we arrived and I had pointed out his bed to him. It was near the window, the least popular spot, for it meant sleeping in its draught. He put down his luggage, straightened, looked me over, and asked,

'What is it like here?'

I was about to give him some meaningless answer, something to the effect that he would feel right at home, never he worry. Then I noticed his expression. There was something in his face that said, *Don't mollycoddle me, don't lie, don't feed me any bull.*

Or I'll despise you for ever.

So I gave him the truth.

'It's like a prison,' I said. 'Like a prison our parents pay for.'

He smiled at that and told me he was 'Thomas'.

We have been friends ever since.

The Trip

They make him wait for his punishment.

It's laundry day the next morning and, having no choice, Thomas throws the sodden, smelly shirt into the basket, along with the week's underwear and bedclothes. The Soot stain has faded but not disappeared.

It is no consolation to Thomas that many a schoolboy adds his own stained clothes to the growing pile. Each transgression leaves behind its own type of Soot, and those versed in such matters can determine the severity of your crime just by studying the stain's density and grit. This is why no classes in Smoke and Ethics are scheduled for laundry day: the master, Dr Renfrew, spends his morning locked in his office, rooting through boys' underclothes. The list of those found guilty of 'Unclean Thoughts and Actions' is displayed in a glass cabinet before lunch, so that each schoolboy may learn what punishment has been levied on him. Two days of dining-hall service; three pages that have to be copied from the *Second Book of Smoke*; a public apology at school assembly. These, for minor transgressions. More serious offences require individual investigation. The boy in question will be called to the master's study, to answer for his sins. There is a chair there, upholstered in leather, that is equipped with leather straps. The boys call it the dentist's chair. No teeth are pulled, but the truth, Dr Renfrew has been known to say, has to be dug up by the roots. For the most serious violations of Good Order even this procedure is seen to be insufficient. They require the calling of something referred to as a 'tribunal'. So Thomas has heard. There has been no such case in the weeks since he's been at school.

In class, Thomas sits distracted and is reprimanded when he cannot recite the four principles of Aristotle's theory of causation. Another boy recites them with glib relish. He is not asked what the four principles mean, how they are used, or what good they may do; nor who this Aristotle was whose marble bust stands in the school hallway, near the portrait of Lord Shrewsbury, the school's esteemed founder. And in general Thomas has found that the school is more interested in the outward form of things rather than their meaning; that learning is a matter of reciting names or dates or numbers: smartly, loudly, and with great conviction. He has proven, thus far, a very bad student.

At lunch, he hardly eats. He is sitting in the school refectory, which has the shape and general dimensions of a chapel and is dreadfully cold. December winds have pushed the snow into the windows. On the outside they are shrouded in dull white that saps the warmth from every ray of sun. On the inside, they bleed cold water from the edges of their metal frames. On the floor, the puddles refreeze and eat away at the unvarnished wood.

Lunch is a cut of hard gammon half hidden under a ladleful of lukewarm peas. Each bite tastes like mud to Thomas, and twice he bites down on the fork by accident, digging the prongs into his tongue. Halfway through the meal Charlie spots him and joins him at the table. One of the teachers held him up after class. Charlie waits until the skinny little boy on service duty has condemned him to his own piece of leathery gammon with its attendant pile of yellowing peas.

'Anything?' he asks.

Thomas shakes his head. 'Nothing. Look at them, though. They are all waiting for it. The pupils, and the teachers, too. All of them, impatient. Yearning for the bloody shoe to drop.'

He speaks resentfully and even as the last word leaves his lips, a wisp of Smoke curls from his nostril, too light and thin to leave behind Soot. Charlie disperses it with a quick wave. He is not worried. Hardly anyone gets through the day without a minor transgression, and there have been days when a teacher could be seen flapping at a thread of Smoke pouring from his tongue. The students tend to like these teachers better. In their imperfection they are closer to their own states of grace.

'They can't send you home.' Charlie sounds like he believes it. 'You've only just got here.'

'Maybe.'

'He'll call you into his office, Renfrew will.'

'I suppose so.'

'You'll have to tell him how it was. No holding back.'

And then Charlie says what's been on Thomas's mind all morning. What he hasn't dared spell out.

19

'Otherwise he mightn't let you join the Trip.'

Thomas nods and finds his mouth too dry to speak.

The Trip is what everyone has been talking about from the minute he arrived at school. It's a unique event: there has been nothing like it in the school's history for close to three decades. Rumour has it that it was Renfrew who had insisted on the Trip's revival, and that he has faced fierce opposition, from the teachers, the parents and from the Board of Governors itself. It's hardly surprising. Most decent folk have never been to London. To take a group of schoolboys there is considered extraordinary, almost outlandish. There have been voices suggesting that it will put the whole school in danger. That the boys who go might never return.

Thomas still has trouble finding spit for words. 'I want to go,' is all he manages before breaking into a dry cough. It does not quite capture what he feels. He *needs* to see it. The prospect of the Trip is the only thing that's kept him going these past few weeks. The moment he heard about it was the moment he decided there might be a meaning to his coming to school, a higher purpose. He'd be hard-pressed to say exactly what he expects from their visit to London. A revelation, perhaps. Something that will explain the world to him.

The cough runs its course, exhausts itself in a curse.

'That bastard Julius. I could kill the bloody turd.'

Charlie's face is so honest it hurts.

'If you can't go, Thomas, I won't—'

Thomas cuts him short because a group of teachers are passing them. They are speaking animatedly, but drop their voices to a whisper the moment they draw level with the boys. Resentment flickers through Thomas's features, and is followed by another exhalation of pale, thin Smoke. His tongue shows black for a second, but he swallows the Soot. You do that too often, your windpipe roughens and your tonsils start to darken, along with what's behind. There is a glass jar in the science classroom with a lung so black it looks dipped in tar.

'Look at them whispering. They are enjoying this! Making me stew in my own fat. Why don't they just get on with it? Put me in the bloody dock!'

But Charlie shakes his head, watches the teachers huddle near the door.

'I don't think they're talking about you, Thomas. There is something else going on. I noticed it earlier, when I went to the Porter's Lodge to see if I had any mail. Master Foybles was there, talking to Cruikshank, the porter. Making inquiries. They are waiting for something, some sort of delivery. And it's important. Foybles sounded pretty desperate. He kept on saying, 'You'll let me know, won't you? The minute it arrives.' As though he were suspecting Cruikshank of hiding it away somewhere. Whatever *it* is.'

Thomas considers this. 'Something they need for the Trip?'

'I don't know,' says Charlie, thoughtful. 'If it is, it better come today. If they have to postpone the Trip, they might end up cancelling it altogether.'

He cuts a piece of gammon like it's wronged him somehow, spilling peas on all sides. Thomas curses and turns to his own lunch. Leaving food on your plate is against the rules and carries its own punishment, as though it is proof of some invisible type of Smoke.

Φ

They send for him after vespers.

It's Julius who comes for him, smirking, Thomas can see him all the way down the corridor, an extra flourish to his step. Julius does not say anything. Indeed he does not need to, a gesture is enough, a sort of wave of the hand that starts at the chest and ends up pointing outward, down the length of the hall. Ironic, like he's a waiter, inviting Thomas to the table. And then Julius leads the way, walking very slowly now, his hands in his pockets, calling to some boys to open the door up ahead.

Making sure everyone knows.

Keeping pace with Julius, trapped behind that slow, slouching, no-haste-no-worry-in-the-world walk: it's enough to make Thomas's blood boil. He can taste Smoke on his breath and wonders if he's showing. A dark gown covers his shirt but he will soon be asked to remove it, no doubt, and expose his linens. He attempts to calm himself, picks Soot out of his teeth with the tip of his tongue. Its bitterness makes him gag.

Julius slows down even further as they approach Dr Renfrew's door. The Master of Smoke and Ethics. It's a new post, that, no older than a year. It used to be the Master of Religion was in charge of all the moral education, or so Charlie's told him. When they arrive at the door, Julius pauses, smirks, and shakes his head. Then he walks on, faster now, gesturing for Thomas to keep pace.

It takes Thomas a minute to understand what's just happened. He is not going to see Dr Renfrew. There will be no dentist's chair for him. It's worse than that. They are heading to the headmaster's quarters.

There's to be a tribunal.

The word alone makes him feel sick.

Φ

Julius does not knock when they reach the headmaster's door. This confuses Thomas, until they've stepped through. It leads not to a room but to a sort of antechamber, like a waiting room at the doctor's, two long benches on each side and an icy draft from the row of windows on the right. They are high up here, in one of the school's towers. Beneath them, the fields of Oxfordshire: a silver sea of frozen moonlight. Down by the brook, a tree rises from the snow-choked grounds, stripped of its leaves by winter. A willow, its drooping branches dipped into the river, their tips trapped in ice. Thomas turns away, shivering, and notices that the door back to the hallway is padded from the inside, to proof it against sound. To protect the headmaster from the school's noise, no doubt. And so nobody can hear you scream.

Julius stands at the other door, knocks on it gently, with his head boy's confidence and tact. It opens after only a moment: Renfrew's face, framed by blond hair and beard.

'You are here, Argyle. Good. Sit.'

Then adds, as Julius turns to leave: 'You too.'

Renfrew closes the door before Julius can ask why.

Φ

They sit on opposite sides, Thomas with his back to the windows, Julius facing them, and the moon. It affords Thomas the opportunity to study him. Something has gone out of the lad, at this 'You too'. Some of the swagger, the I-own-the-world certainty. He is chewing his cheek, it appears. A good-looking boy, Thomas is forced to admit, fair-skinned and dark-haired, his long thin whiskers more down than beard. Thomas waits until Julius's eyes fall on him, then leans forward.

'Does it hurt? The tooth, I mean.'

Julius does not react at once, hides his emotions as he does so well. 'You are in trouble,' he says at last. 'I am here only as a witness.'

Which is true in all likelihood, but nonetheless he looks a tad ruffled, Julius does, and Thomas cannot help gloating a little over his victory. They looked for the tooth late last night when Charlie and he were trying to clean his shirt, but it was gone. Julius must have picked it up himself. It would have made a nice souvenir. But that was then and now he is here, his hands all sweaty, casting around for bravado. Waiting. How much easier it would be to fight, even to lose: a fist in your face, a nosebleed, an ice bag on your aches. Thomas leans back, tries to unknot his shoulders. The moon is their only light source. When a cloud travels across it, the little waiting room is thrown into darkness. All he can see of Julius now is a shadow, black as Soot.

It must be a quarter of an hour before Renfrew calls them in. Rich, golden gaslight welcomes them; thick carpets that suck all sound from their steps. They are all there, all the masters. There are seven of them – Renfrew-Foybles-Harmon-Swinburne-Barlow-Winslow-Trout – but only three that count. Renfrew is tall and well-built, and still rather young. He wears his hair short, as well as his beard, and favours a dark, belted suit that seems to encase him from neck to ankle. A white silken scarf, worn tight at the throat, vouches for his virtue.

Trout is the headmaster. He is very fat and wears his trousers very high, so that the quantity of flesh between the top of his thighs and the waistband dwarfs the short sunken chest, adorned though it is with fine lace and ruffles. What he lacks in hair, Trout makes up for in whiskers. His button nose seems lost between the swell of his red cheeks.

Swinburne, finally: the Master of Religion. Where Renfrew is tall, Swinburne is towering, if twisted by age. He wears the cap and smock of his office. The little one sees of his face is mottled with broken veins, the shape and colour of thistles. A beard covers the rest, long and stringy.

Renfrew, Swinburne, Trout: each of them, it is said, entangled in affairs that reach from school to Parliament and Crown. Thomas has often thought of painting them. He is good with a brush. A triptych. He has not decided yet who belongs at the centre.

It's Renfrew who bids them sit. He points to two chairs that have been pulled up into the middle of the room, making no distinction between them. Compared to the theatricality of Julius's examination last night, the gesture is almost casual. The masters are standing in clusters, wearing worsted winter suits. Some are holding teacups; Foybles is munching a biscuit. Thomas sits. After a moment's hesitation Julius follows suit.

'You know why you are here.'

It is a statement, not a question, and Renfrew turns even as he makes it, reaches into a basket, retrieves something. It affords Thomas another moment to look around the room. He sees a leather settee and a brass chandelier; stained-glass windows with scenes from the Scriptures, Saint George with his lance through the dragon's throat; sees a painting of a fox hunt under a dappled sky; sees cabinets, and doors and a sideboard with fine china; sees all this, but takes in little, his mind skittish, his skin tingling, nervous, afraid. When Renfrew turns back to them he is holding two shirts. He places one over the back of an unoccupied chair, spreads the other between his hands, displaying the Soot stain; runs his fingertips through it, tests its grit.

And launches into lecture.

'Smoke,' he says, 'can have many colours. Often it is light and grey, almost white, with no more odour than a struck match. Then there is yellow Smoke, dense and wet like fog. Blue Smoke that smells acrid, like spoiled milk, and seems to disperse almost as soon as it has formed. Once in a while we witness black Smoke, oily and viscous; it will cling to anything it touches. The variations of texture, density and shade have all been carefully described in the Four Books of Smoke: a taxonomy of forty-three varieties. It is more difficult to establish the precise cause for each type of Smoke. It is a question not only of the offence but of the offender. The thoroughly corrupt breed darker, denser Smoke. Once a person's moral sickness is sufficiently advanced, all actions are coloured by its stain. Even the most innocent act will—'

'Sin, Master Renfrew.' It's Swinburne who interrupts him. His voice, familiar from the thrice-weekly sermon, has a shrill intensity all its own. He sounds like the man who ate the boy who ran his fingernails down the blackboard. 'It is sin that blackens the soul. Not *sickness*.'

Renfrew looks up, annoyed, but a glance from the headmaster bids him swallow his reply.

'Sin, then. A difference of nomenclature.' He pauses, collects his thought, digs his fingers into the shirt's linen. 'Smoke, in any case, is easy to read. It is the living, material manifestation of degeneracy. Of *sin*. Soot, on the other hand, well, that is a different matter. Soot is dead, inert. A spent symptom, and as such inscrutable. Oh, any fool can see how much there is and whether it is fine like sea sand or coarse as a crushed brick. But these are crude measures. It requires a more scientific approach' – here Renfrew smooths down his jacket – 'to produce a more sophisticated analysis. I spent my morning bent over a microscope, studying samples from both shirts. There are certain solvents that can cancel the inertness of the substance and, so to speak, temporarily bring it back to life. A concentrated solution of *Papaver fuliginosa richteria*, heated to eighty-six degrees and infused with—'

Renfrew interrupts himself, his calm self-possession momentarily strained by excitement. He resumes at a different point and in a different voice, gentler, more intimate, drawing a step closer to the boys and speaking as though only to them.

'I say I spent the morning analysing these two shirts and I found something unusual. Something disconcerting. A type of Soot I have seen only once before. In a prison.'

He draws closer yet, wets his lips. His voice is not without compassion. 'There is a cancer growing in one of you. A moral cancer. *Sin*' – a flicker of a glance here, over to Swinburne, hostile and ironic – 'as black as Adam's. It requires drastic measures. If it takes hold – if it takes over the organism down to the last cell . . . well, there will be nothing anybody can do.' He pauses, fixes both boys in his sight. 'You will be lost.'

Φ

For a minute and more after this announcement, Thomas goes deaf. It's a funny sort of deaf: his ears work just fine but the words he hears do not reach his brain, not in the normal manner where they are sifted for significance and given a place in the hierarchy of meaning. Now they just accumulate.

It's Julius who is speaking. His tone is measured, if injured.

'Won't you even ask what happened, Master Renfrew?' he asks. 'I thought I had earned some measure of trust at this school, but I see now that I was mistaken. Argyle attacked me. Like a rabid dog. I had no choice but to restrain him. He rubbed his filth into me. The Soot is his. I never smoke.'

Renfrew lets him finish, watches not Julius but the other teachers, some of whom are muttering in support. Thomas, uncomprehending, follows his gaze and finds an accusation written in the masters' faces. He, Thomas, has done this to one of theirs, they seem to be saying. Has covered him in dirt. Their golden boy. Thomas would like to refute the accusation, but his thoughts just won't latch on. All he can think is: what does it mean to be 'lost'?

'I have had occasion,' Renfrew replies at last, 'to collect three separate statements concerning the incident you are referring to, Mr Spencer. I believe I have a very accurate impression of how events unfolded. The facts of the matter are these. Both shirts are soiled – from the inside and out. The Soot is of variable quality. But I took samples of this' – he picks from his pocket a glass slide at the centre of which a few grains of Soot hang suspended in a drop of reddish liquid – 'from *both* shirts. I could not determine the origin.

'Both shirts,' he continues, now turning to the teachers, 'also bear marks of being tampered with: one very crudely' – a nod to Thomas – 'the other rather more sophisticatedly. Almost inexplicably, Mr Spencer.'

Julius swallows, jerks his head. A crack of panic now mars his voice.

'I wholly reject . . . You will have to answer to my family! It was this boy, this beast . . .'

He trails off, his voice raw with anger. Swinburne rescues him: rushes up, with a rustle of his dark gown, taps Julius on the shoulder, ordering him to shut up. Up close Swinburne smells unaired and musty, like a cellar. The smell helps Thomas recover his wits. It is the most real thing in the entire room. That and a knocking, like a hard fist on wood. Nobody reacts to it. It must be his heart.

'Mr Spencer is innocent.' Swinburne's voice brooks no dissent. He speaks as though delivering a verdict. 'I too made inquiries about the incident last night. The situation is quite clear. It's that boy's fault. His Smoke is potent. It infected Spencer.'

'*Infected?*' Renfrew smiles while the knocking grows louder. 'A medical term, Master Swinburne. So unlike you. But you are quite right. Smoke *infects*. A point only imperfectly understood, I fear. Which is why I insist that both these boys join the Trip tomorrow.'

Perhaps the most disconcerting thing about the roar of shouts and voices that answers this announcement is that Thomas's heart appears to stop: it gives a loud final rap and then falls silent. 'It mustn't be,' one of the teachers – Harmon? Winslow? – keeps repeating, high-pitched, squealing, as though giving voice to Thomas's dismay. A moment later the door is thrown open and the small, dishevelled figure of Cruikshank, the porter, stands on its threshold. He pokes his head into the sudden silence of the room.

'Beg pardon. Knocked till knuckles are raw. No answer. Message for Mast'r Foybles. Ur-jent, like. If yous please.'

The person thus named is mortified.

'Not now, you fool!' Foybles cries, running across the room and dragging the porter out by the arm. Their whispered exchange in the antechamber is loud enough to focus all attention on the pair.

'You says, "*At once*", you did,' Cruikshank can be heard declaiming.

'But to burst in like that,' Foybles berates him. 'You fool, you fool.'

All the same he seems elated when he closes the door on the porter and rejoins the company of his peers.

'The delivery has arrived,' he declares, beaming, rubbing his hands in triumph before the room's atmosphere recalls him to the events that have just transpired there. Rather crushed, he withdraws into a corner and buries his face in a handkerchief for the purpose of clearing out his nasal passages. Like a compass needle momentarily distracted by a magnet, everybody's focus returns to Renfrew, who remains standing at the centre of the room. But the outrage at his announcement has spent itself, and Thomas's mind is clear at last.

He is *lost*.

But he will be going to London.

'There are objections?' Renfrew asks calmly.

Swinburne glares at him, then turns his back and addresses the headmaster.

'Master Trout. That boy is a sickness in our midst. He should be sent down at once.'

Swinburne does not even condescend to point a finger at Thomas. But Trout shakes his head.

'Impossible. He has a powerful sponsor. I will hear no more of it.'

Swinburne makes to speak again, but Trout has heaved his heavy figure out of his armchair.

'It is for the Master of Smoke and Ethics to determine the punishment. The government guidelines are quite clear. If Master Renfrew thinks these two boys will benefit from tomorrow's outing, so be it. Beyond that—' He glances questioningly at Renfrew.

'I will work with each of them upon our return, Headmaster. An intensive programme of reform.' Renfrew's voice sounds notes of reconciliation. 'And, if it will set your mind at rest, dear colleagues, I have a list of pages here from the *Book of Smoke* that I shall ask them to copy. From the third volume.' He glances at Swinburne. 'Passages whose findings have been confirmed by the latest research. Which is more than we can say for much of the book.'

He distributes copies of the list to Thomas and Julius, then lingers at the head boy's side.

'One more thing, Mr Spencer. These midnight examinations. They will stop. I alone have the authority to examine the pupils at this school.'

Swinburne is too outraged to swallow his anger. 'The school has its traditions. Only a fool meddles with—'

Renfrew cuts him off. His tone, now, is cold and brutal.

'A new era is dawning, Master Swinburne. You'd better get used to it.'

He gestures the two boys up and all but pushes them out of the door. Outside, in the hallway, Thomas and Julius stop for a moment, dazed. For an instant something like companionship flickers between them, the sense that they have shared a danger, and survived. Then Julius straightens.

'I hate you,' he says and walks away. Not the slightest trace of Smoke rises from his skin. It leaves Thomas wondering what it is about Julius's hate that is sanctified, and what is so dirty about his own.

Φ

'There you are! I've been looking all over.'

Charlie corners him just before lights-out. That's the thing about school: no matter how big it is, there is no place to hide. Each nook, each hour is supervised. Empty rooms are locked and the hallways swarm with boys; porters in the stairwells, and outside it's too bloody cold.

'They say there's been a tribunal. In Trout's office.'

'Yes.'

Charlie starts to say something, swallows it, looks him full in the face. His eyes are so full of care for him, it frightens Thomas.

'What did they do to you?'

'Nothing.'

'Are you sure?'

'Yes.'

Because how can Thomas tell him? That he's *infected*. That there is an evil growing in him, so dark and ugly it frightens Renfrew. That one day he will wake up and do something unspeakable. That crime runs in his family.

That he is a dangerous friend to have.

So he says, 'They are letting me join the Trip.' And also: 'The delivery arrived. The thing they have been waiting for. Cruikshank came and told them.'

Charlie hoots when he hears about the Trip, from relief and from happiness that they'll be going together. It's a joy so simple and pure, it makes Thomas ashamed before his friend. He might have apologised – confessed – had not Charlie put a hand on his arm and said, 'Let's go see him. Cruikshank. We have a few minutes.'

He starts running, tugging Thomas along.

'He likes me, Cruikshank does. I chat to him from time to time. He'll tell me what it is.'

And as they race down the stairs, their feet clattering, each matching the other's stride, Thomas forgets, almost, that he is a sick boy, a walking blight, the son of a man who has killed.

Porter

Two boys. They come to me with questions. One who strips the truth off things like he's made of turpentine, and the other with eyes so frank, it inclines you to confession. I talk to the second, naturally, though I keep track of the first. He's the type you don't want sneaking up on you from behind.

'The deliv'ry?' I ask, like I don't quite recall. It's how you survive in this world. Play dumb, thicken your accent. Makes you invisible: one look and they dismiss you from their minds. The powers that be. But not these boys. Smarter than their teachers, they are. They simply wait me out.

'Oh, nothin' special,' I say at last. 'Sweets, you know. Tea. Biscuits. From someplace in London.'

That's all I give them, that and the name, to see how they react.

'Nice big stamp on the crate. Beasley and Son. Impor' and Expor', Deliv'ries to the Crown.'

They don't bat an eyelid, not one of them. Innocents, then. Though the quiet one looks like he was born with a knife in his fist. Like he had to cut his way out, and didn't much mind.

'You goin' on the Trip, t'morrow, lads?' I ask, though of course I already know.

'Yes, Mr Cruikshank. Will you be joining us?'

Mr Cruikshank, my arse. Polite little bugger, laying it on nice and thick. Though he certainly looks like he means it. If he puts that sort of look on the right wench down in London, she'll clean his piping free of charge.

'Oh no. I daresn't. Too scary for the likes of me. Wouldn't for all the world. Rather fly to the moon. Safer, that.'

Like I haven't been to London. It's not fifty miles down the road. Two days' walk, when I was young. Now all you needs to do is sit yourself on a train. Bring a little roast chicken along. Enjoy the ride.

Still, it's an odd venture, this Trip of theirs. Times are a-changing. Renfrew's been receiving letters. Three or four a month. No name on the flap but I can tell it's the ministry writing from the postal stamp. Richmond upon Thames. You get your map out, you'll see what you find. New Westminster Palace. The centre of power. Though there's talk of Parliament moving once again. Further from London: the walls are already going grey. Trout gets post from the same little post office, but the hand that writes out the address is different, round and feminine, where Renfrew's man writes like a spider dragging its black guts. Hold it up to the light and you will see the outlines of a rubber stamp. 'Victoria Regina', a fussy signature underneath. A civil servant's, no doubt, acting for the Crown. Bureaucrats versus lawmakers, then; different corridors of power. Makes you wonder what's inside the letters. And whether Trout and Renfrew ever care to show and tell.

I turn the boys away, in any case, ring the bell for lights-out. And in the morning the coaches arrive, all eleven of them, to carry fifty-eight upper-school boys to the train station. It's snowed again and the horses are steaming, and don't one of them shit just as old Swinburne goes walking past. Lovely smell that, fresh horse dung on snow. You want to bottle it and sell it to yer sweetheart.

I watch them go, wrapped in my old blanket. One of the boys looks back at me all the way to the end of the driveway. He don't wave.

Neither do I.

When they're gone, I go inside, shovel some coals into the stove, put on a bone for soup. By the time it's cooked they'll be pulling in at Oxford.

Infection

The country stretches before them, white and serene. The sun emerges, seeks out the snow, ignites it. Hedgerows stand out against the blaze, cut up the valleys into irregular parcels; shade trees rising black and crisp, mirroring their shadows: frost for foliage, bereft of birds. Charlie sits, his scarf tied around his ears, hanging out the window of the coach, glorying in the sights. He cannot remember another December this cold, this beautiful. A mile from Oxford one of the wheels gets stuck in a drift and the boys spill out to dig it free; throw snowballs, but make haste, too, afraid of missing the train.

Oxford itself is a row of fairy castles embroidered by college crests. The streets are full of ladies and their attendants, making purchases. They halt at the station, a procession of coaches, and the whole street stops to watch them get out: young women in fur stoles and muffs pointing them out to one another. Nervously, but also with a sense of joy, Charlie tugs at the nicely tailored jacket of his school uniform and reties his white scarf. There is something very pleasing about walking into the station and tipping one's hat to the gentlefolk waiting at the ticket counter and watching them respond in kind. School seems many miles away all of a sudden, a thing of the past. They have re-entered society and are welcomed as equals, as adults. Charlie is not alone in his reaction. All around him he can see the boys walking taller, smoothing the hair down under their caps and abandoning all horseplay; looking about themselves with a shy sort of pride. Only Thomas appears untouched by this feeling, walks gloomy, head bowed, forever apart. For a moment Charlie is angry with him, at his inability to enjoy the morning. Then a more generous feeling wins out. He walks over to him, attempts to draw him into conversation.

'I wonder what platform it is, to London.'

Thomas looks at him caustically. *Don't pity me*, his look is saying. *Don't you dare pity me.*

'We are with the swine.'

32

It takes Charlie a moment to understand the remark. Then he sees them, a mass of goats, sheep and pigs, standing in the filth of their excretions. They are at the far end of the station, on a platform separated from the others by a barrier and a gatehouse, and are being herded onto a series of carriages. Once the doors are shut on them, snouts appear at the breathing holes, pale, almost colourless nostrils sucking on air. Even from this distance, Charlie can sense their fear.

'But that's a freight train.'

'Most of it is. Food for London. But look.'

Thomas's finger points at two passenger carriages near the front of the train, recognisable by their rows of windows. Workers mill about on the platform, their chequered caps and waistcoats stained by old Soot. It is a shock to find children amongst them, some as young as nine. Puffs of Smoke trail them. One, a girl of twelve, thirteen years, is dressed only in vest and trousers, despite the cold. Her vest is so drenched in Soot, it hangs heavy off her narrow shoulders. She notices the schoolboys lining up near the barriers and flashes them a harelipped grimace, followed by a shout that's lost in the distance.

'What did she say?' he asks Thomas.

Thomas looks at him, starts to speak, blushes. It is a startling moment, a first. Nothing else has ever made Thomas blush.

'Better if you did not hear.'

'A curse word?'

'Yes. Anatomical. The kennelmaster was fond of it. Back home.'

'Christ.'

By now, Charlie realises, his classmates have cottoned on to the fact that they are heading to the far platform. The contrast between the station behind them and what lies beyond the barrier could not be starker. On one side gentlemen in frock coats are reading *The Times*. On the other—

'It's just working people,' Thomas says, as though he has read Charlie's mind.

'Yes, but the children . . .'

'They ride the train, I suppose. To London and back.' Thomas shrugs. 'Not everybody can be so fortunate as to be sent to our school.'

It's the first time all morning that Charlie sees him smile. Soon they are both laughing, laughing out loud, with the other boys looking at them like they are madmen.

Renfrew has approached the little gatehouse. He produces a letter. Even the paper it's on looks important; a red rubber stamp circles the signature. The stationmaster reads it carefully, then performs a head count. The boys have fallen silent by now. All boisterousness has left them. As they are finally waved through the barrier, a scream sounds, from somewhere deep in the train, an animal bleating out its distress. It sounds like the train itself is screaming. The workers withdraw as they see the schoolboys coming, watch them board from afar. Grains of Soot drift in the air. One such flake settles on the sleeve of a boy near Charlie; he wipes at it but only manages to smear it.

'Master!' he calls, tears in his voice if not on his face; afraid of being punished.

Renfrew turns briefly, pushes him along.

'It does not matter,' he says.

The statement unsettles Charlie. They are entering a realm with an unknown set of rules.

They reach the train, walk alongside, towards the front. For a moment it seems to him that it has been painted a matt black. Then he realises it is literally encased in Soot. He reaches out a finger, touches it, recoils.

'Soot is inert,' Thomas mutters quietly.

Charlie is not sure what it means.

Inside, the train is freshly cleaned, cosy. They are travelling in an open passenger coach, in shape and dimensions not unlike the inside of the horse omnibuses he saw in Bath the previous summer. Sitting on the hard benches it is almost possible to pretend one is in school.

Φ

It takes about half an hour until the landscape starts to change. Then the perfect blanket of white begins to give way to dark blotches of grass more black than green; puddles of meltwater reflect a murky version of the sky. Within two miles the snow stops altogether. Winter oats stand low in the fields, flanked by leafless sycamores and oaks. Everything has a stunted, sickly appearance.

'Has the weather changed?' Charlie wonders aloud.

'I doubt it,' says Thomas.

'Then London is hotter than Oxford?' Charlie chews on the

idea. 'All the people. And all the factories, I suppose, running their engines.'

'That. And the Smoke.'

Thomas points, and as Charlie follows his finger he sees for the first time a smear of grey in the air up ahead. Not the dark plume of a fire, nor the clean contours of a storm cloud, but more like a fog, rising out of the ground, wet and stubborn, resistant to the winds. Within a minute, the landscape around them begins to be covered by a film of dark scum. Ahead lies the city: a hazy, dark sprawl from which grow the slender spires of factory smokestacks, their outlines cleaner, sharper than anything closer to the ground. After another minute the first houses start, grime-covered brick and narrow courtyards, washing lines full of linen more grey than white. Soon the Smoke outside the window becomes impossible to ignore: it tints their vision and saps the strength out of the sun. The train has slowed to walking pace and London seems everywhere, boxing them in in the narrow chasm of its streets. Something takes hold of Charlie, an emotion halfway between fear and spite. He wants to return to Oxford. And also: put the match to this city, see it burn. He is about to tell Thomas when Renfrew gets up, walks to the front of the carriage in his deliberate step. The air above his head is oddly hazy. The Smoke has long come inside, Charlie realises, has sniffed out cracks in the windows and doors and risen through the under-carriage, seeped into their clothes, their skin, their lungs.

'Some of you can feel it already,' Renfrew begins. 'The Smoke. It's making you feel – unusual. Afraid. Aggressive. Frivolous. Vain. Your thinking is beginning to be clouded; you dwell on things. The outside world is no longer separate from you but is beginning to insinuate itself into your being. You're feeling small, insignificant, malleable, but are ready to fight anyone who dares to say so; your little store of prudence is eaten away as though by rats. Temptation presses herself on you – to steal, to cheat, to run away. All we have taught you – *all* – is put under pressure. It is as though someone has run off with your coat. You stand in your shirtsleeves, and the day is cold. And this is here, in a closed train compartment, a mile yet to the station. Outside, in the centre, amongst the people of London, it will be a hundred times more intense. Some of you may feel like you must succumb. I have one word for you.'

He pauses, fixes on their faces.

'Don't.'

The word comes down like a blade. Even the other teachers seem startled.

'Smoke is infectious. It begets itself. People are to it nothing but carriers. There is a greater density of people in London than anywhere else on these, our isles. Here Smoke rules, runs rampant, fans theft, adultery, murder. It feeds on the alcoholic, the vagrant, the prostitute; coats the very city in its Soot. Pity those you meet as you pity the sick. But as for yourselves. One word.'

He looks around for a boy who can say it with conviction. Julius obliges him. He is sitting at the front, looking pious, calm, in control of himself.

'Don't,' he says.

Against his will, even Charlie feels uplifted.

'That's right, Mr Spencer. *Don't*. Stay together. Don't talk to anyone. Don't buy anything. Don't pass out any money. And don't give in to the infection. Fight it with every fibre in your body. If you need help, seek it. It is why I and my esteemed colleagues are here with you. To offer support.'

Charlie looks about the compartment, seeks out the faces of the other teachers. All but Trout and Swinburne have joined the Trip; as they roll into the station, back in school the lower-class boys are locked in the refectory, spending the day in silent study. Foybles, the maths teacher, sits on a bench to Charlie's left. He is fingering a tin of sweets, nervously shoving one into his mouth. It is typical of him that he does not offer any to the student sitting next to him. Charlie, for one, could have used something to take the dry out of his throat.

Φ

The doors do not open at once. At another time, in another place, this would have caused complaints and unrest, threescore students wriggling on their bottoms. But the compartment remains as quiet as a grave. Everyone is staring out the window. The platform outside is full of people. There are porters in dirty frock coats holding baggage wagons. Old men, so Soot-covered, their sweat leaves tracks on their temples and cheeks; labourers with tools slung over one shoulder. There is a woman so little dressed it makes Charlie's blood shoot to his face. He looks away and still sees the curve of her white leg disappearing into the long slit of her dress; tastes Smoke on his tongue. *Don't*, he exhorts himself.

He finds it's easier when he speaks.

'If London is full of criminals,' he whispers to Thomas, who remains glued to the window, 'and Smoke begets Smoke, would it not be better if people left the city?'

Thomas does not turn when he speaks.

'Perhaps they don't want to leave,' he says.

'We could make them.'

'We?'

'All I mean is – if they lived in the country, in the fresh air … They can't all be criminals. Sinners, maybe, but not criminals. Some of them are good at heart.'

Thomas turns to him at last. It is a shock to discover how angry he looks.

'And who would work in the factories then? And operate the shipyards? That's what London is, you know. A collection of work yards, around which there's some housing.'

'How do you know all this?'

'Me ma,' Thomas says, a burr of accent surfacing in his voice. He shakes himself like a dog, spits a mouthful of Smoke. 'She used to write political pamphlets, in protest. But look – they're opening the doors. Let's go.'

Φ

There can be no hope of walking in formation. If the platform was full, London's streets are packed. The din is almost as bad as the Smoke: a whole city shouting, or so it seems. Costermongers roam the streets with their handcarts, parting the stream of people like rocks in a river. They sell coconuts, ropes and petticoats, Soot-smeared and drooping; nails, sewing needles and hard-boiled sweets; medicine, gunpowder and coal. Drunks and beggars line the house fronts, slumped against the plaster; they display mangled limbs and open sores, or simply sleep away their stupor. Children dart through the press of the crowd, some in play, some loaded with goods for delivery or sale. The street is made of black muck five inches deep, soggy with meltwater. It takes Charlie a while to realise that it consists of Soot, deposited over decades and centuries. It clings to his shoes as though it were glue. The house fronts are smeared with it to a height

37

of three or four yards: above this, dark brick shines through or else the dappled yellow of sandstone.

Every few minutes the boys are jostled by some person, man or woman, elbowing their way past. Twice Charlie feels hands in his coat and trouser pockets, looking for pickings. He does not try to catch the thief. His pockets are empty anyway. Ahead Renfrew has raised a walking stick high into the air. The boys – isolated, walking in groups of two, or three, or four; drops in the wash of hostile people – keep their eyes trained on this stick. To lose it would mean to risk losing the group. The way *back*. As Smoke sinks into Charlie's lungs this fear transforms into something darker. When another passerby brushes him with his elbow, Charlie pushes him away. All his weight is in the push; the man, old and walking on a withered leg, slips and collides with others. The feeling of triumph that washes over Charlie only erodes when he notices the threads of Smoke that curl out of his coat and shadow him down the road.

Nor can there be any pretence that Renfrew is choosing their route. Tall, self-possessed, formidable though he is, the Master of Smoke and Ethics is, like all of them, subject to the tidal swell that governs the crowd. For there is a definite movement to this stream of people, a movement that can be briefly resisted but not reversed. It leads them across the river, which lies beneath the bridge like a smear of tar. Foybles passes Charlie, his handkerchief pressed to his face.

'Raw sewage,' the maths teacher mutters in horror to himself. 'They are pumping their cesspools straight into the river.'

Indeed the water smells like the distillation of a hundred latrines. Even so, boats and ferries part the muck, and a group of women stand on the riverbank, sifting its mud with bare hands for baubles, lost pennies, cockles and crabs.

They arrive. It is a square of irregular proportions, large enough to hold several thousand people and filled with their heat. The haze is so thick here, it feels like night is falling, though the afternoon is young. The sun stands high above, dirty pink behind this veil of sin. But it isn't the tinted sun that's making people crane their necks. A platform has been erected at the centre, a good two yards off the ground. From it springs a gallows. Its noose frames an oval of dirty sky. The crowd stares at it with a reverence otherwise reserved for the cross. Even the noise is hushed here in the square.

'An execution?' Charlie whispers, not wishing to believe his eyes.

'Yes.' Thomas's eyes look wild. His throat and face show streaks of Soot. There is no telling if it is his own. 'And there's the executioner.'

It takes Charlie some moments to identify whom he means. The crowd shares his confusion. The man who clambers up the platform is not tall nor powerfully built; wears no hood of either black or scarlet; he has not bared his chest over a thick leather belt, and no gristle frames his manly chin. In fact, he is rather slight and knock-kneed, with light, bushy whiskers that stick to his pale cheeks as though they are glued on. He is wearing a frock coat, quite clean given the circumstances, and raises his top hat shyly to the crowd.

'A gentleman?' Charlie asks, surprised and dismayed.

'His Majesty's servant,' Thomas whispers. On his face horror mingles with expectation. Charlie feels it, too. They will watch someone die. His eagerness sickens him.

It's the Smoke, he tells himself.

If so, it is a perversity shared by all.

The victim arrives. For the longest time nobody can see anything other than the tall hats of the guards. The crowd parts reluctantly, letting them through, along with the prisoner hidden in their midst: a jostling that is passed on, from shoulder to shoulder, hip to hip, through the length and the width of the square. At long last the guards reach the ladder leading up to the platform. Smoke rises from their knot of bodies, dark and oily, like they are burning bits of rubber. Shouts are heard, the cry of pain. Then someone is lifted up, bloody and smoking, her body a sheet of paper blotched with black.

'A woman,' Charlie gasps. He staggers under the surge of people starting forward.

She is no longer young, and dressed in a white, ankle-length shift. Across the distance it is difficult to get a precise sense of her features. Big, round cheeks; a heart-shaped face; a mass of greying hair pulled back sharply from the forehead: this is all Charlie makes out. Her Smoke has stained her, face and clothes, but it is as nothing compared to what happens next. The guards position her under the noose; the executioner slips it around her head. He is talking to her, quietly and intently. They are the same age, give or take; they could be man and wife. Just then the crowd starts a chant, 'Murderer, murderer': not for him, who is about to send her to her death, but for her and the crimes she has committed. She turns to the crowd, raises her arms.

And all of a sudden she seems to be burning, her skin an oil slick set ablaze on water. Black, sticky Smoke seeps from her every pore. In a moment the plain white shift is black and sodden, clinging to her chest, her hips, her legs. The Smoke slithers up the executioner's body like a living thing. The transformation is immediate: a wolfish snarl grows over his face; his fingers, still on the noose, grab her hair and tug at it, and he starts screaming something at the crowd, triumphant and cruel.

The cloud of Smoke, heavier than air and hungry for converts, descends into the crowd. You can watch it spread by the yard. In less than a minute it has reached Charlie. It's like breathing in a drug: his heart begins to pound in his chest, his senses open themselves to the crowd. He ceases to think in terms of good and evil, he wants to see the woman die, wants the noose to break her neck, for the sheer thrill of it. And at the same time he admires her, hopes she will drag the executioner down with her, through the trapdoor under her feet; is ready to riot, tastes his own Smoke, grey and feeble on his tongue, and for the first time in his life enjoys its flavour.

All around him the chant continues – 'Murderer, murderer' – but a new note has emerged in it, as accusation transforms into salute. Charlie tries it, quietly at first, then louder and louder: 'Murderer, murderer.' He feels the joy of being one with the crowd, wants to share it with Thomas, wants to link arms with him and run riot, mingle Smokes, and partake of his friend's sin.

But when he looks, Thomas is no longer there.

Φ

Afterwards, back at school, lying awake on his bed, Charlie will be pleased to realise that his concern for his friend was stronger even than the woman's Smoke. A breeze helps him, too, blowing in from behind. It shifts the centre of madness to the other side of the square. The executioner, his features twisted into a mask of hate, is kicking the woman, then throws his weight against the lever that triggers the trapdoor. Charlie turns and breaks his connection with the gasping crowd. He hopes Thomas is behind, away from all this, in safety. But it is hard to make out any one person in this ocean of faces, all trained in the same direction, all blackened and mean. He spins, catches a sickening glimpse of her body, dancing, twisting at the end of the rope, looks in all directions and sees nothing but the heaving, shouting mass, all individuality dissolved, each face reflecting the emotion of its neighbours and retaining little feature of its own.

Then his mind snags on someone, the way a fingernail may catch on fabric. It isn't Thomas, and he does not know him, but all the same his separateness commandeers Charlie's attention. It isn't immediately obvious why. The man is in his forties or thereabouts; stout but not fat; the head sloping sideways, like he's twisted his neck. A face like a dozen others; his clothes shabby and stained. And yet he stands apart. It's his movement, for one thing. Like Charlie's, his eyes are not on the execution. He is slinking through the crowd, trying to exit the square unobtrusively, pushing past those who will move aside and rounding those who won't. Something else, too. It takes Charlie the longest time to see it. He is not smoking. Smoke surrounds him, Soot clings to him in streaks and blotches. But he: he is not smoking. When he passes not two feet from Charlie, the boy, taller by some inches, sees the man's neck, where its sideway crick exposes the inside of his collar. It is clean, though the outside is quite black. As though feeling a stranger's gaze on him, the man pulls at his loosened handkerchief, ties it tightly around his throat. In another moment he has reached the edge of the crowd and is walking more boldly, away.

Charlie hesitates. He wants to chase the man (not *chase*, says the Smoke that's coursing through his blood: *hunt*), but he is worried about Thomas; glances around for him with no success. Then he is gone, the man who did not smoke; swallowed up by the city.

Charlie spins and looks and pushes, all to no avail. As the press around him eases, it's becoming less difficult to move and at the same time harder to see, bodies shifting across his field of vision. Within minutes there is a general movement outward: the crowd disperses, a strange kind of exhaustion in their faces. Charlie realises that it is over. The woman is dead, cut down from the gallows. The spectacle has run its course. Thick flakes of Soot are floating in the air like snow; living evil has turned into mere dirt. As the townspeople leave – to work? to tea? – the only figures remaining on the square are some sixty schoolboys in blackened uniforms and the small huddle of their teachers. As for Thomas, Charlie finds him on his hands and knees, not far from the scaffold, retching. He walks over to him, crouches, waits for Thomas to look up.

'Quite a Trip, this,' he says at last, as lightly as he can.

41

Thomas nods, spits, smiles. 'Yeah. Not bad.'

But his eyes are full of fear.

Φ

They walk the city for several more hours, visit a bottle blacking factory, and admire the grand husk of Buckingham Palace, now locked up and abandoned. A factory bell marks the end of a shift, and Julius, against Renfrew's instruction, stops a flower girl and buys a bouquet, then presents it back to her with a gallant bow. Not even his cronies grant him applause: the boys have withdrawn into themselves, walk in a state of nervous exhaustion. Smoke continues to waft through the air, but it is lighter now, or else Charlie has gotten used to the feel of his own meanness. There is no lunch or dinner, but neither students nor teachers complain. They have but one need: to go home.

On the way back to the train a group of men passes them, in good if Soot-stained clothing, holding rolls of charts under their arms and protected from the crowd by the ministrations of two burly servants who clear the way with the liberal use of their elbows and arms. Renfrew tips his hat to the well-dressed men, and they tip theirs, look after the boys for a moment, before moving on.

They ride the train in silence. Inside the compartment it is very dark. The gas lamps have not been lit, whether by oversight or on purpose it is hard to say. Some whispers travel, boys with their heads thrown together, in conspiracy and shame. A few boys are crying, quietly, their faces to the window. Charlie can tell because of how still they hold themselves. Thomas, too, keeps his face averted. Charlie would like to ask his friend how he is feeling; how it was that they got separated at the market square and what it was that made him sick. He would like to tell him about the miracle he, Charlie, witnessed. *A man without sin; crooked about the neck.* Just thinking about it makes his heart pound with hope.

But Charlie does not trust himself to speak. A trace of Smoke remains in his blood, feeds a feeling of irritation and impatience. He's afraid it will show in his voice. There is more to it yet. Charlie's whole sense of who he is lies disturbed and the calm that returns to him feels strange, like a mask grown stiff from want of use. When he finally does speak, his voice surprises him, is gentle, unchanged.

'We look like miners, coming back from a shift,' is what he says.

42

He has been looking at his hands. The skin beneath his fingernails seems unnaturally pale next to his blackened fingers.

Thomas turns, cheeks shiny with Soot. There are no tear tracks linking eye and jaw.

'There was someone there,' he says. 'Underneath the scaffold.'

'*Under* the scaffold? Who?'

'Don't know. A man. He was stripping the dead woman's body.'

'Stripping her.' Charlie's mind recoils from the image. 'For valuables?'

Thomas shakes his head, glowers at the memory.

'For her Soot.'

He turns his face back to the window before Charlie can ask him to explain.

Φ

At Oxford station the lights are burning. The boys take stock of one another. They are, each of them, splattered with sin. Renfrew and the other teachers do a head count, the third since the execution square. It is a miracle they have not lost anyone. A porter leads them to a room at the far end of the platform. Behind the double doors yawns a bathroom twice the size of the one in school. Four rows of shower-baths stand in military formation. Some gas lamps are lit but turned down very low. On a counter there sit a hundred little towels, neatly folded and piled chest high. Renfrew crosses the room, opens a metal hatch on a large stove in the corner. A fire roars beyond. The heat is so intense he retreats two steps before speaking.

'First,' he says, 'you will retrieve a towel. Then: strip. Pile your clothes here.' He points to the floor. 'They will be incinerated. We deposited a change of clothes for each of you there.' He points to a door marked Changing Room. 'Make sure to wash thoroughly.'

A murmur goes through the room. *The clothes will be burnt!* No inspection; no investigation. Whatever happened that day, it will not be added to any ledger of transgression. As relief floods the students, they grow chatty, almost giddy. Clothes are ripped off bodies; cotton tears, buttons pop; boys can be seen running half-dressed through the room, flicking at one another with towels. As they push into the shower-baths and scrub at their skin, their noise begins to fill the entire hall. They are sharing the wonders they beheld in London, cleansing them of fear in the process; their day recast as adventure.

Charlie listens to them distractedly, his own face raised into the tepid stream of the shower.

'Did you see the Negro street sweeper? He had but one hand. He was so black you could hardly see the Soot.'

'I swear she was selling heads, that one, only they were shrunk somehow. Size of a cricket ball, each of them, tied to a stick by the hair.'

'And as I was looking at her, she opens her coat all of a sudden, and underneath she's starkers, I swear. Only she was so dirty you couldn't see a thing.'

It takes but half an hour until everyone is clean, kempt, dressed in fresh clothing. The teachers, too, have cleaned up in an adjoining bathroom; some have found time to shave. A servant has come and is shovelling their dirties into the incinerator with a pitchfork, much as though he were moving manure. The fire's heat has spread throughout the room and is bringing a rosy hue to Charlie's cheeks. Nothing is left of the delirium of London other than the vaguest of yearnings: for irresponsibility, perhaps, for some hours spent in the thrall of base instinct. He wonders briefly whether all delirium leaves you with this trace. Then Renfrew calls them together, teachers and pupils, assembles them by the door.

'Well then,' he says, gently, triumphantly. 'We have survived.'

The mood is such that the phrase is met by applause. Renfrew basks in it then silences the boys with a gesture, a conductor working a willing orchestra.

'There were those who doubted that we would. And more, many more' – his gaze wanders over his fellow teachers – 'who doubted we should go in the first place. Why, after all, did we have to climb down into this pit of filth and infamy; breathe the air of crime; rub shoulders with the mob; and see our blood poisoned by their lust and hate and greed?'

He pauses for effect. Charlie is watching Renfrew's hands. They are small, handsome, freckled hands covered in fine, reddish hair. When he speaks, they dance in front of his body.

'The answer is that we had to go, because we may be called upon to do so again.'

He shuts off the murmur of ill will before it is conscious of itself.

'Two hours ago, as we were leaving the city, all of you saw some gentlemen walking through the city with charts. They were

44

engineers, charged with remodelling the sewage system. Yes, the sewage system. The dirtiest place in a dirty city; the place where all muck and filth collects. They do so not from need, not for profit, nor because they are bound by contract. They do so because it needs doing. Because, like you, they are gentlemen from the country's finest families. Because they see a cesspool and wish to clean it, improve it, reform it.

'To do so, they must stay, sometimes for days and weeks, in the very centre of London. They must breathe its Smoke and taste its infection. They must endure having their senses clouded, their skin stained, their clothes turned to rags. They must fight temptation, must fight weakness even in their sleep. But they are gentlemen and they are strong. And each time they go, they are stronger, better prepared. More determined, more steeled in their convictions.

'These gentlemen are you. After your studies – as engineers or as doctors, as men of politics or scholars of political science, as scientists and architects – you will be called upon to serve your country and to improve the lives of those miserable wretches we beheld today. When the day comes, do not hide from this responsibility. Do not hide behind fear, or comfort, or the claim of ignorance. When the day comes, stand proud and answer the call of duty. I know you will.'

Renfrew scans his audience's faces. His certainty is like a force. Like Smoke. It travels through the air and settles in your bones.

'I – we – took you to London today so you would see it for yourself. Infection cannot be explained. It must be felt. Today you are afraid of it. You felt its power and quivered before it. But tomorrow – tomorrow you will face it like an enemy. Tomorrow you will begin thinking about what you can do to change things. To take up the fight. It is your duty as Christian men. As men, I say. For you return from London, no longer boys.'

The roar that follows his last statement surprises even those who stand cheering. Even Thomas falls in with it, stands next to Charlie hollering out a triple 'Hurrah!' For once it is Julius who stands apart. Charlie watches him, at the edge of the circle of boys, face drawn, chewing on his tongue.

Renfrew does not bask in his glory but rather shushes them, rushes them out, onto the platform and out of the station, where their row of coaches is waiting for them. The weather is milder than it has been in days, a warm wind blowing from the west, the snow slowly melting and catching the streetlights in puddles.

Φ

Renfrew does not ride back with the teachers. Instead he climbs into Charlie and Thomas's coach. He takes his seat between them as though he were but another boy; butts in, lifting his suit tails, so they are forced to scoot apart. Immediately all conversation dies. The slush outside makes progress slow as each revolution of the wheels requires extra effort from the horses, and the gentle rocking coupled with the warmth of their recent bath sends them asleep one by one. Charlie feels cut off from Thomas by their teacher's rigid form and is too self-conscious to lean across Renfrew to see whether his friend, too, has nodded off. He attempts to catch glimpses of Thomas from the corner of his eye, but all he can see are his legs, angled in front of him, the stillness of his feet, the hands that are spread out on Thomas's thighs. He is so very motionless, in fact, and for so very long, that it comes as a surprise when Thomas speaks.

'Smoke is a disease,' he says.

It takes Charlie several moments to register the words are not for his benefit but for Renfrew's, and that they form a question, not a statement.

Like Thomas, Renfrew speaks quietly, neither turning nor moving his limbs, his hands resting on the top of the walking stick that juts from between his knees. It occurs to Charlie that he has chosen to ride in their coach just for this, a conversation with Thomas.

'No,' says Renfrew. 'Smoke is no more a disease than a fever is the flu. Both are symptoms.'

'Smoke is a symptom,' Thomas reiterates, slowly, carefully. 'Either way. Smoke is not from God.'

Now Renfrew turns, bends down to Thomas, his voice warm and earnest. Charlie strains to understand, bending sideways with him, his cheek almost touching Renfrew's coat.

'Why not?' he asks. 'Measles are from God. Swinburne's religion is outdated. Unenlightened. He does not understand that a scientist can have faith. That science is a form of worship.' Renfrew pauses. 'But there is something else you want to ask, isn't there?'

'If it is a disease. That for which Smoke is a symptom. Does it pass from father to son?'

46

Before Renfrew can answer the coach hits a pothole and throws them out of their seats. In a second everyone's awake, jumbled, pushing themselves up, away from awkward contact with their teacher. Charlie waits for the conversation to resume, but it doesn't. When he looks outside, he sees an owl sitting on a moon-washed hedge, its eyes fixed on his and ringed by fine light feathers that give its stare a look of callous wonder.

Φ

They arrive. As they clear the last hillock, the school lies beneath them, dormitories, schoolhouse and shed forming a black cross in the wet snow, the dark brick evading the eye's attempt to impose details. The boys need no prompting to file inside. They head for the dormitory; some fling themselves down without undressing, an eerie silence in the room where whispers, laughter, little squeals mark bedtime on any other day. Charlie waits for half an hour after the last candle has been blown out, then gets up and sneaks into the bathroom. Thomas is already there, sitting on the floor wrapped in a blanket, his back slumped against the wall. Charlie slides down next to him, the tiles very cold under his bottom.

'Me first or you first?' he asks.

'You,' Thomas says. Charlie is unprepared for how weary he sounds. More than just weary. Resentful. Sick of life.

'Unless you'd rather not. It can wait till tomorrow.'

Thomas shifts enough to find his eye. 'You want to talk, Charlie, and I am your friend. So let's talk.'

He does not say: That's the price we pay. *For friendship.* But it's there in his voice.

It sickens Charlie that friendship should have a price.

47

Thomas

Charlie tells me. About the miracle he has seen. And I tell him what I was up to, back there on the market square. An accounting, you might call it; honest as two Dutchmen settling up. Then we go to bed. Neither of us reacts in the way the other needs him to. Charlie wants me to be excited; to spin theories with him; devise a plan to return to London, sniff out his man.

But it is difficult to believe what he is saying. A man immune to Smoke, hook-necked and all. It's impossible: like seeing a ghost. I don't think he's lying, of course. Charlie wouldn't lie. It may be he can't. But this was the city: a thousand people pushing, pressing, trampling one another's feet; no air to breathe; and so much Smoke in your blood your senses are screaming. To fight, mostly, smash someone's face in. That, and the other thing. Find a girl, I mean. Rip her clothes off. It's like your pulse has slipped into your pants. Chaos, in other words, not just in the square but in you, rage and lust and laughter, too, a mad sort of laughter, weightless and simple, and your stomach tells you it wants food. To see a man in all that, one that doesn't smoke, because his collar is clean on the *inside*, you notice it when he walks past, well—

There're things you have to see for yourself, I suppose. It's not a matter of choice, or even friendship. You cannot help but doubt. *We are lonely creatures*, Mother used to say. *We live in our heads*.

And when I tell him what I saw – and I do, as honestly as I can, though my stomach heaves with it and I keep spitting up black – all Charlie wants to know is, am I all right. I'm not, but that isn't the point. Charlie saw an angel walk past. I think I saw the devil. There's none of us going to be all right ever again.

Here's what I tell Charlie. When the Smoke spread – *her* Smoke, the woman's, the murderess's – I pushed closer to the scaffold. What drove me there was this: if Renfrew is right, if there is a cancer of sin growing in my guts, my heart, my brain, then she is what I will become. My fate, my patrimony. So I wanted to look her in the eye.

For a sign of kinship, or something. That and there was this flavour to her Smoke, something I have noticed before but never this clearly. It tasted *good*. Bitter of course, sheer murder on the lungs, but good, too, like spirits I suppose, if you ask a drunk. Seductive. So I pushed ahead. Dealt out a lot of thrusts with my elbows. Earned just as many, my arms black and blue, but kept on pushing.

Right up front there was a yard-wide gap ringing the gallows: only a few people there, and those that were, were pushing back, into the crowd. It makes sense: everyone wanted to be close – see her hang by the neck, her tongue sticking out – but if you got too close, you got pushed up against the scaffold, a big wooden box, really, man-high, square and covered with a large sheet of nailed-down canvas, somewhere between brown and black. And there, flush against its wall, you couldn't see a thing. Even the Smoke was thinner here, travelled over your head.

So I tried to fight my way back into the crowd, charged it really, headfirst, half mad. And got kicked in the gut for my trouble, Soot and stomach juice mixing in my mouth. Next thing I knew I was on my knees in the dirt, back in the no-man's-land near the scaffold, leaning on it as I struggled up. That's when I noticed that there were gaps beneath the canvas, that the box that held the gallows was more lattice fence than crate. And the evil thought flashed in me that it was there, inside, where the hole would open, the trapdoor, I mean, through which the woman would fall. And – it pains me to say it, it was the Smoke, the Smoke, only perhaps it wasn't – I wanted to see it, see *her*, even if it were only her feet kicking as the breath was being choked out of her, and her stiff bloated face when she was dropped through the hole once she was dead.

So while the crowd was chanting, and the Smoke got so black you could hardly see the sky above, I ran my fingers up and down the side of the scaffold, looking for a gap large enough to slip through. I found it right at the bottom, got flat on my stomach (like a worm, I remember thinking, like a nasty little worm), jimmied two nails out of the canvas cover, and scooted through.

Inside the only light came from the open trapdoor above. I was too late, I realised it at once. The body was already on the ground, cut down, the knot of the noose jutting up from her neck like a knife handle. Already her Smoke had ceased; she lay on her stomach, legs splayed, the shift so caked with Smoke it cracked like icing.

It didn't crack by itself, mind. There was someone there, crouching by her side, his back to me. Holding a razor. He cut the shift away in two quick jerks. The naked body underneath remained as though dressed in Soot. The figure – wearing a suit, a lumpy overcoat, dirty, patched tweed – produced a jar from out one pocket, squat and wide-mouthed, its glass tinted like an apothecary's bottle. Then he bent over the body again, razor in hand, and with its three-inch blade began to scrape away Soot.

Not everywhere, mind. The figure knew exactly what it wanted. He started at the face, unclenching the woman's jaws, wedging open her mouth; then, with gloved fingers pulled out the tongue as though to cut it off at its roots, only to run the blade along its underside, taking shavings of the Soot trapped there, more liquid than powder, then transferring it into the jar by sliding the blade along the inside of its rim, the way you'd clean a butter knife of jam. The sound of steel on glass. It seemed louder than the crowd outside.

I watched all this silently, lying on my stomach, afraid not of the knife but of this man with a dead woman's tongue between his fingers. He harvested Soot from two more places, the depth of both armpits, then (I turned away here: London's Smoke in my brain and lungs, and still I turned away, could not bear it, was ashamed) from the scissor of her thighs: scraped the knife again and again against the rim of his glass, then screwed it tightly shut. All told it took him no more than a few minutes. He never turned around, worked with precision, never more quickly than the task merited, but with an efficiency that hinted at practice.

Then the light changed, down in this coffin that formed the base of London's gallows, grew darker. It was the face and upper body of the executioner bending over the trapdoor and thus blocking much of its light. He did not say anything, but I saw the figure nod to him and pocket its jar. Immediately, the executioner rose again, barked an order at the guards, to fetch the cadaver.

I had but one thought now, and that was to crawl back out. I moved, rolled back towards the canvas flap I had prised loose. I turned once before pushing through. The figure was at the opposite side, crouching in front of a little door that served as its exit. He, too, turned. It was dark, and it was smoky, and yet I swear we would recognise one another again. An odd face, lined and old but also boyish, the chin closely shaved under a bloom of whiskers, with a fine, bony nose and graceful eyebrows; large, heavy-hooded eyes. A gentleman's face, I remember thinking; or a gentle-born boy's who's been aged in his sleep. Like an evil Snow White. Then the man stepped out, closing the door, and I rolled through into the street, where the vomit jumped out of me like a living thing that wanted to get out, out, out, as though association with my body was shameful even for my half-digested dregs of breakfast.

Charlie found me there, a quarter of an hour later. Time to watch the guards drag the body out from underneath the scaffold by its feet, wrap it in sacking, strap it to a plank, and carry it off. That, and to wipe my mouth. My sleeves were so Soot-stained, it was like dragging charcoal across your mug.

The taste of it, though, stayed with me all the way back to school. It's still there in the morning, when the school bell pulls me out of a dream the only part of which I remember is a snowman, its button eyes slowly sliding down the blank of its face one by one. I make it to the toilet before I am sick.

And later – later I go to see Renfrew, for the first of many such sessions. 'An intensive programme of reform.' Those were his words to Trout. It's Cruikshank who fetches me, at five o'clock sharp. Renfrew does not say anything when I enter his office. That's all right; I don't need instructions to know what to do. The dentist's chair is awkward to climb into but turns out to be surprisingly comfortable: upholstered red leather, turned dark and smooth where other boys have sat and squirmed and sweated, leaving behind the hazy outline of a ghostly boy into which I fit myself quite naturally.

'Do I put the straps on?' I ask, doing my best to sound calm.

Renfrew smiles.

'That's what all the boys ask. I think secretly you really want to.'

And I relax a little. After all: Renfrew already thinks the worst of me. That I am growing murder inside myself, the way a woman grows a child.

Nothing I can say or do will ever disappoint him.

51

Sweets

School is different after London. The change is everywhere and, as such, hard to pin down. Charlie tries to make an inventory, but the more he writes down the more he feels is slipping through the cracks, the gaps between words and lines, until he throws away the piece of paper in disgust.

For one thing, the upper-school boys are having dreams. Nightmares. Not all of them, naturally, and not the same ones night after night. Actually, nobody is sure they are nightmares, because nobody remembers a thing. But they wake up, these boys, with rings under the eyes, bruises almost, their pillowcases stiff with Soot. Renfrew does not punish them. This in itself causes a stir. A gentleman never smokes. He dreams, it is said, as he lives. In the lower school, by contrast, the pale grey smears found in the bedding in the mornings continue to exact their price: the boys are disciplined, if mildly.

Then, just four days after their return – Christmas is approaching, and the boys have taken to counting days – an upper-school boy breaks through the ice while playing on the school pond. They are in the midst of a cycle of rapid melts and sudden freezes, and the boys have been warned to be careful. Charlie happens to be present: it is the afternoon break and he is returning books to the school library. The water in the pond is less than a yard deep, but the bottom is littered with rocks and discarded old junk. In summer, when the water is low and the sky clear, one can see the shape of an old bedstead rusting at its bottom, like the wreck of a steamer lost near the shore.

It's this very shallowness that causes the injury. The boy's skate hits something at an awkward angle, and his ankle and knee buckle. He is screaming so much, they have a hard time dragging him out of the hole and onto the thicker ice. There is blood on his trouser leg, hard to see at first, then dyeing the ice a vivid crimson. Low down on the shin, a thick, jagged spike pokes a bulge into the wet wool that nobody dares touch or even name. Worst of all is the pungent yellow Smoke that comes out of him, out of his mouth chiefly, along with

52

his screams. It does not rise like a plume but rather crawls along at ankle-height then falls to the snow as a fine yellow powder, impossibly bright, like the jar of sulphur on the shelf in chemistry class.

It's Charlie who beds the boy's head on his knees until the school nurse arrives. His name is Westwood. Peter. They share a bench in Greek.

'Help me,' Peter keeps shouting up at Charlie's face, not five inches away, and Charlie strokes his hair and promises he will be fine. By the time the nurse gets there, Westwood has passed out, his blood steaming in the cold air.

The boy is saved, but for several days the school lives in suspense over whether his leg will come off. It doesn't. When Charlie's trousers return from the laundry, he can trace the outline of the boy's Soot as a faint yellow line that runs from knee to mid-thigh. Disquieted by this, Charlie requests special permission to deposit the trousers in the school's charity box, destined for an orphanage in London. He'd rather burn the pair but this, he is reminded, is against the rules. Charlie recalls the incinerator at Oxford station. They broke the rules easily enough on their return from London.

Φ

Then there is Thomas. He is being sick. Every morning, like clockwork, a full hour before the bell is rung. The sound travels, the toilet bowl amplifying his retching like a trumpet, sending it down the corridor to where Charlie crouches, waiting for him, a handkerchief at the ready.

'Are you all right?' Charlie asks him in what has fast become a ritual.

'Right as rain,' Thomas always responds. 'Something I ate.'

They laugh, as the ritual demands. Gallows humour, one calls it. Only now that they have seen a gallows, the phrase is not one they use.

And every day, at four o'clock sharp, when the others sit down for study hall in the upper assembly room, Thomas goes to visit Renfrew. It's part of his punishment for fighting Julius. Thomas does not seem to mind these sessions. No, that's not quite true. He dreads them and seems eager to go, all at the same time.

Charlie asks him about what happens at these meetings. There is too much between them – too much respect, for one thing; too much trust; too many hours spent exchanging confidences – for Thomas to button up entirely. But Charlie sees him guard his words.

'What does he do to you?' Charlie asks. 'Renfrew.'

Thomas shrugs. 'He asks questions. I answer.'

'Do you show?'

'Very little.' Thomas seems surprised by this himself.

'What does he ask about?'

'This and that. Family, a lot of the time. My mother and father.' His face darkens, grows pensive.

'It's the way Renfrew asks,' he continues. 'In *earnest*. Like he really wants to know. Sometimes I almost trust him. Sitting there on his inquisitor's chair.'

Thomas looks up, forces a smile through the tension on his face.

'He's an arsehole, of course, a gaping arsehole. But there are worse.'

Φ

There are other, confusing aspects to life after the Trip. For all the darkness they brought back with them, a new spirit has taken hold of the upper school, a sort of pride. It takes Charlie a while to understand it is the afterlife of Renfrew's words, his demand that they return to London when they come of age. Students can be found standing in huddles discussing 'politics'. It is time, some say, to join the movement for 'reform'. Parents are criticised, not individually but as a generation, and slogans are bandied about. These are seductive and evade concrete meaning. 'The return to the cities' is one of them. 'Scientific theology' is another. 'Meritocracy'. 'Rationalism'. 'Regeneration'. Even (more quietly, with guarded smiles): 'Revolution'. On occasion one of these impromptu speeches results in a belch of fine, light Smoke. The boys so chastised by the emission of their bodies observe this Smoke with genuine shame. It is, they say, a judgement on the purity of their motives. They invent punishments that they impose on themselves long before Renfrew has had the opportunity to study their Soot.

Interestingly, the ringleaders of this talk are boys who have been at the periphery of things before. Not one of them is a member of the highest aristocracy. Charlie, usually popular across factions and cliques, finds himself avoided: his father is a prominent Tory. Julius, too, is sidelined, participates only by listening, an odd little smile on his face. In fact, his whole behaviour appears changed, especially as regards his treatment of Thomas. The first few days after the Trip he was his usual self: jeering, pompous and hostile, baiting the younger boy at every opportunity. Now he is watching; seems omnipresent in fact, always at the doorway or standing halfway down the hall, his hands in his pockets, his dark eyes everywhere. He, too, is having daily discussions with Renfrew. It may be that it is these that account for the change.

Whatever the reason, it has caused considerable confusion amongst Julius's cronies – the whole complex web of guardians, prefects and informers that upholds the structure of the school more surely than the teachers or the bricks and mortar. They have grown unsure of themselves, less inclined to impose their authority. In the lower school in particular, Charlie hears, it leads to more horseplay, more pushing of the rules, more arguments, more quarrels, more Smoke. But then, it's almost Christmas. Everyone will be going home soon. Perhaps it is nothing more than this.

Φ

With Thomas busy and preoccupied, and he himself adrift between the group of 'rebels' and those representing the 'old order', Charlie finds himself with time on his hands. For a full week he searches for a sense of purpose, sits around, mopes, turns pages in books he fails to read.

Then he finds it.

It starts with a letter to his parents. The letter is overdue – Charlie is to write every Sunday without fail – but he did not feel up to it before. Even now each sentence crawls reluctantly out of his pen. The words sit on the page with a clarity that feels unearned and mock the chaos of his emotions. Part of the problem is that he does not know what to say about London. 'I was very saddened to see the preponderance of sin,' he writes then crosses it out immediately. Not only is it inaccurate but it reads as though he is eighty years old and lives between the covers of a book (and a dusty book at that). 'I hated it,' he tries again, but again crosses it out, because this, too, is false, inadequate, short of the mark. It takes six drafts in all for him to produce a satisfactory version. In not one of them does he mention the execution.

Near the end of the letter, in the only paragraph he writes with ease and pleasure, for it conveys well-wishes to his sister and his excitement about coming home, he includes the following passage: 'A week or two ago the teachers here received a shipment of tea and sweets from Beasley and Son. Naturally this caused some interest amongst us pupils – especially the sweets! Would it be cheeky for me to ask whether a packet of B&S's might not also find its way into my Christmas stocking?'

He finishes with a postscript asking whether it would be agreeable if he invited a schoolmate to join the family for all or part of the holiday. 'I do not know what his commitments are,' he adds, punctiliously, 'but am anxious for you to meet him. He is my best friend.'

He sends the letter by the afternoon mail and receives an answer with the customary promptness the day after next. Yes, the family are looking forward to his coming, his mother writes, and are planning a trip to their house in Ireland, weather permitting. Yes, he may bring home whomsoever he wishes, however obscure his family name; and all the more so if the boy in question is dear to his heart.

As to the sweets, Charlie has to read the letter twice until he finds an answer to his request. It is hidden away in a paragraph describing Christmas preparations and in particularly the tree that the servants put up 'only yesterday' and whose branches are 'so rich and wide that there will hardly be any space for the family to fit beside it'; 'nor is there hardly any chance that Father Christmas, who in some picture books appears a rather portly fellow, will be able to squeeze his girth into the room to deliver any presents.' 'It may be just as well,' his mother goes on, 'that, by the evidence of your letter, you are growing up very fast and have no more need for superstitions. It is all the more important that your maturing desires, regarding Christmas presents and otherwise, be married to your discretion, both in public utterance and private.' There the paragraph ends. The next spends an inordinate number of words reminding Charlie to wear warm socks and underwear, and to dry off properly after taking a bath.

Charlie wishes that his mother could put matters more simply, but has learned that it is the nature of letter-writing that one must state things in a roundabout and somewhat poetic way; otherwise letters would become frightfully short. All the same he finds himself returning time and again to that curiously worded admonishment concerning his 'desires'. It appears his mother is telling him to shut up. This is unusual in itself; as an answer to his lighthearted request it is also rather odd. More than odd.

A riddle.

It is fair to say that Charlie is intrigued.

Φ

The following afternoon finds him setting out to the little market town about half an hour's walk from the school. Visits there are one of the privileges he enjoys as an upper-school boy in good standing, though they are limited to a single outing a term. The day is grey and cold, the skies threatening snow. Charlie walks briskly, trying to keep warm, but there is no way to keep the frost out of his hands and feet. Town is a butcher's, a baker's, a greengrocer's and a haberdashery. There is also a public house near the river and a Saturday market, though none of the boys have been to either, their privileges extending neither to weekends, nor to pubs. In a side street, not far from the market square, there is yet one other establishment. By three in the afternoon, when the bakery's bread is all sold out and no longer dominates the smells of the town centre, one can find it by scent alone. A sticky smell: baked apples, cloves and cinnamon along with something darker, black treacle burnt solid on the iron of a red-hot hob. HODGSON'S SWEETS, DRIED FRUIT AND NUTS. The sign of a date tree, stooped low under its load.

Inside the shop the smell of sugar is near-overpowering. The shop's heat, too, rushes in on Charlie, puts a tingle in his fingers, toes and cheeks. A young gentlewoman is there, buying candied fruit and almonds. Her waist, seen from behind, is impossibly slender and accentuated by the bundled opulence of her skirts. Attending her is Mr Hodgson: a short, balding man with pockmarked cheeks and tidy movements. At his feet, rolled up snout to tum, lies a runty whippet, as skinny as they come. The dog appears to be sleeping, dreaming; sweeps its tail across the floor in jerky crescents and sounds quiet, high-pitched yelps. It is, it occurs to Charlie, a very good thing that animals do not smoke.

Charlie keeps to the back of the shop until the woman is finished. The schoolboys are warned not to have any contact with the opposite sex other than the school nurse, though greetings, of course, are allowed. He takes off his cap when the lady turns to leave and holds the door for her; sees her smile with pleasure. Outside, she crosses the

57

street holding up her skirts to avoid dragging them through muddy snow: a movement to the hips underneath that wasplike waist that puts a blush on Charlie's cheek. The shopkeeper, too, looks after her with a certain fixity, a wisp of Smoke curling from somewhere at the back of his neck.

'Corsets, eh? Like tying a belt around a balloon. You always think it's goin' to blow. Above. Or below.' He makes a violent gesture that brings to mind a man with a garrotte. Then he recalls he is speaking to a gentleman, albeit a schoolboy, tousle-haired under his cap. 'Begging your pardon, of course. I was only speaking in jest.'

Charlie is unsurprised by his sudden deference, at once strategic and real. No police, no magistrates are needed to enforce it. It is written into their complexions, the man's Soot-coarsened, Charlie's soft and smooth. All the same, the grocer's comments about the lady have put Charlie in a difficult position. As a gentleman, it is his duty to reprimand the man. But Charlie is also a minor, instructed to respect his elders, irrespective of their station. That, and he is here for a purpose.

A new customer relieves him of his uncertainty. It is the vicar, come in for a tuppence-worth of humbugs. Charlie immediately cedes ground to him, stands by the door with his cap in his hand, listens to their small talk. On his way out, the vicar stops, places his eyes on Charlie, and leaves them there for longer than is comfortable. He is an old man, close-cropped white whiskers meeting underneath his chin.

'Skiving?' he asks at last.

'I have a pass. From the school.'

'Ah. A good boy then.' The vicar digs in his paper bag. 'Here, have a humbug.'

His eyes won't leave Charlie until he has put the stripy sweet in his mouth. Then the old man sniffs the air.

'It smells of Smoke in here. Underneath all the sweet. Not yours? His then. Well, his kind are meant to. Go to hell, I mean. God's natural order. Good day.'

He says this quite loudly, even cheerfully, then walks out of the door. Again both Charlie and the shopkeeper find themselves looking out the big front window, watching after the flutter of dark skirts.

'A true man of God,' Mr Hodgson declares, rattling the vicar's pennies in his fist. 'Righteous. If not as charming as the lady.' His tone remains oddly poised between deference and derision: accepting the truth of the vicar's words, yet enraged by them all the same. 'And what would you like, then?'

Charlie has anticipated the question and has worked out his answer, word for word, on the way over; has gone so far as to try it out on the empty country road where there was no one to hear. But now, faced with this man, his wheedling manner, the coarseness of his pockmarked cheeks, and the heavy atmosphere of the shop, he hesitates.

'Sir?'

'Liquorice,' Charlie improvises. 'A penny's worth.'

'Sweet or salty?'

'Salty.'

'I've snails and coins.'

'Snails, please. And a quarter pound of hazelnuts.'

'Anything else?'

Again Charlie hesitates, then is grabbed by the sudden fear that the vicar will return, or some other customer, and make his query impossible.

'A tin of sweets.' He is rushing through the words so fast, he himself can hardly understand them. 'Beasley and Son. If it's no trouble.'

'What's that?'

'Beasley and Son. A tin. Or just some loose sweets, if that's how they come.'

The shopkeeper's reaction is curious. The first thing he does is step away from Charlie, look him up and down. Reassess him. But he is still the same skinny schoolboy in the same tidy uniform, his collar freshly starched. Then the man looks behind Charlie, as though he suspects him of hiding a second person behind his back; then on past him, at the desolate street. His face is a mask of calculation.

'Don't know what you're talking about.' Smoke frames the words like a shroud. 'You better pay and get out.'

And then, as Charlie stands counting out coins: 'Who sent you here?'

'Nobody. I just . . . The teachers have them. I have seen the little tins. Just ordinary hard-boiled sweets. Like caramels, only clear. There was a delivery not long ago . . .'

Charlie trails off, unsure how much information he should part with. The school's affairs are private. Nobody has ever instructed him to treat them as such, but it is a rule all the same. It's like any other family. When there are guests at dinner, certain things are not to be discussed.

'Look here,' the shopkeeper barks with particular emphasis, as though defending his good name, 'if there was a delivery it wasn't from here.'

More Smoke pours out of him, not thick but oddly smelly. It paints dark blotches on his collar. Again he looks Charlie up and down; again he stares past him, out at the street, searching it for accomplices.

'How much was there, boy? How many tins?'

Charlie shakes his head. 'I don't know. A crate, I believe.'

All at once the man is shouting, sweeping Charlie's pennies off the counter so they scatter on the floor.

'You're a liar, you are. Out. I will make a complaint, don't think I won't. Out, out!'

The noise wakes the dog. It jumps to its feet, presses its ears flat against the side of its head, arches its back, then spins on its feet, trying to identify the source of danger. But Charlie has already re-treated to the door. He lets himself out, the brown paper bag with his sweets in one hand. Outside, released from the atmosphere of boiled sugar and caramelised nuts, the cold air hits him like a slap. Through the window he sees the man shouting, shaking his fist above his head. The high, quivering yelp of his dog falls in with the man and follows Charlie down the street. Then the wind picks up and scatters their noise. All the same, it's only at the edge of town that Charlie stops running.

The road to school seems longer on his return.

Φ

Charlie tells him everything, starting with the letter. Thomas listens distractedly at first, then with ever greater intensity, biting off pieces of liquorice from an uncoiled snail.

'So what do you think?' Charlie asks when he's finished his account.

'These are disgusting. You should have bought sherbets.'

'Be serious, Thomas.' But he can see from his friend's face that he is, really; that he is thinking it over.

'I don't know,' Thomas decides when the liquorice is gone. 'Some sort of drug, maybe. Like opium.'

'Can't be. You can buy opium in any pharmacy. Or laudanum, which is the same thing.'

'Something different then. More powerful than opium. Hence: forbidden.' Thomas shrugs. 'We won't really know until we get our hands on some. Here's the thing, though. The shopkeeper knows about it. And so does your mother.'

Charlie bites his lip.

'Yes,' he says. 'I think so too.'

'So everybody knows. It's only we idiots who are kept in the dark.'

Φ

Two days later Trout summons Charlie. He does not send Cruik-shank: it's a note he finds in his pigeonhole, unsigned. *Report to the headmaster. Seven o'clock sharp.* The note is so beyond precedence that right away Charlie knows he is in trouble. There is nothing, of course, that can be done. He will have to go. Trout will ask him how he came to hear of Beasley and Son. If Charlie mentions Cruikshank, Cruikshank will get the sack. If he does not, he will be in disgrace and make acquaintance with the dentist's chair. A tribunal seems possible. A letter to his parents will already be in the post.

As he sits at dinner, sawing forlornly at the lukewarm cutlet in front of him, Charlie watches an invisible wall spring up between him and his fellow students. Already he is set apart: they just don't know it yet. Thomas would understand this feeling, but Thomas isn't here. Charlie has not seen him since breakfast. There is no one to help him make sense of his fall, from good boy to pariah.

Φ

Charlie arrives early at the headmaster's door, then sets to pacing, up and down the long empty corridor. Dust balls attend him with the solicitude of pets, withdrawing some inches as he draws close, then following in his wake, sometimes as much as a yard. The moment he becomes conscious of this game, the headmaster's door swings open and the fat, rosy dome of Trout's head leans into the hallway.

'Cooper!' he calls and is answered by the prattle of footfalls.

'Here, sir.'

Charlie's haste scatters the dust.

61

Past the door and the antechamber, logs smoulder in the fireplace, spreading the smell of pine. Two armchairs have been arranged before it, inclining to each other confidentially, as though they are in conversation. Trout pats the seat of one, before sitting down on the other. His weight is such that this is a delicate operation: he stands in front of his chair like a diver on the platform, his fundament thrown back and the chest forward for balance, then topples backward with a grunt. Charlie draws closer suspiciously, sits on the edge of the other chair, his weight still in his thighs. A coffee table fills the narrow gap between the two chairs' armrests. It holds a decanter and a silver tray with glasses.

'Port or sherry?' Trout asks blandly. Behind the blandness, and the fatty half spheres of his cheeks, the headmaster's eyes are shrewd.

'Nothing, sir.'

'Nothing? Nonsense. Some port then.' Trout fills two glasses. 'Taste must be cultivated. Just like good habits. A gentleman appreciates his wine.'

Trout seems intent on waiting until Charlie has taken a sip before saying anything further: he sits with his own glass raised halfway to his lips, sniffing at the liquor. For a mad instant Charlie grows convinced that the headmaster is trying to poison him. But even if he is, Charlie has no choice but to drink. Unlike a pill, you cannot hide liquid under your tongue or in the pocket of one cheek.

'Well?' Trout asks when Charlie puts down the glass.

'It's sweet.'

'Yes. Hints of plum. And something earthier. Truffle, perhaps.'

Charlie cannot tell whether he is making fun.

'I suppose you have guessed why I invited you here.'

Trout does not say *summoned*. There is no need. They both know the truth.

Charlie manages a nod.

'It is an unusual situation, Mr Cooper. Unusual. I cannot recall the last time I had to ask a boy for such a tête-à-tête.'

'Yes, sir.'

'But then, what is to be done? After all, you are his closest friend.'

Charlie looks up, confused. 'Whose?'

'Argyle's.' Trout eyes him suspiciously. 'Do I have the wrong boy?'

It takes Charlie three breaths to adjust his expectations. He tries to ward off the feeling of relief, but it is there. His body slides deeper into the armchair.

Perhaps, though, Trout is merely toying with him.

'No, sir. I mean I am. His best friend.' A new worry takes hold of him, its texture different from the old. 'Is he in trouble?'

'You know he is. But perhaps you don't understand the full extent of it. He may have been ashamed to share it.'

Trout wets his lips. Fat lips and a fat tongue; the glow of spittle on soft pink skin.

'We are worried about Argyle. There is something growing, you see. Inside him.'

'He is sick?' His own voice sounds normal in Charlie's ears, controlled. But his stomach is a knot. No, not his stomach. His entrails, from colon to diaphragm. A knot. It will take hours to unpick.

'Sick? In a manner of speaking. There is a darkness growing in him. Corruption. No, more than that. *Evil.* Yes, I think we cannot do without the word. Evil. It's like your friend is carrying a bomb. When it blows, well . . .' Trout swirls the wine in his glass. 'Dr Renfrew has found evidence, you see. In his Soot. It's *scientific.*'

The word is given a certain weight, a certain note. Not resentment, exactly. Wariness?

'And it can't be stopped?'

'We mustn't lose hope. Mr Swinburne recommends prayer. It has been known to help. For instance—'

But Charlie is not listening now. He is thinking, remembering Thomas's conversation in the coach back from Oxford, picking through its terms. *Smoke is a symptom*, Renfrew said.

What then is evil?

Trout sits watching him. His tongue is restless within his mouth. Charlie can see it move around, probing his teeth, his gums, the insides of his cheeks. Or haunting them. It distracts Charlie.

'If it's a disease,' he asks at last, forcing his thoughts into words. 'Evil, I mean. Then it can be cured.'

Trout spreads his hands on his thighs. 'Dr Renfrew believes so.'

'You don't?'

'Can we cure tuberculosis? Cancer? The common cold?'

'We might, one day.'

Trout sighs. 'One day. Perhaps. But you go out there, whisper it. That there is a *cure*. Watch the world go up in flames.'

They both lapse into silence, each draining his glass. The heat from the fireplace is so intense, it climbs up their limbs, filling them, consuming their strength: a fat man and a boy, sprawling side by side.

Charlie fights it, sits up again, returns to the edge of the seat as though preparing his departure.

'Headmaster,' he asks, sounding adult to his own ears, 'sir. Why did you call me here?'

'Ah, that.' Trout reaches into his coat pocket, produces a sheaf of papers. 'Your friend Argyle has received an invitation. From his uncle, in Nottinghamshire. Asking Argyle to join him and his family for Christmas. He insists, in fact.'

Charlie stares at him, shocked.

'You open our mail?'

Trout flushes, laughs. 'God, no. That'd be against the law. He wrote to me, naturally. Baron Naylor. Argyle's uncle.' He waves the envelope at Charlie, too briefly to see to whom it is addressed. 'I'd like you, Cooper, to go with him. As his friend. Keep him out of trouble. In light of things, I mean.'

A gaggle of questions rises up in Charlie. They spill out unsifted, in fragments, each word very fast.

'But I have already written to my mother to ask whether Thomas can come – Besides, won't he want to go home – And after all, I can't simply invite myself, can I?'

'Order, Cooper, order. One thing after the other. No, Argyle won't be going home. It's quite impossible, he'll tell you so himself. And as I've already said, his uncle *insists*. So there cannot be any question of his spending the holiday at your parents' house. As for you, all it will take is another little letter to your parents. After all, Baron Naylor is the head of one of the most prominent families in the country. Just like your father. Your people will approve of your wishing to make social connections. They will send a letter to Baron Naylor explaining that you and his nephew are very fond of each other and had hoped to spend the holidays together. All it takes is a hint. He, no doubt, will respond with a formal invitation. It's all very simple indeed.

'Naturally,' Trout adds, so casually he does not even feel the need to look at Charlie when he speaks, 'naturally, there is no need to alarm Baron Naylor about young Argyle's predicament. His *condition*. Nor yet your family. It would make it harder for Ar— that is, for Thomas. Once stigmatised, it will be twice as hard for him to ... especially given his father's disgrace. But I don't need to go on. You understand very well how it is. Which is why I think your presence will be an invaluable asset to your friend.'

Trout heaves himself out of the armchair. The leather's groan might have been comical under other circumstances. But the head-master's eyes are too shrewd to mistake him for a buffoon or a kindly relative troubled by wind. He walks Charlie to the door.

'I enjoyed our talk, Mr Cooper, really I did. We should do it again. Perhaps after your return. You can tell me then how it went. Yes, I think that's an excellent idea. A debriefing of sorts. Like in the army.'

Outside, at the top of the stairwell, Charlie nearly runs into Swinburne, lurking in the darkness of the landing and breathing heavily, as though he's been running. Charlie passes him quickly, telling himself that it is merely a coincidence. No dust dances in the gaslit stairwell beneath: it's only when the boy passes that it rises and hovers, like inverted snow.

Φ

'So are you coming along as my nurse or as Trout's spy?'

They are sitting on the bathroom floor again, making themselves small amongst the row of tubs. Above them, where copper pipes crisscross underneath the ceiling, a spider is sitting in a wedge of web. It may be dead, trapped in its own design. Then again, it mayn't.

Charlie ignores the question. If Thomas is angry, so is he. They have both taken off their shirts, in case they Smoke. They mustn't stain.

'You should've told me, Thomas,' he says. 'I'm your friend.'

Thomas responds without looking at Charlie.

'Yes, Charlie, you are. But will you still be my friend when I end up killing someone? When I turn into that woman underneath her noose, and you feel your own heart blacken with my filth?' He spits, angry, the spit steaming with white Smoke. 'I'm rotting. Inside. Like a cancer, growing in here.' He rubs his chest, his guts, his hand a fist that he forgets to unclench. 'Renfrew says there's a machine, on the Continent somewhere. You step behind a sort of mirror and then they can see inside your rib cage. The bones show snow white. And your Smoke shows like fog. The blacker it is, the lighter it shows.'

He spits again, watches it steam. 'Another year and I'll glow like an angel with my darkness.'

Charlie does not know what to say. He has rehearsed his conversation with Trout for Thomas. *There is a cure*, he wants to say, but the words get stuck in his throat.

There may be a cure.

It isn't the same thing at all.

'Do you know him?' he asks instead. 'This uncle who has invited you?'

'I met him as a child. Him and his wife. I only saw them from across the room: a bald man and a woman in a fancy frock. I was too young to be introduced. You know – *the childhood years of sin.*'

Charlie watches Thomas spit once again, hears his own voice drop to a whisper.

'Why can't you go home for Christmas, Thomas?'

A snort, tinged with dark. 'Nobody there. Mother's dead.'

'And your father?'

'Dead.' Smoking now, breath and skin: 'Disgraced.'

'What did he do, Thomas? Tell me.'

'What did he do? He beat a man to death.'

The words are hard, curt, devoid of pity. *Here I am*, Thomas seems to be saying, *exposed*. But also: *Don't push me, not now. I might break.*

Charlie hears it, fights a shiver.

'He beat a man,' he repeats, no weight in his voice. 'Very good. Thoughtful of him. This way we can spend Christmas together.'

It takes Thomas a heartbeat to react. A transformation in his Smoke, a lightening, colour entering the grey; a parcel of emotions exhaled by one boy and inhaled by the other; infection: the sharing of a burden.

'Prick!' Thomas says softly, shaping a Smoke ring with his mouth.

'You're welcome.'

Charlie waits until both their breaths have slowed and Thomas's Smoke has cleared out of his blood. It's like stepping inside after racing through a tempest; as such not without a sense of loss. Then he changes the subject.

'Where were you all day? I was looking for you.'

It does something for Thomas, this question, completes his transition from desolation to wry humour.

'Well, first I had to see Renfrew. Kept me for a full three hours.

And then I went over to Foybles's rooms to ask him whether he would help me with my maths.' Amusement flashes in Thomas's eyes. 'Made him rather nervous, I think. The demon boy coming to visit.'

'Maths? But you are doing fine with—'

In answer Thomas opens his right hand which has been curled into a fist from the moment they left the dormitory. Inside sit two little cubes, clear like icicles. For two heartbeats Charlie does not know what they are. Then it dawns on him and his stomach contracts with excitement and fear.

'He will know who took them,' he whispers.

'Maybe. There were five pieces left. He may not know the count.'

'He's sure to.'

Charlie pictures it, Thomas searching the desk in Foybles's office, while the latter had his back turned. It seems impossible. Thomas picks the thought off Charlie's face.

And dares a smile.

'Foybles left me alone in his living room. The question I asked, it turned out to be rather complicated. He needed to consult his books. It appears Foybles has his library under his bed. At least that's what it sounded like. Like he was moving all his furniture about. Hunting for Newton. He left me alone for a full half hour.' Thomas shakes his head in disbelief.

'Did you smoke?'

'A little. But I opened the window. By the time he came back, it was barely noticeable. And he was very focused on the problem.'

Charlie tries not to think it. *Thief.* But there is admiration in the word, too. It has long been a puzzle to him how often sin aligns with pluck.

'Shall we?' Thomas asks. 'Together?'

They each pick up a sweet. Held up to the light Charlie discovers a pattern stamped into one side. 'B&S' underneath a stylised crown. The Queen's stamp.

There is no smell to the little cube.

'Let's do it then. On three.'

Thomas counts them down and they each place it on their tongues, like sugar lumps, gently pressing it against the roof of their mouths waiting for it to melt. It takes a while for the taste to spread. Lemon and the sharp herbal notes of Chlorodyne. The sweet dissolves very slowly, one has to suck on it, chew it, wear it out with one's tongue. Charlie is waiting for something, a tingling, a giddiness, some sensation of change: a surge of strength, a sudden sleepiness, the elation of alcohol. But nothing happens, nothing at all. A look at Thomas tells him it is the same for his friend. At long last they swallow the final few shards. All that remains of the sweet is a medicinal flavour clinging to their gums, like they have just cleaned their teeth.

They both sit in silence, feeling crushed.

'So what does that mean?' Charlie asks when he can no longer bear it.

'It means,' Thomas says, 'that we don't understand anything. Not a thing.'

The spider above them quivers when they rise, in imitation of life.

Swinburne

The boy asks me after vespers: name of Kreuzer, Martin Herman. First year upper school. A German. Naturalised, I suppose, the whole family, for generations.

But still.

'Sir,' he asks, nervous, perhaps on a dare. 'What is theatre?'

He does not smoke when he says it, so he thinks the question must be safe. I make him kneel in the pew. Sore knees. Good for the soul. He's been reading Mr William Shakespeare, he admits after some probing. A book of plays. Where does he have it from? This he is not supposed to say.

His crying is unbecoming.

I bring all this to Trout. His brother gave the book to him: Kreuzer, Leopold Michael, five years the elder. I remember him well. Daft little shite. Wouldn't have thought him capable of something quite so monstrous.

'There has to be a letter,' I say. 'An investigation.'

Trout won't have it. Soft, he is, or else *adaptable*. Changing times: turning with how the wind blows.

'Confiscate the book,' he says, 'and let it rest.'

Let it rest indeed. He didn't hear the boy: 'Please, sir. I don't understand. Why is it forbidden?' Snot on his lip from all the crying, sitting there like a wet moustache.

I could have told him, of course, could have recited the Stratford Verdict, chapter and verse (*Seeing that theatre depicteth sin and maketh it a matter of entertainment; that it maketh bad actors commit the action of sin without the sign of Smoke, and good actors inhabit sin so thoroughly that their crime showeth on the skin; that the former createth an illusion that sin be possible without Smoke, and the latter forceth paid servants to distort their souls for the sake of spectacle; that in short the whole enterprise be lewd and filthy, unbecoming to gentlemen and dangerous for the crowd; that its lessons and morals, however pious, be lost behind intemperate words and idle shouting; and theatres be cow barns plastered with Soot; for all these reasons, and by the power invested in us by the Crown, we henceforth forbid and banish the performance, circulation, writing and reading of theatre plays, be they comedy or tragedy, history or romance, from this our realm from this day forward etc. etc.*), but that is hardly the point. Obedience is. A boy must not question. A new wind is blowing indeed. Renfrew's kind of wind. Some mornings one can smell its stench all the way from London.

There are other portents. Spencer has begun to smoke. Julius, the head boy, *primus inter pares*. He has been seen, coming out of Renfrew's office, with Soot on his sleeve. A pure boy, the purest we've had. Corrupted by his own master.

And by the presence of that other boy. Argyle, Thomas Winfried. A child of sin. He smokes most every day, like a workman's boy in puberty. Even the servants avoid him, the kitchen hands, the groundsman living in his shed on the south field. Noble by birth, Mr Argyle is, if we have faith in the honour of his mother. Yet common as dirt. There is some mystery attached to his father's name, but Trout forbade all questions and discussion on pain of suspension. Argyle must have a powerful sponsor indeed.

For now he has been summoned by one of the highest in the land. Baron Naylor, lord of Stanley Hall, Marquess of Thomond. Nobody's seen hide nor hair of him for nigh on ten years. Fell out with the Queen, some say; lost her trust. Trout's sending Cooper, Charles Henry Ferdinand. The future Earl of Shaftesbury. A redhead, more pedigree than a prizewinning bitch; his father a beacon in this, our dusk. He must be disappointed with his son.

Naturally Trout will want a report from the boy. I wonder: is it the state's business, or his own? And if the state's, which corner of its civil service? There are divisions now, where there once was unity: the commonweal crumbling like a slice of sailor's rusk.

The New Liberalism. Science. Self-Governance. Progress. Fancy words harbouring heresy. A sin turned political movement. Sitting there, in Parliament, in plain sight.

Renfrew is a liberal.

Ask yourself: who studies *his* linen?

Part Two

The Manor

The crew, man, the crew! Are they not one and all with Ahab, in this matter of the whale? See Stubb! he laughs! See yonder Chilian! He snorts to think of it. Stand up amid the general hurricane, thy one tost sapling cannot, Starbuck! ... (*Aside*) Something shot from my dilated nostrils, he has inhaled it in his lungs. Starbuck now is mine; cannot oppose me now, without rebellion.

Herman Melville, *Moby Dick* (1851)

Lessons

They take a late-morning train. Thomas calculates they should get there well before nightfall, but they have to change twice and miss their connection at Rugby. The station is dreary and empty, the waiting room a row of wooden benches clustered around an oven without heat. A conductor tells them there will be a train within the hour, but three o'clock passes, then four, then five, before he reappears, buttoned up tight and smelling of Smoke and brandy, informing them there has been a delay.

It is eight by the time they board the train and they are frozen through. In their compartment a stack of blankets sits folded on the luggage rack. They fetch them down and wrap themselves in the plain brown wool which appears clean but gives off a bitter, funky smell, as of soiled sawdust.

Thomas and Charlie have spoken little in the past hour. The long day of waiting has exhausted their conversation and they are both busy with their hunger, having shared the last sandwich and the last apple not an hour after pulling out of Oxford, taking turns, bite for bite, each making sure he did not get the last. It left them nibbling at scraps in the end, laughing, passing the wretched piece of apple core back and forth, until Thomas swallowed it, seeds, stem and all, and nearly choked himself with laughter. Now their silence sits with them in the compartment while, outside, high winds batter the train.

'You hungry?' Charlie asks at one point, his own stomach growling in the dark.

'No,' Thomas lies. 'You?'

'No.'

'Tired?'

'Not a bit.'

'Same here.'

Φ

They both startle awake as the train comes to a stop. Mechanically they shake off the blankets and fetch their luggage down only to realise it isn't yet their station. It is hard to say how much time has passed. Darkness presses in on them, seems confirmed rather than relieved by a single gas flame shivering in its glass cage on the station platform. The wind is like a living thing, searching their windows for purchase, pushing fingers, tongues in through the cracks.

As his eyes adjust, Thomas comes to realise that the platform is not as deserted as he had assumed. A group of men, women and children huddle against the wall at the far side of the building, downwind from the storm. There may be as many as a dozen of them; they have formed a circle, their faces focused on the centre. When the train starts up again, they draw level. It is too dark to read any features, but their gestures and stance speak of a violent excitement, clenched fists and wide-open mouths, the feet planted wide apart. At the centre of their man-made ring, two figures are wrestling, one atop the other, the upper stripped to his waist. They pass too quickly to say whether it is two men or a man and a woman; whether they are fighting or engaged in something yet more intimate. The whole group is steaming with a misty Smoke, snatched off their bodies by the storm and blown down-country where it will plaster a barn, a house, a shade tree with their wind-borne sin.

Then they are gone.

Charlie and Thomas go on looking out the window long after they have passed the group, though now, coated by country dark, the pane has turned into a rain-streaked mirror.

'Pedlars?' Charlie asks at last. 'Circus people? Irishmen?'

Thomas shakes his head. 'Who knows.'

The words are laced with a familiar flavour; the mirror shows a shadow darting from his mouth.

'A group like that,' Charlie goes on, 'they infect each other over and over. Like a tiny, travelling London.' He sighs. 'I wish we could find a way to save them.'

'Save them? Whatever for? Leave them in their filth. They deserve it. Isn't that the point of Smoke?'

The words come out wrong, hard and flat and ugly. Charlie looks at him in shock. Afraid that Thomas means them, aware of the smell that's filling the compartment. For a moment, Thomas searches for a phrase that will explain. But you cannot unsay the said. And how

74

do you account for the yearning, distinct in his chest, to go back and join the men and women in their circle, find out what it was that those two figures did, half naked on the freezing brick of the station platform?

'We better get there soon,' he says, wrapping himself into the blanket, and leaving Charlie to worry for his, Thomas's, soul.

Φ

It must be past ten when they arrive at their destination. It is hard to be sure. The station clock is not working; Thomas has no watch, and Charlie quickly realises that he has forgotten to wind his. Baron Naylor's coachman welcomes them on the platform. He is tall, bearded, half frozen and nervous; stands muffled into a greatcoat; insists on carrying their luggage, then sets it down again after a dozen steps.

'It's too late now to harness the horses,' he explains, both in accusation and apology. 'You were expected at three. Even then, the light would have been bad. It's quite a ways, you see.'

'Then we'll stay the night,' Charlie suggests reasonably.

The man nods, bends for their luggage, hesitates.

'There is no inn.'

'And the waiting room?'

'Locked.'

'Then where will we—'

The man sighs, picks up the suitcases again, leads them down the platform steps and across the station yard. Here the horse stables form two shabby rows, shielded from view of the travelling public by a high brick wall. No streetlamp lights their footing here, and as they make their way down the alley in near darkness, Charlie becomes eerily aware of the animal eyes looking down at him across the stable gates, his ears alert to the shifting of hooves and the sudden shakes of horses' heads; the exhalations of hot air; the smacking of lips and meaty tongues. When a horse bares its teeth not a foot from his ear, they catch the little light there is: crooked, yellow teeth like stubby fingers, sticking out of colourless gums. Startled, Charlie stops. Thomas bumps into him, swears, then places a hand on his shoulder.

'Spooky, eh?'

'Just lost my footing,' says Charlie, thinking that this is what it must feel like to have a brother. An older one, willing to stick up for you in times of danger.

75

They arrive at a door that the coachman wedges open with some difficulty. Inside, the scene is lit by a single tallow candle. The room is tiny, smells of hay and horse. Three men sit propped up against the wall, smoking cheap little pipes; two others are stretched on the freezing ground under shabby blankets, resting, sleeping, or dead, it is impossible to say. Nobody speaks: not to welcome them, not to communicate with one another.

'The coachmen sleep here,' Baron Naylor's man informs them. 'I'm not supposed to . . . That is, gentlemen don't usually come here.' He sets down their luggage on the little floor space there is, unwraps his scarf to free a throat marked by an old burn scar. 'But I don't know where else—'

'It'll do,' Charlie says, and Thomas sits down wordlessly, then spreads his coat out underneath him. The room is so small that once Charlie has joined him, they lie wedged between the prostrate men and the smokers. Charlie's face rests not an inch from the hand of a stranger. It is a large hand, with a tattoo in the wedge of skin between thumb and index finger, and knuckles blackened by either dirt or Soot. The tattoo is some sort of picture. Charlie cannot make it out until the hand spreads itself upon the wooden floorboards like an animal seeking purchase for a leap. A mermaid, bare-chested, smiling.

'We will freeze to death,' Thomas whispers next to him, only half joking, and closes the gap between their backs so their spines can pool their bony warmth.

They lie like that for half the night, strangers coughing around them, a mermaid dancing on dirty skin, her breasts shrivelling, expanding, winking with every twitch of the coachman's mighty hand.

By dawn, the boys are so stiff, they have to support each other as they limp into the coach. They crawl onto padded benches and drift into a state more stupor than sleep.

Φ

The coach ride has the texture of a dream: half a dozen impressions sewn together with no reference to time. They set off in twilight, amongst undulating hills; pit towers and smokestacks dotting the horizon. The sounds of travel seem to reach them through their skins as much as their ears, clot together into lumps of noise they are too tired to unpick: the churning of the muddy wheels, the crack of the

76

coachman's whip, the frightened whinny of the horse when it slips in a puddle. Once, Thomas wakes to see the ruin of a windmill studded with tiny birds: the sun at its back and the coach riding through its mile-long shadow. Then, the moments miles apart but adjacent in his consciousness, separated only by the closing of his eyes, they arrive. The coach halts before the long flank of a stone building painted dark by rain. A butler runs out, umbrella in hand, and escorts them the ten steps from coach to side door, gravel crunching under their feet.

'Delighted to see you have arrived, Mr Argyle, Mr Cooper. You will be hungry, I presume? If you'll follow me to the breakfast room.'

At the mention of breakfast, Charlie's stomach growls like an ill-used pet.

Φ

They sit at breakfast. The room is large and formal, the tablecloth starched; the chairs high-backed and stiff; the cutlery elegant silver. The table seats ten, but the boys are the only ones in attendance. They perch shabbily – their clothes rumpled, their hair unkempt, their hands all too hastily washed – afraid they'll stain the uphol-stery. The butler has left them. A door to their left admits kitchen smells but has not yet produced any food; cold heavy rain running down the glass veranda doors.

Then a serving girl arrives. She may be eighteen or nineteen; casts a glance at them from large, thick-lashed eyes before kneeling in front of the fireplace and setting to lighting it. She strikes a match, holds it to a scrap of newspaper already crumpled amongst the coals, repeats the action; cowers down, still on her knees, her chin now almost touching the floor, to blow into the hearth. The boys – dazed, blurry-eyed, travel-weary – feel they have no choice but to stare at her. At her bottom, to be precise. In this position, stuck in the air with most of the skirt's fabric trapped under her knees, it is most awfully round. When a stomach growls (Thomas's? Charlie's again?), it sounds pleading, forlorn. And still the girl kneels, blowing at coals.

'I believe the fire is quite lit.'

They did not hear her enter. Thomas and Charlie move as one: reflections in a mirror. Both heads swivel; both faces fill with blood.

Charlie's blush is the darker. A redhead, he is, copper-skinned. To those of his complexion, nature is not kind. It's like a different type of Smoke, marking a different type of sin. There is no chance at all that the lady does not notice.

For she is a lady, though she is no older than they. Not tall, but holding herself as to appear it, her long, plain dress cut almost like a habit. A small face: pale, rigid, self-possessed, cold.

And pretty.

Her lips are naturally very red.

'Come here, please,' she says, not to them but past them, at the cowering form of the servant.

The girl obeys with haste but no enthusiasm, her large eyes on Thomas, then the floor. Her blouse is tight over her chest, the skirt rides up a little where it has caught at the swell of her hips.

'It appears your clothes have shrunk in the wash.'

The young lady's voice is neither cruel, nor loud, nor yet commanding. Notes of patient sadness underlie it; humility forced into action against its will. Next to the serving girl's large, florid frame, she appears dainty, almost fragile.

An elf, Charlie thinks.

Thomas thinks: a nun.

'It would be better if you returned to scullery duties for the moment. Until you learn to be a little less obtrusive.'

'But Lady Naylor promised me—'

'Until the New Year.'

'But she said I could—'

'Spring, then. You are excused now.'

There is a sequence to what follows. The Smoke comes first, a sudden little plume that rises from the servant girl's chest and leaves a smudge in the starched cotton. Then tears start running, clear and silent, from dark eyes to chin. A sob follows, starts in the depth of her and shakes her frame. Next she flees, all grace forgotten, the sound of her flat shoes travelling through the closing door.

'My apologies. Miss Livia Naylor. Mr Argyle, I presume? And Mr Cooper. How do you do? We were expecting you last night. It is, of course, long past our breakfast time. Never mind, here comes the food. Sit. I shall keep you company.'

Φ

They sit and eat under her scrutiny. Her gaze is all the more disconcerting for being patient, judicious, meek. Charlie finds it turns the toast to ashes in his mouth and the tea to bilge water. A well-brought-up boy, he forces himself to make conversation.

'Thank you for welcoming us so kindly, Miss Naylor. Will your father – the baron – will he be joining us this morning?'

But the girl gives him no help. 'I am instructed to tell you he is unwell.'

'That's too bad. Your mother, then?'

'She has ridden out.'

Charlie feels rebuffed but is not ready yet to admit defeat. He adds with an increasing air of desperation: 'I assume you're home from school. Just like us. Not that we are at home, of course. But all the same . . .'

She waits attentively, patiently for him to finish, but he no longer knows where he is going, is hiding behind his cup of tea, appalled at the noise he makes when he tries to take a quiet sip.

Thomas rescues him.

'You are not a prefect, by any chance?' he asks, his mouth full, a dangerous note to his question. 'Back at your school?'

She meets his eyes calmly. 'I have that good fortune. How did you guess?'

They cannot help themselves. Both boys start to giggle, furtively at first, then, their frames shaking, with blushing abandon, while she watches on, calm and meek and disapproving, until their hysteria dries out along with their appetites, and the butler reappears to see them to their room.

Φ

'We'll have an early dinner at five.'

These were Livia's parting words. The only thing of substance that the butler added to their stock of information was the location of the bathroom, right across from the room in which they have been housed, and the exhortation that they may feel 'more comfortable once they have had a moment to refresh themselves', which Charlie takes to mean they stink. The room is prettily but sparsely furnished. It holds two beds, a press and a little desk and chair. They remain on the ground floor; a large veranda door grants access to the gardens. The clock shows a quarter to eleven. When Charlie returns at eleven twenty from his bath, he finds Thomas at the open veranda door, watching a pheasant striding up and down the garden path. He leans out, into the pouring rain, and Charlie hears him count the windows along their wing of the house. He breaks off after three dozen, turns, his hair wet and his face streaming with rain.

'Is your house like this, Charlie?' He points for some reason at the marching pheasant who is on yet another of his rounds.

Charlie thinks about it.

'You mean this big, with gardens like that? Yes, I suppose it is. Grander, even.' He shrugs. 'How about yours?'

'More like that.'

It takes Charlie a moment to see the garden shed through the sheets of rain, standing with its back to the dark treeline beyond.

'Do you miss it? Home?'

Thomas's eyes turn hard. 'No.' He gathers up a dressing gown and towel. 'My turn for a bath.'

Φ

Their afternoon passes turgidly. Five seems an eternity away. The rain continues unabated, making exploration of the garden impossible. When they step into the corridor instead, they find most of the doors closed, the house all but abandoned. It seems rude to climb stairs and look around in earnest, and after running into the hard stare of the butler at what appears to be the stairwell down to the servants' quarters, they retreat, watch the clock move in painfully slow spasms. At three thirty they change into their formal attire. It is only now they realise they have forgotten to hang their clothes or ask someone to press them, and their shirts and jackets look hopelessly rumpled. Thomas's dinner jacket is not only cut according to some long-abandoned fashion but appears to have been attacked by moths. The cloth underneath the left arm is all but worn away. This leads him to walk around awkwardly, pressing one elbow into his flank so as to hide the bald spot. When the clock hand finally twitches onto five, their nerves are exhausted with boredom. At three minutes past, the fear takes hold that nobody will come to collect them.

'We could ring for a servant,' Charlie suggests.

'*She* might come. Tell us off.'

'*She* doesn't seem the type to answer bells. Maybe the other girl will come.'

'The one with the big—'

Thomas is stopped short by a knock on the door.

'Dinner,' says the voice of the butler. 'Lady Naylor is waiting.'

Φ

Lady Naylor is resplendent in a floor-length evening gown of velvet and silk. She gets up from a chair when they enter, shakes their hands, gives Thomas an odd searching look. Charlie does not know how to gauge his friend's reaction: a thoughtfulness comes over Thomas that is not quite recognition. He takes his seat at the large, formal dinner table with a frown on his brow. Charlie sits across, separated by four feet of starched damask. Rows of cutlery five-deep flank their china plates.

'I trust you had a pleasant journey.'

The boys look at each other. Both remember the coachman's waiting room with its unheated floor; the anxious look of their driver as he explained there was no inn.

'Very pleasant,' they say, almost in unison.

'I am pleased.'

Miss Naylor enters. She is wearing the same nunnish dress she wore at the breakfast table, though she has added a string of pearls. The boys rise, somewhat clumsily, dropping napkins, until she has taken her seat across from her mother. Right away a servant appears carrying a tureen of soup.

'Please,' Lady Naylor says, after a perfunctory grace, 'begin. We don't stand on formality here.' The smile she flashes highlights the absurdity of the claim. Her daughter scowls and spoons the soup with such noiseless precision that Charlie, sitting next to her, feels like a pig at the trough.

'I trust your parents are well, Mr Cooper.'

'Very well, thank you.'

'It is generous of them to share you with us in this festive season.'

Charlie blushes. 'Not at all.'

'Livia, you forgot to mention to me what a perfectly charming young gentleman Mr Cooper is. And Mr Argyle, too, of course.' She flashes another smile, subtle and naughty. 'Her report, I must tell you, was rather libellous.'

'Mother! I really must insist that you don't lie.' A flush of colour has entered the girl's cheek.

'See how we live here,' her mother appeals to her guests. 'Under the heavy thumb of a prude.'

Φ

Dinner is interminable. The soup is followed by jellied tongue, followed by duck in red wine sauce, then roast pork and parsnips, plum pudding, cheese and coffee. For all Lady Naylor's charm, she is unable to draw more than half a dozen words out of her guests. Even her daughter refuses to be drawn into extended skirmishes. She checks herself at several points and accepts her mother's barbs with the patience of the martyr. Charlie watches them all very closely: Thomas, awkward in his moth-worn jacket, eating little, chewing over some thought; Livia, thin, pretty, embarrassed by and for her mother; and Lady Naylor, a well-kept woman of forty, her hair piled high above her mobile, made-up face, the thin lips thickened by a rich hue of lipstick. She is speaking to him, Charlie, mostly; seems less interested in Thomas. Only now and again her eyes steal over to him, an odd sort of question in her gaze. It busies Charlie so much, this gaze, he too nearly forgets to eat.

At last the final plate is cleared away. Lady Naylor stands. Charlie and Thomas quickly scramble to their feet.

'Thorpe will see you back,' she announces. She gestures behind them. Thorpe, the butler, proves to be already in the room, having appeared from God knows where. His face is the perfect façade of lifelong service: so devoid of expression that one must assume his total indifference towards all matters grave and light. Certainly towards the comfort of guests.

'Please let him know if you require anything else.'

Lady Naylor shakes both of their hands again, again holding Thomas's eyes for the fraction of a moment, then takes her daughter's arm and walks away.

'Goodnight,' Charlie calls after them, too late to elicit an answer.

'This way, if you please.'

The butler escorts them like a jailer. Back in their room, Thorpe hands over custody to the great clock whose ornate hands will keep measure of their sentence. It is barely seven o'clock. Dinner is finished, they have been sent back to their room.

It feels worse than school.

'What do you make of them, then?'

Charlie thinks about his answer. Why not? They have time to spare.

'The mother is all perfume and charm. And the daughter—'

'Tar soap and prayer books!'

They laugh but there is no mirth to it. The room already feels small to them, the two beds narrow and far too soft. They have opened the veranda doors and sit there freezing, facing the rain-dark night. Letting the wind in.

Just to feel alive.

'Did you recognise her?' Charlie asks, getting up and inspecting the bookshelf. There is an incomplete encyclopaedia, volumes Aa to Pe; a Bible; a chess game in a wooden box; playing cards; dust. 'Lady Naylor, I mean. You looked like you might have.'

Thomas begins to shake his head, then shrugs.

'I'm not sure.'

'A distant memory? From childhood?'

'No, it's not that. Something else.' He searches for it, pulls a face at not being able to put his finger on the feeling. 'She reminds me of someone. Her face, her bearing. Someone at school, I think.'

'One of the teachers?'

'Perhaps.'

They sit for a while, get up, open the door on the draughty silence of the corridor, close it again, step out onto the veranda, get wet. No sound travels through the night. They have been abandoned even by the peripatetic pheasant. Whatever lights may be burning within the house are blocked by curtains and blinds.

Thomas closes the veranda door at last, flops onto the bed.

'It's not how I imagined it. Coming here. I thought there'd be, I don't know. Some sort of confrontation. Another dentist's chair. Or maybe the opposite. My uncle explaining the world to us. Confiding secrets.' He scowls at his own naïveté. 'Some kind of adventure in any case. But it looks like he has some other plan in mind. They'll bore us to death.'

'Perhaps we are to serve as bad examples to his daughter.' Charlie rouses himself from their gloom, walks back over to the bookshelf. 'Chess then? Or draughts?'

But Thomas is too disconsolate to answer.

He wakes not an hour after they've gone to bed. It's not a dream that wakes Thomas but a thought. He knows where he knows her from.

Lady Naylor.

He leaves the room in his nightshirt. His clothes are piled onto the chair, and there is a dressing gown hanging off a hook somewhere, but he does not want to wake Charlie by rummaging around.

The corridor carpet is soft under Thomas's feet. He asks himself what it is he is searching for. Proof, he supposes; something that will turn conviction into fact. It isn't clear what can furnish such proof. All the same: staying in the room, staring wide-awake into the darkness, alone with his thoughts – it is impossible. He walks slowly, shivering. After a while he realises it is not from the cold.

The house isn't totally dark. Here and there some embers are smouldering in fireplaces. In the dining room, a gas lamp has been left burning, turned very low. In the kitchen, a shimmer of light has fought its way up from the cellar, the servants' quarters, and carries along with it the soft, high giggle of one of the girls. He stops for a moment, savouring it: tiles underfoot now, vivid with cold.

Out in the front hall, Thomas locates the great spiral staircase. Its banister is a sweeping black curve, reassuring to his touch. Upstairs he finds another light, brighter than the others: it draws a tidy white line underneath a door. He stands in front of it and listens; raises a fist to knock, then stops himself and turns the handle. He might be walking into Livia's bedroom; into a toilet busy with an occupant. But to knock and don the role of supplicant (for what is a knock, if not an invitation to be turned away) is not palatable to him. Not now. The taste of his Smoke is so bitter in his mouth, he does not need to look down his nightshirt to know he is showing.

The room is a lady's study, large and well appointed. It has no occupant but its owner is disclosed by the patterned wallpaper of purple and gold, too playful to be a man's, too opulent to be the daughter's. The desk confirms it, ornate rosewood inlaid with other, lighter woods. A letter opener catches Thomas's eye, the brass blade shaped like a dagger, and heavy enough to serve as a weapon. He picks it up, sits down, insolent now, his eyes on the wall with its two dozen paintings, hung close together, crowding the wall. Sits looking at them, unseeing; Smoke rising like a mist in front of his face.

It isn't long before the door opens and its owner enters the room. Lady Naylor appears unsurprised to find him there.

'Thomas! I am glad you are enjoying my art.'

His voice finds a timbre he recognises as his father's, gravel rasping under heavy boots. It's years since he has heard it, and never in himself.

'I was looking for your cutthroat, milady. And your fake whiskers. I was lying awake, trying to fathom what you did with the dead woman's Soot.'

'Ah. So you did recognise me.' Lady Naylor is wearing a silk dressing gown; its rich colour sets off her dark hair. She looks at him intently, then drops into a chair on the far side of the desk; smoothes the fabric over her thighs. 'Did you know already at dinner?'

'No.'

'I didn't think so. But it was hard to believe.'

She laughs: it's a brief laugh, almost a cough, but there is genuine humour to it all the same.

'Well, I'm relieved,' she goes on. 'A boy who wears such a perfect mask of composure – no, I confess I did not like the thought.' She shakes her head, still laughing, with her eyes now rather than her voice. 'And I was so very sure you knew right away. You see, I recognised you at once. Under the scaffold. You looked just as you did when you were a child. The same eyes, the same cast of the chin. Belligerent. And the face you made! Frightful! I was sure you would start screaming my name and accuse me in front of the whole mob. But then you didn't tell anyone. Not even at school. I had you watched, you understand, worried that you'd be sullying my name. It cost me some sleep. In the end I decided to invite you here and have it out in the open.'

Thomas does not trust himself to respond. He sees her again, in men's clothing, the hair hidden underneath a cap. The face dirty, looking boyish in its feminine grace but also old. He flinches when she gets up and draws to the wall.

'I trust you have been admiring my paintings. Fascinating, are they not?'

He shrugs, trying to fathom her, the letter opener clutched so tight it is hurting his hand.

'You don't think so. Well, look again. Trust me, Thomas, you have never seen any pictures like these before. Tell me: what do pictures usually show?'

Her voice is oddly soothing. It slows his heart. He answers sullenly; rises, gauges the distance between them.

'All sorts of things. Landscapes. People.'

'Describe them to me. The pictures you know from school, for instance.'

'There are only a handful. The headmaster has a few, in his study. A hunting scene, I think. Gentlemen to horse. And a coastline. Sun and water.'

'And these?'

Almost against his will he steps forward, to where picture frame hangs next to picture frame, nearly hiding the wall.

'People. Street scenes. Commoners.' It dawns on him. 'The city. But—'

'Yes: *but*. There is no Smoke.'

Thomas looks again from picture to picture. Some of them look very old. There is a market scene, people haggling over wares, a young child stealing an apple while his brother looks on. Next to it, a village square, some sort of carnival, people dancing, drinking, rolling in the dirt. Another picture shows a soldier, studded with arrows. His tormentors surround him, faces full of hate. In yet another picture, frameless, the paint thick upon a panel of wood, Jesus hangs from his cross in between two others. Thomas has seen the scene before, in a stained-glass window of his old parish church. Golgotha. There – most vivid on clear winter mornings when the slanting sun pours warmth into the glass – dark plumes rise from the shoulders of the two thieves and their cheeks are marked with two black boils of Smoke. Here they hang as sinless as the Saviour in their midst.

'How can that be?' he asks, his eyes darting amongst pictures. He flinches when Lady Naylor steps next to him.

But he does not run away.

'There are only two explanations, aren't there? The first is that it is a matter of artistic licence. Fantasy pictures. Outlaw artists, dreaming about a different world, hiding the Smoke. Such pictures exist and I have a few in my collection. But none are hung here.

'The truth is that all pictures used to be like this. Until a certain year. It's hard to pinpoint exactly, but I make it 1625 or 1626. No

Smoke. In not a single painting. Showing rapes, tortures, war and execution.

'Then comes a period without pictures. Thirty, forty years, and not a single brush stroke anywhere in Europe. Perhaps nobody felt moved to paint. Or they have all been destroyed, as so many of the older ones have.

'And then, after a whole generation of silence, we finally get pictures again. Nature scenes. Creeks, mountains, storm-tossed seas. It takes another generation before anyone paints people. Gentlemen, gentlewomen – not a commoner in sight. Unless it's a religious motif. A martyr boiled in a pot: lily-white in dun water. The men firing the pot are as black as a boot, the air dark with their filth.' She smiles. 'Like the air in here, I suppose. Do you mind if I open the window?'

She turns her back, slowly, deliberately, as though to taunt him who is still holding the blunt blade of a toy dagger. It's when he raises it to place it back onto the desk that he realises his fingers are numb. He has squeezed the life out of them. She waits, patiently, for his tongue to catch up with his feelings; like a nurse leading a sick man, waiting for him to place his foot.

'You're saying there was a time before Smoke,' he manages at last. 'But it's impossible. All the history books—'

'Were written later. By schoolmasters. University dons. Ask my husband. He wrote books like that himself.'

'But everyone would know. They'd remember, surely. People would tell their children, and they in turn would pass it on. You can't forget something like this.'

'Can't you? Not even if every painting was destroyed and every book burnt? If there was not a shred of evidence to support old people's stories? If you were taught that it's a sin to speak the truth – and burnt at the stake if you did? Almost three hundred years, Thomas: it's a long time. A very long time. But you are right. Some people *do* know. On the Continent, mostly. They weren't as thorough there. There are a few universities with some well-guarded collections. Even a monastery, in Germany, where—'

'The Bible,' Thomas interrupts her, his voice over-loud, almost shouting. 'Smoke is mentioned in the Bible. It's everywhere. Old Testament, New Testament. Every chapter and verse. And the Bible was written in – you know. The dawn of time.'

'So it was. The dawn of time. Do you remember where Smoke is mentioned for the first time?'

'Genesis,' he answers without hesitation. 'The Fall of Adam and Eve.'

'Yes – Genesis 3:7. How does it go?'

Thomas quotes: '"And when the woman saw that the tree was good for food, and that it was pleasant to the eyes, and a tree to be desired to make one wise, she took of the fruit thereof, and did eat, and gave also unto her husband with her; and he did eat. And the eyes of them both were opened, and they knew that they were naked; and shame filled them, and the air grew thick with Smoke. And so they sewed fig leaves together, and made themselves aprons, and the aprons turned black with their Soot."'

'Very good! I did not know you were such a scholar. Your mother taught you, I suppose. A feisty woman, a reformer. But pious.' Lady Naylor walks over to a glass-encased shelf. She opens it, waves him closer. 'I have a few bibles here. Go on, pick one. Read me the passage.'

Thomas does as he is bidden, pulls a small, brittle book down, opens it to Genesis.

'It's in Latin. "*Et aperti sunt oculi amborum cumque cognovissent esse se nudos consuerunt folia ficus et fecerunt sibi perizomata*".'

'Translate, then. You have Latin in school, don't you? At least I hope so. I'm paying your fees.'

He stares at the words. His voice is halting, his brain numb with what isn't there. 'And opened were the eyes of both of them. And when they realised that they were naked, they joined leaves and made for themselves clothes.' He leafs back, to the book's beginning, almost tearing the pages. The cover print incorporates a number in Roman numerals. MDLXII.

1562.

Thomas looks up, tears in his eyes.

'They changed it, the bastards.'

'Yes, they did.'

'And everything – everything! – is a lie.'

'Yes.'

She prises the book out of his hands, lays it back on the shelf, then stands facing him, at an arm's length, reading his face. He waits until the tears have rolled down his face, wet his lips; tastes it, his sadness, finds it tinged with Soot.

'Does your daughter know all this?'

Lady Naylor's face grows hard. It's the first time since she's entered that he sees it amongst her features: that other face, the person who scraped fresh Soot off a woman's corpse.

'I told Livia a long time ago. She says it is heresy, and my research an abomination.' She laughs, draws her dressing gown tight around her body, looks scrawny for a moment, diminished, old. 'My daughter tells me that if the old books were burnt then there was a good reason. That no plague comes amongst us unless God has sent it, and no dog rips out a badger's throat without God holding the end of the leash.' Lady Naylor pauses, calms herself. 'But she has not reported me yet.'

She walks over to the desk, sits down, straightens papers.

'My daughter,' she declares abruptly, 'lives like she is a china doll. Holding very still. Listening into herself, stiffly, stuck in one posture. She's waiting. Waiting for something to break, you see, and reveal a secret reservoir of Smoke: an impurity, deep in herself, that will mark her as a sinner. You saw how she was at dinner. She tried to laugh, once or twice. But she isn't sure how. And whether it's allowed.' Lady Naylor waves a hand, as though to dispel the thought like a bad smell. 'Enough about Livia. She's made her own bed. How about you? What will you do, now that you know?'

Thomas feels his heart pound in his chest. The enormity of it all comes crashing down on him, squeezing the air out of his lungs. He searches for something simple, some corner of it he can understand.

'What did you do in London, Lady Naylor? What is it for, that woman's Soot?'

'Experiments.'

'You are looking for a cure. For Smoke.'

'Yes.'

'How?'

She laughs. 'How? That's a very long story. Too much for one night.'

Panic grabs Thomas. Panic that he will wake, and it will all have been a dream. 'But you will tell me, won't you? Everything!'

'As much as I can. But not now. I need my sleep.' She looks in his face, finds a plea written there. 'One more question then. Something quick.'

Thomas chews his cheek, afraid to waste his question, like those people in fairy tales who part with their wishes like fools. Then he knows.

'Sweets,' he says. 'Beasley and Son. We ate some but nothing happened. What are they? How do they work?'

Φ

When Charlie wakes from pleasant dreams in the early hours of the morning it is still quite dark outside. It takes him some minutes to realise he is alone. No sound issues from Thomas's bed. Curious, he rolls off the mattress, tiptoes forward in the dark until his shin bumps into the other bed. He feels the pillow and finds it quite cold. As he stands, pondering this fact, a light passes the door. It slides through the crack like an inverted shadow, licks a yard of floorboard, and is gone.

By the time Charlie has stepped out into the hallway, the light is seven or eight steps ahead. The figure that holds it is moving briskly. It blocks the bulk of the glow and hence is visible only in outline, a darkness traced in hues of gold. Fittingly enough, this halo is most radiant around the head.

Charlie recognises her by her hair. As his eyes adjust, Livia gains solidity, transforms from lamp-sketched apparition into a more corporeal sort of ghost. If the previous day her dress was plain it is now austere: an apron worn over an ankle-length smock, both garments startlingly white. Her hair is honey-thick by gaslight. From her hand swings a porcelain jug.

Charlie follows her without hesitation and has taken three steps before even being conscious of his decision. He does so neither furtively nor wilfully announcing his presence, but simply follows, his nightshirt fluttering as he rushes to keep step.

She leads him to stairs: the main stairwell first, then – a long corridor later, lined with portraits, vases, animal heads – a narrower flight that leads them to a barren corridor under a slanting ceiling. The attic. It isn't clear to Charlie whether Livia has noticed his pursuit. She has not slowed or turned but when she stops before a door ten steps ahead, it appears to him that she is tarrying just long enough to make sure he won't mistake it for another. Then she disappears inside. A sound greets her, an animal braying, and slows Charlie's step.

It is the sound of a beast in pain.

The room beyond the open door is dark, despite the gas lamp. At first Charlie thinks the walls are painted black. But when his hand brushes one side, the black smears and crumbles and leaves his fingers dark with Soot. The room is large and furnished only with some chairs, a table and dresser and a large, iron-frame bed. On the bed lies a figure, manacled at wrists and ankles with wide leather straps. Again the strange braying sounds, filling the room. Charlie's skin puckers when he realises it issues from this man, his arms and legs tugging at the leather binds.

'He gets agitated in the mornings.'

Livia's voice is calm, matter-of-fact. She stands at the table between bed and window, pours water into a washbasin. Already her apron is stained with Soot. When she bends down to run a wetted washcloth over the man's forehead, he cries again and his body exhales a dark-green burp of Smoke. Slack-mouthed, leering, he wears a mask rather than a face. Whatever features he might call his own are cancelled out by his condition.

'Mother thinks we must keep it a secret,' Livia goes on, still in the same nonchalant tone. Her eyes are on her work. All the same Charlie has the sensation of being closely watched by her, his every move registered, analysed, judged. 'But I say we must accept Providence humbly, without shame.'

It is only now, as she says it, that Charlie understands.

'Baron Naylor.' It tumbles out of him. And is followed, with an alacrity that clearly pleases her, for Livia's eyes light up within her small, finely drawn face: 'How can I help?'

'We must wash and feed him.'

It proves an awkward, difficult procedure, in part because it necessitates the removal of the leather restraints. Baron Naylor fights them. He is not a young man, perhaps as much as twenty years older than his wife (though it is possible, too, that his illness has aged him, for he is thin and dishevelled, and his molars are dark within his mouth, there at the back where they are hard to clean). For all that, he is as strong as an ox and the presence of a stranger appears to upset him. No sooner have they freed his right hand than he snakes it around Charlie's wrist. Again the baron brays and thick, viscous Smoke crawls out of his skin and works its way up Charlie's arm. A moment later it is in his nose, his lungs. He begins to struggle with the man, begins to loathe him; disgust floods Charlie and when the madman's hand reaches up, searching for his throat, Charlie slaps it away with coarse brutality. It is only then, spitting out his anger, that Charlie realises he, too, is smoking.

Shame cuts through him, winds him, stoppers his Smoke. He backs away, to the wall, where the man's infection does not reach; stands panting, pressing his back into the wall like a burglar caught red-handed; looks over at Livia and hangs his head.

'I can't do it. I'm not strong enough.'

Livia returns his look. Her hands remain upon her father's body, she is buried to her elbows in the old man's Smoke, but her head turns and he can see how difficult it is for her, how magnificent her self-control. Her own Smoke is minimal, fine white wisps that escape her lips and colour them grey. It is as though she's been spoon-fed ashes. Her gown is white, Charlie realises, because she wishes to test herself. Nothing must be hidden. It makes him marvel at her: a feeling not unlike fear. She, for her part, does not hide her disappointment in him; lets go of her father's limbs and reaches over to the table where she finds a tin box and throws it across to Charlie with a quick, disdainful flick.

'Here. Mother uses them when she is up here. Take one.'

Charlie opens the tin and finds a dozen sweets inside. Clear, knuckle-sized, stamped with the familiar symbol: B&S underneath a three-pronged crown. He fishes one out, shakes his head.

'What do I do? I've tried one before but nothing happened. All it did was taste of soap.'

She does not turn with her answer.

'Put one in your mouth. Don't chew it. It'll pull the Smoke out of your breath and blood, and bind it, long before you show. Before it can infest your mind.'

Charlie does as instructed, then gingerly, not quite trusting himself, steps up to the bed. Livia has her hands full: her father is fighting her every movement, is spitting, biting, kicking. But this time Charlie's blood remains cool and his mind clear, almost detached. He takes hold of Baron Naylor's arms and pins them very gently, speaks to him in low soothing words, much as one would speak to a frightened pet or an infant; takes the cloth from Livia and cleans his face, his neck and ears. Within minutes the old man calms down, becomes pliable and almost childlike, his features composed.

The face that emerges is not unlike Livia's, fine-boned, heart-shaped and noble, if old.

'What now?' Charlie asks.

'We need to take off his nightshirt, wash his legs and – the rest of him.'

Livia blushes, points to her father's midriff. It alerts Charlie to the whole sadness of a situation in which a mother and a daughter have become nurses to their husband and father.

'I will do it,' he says. 'You take a rest.'

Φ

Washing a man's legs and body proves surprisingly straightforward once Charlie gets past the simple fact of his nudity. It is, in the end, rather like cleaning yourself. Baron Naylor is so calm now, he even lets Charlie shave him, very slowly and carefully, until five or so years of premature age have been scraped off his chin. Afterwards, the baron dressed in fresh clothes, his bedsheets changed, Charlie joins Livia by the window. Dawn is breaking, the lawn still grey with shadow, the nearby wood a black square framed by lighter fields.

'Can you see a woman out there, walking out of the woods?' Livia asks in a whisper, then carries on, not expecting an answer. 'The servants, the old ones, they have a story about a woman wandering the woods. Lost, they say, living on the edge of them, half in darkness, half in light. They say she is father's lost soul. His sanity.' She smiles sadly at the windowpane. 'But I've never seen her, not in a thousand mornings of looking.'

She turns to Charlie then, studies him, frankly and systematically.

'You are shocked, aren't you? Shocked and disgusted. I can see it here.' She points to where his eyebrows have knitted over the bridge of his nose.

Charlie is silent for a moment, gauging her expression. He knows it is important to give an honest answer.

'No, I am not,' he says at last. 'I have been thinking. It came to me just now, looking out the window with you. This is what Smoke is, isn't it? Smoke is madness. It's as simple as that.'

When she answers, there is a catch of excitement in her voice. It is as though Charlie has just spelled out a long-cherished thought.

'Plato writes that evil is having a disordered soul.'

She is about to go on, but breaks off instead. She does not trust him yet.

'We never read any Plato,' Charlie tells her. 'We only learned his dates.'

Livia chews her lip.

'Father has his books downstairs, in the library. In Greek. He translated some of them. When he was a professor at Cambridge. I found his notes.'

Livia looks over at the man in his bed, shackled again, placid and vacant. Her eyes fall on the razor on the little table. Charlie has washed and wiped it, and left it open to dry. She walks over, folds it, weighs it in her hands.

'You shaved him,' she says suddenly, as though she has only just discovered the fact. In her head it's connected, somehow, to Plato, and madness and sin. He does not quite fathom how. 'You have good hands, Charlie Cooper.'

He masks his embarrassment by shaking his head.

'Only because of this,' he says, picking the candy out from under his tongue. It has diminished in size and turned dark, almost black, and looks for all the world like a rotten tooth.

She stares at it in distaste.

'Throw it. It won't hold any more Smoke.'

He nods, closes his fist on the candy.

'Where do you have it from?'

'Mother. The government produces it, or rather there's a special factory that has a government contract. It used to be that it was a big secret. Only very few people were issued them, people in certain positions. Churchmen, for one. Government officials.'

'Teachers.'

'Yes. For emergencies; and to ward off infection when they are dealing with common folk. But Mother says that this is changing. Beasley and Son sold the monopoly, and the new owners, they are selling sweets, secretly of course, to whoever can pay. A black market. Mother says they even sell to commoners. Soon, I suppose, greengrocers will sell it, along with tea and soap.'

Charlie whistles. It sounds brighter than he means it to. 'Or along with their liquorice and nuts! But this is good, isn't it? It means people can fight their Smoke. Suppress it.'

She grows angry, fierce, her eyebrows knotting.

'It's a sin, is what it is. A crime.'

She stares at him as though she holds him guilty too. In his fist the spent sweet lies sticky against his skin.

'I better go.'

Livia does not stop him. All she says, as he walks through the door, is, 'Merry Christmas.'

He turns.

'Already? I lost track of time.'

'Christmas Eve at any rate. Mother grew up abroad. She keeps to Continental traditions. We'll have a formal dinner, followed by carols at the tree.'

'I have no present for you.'

'It isn't expected.'

Her voice, when she says it, is cold and distant. It is as though the morning never happened.

Φ

'Smoke is madness,' Charlie repeats to himself on the way down the stairs. 'That's why she is how she is. She is her father's daughter. He lost his reason. So she is afraid.'

The thought is still with him when he enters the guest room and finds Thomas straddling the threshold of the open veranda door, looking gaunt and sickly in the early-morning light. Rain has soaked one sleeve of his nightshirt and glued it to his arm.

Charlie closes the door behind himself before he speaks.

'I know what sweets are. And I understand Smoke.'

Thomas looks over, water streaming down his face.

'I know more than that, Charlie. I've read the Bible.'

They sit down on the floor shoulder to shoulder, and explain.

Livia

We spend Christmas with our guests. Mother, in keeping with the customs of her family, serves carp in black plum sauce and buttered potatoes. She roundly ignores my objection that dressing fish with fruit turns a dish that should at least remind us of a fast into something sweet and gluttonous. We have guests, she says, we can eat convent food when they are gone. The evening is further spoilt when Lizzy, the kitchen maid, is caught attempting to steal a present from under the tree. It is I who have the misfortune to catch her. The silly goose of a girl gets tangled in a crude lie, then immediately bursts into Smoke. Mother has little choice but to dismiss her, and we all watch as she runs off, her thick shoes making a racket on the floor and her skirt riding very indecently up the back of her calves.

Despite this, a certain solemnity prevails throughout the holiday. I am delighted to discover that Mr Cooper – Charlie, as he insists I must call him – has a lovely voice for carols. He is a well-mannered, even charming guest. On the morning of Christmas he surprises me by waiting outside my father's room when I arrive. He does not explain but blushes rather becomingly, takes the jug and the wash-cloth out of my hands, and sets to helping me. I like him for that blush. He insists on not taking a sweet this time and humbly steps outside when the Smoke overwhelms him, until he has reclaimed his calm. Father has taken a shine to him and can be heard humming a nonsense melody as we leave. Mr Cooper falls in with it and starts skipping down the corridor like a fool.

Mr Argyle is a different matter. He humiliates me. There is something to his gaze, something forceful and insolent and searching that makes me aware of the plainness of my dress and hairstyle, the scuffed old shoes I wear around the house. It is not that I wish to appear prettier for him – God knows I would rather be spared his stares – and yet I have found myself donning the odd piece of jewellery for dinner and have slipped into the silk gown Mother gave me for my birthday, just to put him in his place. Not that I see much of this dark cousin of mine. Mr Argyle spends his afternoons shut up with Mother, who is filling him with her theories. It is hard to tell whether or not he believes her: she, too, is subject to his gaze. Its force is such that it leaves his own face inscrutable. He must be a most unpopular boy at school.

However, perhaps I should be grateful for his presence. It helps me guard against complacency. Each evening I sit down after my prayers and examine my feelings. The visitors – Charlie Cooper; his presence at my father's bedside – have enriched my life and I find myself, for once, content. But I am pleased to report that there is no joy in me when I rise in the morning to attend to my work. Joy is not a sin. But it is always better to act from duty. What one does from inclination one may do thoughtlessly. Inclination is fickle. More than that: it may lead you astray. One day, you might find yourself smoking, thinking you are doing good.

Mother says that I am obsessed; that far from dismissing Smoke, I have made it my idol. Indeed I am grateful for the Smoke. It tells us when we err. Imagine a world in which we err and nobody notices. Not even oneself. Until one goes to seed by increments and slides into the madness of villainy. Smoke eats our reason with a charcoal spoon. We measure our humanity against its darkness. It is good it leaves a mark.

On the second day of Christmas, Mother sits up late with our guests, lecturing on history. *The day the Smoke came.* She has sent the servants to bed. Her heresy is not for them.

Smoke, I remind her, comes from God.

So, she says, does cancer.

There is a lesson, I say, in cancer, too, and Mr Argyle glares at me with such an intensity of anger that it makes me want to quit the room. I had forgotten his mother succumbed to that disease. Once again it is Mr Cooper who saves the evening by suggesting a game of whist. During the game, he draws out Mother into telling stories from her time in Paris and Vienna. It is years since I have heard a laugh and, against my better judgement, I am happy.

For five whole days we are content in this manner, from Christmas Eve to the Feast of the Holy Innocents. I mark each day with a candle in the chapel. Five candles, each a foot long, wrist thick, burning at the altar of the Virgin. Then my half-brother arrives. He comes on horseback, unannounced, his manservant in tow, and the next thing we know the whole house seems to be thick with him, his voice, his boisterous laughter, the chink of his spurs. He came to warn us about marauding Gypsies, he says. He brags and skulks and monopolises Mother.

I wish he had sent a letter instead.

Sparring

He arrives while they are sitting at lunch. Lunch is a frugal affair of cold meat jellies and some kind of lentil porridge: a rebuke to the senses; Livia's idea. Thomas chews each spoonful like the dreary ordeal it is, ignoring Charlie's kicks under the table. The porridge has been thickened with cornstarch and has the consistency of frozen mud.

Then Thorpe, the butler, steps up to the table and whispers something into Lady Naylor's ear. The emotions that attempt to gain purchase on her features are hard to read, but annoyance sits topmost, rules the slant of her mouth. She rises without a word, forcing both Charlie and Thomas to scramble to their feet (for one must not sit when a lady stands), then takes three long strides that carry her out of the room.

Curiosity easily defeats their lentil-smothered appetite. Already on his feet, Thomas follows Lady Naylor at once. Charlie is only a step behind. Livia remains at the table. Looking back, Thomas catches a glance of her: stiff-backed, chin tucked into her throat, resigned to this latest of humiliations.

They find milady in the front hall. She has taken up position at one of the big windows looking out onto the driveway. There, two riders have just climbed off their horses. The first is a tall, lumbering man in a greatcoat with close-cropped hair and hard, flat features. He is closer to fifty than forty but moves with the confident ease of a younger man. His cheeks are raw with wind and cold.

As for the second man: it is disturbing to see him out of school clothes and dressed instead in a gentleman's hunting gear. Thick chequered tweeds in muddy greens with a matching cap and knee-high boots. A smudge of dark down twitches on the upper lip. Julius Spencer has been growing a moustache. He has brought a further horse, a pack horse, laden with trunks and leather-cased rifles. From his wrist a riding crop dangles by its loop.

They cannot hear Julius's voice through the window. Judging by his gestures he is instructing Lady Naylor's servants to help the older man lift down the trunks. He is his valet, then. When a stable hand leaps forward to catch the reins Julius has tossed at him, a shadow darts out from behind the horse's bulk and sits down waist-high to its master. Dark copper fur draped in abundant folds over a thickset body; the eyes red-rimmed and small within their face's droop; the lips rolled back to disclose mottled gums of black and pink. The dog howls, a sound loud enough to carry indoors; is petted for its trouble, or rather cuffed across the head and snout, then leans its slavish love into its master.

'Milady!' Julius shouts, at the door not at the window, though he can plainly see her, see all of them, standing in a row, their eyes riveted to his figure. 'Mother! Come greet your beloved son.'

At the word, Thomas turns away in disbelief.

'Surely—'

Lady Naylor's face is stony.

'Indeed. My son from my first marriage. And you are my second husband's sister's child. I tried to work it out the other day. The correct *terminus*. Some manner of cousin, I suppose. In a roundabout way.'

She eyes Thomas blandly, then walks over to the door. 'I see he omitted to mention it to you at school. An oversight, no doubt.'

She pauses before opening the door. 'Well, unless you are dying to greet your schoolmate, I suggest you and Charlie return to your luncheon. I expect my little *Jules* will want to talk in private. He and I have business to discuss.'

Φ

For the next few days they see little of Lady Naylor. She spends hours locked in with her son, then withdraws to her private quarters for all but meal-times, where she presides with grim politeness over a table split in half between her children and her guests.

Thomas expects to feel annoyed by her change: shut out, rejected, replaced; more than half his questions still unanswered. Instead, something else sets in, a newfound sense of freedom. For the first time since the day of their arrival, he and Charlie find themselves thrown together, with time on their hands. That, and Julius's presence – his smug malice; his strutting grandiosity – makes it feel like a weekend at school.

More familiar now with the routines of the household, no longer worried about causing offence by poking their heads where they don't belong, they go tearing through the estate. Initially, the explorations dispense with talk. It is a relief to Thomas. There has been so much talk since their arrival, so little time for the words to settle.

Their exploration unearths a whole series of wonders. The stables, for one thing, turn out to be a whole system of sheds, workshops, kennels and living quarters, so extensive they feel like a roofed and rambling village all their own. Amongst the three dozen or so hunting dogs there is a Russian borzoi with a chest so deep, its fur almost brushes the ground. Further back the body tapers into a waist so narrow, a child could encircle it with its hands. In another shed, uncaged, unchained, Lord Naylor's mastiff whiles away its days, sleeping with both paws draped over an axe handle he has claimed, they are told, from earliest puppyhood. The dog is said to weigh one hundred and twenty-three pounds, and is kept on largely because 'it's bloody hard to shift'.

In the house itself they find bedchambers and drawing rooms that have not been used for generations, their floors made monochrome by inch-deep dust. The furniture is wrapped in sheets and blankets. In some rooms it is stacked, ceiling-high, and trussed up with ropes. It gives an odd bulk to sofas, chairs and tables, turns them into mist-moored ships: a sea of dust tranquil beneath their prows. The boys' feet upset this peace. Leaping backwards and forwards, hopping on one foot, they write demonic dances into the rooms' memories, for servants to puzzle over in years to come.

Then there are cellars filled with barrels and bottles, others crammed neck-high with mighty rounds of cheese; a suite of rooms in an upper wing, in which all floors are tiled in chessboard patterns and all furniture has been removed; a big brass telescope that stands in an abandoned corner study and pokes its lens through the removable pane of a narrow window, taking aim at the winter sky.

Through some unspoken agreement, they do not venture to the attic. It is understood that the attic is Charlie's space, Charlie's and Livia's, and, of course, their patient's. Thomas does not tell Charlie that he has no need to go exploring there. He has already been. He went up to the attic the very day Charlie described his discovery to him, driven by a private need. It was the early hours of the evening.

Thomas hid in the shadow of a doorway while two servants, a man and a woman, were taking their turn looking after their employer, the sound of their voices travelling into the corridor if not their words. When they left at last, Thomas walked up to the door and opened it silently; stood on the threshold, looking in. The servants had left a gas lamp behind, turned very low and hung from a hook far from the bed. It had taken several minutes before Thomas's eyes learned to distinguish man from bedding. In the meantime, he listened to the baron's breathing, even for the most part, a little too laboured to suggest sleep. The breathing reassured Thomas. He had come there to look into his own future: the flowering of the seed that Renfrew had detected in him and not been able to dislodge. Thomas had expected the raving lunacy of London, curable only by the rope. This was another outcome of his sickness, a calmer end.

If it comes to this, it crossed his mind, *I can ask Charlie.*

To help me end it.

Then the baron's face began to peel itself from out of the shadows. First came the eyes: large white orbs, their irises dark like punctures. Moving, staring. Aware of being watched. Agitation began to shake the sick man, drenching his nightshirt in fresh black. Thomas ran away at once. He did not want to frighten the man. Nor have his last illusion shattered about the day of reckoning that will be his.

Φ

On the third morning of explorations, Charlie and Thomas find the billiard room and the gymnasium. The first is a narrow, wood-panelled room, with the playing table at one end and a drinks cabinet at the other. The atmosphere is so snugly masculine – from the glass case well-stocked with cigar boxes, to the row of decanters filled with sherry and port – that it feels as though a group of gentlemen in frock coats must be standing just around the corner. Paying tribute to the ladies. Looking for excuses to return to their games.

Across the corridor lies quite a different room. Spacious and well-served by windows, it is uncarpeted and virtually unfurnished apart from four chest-high posts that form a square made more explicit by the double line of rope stretched between them. Two stools stand in the ring, in opposite corners. A long bench lines the windows and a single wardrobe leans opposite, slumped to one side, where a leg has given out with rot. On its left hangs a mirror, so corrupted by age that the dirt seems to have grown into the very glass. On its right, a daguerreotype whose glass is black with dust.

They open the wardrobe first. Inside is dirt, a pile of mildewed towels; a candyfloss cone of spider's webbing; a brass bell to ring in the rounds; and a dozen or so boxing gloves, with worn, knotty laces, split thumbs and fraying seams. Without discussing it in the least, they set to trying on gloves, exchanging pairs, shaking out dirt and insect remains, discarding those whose torn leather might cut the skin on impact. They have no gym tights but roll up their trousers; no gym shoes, so decide on bare feet; no jerseys, so strip off their shirts and coats; stand freezing, the gloves hanging heavy from their wrists, and eye the ring.

Before they climb in, Charlie reaches up and wipes the tip of his glove through the daguerreotype's murk. A face emerges, then a second. The first is handsome and composed, a man past the half-way point in life, but proud, well-kept, his longish hair swept back from his brow and tucked behind his ears. Livia's face is imprinted in his features. It is by this, rather than his excursion to the attic, that Thomas recognises the baron.

The second face they do not expect to find in this place. Hence it eludes them, yet also calls to them, sufficiently so that Charlie reaches up and, still in boxing gloves, fishes the picture off its hook. They take it to the bench, lay it out flat, pore over it like over a book. The body is slender, there is no beard, and the features have the softness of those early years of manhood. It is a stage of life that still lies ahead of them but is so close now, its contours have already been sighted.

In black-and-white the man's hair does not shine in its familiar colour of young corn.

'Renfrew,' Thomas says at last, when he is sure.

As they wipe away at the blighted glass, they find pale skin. Like themselves, the pair they see are stripped to their waists; wear gym tights and gloves, the latter raised in front of their chests. The backdrop is this very gym. The men's shadows are thrown behind them, deep into the ring.

'Where did Renfrew go for his studies?' Charlie wants to know.

'King's, at Cambridge. He says it's the finest college there is.'

'Livia told me that Baron Naylor used to be a don. At Cambridge. He must have been Renfrew's tutor.'

'Trying to knock some sense into him, by the looks of it. Shame it didn't work.'

The joke is feeble but it helps them reconnect to the mood that made them put on the gloves. Besides, they are cold. Thomas replaces the picture; climbs into the ring. Charlie is about to follow when he stops himself, races back to the wardrobe, retrieves the bell. He rings it. The clapper is so caked in dirt that the sound resembles a clucking tongue.

'First round,' he announces.

They square off and begin to spar.

Φ

For the longest time neither of them lands a punch. Instead they are shadowboxing, keeping their distance, dancing sideways, only to suddenly lunge forward and deliver devastating hooks into thin air. When they are good and winded, Charlie races over to the bell, takes a clumsy hold of it between glove-swollen palms, then augments its sound by singing out three rings.

It takes until halfway through the second of these rounds before Thomas divines the reason for their reluctance to connect their punches. It isn't just that they are friends, averse to causing each other pain, even in sport. Charlie, he realises, is afraid. Afraid he will wake Thomas's Smoke; afraid that one well-placed punch will break something in him, and wake it up. The monster inside. And it isn't just Charlie. He himself is holding back. The danger, he senses, lies not in being hit but in hitting: the joy of crushing padded leather into flesh and bone. Lady Naylor's words about Livia hang in his head all of a sudden.

She lives like a china doll. Listening into herself.

Waiting for something to break.

The thought alone coats his mouth with Smoke.

And so he snarls, steps into Charlie, and delivers a clean hard hook into his shoulder, then follows it at once with a quick cross. His friend grunts, retreats, jiggles the arm just hit as though testing it for injury – and grins. His gloves rise, he steps forward, toe to toe, and loosens three quick jabs into Thomas's chest, before stepping in to sling an uppercut into his stomach. A brawl follows in which shoulders are beaten meat-loaf red, and chests given a good pounding; the odd rib is rung and one lowish sucker punch leaves

104

Thomas gasping for sweet air. They dispense with the bell, hammer away at each other until they are both breathless, sweaty, slumped over on the bench and radiant with joy. If there has been any Smoke, it has been so light, requited and playful as to have been part of the game.

'We should come here every day,' Charlie says at last, slipping his coat over his shoulders against the window's draught. A letter sticks out the coat pocket. He notices it, smiles, pulls it out.

'I wanted to tell you earlier. The post finally arrived. It's from my sister. She sent it well before Christmas, but it only got here today. She says she hopes we will make it in time to join them on their trip to Ireland. She is dying to meet you.' He rubs his sore arm. 'I must have given her the false impression that you are very handsome. And kind.'

Thomas returns his smile, then grows serious and begins to pull on his socks.

'You should go home, Charlie. I can't. Not yet. I need to hear what else she can tell me. About Smoke.'

Charlie does not dispute it. It is one of his talents, Thomas thinks: not to put himself at odds with the truth. What Charlie does do is question the value of Lady Naylor's conversation.

'When all is said and done,' he asks, 'what has she told you this past week? What have you really learned?'

Thomas recognises the doubt at once. It is his own, fought nightly, when he reviews with impatience the sum of his knowledge about Smoke.

'It's hard to say, Charlie. She never quite tells you what you want to hear. I ask about Smoke and she'll start talking about politics. How the country used to be liberal but has swung Tory these past twenty years; how the new liberals are gaining ground but they are all terrible puritans at heart and just as bad. That and the Queen is ailing, leaving the business of governing to her civil service. But it's not just politics. The other day she got stuck on science. The Books of Smoke are outdated, she says; they are literally riddled with mistakes. Everybody knows it, but all the same it's illegal to change them because it would imply that we don't have a clue as to what Smoke actually is. Then two whole hours on inventors, German periodicals, the laws of optics, reeling off names so fast it makes my head spin. Apparently there is decades' worth of new technology Parliament has outlawed and won't allow to be imported. Factory machinery, weapons, new photographic emulsions. It's a total embargo: every ship's searched for machines, blueprints, scientific papers, everything. It's because the government fears change. The new technology might challenge social order, or something. Make new people rich. While in Italy or somewhere they have a thing now called a "telephone", where you can talk to people who are miles away from you, just by speaking into a box. The box is connected to another box by a long wire. The wire transports the words, somehow. As though by magic.'

He watches Charlie picture it. Charlie is not impressed.

'Even if it worked, what use could it be? You'd have to connect all houses in the world with wires. And that's impossible.'

Thomas shrugs. It is hard to argue with that.

'Then there are all sorts of medical breakthroughs. Vaccinations, drugs, that sort of thing. A new type of microscope.' Thomas leans forward, lowers his voice. 'She has a laboratory somewhere. Here in the house. She says she will show me. When I am *ready*.'

It dawns on Charlie that the past few days of exploration were not as innocent as he had assumed.

'You've been looking for it.'

Thomas nods, then hesitates. 'Yes. But if I find it, and go inside, it'll be a breach. Of the rules or something.' He leans back against the wall, throws one of the boxing gloves across the room, aiming for the wardrobe. 'I have a feeling Lady Naylor is the type who is a stickler for rules.'

Charlie emulates his throw. His aim is better, but the glove falls a yard short. He wants to know: 'Do you trust her?'

Another throw, Thomas's turn. It hits the wardrobe door, slides down, lies on the ground, laces sprawling.

'I trust her sometimes. Other times I look at her and think she is the devil.'

'Because of London.'

'Yes. To do what she did there . . .' Thomas mimes scraping a razor down the length of his tongue. 'But then, of course, the woman was already dead.' His face grows hard. 'In any case, it does not look like she will talk to me now, not until her *son* is gone.'

At the mention of Julius, Charlie throws the fourth glove. The throw is wild and it hits the picture frame by the side of the wardrobe, dislodges it, brings it crashing down. They pick the print out of the shower of broken glass. Renfrew grins at them, chin tucked, fists raised, itching for a fight.

Φ

They don't pick up the conversation again until they are back in their room. They have each taken a bath and dressed in fresh shirts; their hair damp and frizzy from being towelled dry. A game board is between them, lined with ivory figurines. Chess. It's Thomas's turn. He picks up his queen, twirls her in his hand.

'I still can't believe I am related to him.'

Charlie waits with his answer until the move is complete.

'Why not? Amongst the old families, almost everyone's related to everyone. I am sure I have some Spencers in the family tree. There may even be an Argyle somewhere.' He pauses. 'Anyway, I asked around. How come Julius does not live with her, his own mother? I tried Thorpe first, but he merely frowned. Disapproving of my curiosity. So I spoke to the coachman, the one who drove us here. He says Lady Naylor married very young. A political marriage, apparently, not a love match. Her husband died less than a year after the wedding, somewhere abroad, in the colonies. When Julius was born, his father was five months dead, and she was living with his parents. He made it sound as though she was kept almost like a prisoner there. You know how it is with some of the more old-fashioned families, the women don't really have much freedom and when there is a son involved, an heir . . . In any case, when Baron Naylor began to court her, they would only consent to the match if she left the child to be raised within the Spencer household.' Charlie pulls a face. 'Imagine being faced with that choice. She must have really wanted to get away.'

'Poor Julius.' There is, to Thomas's voice, not a hint of sympathy. 'You are telling me this is why he is such a turd.'

Charlie colours, nods, moves a pawn.

'Yes. Maybe.'

'And why he skulks around with a bloodhound and a valet that looks like a cutthroat.'

'Ah. About that valet. Mr Price is his name. Here's something else I heard, also from the coachman, though this one comes via his wife. God knows how she would know, it's straight from the Spencer family vault. In any case, the coachman says that his wife says that

107

the valet used to be Julius's rook, his bond servant, back when he was a child.'

'So?'

'So? Did you have a bond servant when you were small, Thomas?'

'No. My parents didn't bother.'

'You know what they are, though.'

'Of course. They get hired to watch over you when you are ten. It's a ritual position. For the final year before you are held to be responsible for your Smoke.'

'Oh, it's not so ritual as all that. They watch over you, day and night. If an accident should befall you, the same injury will befall them. It's a holy oath: they have to take it in church. My rook, he was my first proper friend. Taught me half the things I know. For a year and a bit he was there, around me, for every breath I took. Slept right outside my room, on a sort of pallet. Picked me up when I fell off my horse. And then he was gone. On to the next job. It rips a hole in your life.' Charlie's voice has grown hard. It is a tone so unusual in him that Thomas is startled.

'Did you ever see him again?'

'Once. A year or so ago.'

'And?'

'And nothing. We hardly spoke. He seemed coarse and stupid and overbearing. Riddled with sin. Reeking of old Smoke.' Charlie shakes his head at the memory. 'The fact is, they spend their lives around children. Undisciplined, smoking, silly, ten-year-old children. It rubs off, I suppose. And at the same time, they are bodyguards. Strongmen. Mine, I remember him beating a servant girl who was teasing me. He just took her by the hair and started hitting her, laughing at me over his joke. I had to beg him to stop.'

'You are saying he wasn't valet material.'

'No. He was a professional brute.'

'Well, it seems Mr Price is both.'

They finish the game. Charlie wins. He mostly does with games of strategy. Thomas is better at cards: games where your strength is hidden and subject to your opponent's speculation. He does not particularly like what this says about him.

Thomas says, 'I too learned something about Julius. Something you don't know. Last night, I followed the maid when she was fetching his hot water.' He smiles. 'I know where he lives, Charlie. And guess what. His door is just like ours.' He gets up, pushes on the handle, swings it open. 'It has no lock.'

Charlie is appalled. 'You didn't!'

'No. Not yet. But I think he must be speaking to Lady Naylor now. And the servants will be having their tea in half an hour. As for the dog, it's kennelled. I checked.'

'But you can't—'

'Can't I, Charlie? He is my enemy. And I want to know why he came.'

Φ

The room is in the west wing. If their own room is witness to sunrise and a view of the gardens, Julius's catches the evening light spilling over woodlands and a rain-swollen brook. Like much of the house, the corridor that leads to his room stands empty and silent. Thomas wonders whether all great houses are like this: stone deserts, traversed by servants in livery at set times of the day. Within these deserts there are small islands of habitation. In their week here, he has only ever seen Lady Naylor in the context of three rooms.

They walk up to the door, already feeling like thieves. Though their gait is no different than usual – or is it? – Thomas feels as if their intention is written on their skin. He sniffs the air, studies his breath to make sure he isn't smoking. But it isn't Smoke that's troubling his blood, it's a self-consciousness bordering on shame. All the same, he feels no doubt concerning what he is about to do. Julius coming here is an act of aggression, like a move on the chessboard they have just abandoned. It requires a counter.

They arrive at the door. Thomas knocks, loudly, boldly. Charlie winces at the sound. The knock receives no answer.

'You can wait here. At the end of the corridor. Whistle if someone comes.'

Thomas can see Charlie is tempted. He is uncomfortable with this. Not from want of courage. It simply appears wrong to him, not so much a crime as ungentlemanly, against the rules of civilised conduct. Thomas wonders if Charlie would have fewer qualms if Thomas had suggested searching the valet's room.

'Let's go,' Charlie says at last. 'If they catch us, we are in it together.'

The room is much bigger than the one they share, and more opulently furnished. There is a four-poster bed, a bureau and several couches; a dozen artful models of sailing ships from the Royal Navy, displayed on shelving that is built into the wall panelling. Julius's travelling trunk has been unpacked and stored at the top of the heavy chestnut wardrobe. A painting of a fox stalking a chicken graces one wall, an old map of England covers another. The washstand is lined with bottles of scent and silver-handed brushes. It isn't what Thomas expected – a bunk and an open trunk; a pile of belongings that could be sifted in a few minutes – and for a moment he is unsure what to do. If he has fought the knowledge until now, the room puts an end to his denials. Julius is Lady Naylor's son. He may not have grown up with her, but this is his space, has been from childhood, each sailing ship a birthday perhaps, until he tired of models and graduated to hunting dogs and rifles and cricket pads hand-tailored to his legs.

Charlie looks at Thomas and recognises his confusion. 'Where do we start?'

What he is really saying is: *We shouldn't be here.*

'The wardrobe,' Thomas says, walking over.

He does not expect Charlie to do any searching himself.

Φ

There isn't much that would be of any use. No diary hidden under the pillow; no papers or letters on top of the bureau, nor in its shelves, nor in the wastebasket. There is a surprising number of shirts, more than thirty in all, each freshly pressed and of such radiant crispness as to appear unworn. Thomas also finds three pairs of leather gloves; a toy foil and a real sword stick, both carelessly thrown into the back of the wardrobe; an ivory fountain pen with a gold nib. Spurs, a riding crop, a slender horn-handled penknife with a four-inch blade. But no clue, no explanation of why Julius has come there, no secret about his character revealed.

There is one thing though: a wooden box. Thomas notices it because it has the air of something that does not want to be noticed. It is kept on the bedside table in plain enough sight, but is stacked amidst a pile of books. Almost as though by chance. But somehow too neatly all the same.

The box is quite small and made from a curious varnished wood that shines red in the evening sunlight. It is not light enough to be empty but neither is it particularly heavy; has the wrong sort of dimensions to comfortably hold letters or papers; and emits an ever so slight smell, not unlike that of old leather. That, and it is locked. There is a small silver keyhole, and no key.

Thomas carries it over to the bureau, opens the penknife, inserts its tip into the lock. It takes some fiddling, but the lock is a simple one and turns under pressure. He can feel Charlie frowning at his back, bending forward to see. Thomas opens the box with a flourish and finds (his stomach lurches with the disappointment): cigarettes. Neat rows of them, perhaps as many as six dozen, looking pale and fragile against the lustre of the wood.

'Damn,' he whispers and closes the box.

But Charlie stops him. 'Reopen it. Smell them.'

Thomas does so, pushes his nose right up to the cigarettes, then takes one out, runs it under his nose. He has never smoked a cigarette and, come to think of it, has never held one. Even so he recognises the smell of tobacco, can imagine its aroma when lit. Underneath it, though, there is another smell. Darker, tarter, hard to place. Charlie, hanging over his shoulder, has his eyes closed; is rooting through his memory for a trace of this smell.

'Like your undershirt,' he says at last, 'when it came back from the laundry. When we were children, I mean. Before Discipline started. The smell of lye, there, at the centre of the chest, and between the shoulder blades, the places where the maid had rubbed away your Soot. But underneath the lye, something else – not Smoke, not sweat, a smell all its own. *This* smell.'

Charlie's words take Thomas back to his childhood room and a scene precisely like this one: him sitting on the bed, naked to the waist, taking his undershirt from the clean laundry pile; sitting there, sniffing it before putting it on, sorting the flavours; a vase with flowers in the open window and birdsong. It's a smell like mushrooms, and ashes, and rain-moistened dirt. A dangerous smell.

'These aren't cigarettes,' he says, and immediately stuffs four or five in his jacket pocket. Charlie does not object. It is thieving, but there are so many here, a few cigarettes won't be missed. It's unlikely Julius keeps a precise count.

This thought catches Thomas short. He hesitates, reaches into the box for one more cigarette and breaks it in half. Some tobacco flutters out, and something other than tobacco, also brown but darker and grainy like salt crystals. He lays the broken cigarette crosswise over the neat rows underneath, closes the box lid, fiddles the lock until it snaps shut. Then he returns the box to the bedside table, stacks it in between the books. Charlie observes all this, the setting sun bright on his face and narrowing his eyes into dark slits.

'You want him to know.'

Thomas shrugs. 'You were right all along. Breaking in here, it's wrong. A violation. Let's see what he does about it.'

He imagines the chessboard again, moving his king out from behind a wall of pawns.

Perhaps there is a type of chess where it pays to bluff.

Φ

They take the stolen cigarettes back to their room, line them up on one of the starched pillowcases. Sit on the other bed, staring at them. After some minutes, Thomas gets up, searches his pockets, digs out a box of matches. He fetches one of the cigarettes and sits, holding it under his nose. Smelling it. His stomach cramps. It takes him a while to admit it is from fear. Thomas does not understand it. His body is rebelling against this smell. He wonders if it would be the same if you held a poison mushroom under your nose. If, smelling it, your body would scream at you not to take a bite. Charlie is watching this silent struggle. It should be frightening, the fact that someone can read you like this, simply, like a book. But it isn't. Not when Charlie does it.

He reaches over, takes the cigarette away from Thomas.

'I'll do it. Light me a match.'

Thomas does, then sits motionless, the flame burning brightly, curling the spent wood. When he lights the second match, Charlie quickly reaches over and takes it from him, but the speed of the motion extinguishes the flame halfway to his mouth. Thomas strikes a third match, then pinches the flame dead before the cigarette is lit.

'Don't, Charlie. It does not feel right. There must be another way of finding out what they do.'

'What other way?'

'I will ask Lady Naylor.'

Charlie nods, then frowns.

'Ask Livia,' he says. 'She knew about sweets. She may know about these.'

'The little nun?'

'She'll help us.'

112

Thomas repeats the question Charlie asked him earlier, concerning Livia's mother.

'Do you trust her?'

Charlie does not hesitate. 'Yes.'

'You like her?'

'She makes herself hard to like.'

Thomas accepts this. He remembers the letter that's still sticking out of Charlie's pocket and points to it now.

'What would your sister say about her? The one who is convinced that I am handsome.'

'Oh,' says Charlie, 'she'd despise her from the bottom of her heart.'

Φ

They find Livia in her own quarters. Thomas is not prepared for how playful her rooms seem, with their patterned rose wallpaper and china figurines, the rich burgundy curtains that frame the windows. Livia interprets his look and scowls. In one corner, a dark, heavy lectern stands, quite out of keeping with the rest of the furnishings. It's a piece from a monastery dragged into a princess's chambers. A copy of a book lies open upon it, the pages held down by a lead ruler. Thomas notes distractedly that Livia must read standing up.

She leads them to a group of sofas and chairs near the window and begs them sit down. It is as though she is about to serve tea. But her face is cold and hostile, her attention on Thomas. She is making him responsible for the intrusion.

'What can I do for you?'

Charlie speaks before Thomas can answer. 'We broke into Julius's room.' He says it like it was his idea; does not soften it or excuse it, simply presents her with the fact. 'We found these.' He nods to Thomas to pass over one of the cigarettes. 'They are not what they seem.'

Livia takes the cigarette from Thomas, smells it, then immediately returns it. It is clear that she has recognised them at once.

'And?'

'What are they?' Charlie asks.

'You didn't try one?'

'No.'

'Nor you, Mr Argyle?'

Thomas shakes his head, holds her eyes. 'I was afraid.'

113

'Do it,' she says. 'I understand the effect is not permanent.'

Again Thomas produces the box of matches, again he hesitates, his blood rebelling against the smell. Or is it? There is, mixed into his fear, the faintest thread of longing.

Again Charlie intervenes.

'I will try it,' he announces. 'If Livia says they're harmless, I will.'

She shakes her head, as though wishing to stop him, then thinks better of it.

'All right then, Mr Cooper. Here, I will hold the match.'

Charlie takes the cigarette from Thomas's hand; Livia reaches over and snatches up the matches. Her face, as she looks at Charlie, holds a peculiar expression. Renfrew looks like that, when he asks one of the clever boys a question that is particularly difficult. Hopeful. But expecting failure all the same. Between them, they have turned Thomas into a spectator. It sits ill with him, but he does not intervene as Charlie holds the tip of the cigarette into the flame. Charlie coughs a little, exhales the barest breath of grey, takes another drag.

'And – how do you feel?' Livia asks.

Charlie speaks very quickly.

'I feel normal,' he says. 'Just the same as before.

'Good,' he adds. 'I feel really good.'

He gets up from the chair, starts pacing the room. Livia is not looking at him, speaks to her hands, folded in her lap as though in prayer. The words are so meek, it takes a while to digest their meaning.

'Mother says it makes boys "amorous". Girls too, but I think she is referring to something anatomical.'

Charlie frowns at this, turns away from them, paces.

Thomas, unnerved, walks over to him.

'Are you all right?'

When he places a hand on Charlie's shoulder, his friend shakes it off with sudden violence, steps close to Thomas, presses his forehead into his.

'Am I all right?' His voice is joyous, but there is an edge to it Thomas does not like. 'Never better.' Charlie leans his weight into him, pushes Thomas back a step. 'You should take a drag.'

There is something to Charlie's eyes as he turns his attention from Thomas to Livia. Something lewd, suggestive: so unlike Charlie that for a moment he is as though transformed.

'Or *you* should, little Miss Prim. It'd do you a world of good.'

Charlie moves the cigarette back up to his lips. Thomas slaps it out of his hand before he can inhale. Next he knows, Charlie has pushed him into the wall. The strength of it surprises Thomas, knocks the wind out of him: an unfettered Charlie, his strong young body free of restraint. Three heartbeats they stand eye to eye.

Then the real Charlie returns. There is no other phrase for it. It's his kindness, his patience, rising up again through his features. They settle around the eyes, inflect the curve of his mouth. Within another second they are followed by shame. Charlie bends to the still-burning cigarette, pinches the tip then crumples it in his fist. Livia is watching him.

'That's like throwing away pure gold.'

But Charlie's mind is elsewhere.

'I didn't smoke,' he says.

Even as he speaks a shiver goes through him. He reaches inside his shirt and his hand comes back stained. It isn't Soot and it isn't Smoke but something in between: a black, oily smear that oozes a fine stream. Then, the very next moment, it is as though it catches fire, and in the blink of an eye, Charlie's hand emits a tar-black breath of Smoke. The Soot that forms is a fine white ash. It scatters by his feet like flakes of chalk.

'Like pure gold,' Thomas repeats. 'These cigarettes are expensive?'

Livia nods. 'So I am told.'

'Who makes them? The same people that make sweets?'

She shakes her head. 'No. Sweets are a government monopoly. It used to be held jointly by three or four families, before the Spencers bought it up. These' – she stabs a finger in the direction of Charlie's fist – 'are illegal. Officially they don't even exist. Nobody knows where they are made. Or how.'

'The Spencers own the sweets monopoly?'

Thomas would like to hear more about this, but Charlie talks over him, his voice bewildered, struggling to make sense of things.

'It was like London,' he says. 'Like a fever. Only it didn't come from the outside. It came from within.' He shudders, lays his palm on his throat, as though the infection were stuck there, poisoning his breath.

'But why?' he asks, still in the same panicked tone. 'Why would anyone pay money to buy Smoke? It makes no sense.'

Livia explains it to them. They are sitting on the settee again. She has poured Charlie a glass of water. No glass for Thomas. But then: Thomas isn't convalescing.

'You went to London,' she starts. 'We heard about it, of course. My whole school was talking about it. Your *Trip*. A daring experiment for a better future. Most of the girls were jealous.'

'That's because they don't know what it is like,' Charlie interjects. 'It was horrible.'

'Was it?'

Livia says it with peculiar emphasis. Her eyes are on Thomas. He thinks about it.

'It was horrible,' Thomas repeats Charlie's phrase. 'But also: a liberation. You could not help but sin. So you are free to behave like a cad.'

Livia nods. 'Mother says, when there are government contracts for work in the cities, the gentlemen line up to do it. Of course, the official line is that it is a sacrifice they are making, "for the commonweal". Sometimes, Mother says, ladies go on weekend jaunts to London. For "charity".'

There is contempt in her voice. She seems to hate hypocrisy as much as Smoke.

'That's crazy,' Charlie insists. 'It turns you inside out, the city. You lose yourself, become someone else. It makes you *evil*.'

'Just so. Apparently one view has it that evil has its joys. But of course one cannot risk total dissipation. Nor undo all those years of schooling the senses.'

Livia's anger is so palpable now, Thomas almost expects her to smoke.

Almost.

'Since going to London is inconvenient, many a gentleman has looked for a more controlled way of sampling vice.'

'A cigarette's length of sin!' Thomas shakes his head, half amused, half disgusted. 'So school really works, eh? They take you in at eleven, and for every wisp of Smoke you get a black mark against your name. By the time you finish, you've become so very disciplined, you are incapable of letting yourself go. Oh, sure you smoke on occasion, but it's weak, a mere hiccup. Even

116

when you long for it, you can no longer find it, your inner pig.'

He looks from Livia to Charlie. Charlie didn't need much schooling to become good, Thomas thinks. He was born that way.

Thomas is less sure about Livia.

'So it's sweets when you want to avoid infection and cigarettes for leisure,' he continues. 'And just like that you have mastered the Smoke! So when do they do it, then? These gentlemen you're talking about? And gentlewomen. When do they decide it's time to take a holiday from being good?'

He has Livia's attention now. She is unflinching. 'When they want to seduce their chambermaids. Or their husband's valets.'

'Or rob,' Thomas adds. 'Or kill.'

'You could kill without Smoke,' Charlie whispers. 'If it were righteous.'

It is hard to say what he is thinking about, but he looks stricken, more so than when Thomas explained to him that Smoke is a lie; that it came to them a quarter of a millennium ago; that the powers that be rewrote the past. Charlie does not want to live in a world where sin is a sport dabbled in by the rich.

'I am not sure you could, Charlie,' he says gently. 'Even the executioner in London first worked up a Smoke. What do you think, Miss Naylor?'

But the girl does not seem interested in the question; turns away from them both, walks over to the lectern, and bends over her book. She reminds Thomas of her mother then: dismissing him at the end of one of their talks. If it was only Charlie there, perhaps she'd let him stay. But Charlie accepts her decision, walks over to the door. Thomas follows more slowly. He isn't quite done yet.

'I've been calling you a nun,' he says, still looking at Livia. 'But there is more to you than that. The nun has a brain. And teeth.'

His voice is respectful. He thinks of his words as a compliment.

Livia does not stir.

'Do you know where your mother's laboratory is?' Thomas asks.

'Yes.' She speaks without looking up.

'Will you show it to me?'

'No.'

Thomas nods, studies her, hunched over a lectern, the ruler marking her place.

'Thank you for your help.'

Thomas closes the door behind them with more force than he had planned. He hopes it does not undo his words of thanks.

Φ

One floor down, they walk into Julius's valet. Mr Price. The man enters the far end of the hallway just as they step off the stairs. Thirty steps separate them, muffled by carpet. They walk towards each other like two armies in the field.

Price is an imposing man, tall, broad-shouldered, not fat but massive, each limb a tree trunk, heavy with muscle and bone. A line running parallel with his hair marks the place where he habitually wears a cap: below, his face is wind- and sunburnt, brown like a root. On top, it is pale, the skin strangely tender, like a mollusc's, living in its shell.

There is such purpose to Price's movement that Thomas begins to wonder whether Julius has found the broken cigarette yet. He is walking without haste but with a mechanical precision that eats up the yards. It takes Thomas an effort of will not to slow his own step, defer their meeting. Instead he mirrors the man's movement, walks chest out, at the centre of the corridor. Charlie notices his change of gait and keeps step at his side.

The closer they come, the more they see of Price's features: the stubble-framed mouth, the blunt, broken nose, the deep dimple that marks the chin as though someone pressed his thumb in it when it was being baked. It's a handsome face, in its own way, strong-featured and not unintelligent. But the eyes are ringed with something. Resignation. Implacability. A lifetime of violence. A sliver of red is visible where the lower lid curves around the eyeball. Not bloodshot eyes, then, but blood-lined ones: as though for emphasis, with a razor-edged pen. The brows that frame these eyes slope downward, from temples to nose. A frown splits them. It is not for their benefit, has been written there by the facial habits of a lifetime, by anger, concentration, or by pain. Five steps apart his smell becomes noticeable, of leather and sweat and an edge of old Smoke. In a moment they will push together chest to chest. Again Thomas thinks of the broken cigarette. If there is to be a fight, neither of them is the man's match. He wonders whether he'll be able to busy Price while Charlie runs for help.

And if anyone will be willing to help.

118

One step before their collision, Price veers aside. He never slows, walks past them, his heavy boots making remarkably little noise. At the end of the hallway, Charlie stops, looks after the man. His face is flushed. It has not been often that Thomas has heard his friend speak in anger.

'That man drowns kittens for sport,' Charlie says.

'Not for sport. Only when he's told. But then he drowns them by the sackload.'

Thomas means to say it lightly, but his voice catches and a shiver runs the length of his damp back.

Mr Price

He calls me to his rooms late that night. Key-sar. That's what they call him at school. Emperor-to-be. Julius Paul. *Jules* to his mother, after the manner of the French. To me he has always been Mr Spencer, even when he was knee-high to a goose. I have known him half his life. I am father and mother to him, and also: his son. I see at once that he is angry. A riding crop is in his hand.

Go on, I say. Beat me if you must.

He does, works me over wordlessly, hitting my shoulders, back and thighs, while I shield my face and eyes. We smoke together, he from anger, I from pain; breathe each other in. Far from estranging us, it affirms our bond. It's what family is: the sharing of one another's Smoke. Everything else is like a handshake: cold, formal, keeping a step apart. Isolation. Man is not born for such a thing.

Afterwards, still breathing heavily with the exertion, he explains it to me. That they sneaked into his room that afternoon and stole his cigarettes; that they broke one and lay it topmost, in order to let him know. He is pale with his anger. A handsome boy, always was. I run a bath for him, so he can scrub off the Soot. While he sits and soaks, I tidy the room. The cigarette case stands open. I close it and lock it away.

He does not share his cigarettes with me. Each of these, he often says to me (he likes to handle them, point with them, stab one at your face: a scarecrow's finger, stuffed and bent, bleeding tobacco from its tip), each of these is worth two years of your salary. For five your own mother would sell you to the hangman.

I object.

I have no mother, I say.

It never fails to make us laugh.

What will you do? I ask him when I tuck him into bed. How will you punish the thieves?

Discipline, he says. A gentleman does not punish.

I wait until he falls asleep. After some time his features smooth and you can see the boy in him, one hand tucked under his cheek.

Late that night, I burn the clothes. There's a disused kiln behind the house that's perfect for the purpose. Mr Spencer never wears soiled clothing. The lye, he says, makes the fabric coarse. The fire attracts birds. Rooks. My kinsmen. Cawing, they walk the perimeter of light, warming their feathers. I fall into step. They scatter when I approach, then reclaim the space as soon as I turn. It's almost like a dance.

On the morrow, after a late breakfast, Mr Spencer sends me to find the butler. Thorpe. Thorpe has his eyes everywhere, Mr Spencer says. The house is his kingdom and he rules it with spies. Thorpe will know where those boys are spending their time.

Thorpe does. He tells me the boys are taking their exercise in the gym. Main house, ground floor, east wing. He is speaking for Mr Spencer's benefit, not mine: his eyes see through me, as through a window, to the man I represent.

I do not like Thorpe. Here's a man who has never smoked in the company of others. A man without family or tribe.

A lonely man.

The stable hands have it different. They say he's a man that's buried children.

It's an odd thing but they never say: his own.

Laboratory

Julius enters the gym while they are still warming up. He is wearing knickerbockers and a blue jersey and soft boots that are laced above the ankle. A little towel is thrown over one shoulder.

Before they even have time to respond to his entrance, he disappears again and runs across to the billiard room. A minute later he is back, an hourglass in his hand, beaming.

'I knew it was somewhere. It'll help us keep time.'

Wordlessly, both Charlie and Thomas turn away from him and start climbing out of the ring.

'Mr Price was right, then. He said you were too much of a pair of sissies to step in the ring with me.'

Charlie watches Thomas's back stiffen at this and speaks at once. 'I'll give you a few rounds.'

Julius smiles. 'Mr Cooper! Excellent. Queensberry rules, I suppose. Though I do wonder at times what it was like in the bare-knuckle days.'

He turns his back without waiting for a response, opens the wardrobe, searches it for a pair of gloves. The pair he settles on are worn across the knuckles. A mosaic of cracks marks the old leather. He punches the gloves together and watches a cloud of dust disperse.

'Shall we say one round, for starters? Just to warm up.' Julius lifts one stool over the ropes into the ring and places the hourglass on top. 'There we go. Ready?'

He turns the hourglass, watches the first few grains of sand slide through its waist, then climbs in the ring and starts circling its empty centre with rhythmic, light-footed steps. Ignoring Thomas's warning look, Charlie nods and climbs in after the head boy.

They spar in silence. The sand shifts slowly in its glass. It is clear from the start that Julius has had training and is, in fact, a very accomplished boxer. Thankfully he seems content to prance around, blocking or dodging Charlie's punches and landing a few soft jabs on Charlie's forehead and shoulders. As time runs down, Charlie finds himself enjoying the exercise. It is not so very different from yesterday's bout with Thomas.

When the sand is all but gone and Thomas is about to announce the end of the round, Julius steps into Charlie. It isn't a very complicated movement: he simply moves his leg inside Charlie's, drops a few inches at the knees, then pushes off from the toes and pours the weight of his body into an uppercut to the short of Charlie's rib. Three quick body hooks follow, all hitting the same spot. As Julius dances away, Charlie crumples to the ground. It is not that he cannot get air. But each breath is agony, a sharp and stabbing pain as though bone has rent the tissue of his lung.

When he collects himself, he finds Thomas by his side, quietly raging. Julius is sitting on the stool inside the ring. He is cool and composed, not showing a thread of Smoke.

'How about three rounds, Mr Argyle? You look like you need to blow off steam. Just give me a second to catch my breath.'

Julius grins, takes off his gloves for a moment, reaches into his pocket, and withdraws a cigarette and matches.

'Some say they are bad for your health. But I find they help me focus.'

He lights it with a flourish. The smell is unmistakable. Charlie waits for some sign of the cigarette's effect but Julius's face remains a picture of calm, his skin clean. It seems impossible.

There must be some sort of trick.

The motion of his jaw gives it away, the way he turns his tongue inside his cheek. A sweet. No, many sweets, tucked away at the side of his gums. Charlie wants to warn Thomas but it's obvious from Thomas's face that his friend has already seen it. More than that. It confirms a theory long adopted.

'It binds the cigarette Smoke the very moment it is produced,' Thomas says, quietly, but not so quietly Julius cannot hear. 'He likes it there, on the knife edge of control. Vicious, but not quite barking mad. And, of course, clean as a whistle.'

Julius smiles at that, steps to the centre, raising his fists and bouncing on his toes.

'Ready whenever you are, Mr Argyle. When you are done talking, that is.'

In his mouth his tongue is turning, redistributing sweets.

Julius boxes with cool viciousness. He hits Thomas almost at will, largely with jabs, at distance. When his opponent swings at him, he slips the punch and counters, all with the same aloof air of control. Thomas, by contrast, is distracted by his own rage. He charges widely, stands flat-footed, off-balance, always a beat behind the dance. Already his breath is showing dark in front of his mouth and an inch-long line has formed between his shoulder blades like the swollen body of a leech.

At the end of the round Julius bends over the ropes that frame the ring and spits out a black rotten sweet. For a split second Charlie is transported back to school, to that initial fight between Thomas and the head boy. There, too, a blackened lump was spat across a floor. It bounced on bathroom tiles.

Back then they took it for a tooth.

They start the second round. Thomas does not stand a chance. Julius continues to box scientifically, inflicting maximum punishment. He works Thomas's body as much as the face, the side of the ribs and the soft of the belly, Thomas looking as though he is drowning. He smokes from pain and helplessness, staggers, rolls, slumps. It does not even occur to Charlie that he is baiting his opponent, making him careless. But when Julius shoves his reeling figure, pushing him into the ropes, Thomas suddenly straightens and out of nowhere lands a hook with such force it sends four or five sweets flying from Julius's mouth, some dark, some still clear as crystal. They are followed by a gob of blood.

Still Julius keeps coming and still he does not smoke. He is more careful now, boxes at distance. Punch after punch hits Thomas: the flat, dry drumbeat of air being forced out of the glove. It isn't until the sand in the hourglass has almost run clear that Charlie understands that Thomas, too, has adjusted his strategy. He is leaning into Julius; is grinning, taunting him; allowing himself to be hit.

Feeding Julius's frenzy.

Exhausting his remaining sweets.

And then, without any warning, with only seconds left in the round, the last of the sweets is spent. Julius *erupts*. Smoke paints him black. It envelops Thomas who screams a viscous cloud of welcome. They go down, one on top of the other, and Julius keeps pounding

Thomas, never tiring, inhuman in his strength, while Thomas keeps on screaming in pain and hatred, his chin dripping with wet Smoke and blood. The round is long over and Charlie is in the ring, trying to pull Julius off. In vain. Julius does not even budge, kicks and elbows behind himself, all the while sending fists into Thomas's black and bloodied face.

Again Charlie tries to pull Julius off. Again he fails, Smoke and panic in his every breath. Then an idea comes to him. He does not hesitate, throws himself flat on his stomach, searches the floor for the unspoilt sweets that Thomas beat out of his opponent. He finds one, then a second the shade of light amber; scuttles over to Julius and reaches, through his Smoke, first for his throat then his chin, his mouth, attempting to force the sweets inside. Teeth cut his thumb, his index finger, the knuckle. Then an elbow to the head sends Charlie flying onto the parquet next to them, and when he gasps for air it is Smoke that rushes in his lungs and turns all thought to madness.

Φ

It works, after a fashion. The fresh sweets absorb and bind the strongest Smoke. It grants a measure of lucidity to Julius's hatred. He rolls off Thomas – to regroup? to fetch the stool from the corner of the ring and bash in their skulls? – staggers to his feet, yells something; then stops short, staring out into the hallway past the gym's open door. The next moment he is running. Where to does not matter to Charlie. He barely hears the footsteps, his own blood is so loud in his ears. All that matters is that Julius is gone.

Charlie retches, watches Thomas's Smoke die out. When his friend sits up, Thomas's outline remains on the parquet. A wood-pale shadow, as though cut into a sheet of perfect black dust. Charlie, still on his knees, draws a finger through the Soot. It is warm, almost hot, and fine like coal dust. He feels he needs to say something, anything, just to return them to normality: a world where people communicate their feelings in words. But all he can find to say is a lie.

'I have never seen anyone smoke like that.'

The truth is that he has. Both of them have. When a murderess swung from a rope in London.

Thomas's features are unreadable under the Soot.

'Do you mean him, or me?'

125

Charlie closes his eyes and again sees the smoking, blackened forms of the two prone bodies intertwined, like the charred remains of lovers discovered in a burnt-down barn.

'Him,' he whispers. But what he thinks is: *Either. Both.*

Compelled by some strange alchemy, Julius's and Thomas's Smoke have reacted to produce something Charlie has no words for. He was inside their Smoke for no more than a few seconds. What he breathed in – what entered his body, took control as surely as a puppeteer's hand shoved into a Punch or Judy – stood all truth upon its head. Over *there*, inside the Smoke, pain was joy and anger peace. Violence was love.

As though hoping it will rid him of the memory, Charlie rises to his feet. The moment he is up, still dizzy, he sees what Julius saw.

Livia is there.

From the look in her eyes she has been there a good long while.

She is standing out in the hallway, half a step from the door, in a frock of perfect white. And looks as though she is going to a party. Her cheeks are powdered, hair pinned into a bun behind her head. It disturbs Charlie that in a moment like this he can notice such a detail. And approve. The hairstyle suits her, underlines the slimness of her neck. In her ears, two pearls swing on silver loops.

'Miss Naylor!' Charlie raises a hand in greeting then lets it drop. All social conventions are as though swept away. His naked, black-ened chest shivers with sudden cold. One side of the hourglass is dusted with Soot as though it has been witness to a storm.

To Charlie's surprise, Livia walks into the room rather than run-ning away. She climbs in the ring, walks past him, and bends down low to where Thomas is still sitting on the ground, the hem of her dress soiling in Soot. Her voice betrays her disgust with what she has seen. But there is something else in it, too. Pity.

It softens her words.

'You must leave this house, Mr Argyle. He will cripple you.'

Thomas shakes his head, croaks something only she can hear. She flushes, stiffens, shakes her head.

'I can't. I won't.'

Another croak. This time Livia straightens. All pity is gone from her voice. 'I will not show you the laboratory, Mr Argyle. And you *will* leave as soon as it can be arranged.'

Only then does she turn to Charlie.

'Clean him up, Mr Cooper, and do it fast. It's New Year's Eve and mother is planning a formal dinner. We eat at six.'

Φ

At dinner, Julius is composed, charming and attentive to his mother. The bruise on his cheek is barely visible. As course after intricate course is served, his mood only continues to improve. He declines to partake in the wine. As he reminds Lady Naylor, he is, after all, still only a schoolboy; his Smoke and Ethics teacher would not approve. Julius beams at Thomas as he says it. The two are sitting directly across from one another.

Thomas's face is red and lumpy, one eye lost behind his swollen brow and cheek. The other eye is smeared by a ring of sickly yellow that is already darkening into hues of purple, brown and black. He will look worse on the morrow. But Charlie is more worried about the damage to Thomas's body. The way Thomas sits, slumped to one side like a listing ship, it is clear he is in considerable pain. Charlie himself winces whenever he takes too deep a breath. His rib is so tender, he eats with one elbow sticking out far to the side, to avoid brushing his own chest.

The afternoon was spent trying to make themselves look respectable. Getting the Soot off took several hours of scrubbing: Thomas so sore that every contact of brush with skin brought tears to his eyes. He struggled with getting into his trousers and shirt and yet refused Charlie's offers of help; sat for minutes over each of his socks, unable to bend down to his feet. In the end, already dressed, his cravat splayed against his chest like a broken butterfly, Thomas had crawled onto his bed and lain there unmoving while Charlie paced the room, looking for something to say.

'Next year, how about we spend New Year's with my parents? It's quieter there.'

Thomas did not smile at this. He may not believe he has another year.

When, at the appointed time, they head over to the dining room, they – crumpled, limping, their shoes unpolished – make a marked contrast to the splendour of Lady Naylor's dress and the elegance of Julius's frock coat. Livia wears a ruby pendant over a high-cut dress. It is startlingly becoming. Neither she nor her mother comment on Thomas's appearance. When a cut on his lip opens during dinner, the baroness leans over and offers her handkerchief.

Half an hour before midnight Lady Naylor and Livia excuse themselves. They wish to be with the baron when the clock strikes: it is a family tradition. This leaves the three boys sitting there alone, at the big table. The first thing Julius does is to help himself to another slice of cake. He lifts his feet onto the chair next to his, makes himself comfortable. A moment later Mr Price enters the room. He walks in in silence and takes up position near the wall, directly behind Thomas's and Charlie's backs. Charlie has the impression he is holding something but does not want to turn. Not one of them speaks. Julius's fork scrapes across the china plate every time he scoops up another bite of cake.

The minutes creep by, midnight approaching. Charlie's back is crawling with the sensation that any second now Mr Price will come at them from behind. He might be holding a whip, a cudgel, a gun. Surely Julius is not as crazy as that. The very moment he thinks the thought, the memory of the boxing ring rises up in Charlie. His hand inspecting the floor after the fight. Soot fine as coal dust.

Who is to say just how crazy Julius may be?

Another minute passes. Julius discards the plate but holds on to the fork, taps his teeth with its prongs. Behind them, Mr Price starts humming 'Rule Britannia'.

At three minutes to midnight, Thorpe joins them. He walks in briskly and starts fussing over the champagne bottle that's been cooling in a silver bucket. A tidy, closed little man, slight and fragile-looking next to the bulk of Mr Price. But immediately all the tension goes out of the room. When Charlie lifts his glass to Mr Thorpe's proffered bottle, he cannot keep it from shaking with anxiety and relief. At midnight the clock in the corner gives a low chime. Into the awkward silence, Mr Price injects a hearty, Scots-inflected 'Auld Lang Syne'.

Nobody else thinks to sing along.

No sooner has Mr Price worked his way through the last chorus than Charlie quickly rises.

'I'm going to bed.'

Mr Thorpe puts down the bottle.

'Very well. I will light the way for you and Mr Argyle.'

It seems to Charlie that he is under instruction to see them safely to their room.

Just as Thomas begins to push himself laboriously up from the table, Julius leans his body across its width and grabs Thomas's wrist. His voice is quiet, untouched by anger.

'Look here, Argyle. Mother's right. I didn't like it when she said it, but there's no denying it. We are kindred souls. We should make friends.'

Thomas freezes, looks him hard in the face, and suddenly spits a jet of Smoke. A foul smell accompanies it, along with a retching that imparts distress rather than anger. Julius recoils, then laughs and makes a sign to his valet to open the windows.

He is still laughing when Charlie and Thomas follow Thorpe out of the room.

Φ

They do not turn off the light. Neither of them has mentioned it, but both are very conscious that their door has no lock. Thomas is lying on top of the bedding, still wearing his shoes. He might be finding it difficult to take them off.

'What if we wrote to Renfrew?' Charlie asks into the silence. 'About all this. Julius. The cigarettes. And what Lady Naylor told you. He, too, is fighting Smoke.'

Thomas thinks, disagrees. 'Renfrew is fighting *sin*. And we don't know enough to go and pick sides.' He furrows his brow, then winces. The movement hurts his bruises. 'Julius has changed, don't you think? I mean, he was always a prick. But now . . . Now he's out of control.'

'Too many cigarettes?'

'Maybe. Who knows how many a day he smokes, a sweet in each cheek. In any case: no letters, Charlie. Not for now.'

Φ

Charlie must have fallen asleep. He did not hear her knock, if knock she did, nor enter the room. It stings him for a second that she should have woken Thomas first. The two are in negotiations.

'You must leave as soon as possible.'

'You are very keen to get rid of us, Miss Naylor.'

'I tried to convince Mother to send you away. But she won't believe me. She says it's just two boys, having an argument. The law of the playground. She didn't see what I saw.

'You must leave,' she says again. 'Or there will be further incidents. The whole house already reeks of your darkness.'

Thomas's voice is hard when he answers. 'You know what I want.'

'If I show it to you, do you promise you will go?'

'We will,' Charlie intervenes, causing Livia to turn. 'Just as quickly as we can.'

Livia nods. 'Do I have your word on that, Mr Cooper?'

'You do.'

'And yours, Mr Argyle?'

'Yes.'

'Then follow me.'

Φ

She leads them to the third floor. Charlie had some idea that the laboratory must be in a secret basement, hidden away beneath a trapdoor in some distant room, but here they are, high up within the main structure of the house, within an easy walk from all its main rooms. The door Livia stops before looks like any other. It is not even locked. Behind it, though, is a second, heavier door, upholstered in black leather.

'Only Mother has the key. I am sworn never to touch it.'

Even as she says it, Livia produces the key from out her left fist. She's been clutching it so hard, its profile is cut into her palm. It occurs to Charlie that this is the first time Livia has ever broken a promise. If so, it does not show in her movements as she deftly unlocks the door.

The laboratory is not one room but a whole suite of rooms, lined up one after the other, like railway carriages. When Livia has closed and locked the door behind them, she lights a lamp and hands it over to Charlie.

'You may look, but don't shift anything. You have a quarter of an hour. This is my mother's life's work. It may be wrongheaded. But we should respect it.' As she speaks, her lips flicker red in the gaslight. Not for the first time Charlie wonders what she would do if he kissed them.

The two boys drift into the room. There are so many tables, bureaus and shelves that it is hard to know where to start. Livia alone remains near the door, as referee and timekeeper.

A large desk draws them. It stands off in one corner, but the pile of books and papers covering it mark it as the centre of the room's activities. The room's most comfortable chair has been drawn up to it, its upholstery dark with use. Topmost on the desk, perched precariously on a whole stack of volumes, lies a large, leather-bound journal stamped with the baron's crest. Inside, the pages are covered with tiny, dense handwriting. Charlie bends to it, but is unable to make sense of the letters. The journal, if that is what it is, is kept entirely in ancient Greek.

As he picks up the volume, two pictures shift within it, each marking a place. One is the portrait of a teenage girl, a little younger than themselves. At first glance it is easy to miss the iron rings around her wrists and throat. She is in chains; her neck attached to the wall behind. Even so she has found enough space to twist her head away from the camera. It smudges her features and leaves her with two heads, one superimposed upon the other. The first faces the viewer, the second avoids him, shows her chin and eye in profile. The girl's mouth connects the two faces, unnaturally elongated by her movement and stretched into a bitter smile. A strand of dark hair has come loose from the knot at her back and cuts across her pallor like a crack. Her features are foreign, hard to place. It is a face, Charlie thinks, that would be hard to forget.

Separated from the girl by some thirty pages rests the picture of a familiar pairing. Master Renfrew and Baron Naylor stand shoulder to shoulder on an open plain of such pancake flatness that the horizon forms a straight, smooth line. As in the picture in the gym, they are both much younger: Renfrew a university student, the baron a man of forty in a thick worsted suit. The light is so bright that the sky above the two figures appears the purest white. It is as though they are standing with their heads dunked into the void. Beneath their heavy boots, the ground is made of coarse, wild grass. There is no landscape in the whole of England as big, as flat as this. It is so barren, they might be standing on the moon.

But it is another detail that has caught Thomas's eye. Haltingly, his fingers clumsy and swollen, each movement painful to him, he reaches over and takes the picture out of Charlie's hand; holds it up to the lamp at a flat angle, then rubs one corner between his fingers as though testing a piece of cloth.

'Feel it, Charlie. This is not a daguerreotype. And look – when you hold the lamp close, it glows like it's shot through with silver.'

Charlie understands him at once. 'Some new technology; from the Continent. Despite the embargo.'

'New for us. But this print must be fifteen years old.' Thomas replaces the picture between the pages of the journal. 'This alone is enough to land Lady Naylor in jail.'

Φ

They continue looking. After a few minutes Thomas, trusting to moonlight, shifts away from the desk of papers, and limps onwards, into the next room. Charlie, meanwhile, has become immersed in what appears to be a ledger, lying open to its latest entry. He is unfamiliar with the high art of bookkeeping, but expenses and income are recorded in different-coloured ink – red and black – and as such are immediately identifiable. The sums listed for expenses are enormous. One particular item draws the eye. The figure indicated is so large, that initially Charlie thinks he must have misread it. The item is identified only as a 'delivery'; a date has been added in pencil: '12 January'. Less than two weeks from now. The baroness has paid for her order in advance. A letter is attached to the page by a pin, taciturn to the point of obscurity. It, too, makes reference to a delivery and identifies the same date. 'Tobacco Dock. The *Haarlem* (La Rochelle). Midnight. Pls collect in person & arrange for transport.' A Captain van Huysmans is undersigned.

As for the ledger's income column, each figure in it is replicated in a separate column marked with a capital D. Charlie cannot make sense of this odd doubling until he chances on the notion that D must stand for 'debt'. A name follows each sum in this column, always the same, always written out in full with such a show of fastidiousness that it takes on the flavour of obsession.

Spencer.
Spencer.
Spencer.
Spencer.
Spencer.

It is as though Lady Naylor does not want to allow herself to forget to whom she owes her money. The figure that is carried over from previous pages is already so large that the implication is clear. The Naylors must be bankrupt. For all intents and purposes the Spencers own them. Which is to say Julius owns them, the moment his grandfather dies. The man is said to be very old, and bedridden with gout.

Φ

Charlie moves away from the ledger, continues drifting through the room. There are other mysteries. There is a desk, for instance, almost entirely covered with technical drawings. Many of them are rendered on dark blue paper of a peculiar texture. The drawings themselves are white. As Charlie tries to spread them out, a few tumble to the ground. He sees Livia wince at the noise; retrieves them, and immediately realises that he cannot reproduce their former order. The topmost shows a warren of long, intersecting alleyways: a system so complex and angular that it is difficult to picture a city built according to its principles. But perhaps the chart is showing a railway system, or an archaeological site. The only clue as to what Charlie is looking at is provided by a single word, printed in ornamental capitals along the drawing's lower edge. *A·S·C·H·E·N·S·T·E·D·T*. Charlie has never heard of a place by that name. But he knows that *Asche* is German for ash, and *Stedt* very nearly the German word for city. A City of Ashes. The phrase conjures images of a thousand furnaces burning in the dark.

A hiss from Thomas snaps Charlie out of his musings and beckons him to follow. The second room appears to be the laboratory proper. The walls here are lined with pharmaceutical equipment: jars and glass tubes, rows of chemicals in dark brown bottles. Several apparatuses are set out on tables, though none are currently in use. A microscope takes pride of place on a separate desk. Thomas stands stooped near it, his hands leafing through a pile of notebooks.

'All her notes are in French. And over there, there's a library of scientific texts. Books in German, Italian, Russian – you name it. Most of them illegal, no doubt. And then there is this.'

Thomas pulls Charlie over to a glass case in one corner. Here, too, apothecary bottles are lined up. Each of them is carefully labelled with a person's name and a date. Each of them contains a black substance, more liquid than powder.

Soot.

Thomas opens the door of the glass case and points to a few of the bottles.

'James Hardy, remember him? No? A legal clerk. Accused of

133

murdering his wife and children. The newspapers went wild about him. Two or three years ago, in Hexham, it was, up north. He was hanged.' He points to the label. 'On my birthday – that's why I remember it. And here, Anne MacNamara. You know about her, surely?'

Charlie does. 'She burnt down a church in Ipswich. More than fifty dead. She said she got the idea from a book. I remember my parents talking about her trial.'

'Sentenced to death. I don't remember the date, but I bet you it is what it says on the bottle. Early last summer.'

Charlie scans the many bottles. There are more than two dozen.

'You think all of them—'

'Yes.'

'And all of them criminals. Murderers.'

'Yes. She harvests their Soot when they are executed.'

Charlie winces at the word. *Harvest*. It's what the devil is said to do with souls.

'What else have you found, Thomas?'

'Slides for the microscope. Soot, blood drops, bits of tissue. Grains from those cigarettes: she has sliced them open and studied the contents. Medical texts, anatomy charts. The only thing in English I saw is a handwritten treatise on some kind of surgical procedure. But it's hard to read by moonlight. Then there's this.'

Thomas takes the lamp out of Charlie's hands, trains it on another shelf. Its beam finds a row of glass jars in which strange, mottled objects hang, as though weightless, suspended in a liquid too viscous to be water. It takes Charlie a moment to identify them as bodily organs. Lungs and livers feature prominently, familiar enough from the school dinner table, where offal remains a staple. Their spongy tissue looks pale and bloated in the preserving fluid.

'From humans?'

Thomas shrugs. There is no need to say it. What interest could Lady Naylor have in animal parts?

Livia's voice carries to them from the front room. 'We must go.'

'One more minute.' Thomas turns his back on the jars and pulls Charlie along, to the last of the rooms. 'Just a quick glance.'

The beam of the light travels before them. They themselves never make it past the threshold of the door.

In size it is a room much like the others: square, wood-panelled, a narrow window closed upon the night. There are more desks here and more shelves; books, scientific tools, a dusty sheet that hides some bulky machine.

But what absorbs Charlie's and Thomas's interest is a sort of alcove or closet at the far end of the room. It is not quite big enough to be thought of as a room in its own right and is separated from the main space by a row of iron bars that turn it into a kennel. A door is worked into the bars, just large enough to admit a person. Inside stand a camp bed, a stool, a chamber pot. Incongruously, a thick little carpet covers much of the floor of the alcove, and its walls have been wallpapered with a design that shows the silhouettes of ladies in ball gowns, each arrested in a different posture, gold leaf on mauve. As the lamp flickers, these dancers appear to twitch and move. The bed, somewhat too short and narrow to be comfortable, is freshly made. At the height of neck, wrists and ankles, its metal frame anchors leather restraints. A ring of steel is let throat-high into the wall.

The boys stare at this alcove for a full minute. Again and again Charlie focuses the lamp on the wallpaper, the bed, the chamber pot. It's this chamber pot that somehow fills him with a particular horror. In the absence of a prisoner it concentrates upon itself all the evil, the humiliation of this cage.

'We must go,' Livia calls again, softly, across the darkness of three rooms.

Without a word, the boys turn around and walk back to her, their faces grim with anger.

Φ

They extinguish the lamp before Livia opens the door. Outside, the long corridor lies dark and silent. She turns, locks up, tension leaving her frame. It is as though she's stepped out of a corset.

As she curls the key into her fist and leads the way back towards their room, a light is turned on, or rather the hood is turned back on a lamp already burning, arresting them in a beam focused by its parabolic mirror. They freeze, blink blinded into the glare, see the outline of a figure behind the lamp, ten steps away. Then, as quickly as it was opened, the lamp hood is shut. Steps move away from them, into the freshly thickened darkness of the house. It all happens so quickly that there is no time to decide between flight and pursuit. By the time their eyes have recovered enough sight for them to consider either, it is too late. They walk back to their rooms with exaggerated slowness.

'I'm sorry,' Charlie says to Livia when they part ways. Sorry they got her into trouble. Sorry they mixed her up in their felony and weren't clever enough not to get caught.

But her face robs all force from his words, her features flitting from self-reproach to a nunnish kind of pride: pride at how thorough the punishment will be that she has already begun devising for herself.

'There will be no need to assist me with my father tomorrow, Mr Cooper. Goodnight, Mr Argyle.'

The words have all the formality of a coroner pronouncing death.

Φ

They cannot find sleep. Lying in their beds in darkness, separated by two steps and the walls we all erect around our thoughts, they listen to each other breathing. Their conversation is halting, interrupted by long minutes of silence.

'Who was it with the lamp?'

'Lady Naylor. Or Thorpe, or Julius, or Price. Does it really matter? One way or another, it means she knows.'

There is a rustle in the room, as of something creeping along a linen sheet. It might be Thomas running his fingernails over the pillow or a mouse scraping at the foot of the mattress. Charlie wants to light a candle and find out. But the room is cold around him, and his limbs leaden. He speaks to say something; to silence the sound.

'What's all the Soot for?' he asks.

'Don't know. But she likes it fresh, from killers, the moment they are dead.'

Thomas's voice shifts with the next breath, grows younger somehow. In the darkness it is easy to imagine him as a child, twelve years old, eyes burning fiercely with fear and defiance.

'She is collecting Soot, the blackest she can get. Then who is the cage for, Charlie?'

Charlie does not answer at once. He pictures the iron collar screwed in the wall, high above the cage's too-short bed. It seems too slender for Thomas's neck.

'She wouldn't,' he says at last.

'We don't know the first thing about what Lady Naylor would or wouldn't do.'

'Then we must do what we promised. Leave. This very day.'

Thomas responds by lighting a candle. He holds it close to his face, shadows chasing upwards, past his swollen cheeks and brows. His voice is calm, pensive.

'If that's what it takes, you know ... To defeat Smoke, I mean, once and for all. If all she's missing is the last bit of Soot, the *right* sort of Soot, tainted from birth ... I mean, if that's what is growing in me, and if she asked me to – I'd do it, Charlie, I would. Even if it comes with that collar. Or with a rope.'

Charlie watches the thought unfold in Thomas. He doesn't try to dissuade him. All he says is, 'She hasn't asked.'

'Maybe she's working up to it.'

'Maybe. If so, she can write you a letter.'

Thomas's expression is stony. Then a smile crawls over his face.

'A letter?'

'Yes. Kindly request your volunteering yourself to be killed. Much obliged. RSVP at earliest convenience.'

They both giggle. It's the sound of relief.

'You're right, Charlie. Let's get the hell out of here.' Then: 'Where will we go?'

'Home. My parents set off for Ireland today. But Lady Naylor doesn't need to know that. We will have the house to ourselves.'

Thomas is quiet for a moment.

'She might not let us,' he says at last.

'No,' Charlie concedes. 'But then we'll know what she is about.

'I am a Cooper,' he adds after some thought. 'Firstborn son of the eighth Earl of Shaftesbury. It'd be hard to make me disappear.'

Φ

They broach the subject with Lady Naylor at lunch. They could not locate her before, ate breakfast alone in the smaller of the three dining rooms. It is Charlie who takes the word. He explains how his sister's recent letter included a note from his parents requesting he come home with his friend; how his mother in particular is keen to meet Mr Argyle about whom she has heard so much; and adds that his father is desirous that they come as quickly as possible so that he can introduce them to a cousin visiting from Ireland.

Thomas interrupts his flow of eloquence.

'In short,' he says, 'we will leave today.'

Throughout all this Lady Naylor sits impassive, stiff-backed, her fork embedded in a piece of cold pork.

'It'll be dark before you get to the station. The roads aren't safe. Besides, you are too late for the express.'

Thomas is about to argue, but she has already turned to her butler.

'Thorpe, please talk to the coachman. And help the gentlemen pack. They leave at dawn.'

Φ

They spend the day in their room, only venturing forth for necessities. Neither of them says so out loud, but it's because they are scared. Scared of something going wrong, someone stopping them, thwarting their escape. When they arrived, ten days ago, the house bored them. Now it feels like a trap. As they sit, counting the hours, Charlie finds his thoughts wandering to Livia. He feels like he owes her an explanation, or perhaps she him. About what exactly, it is hard to say.

After dinner Lady Naylor asks Charlie and Thomas to join her in her study. She sits down behind her desk and makes them swear 'not to speak or otherwise mention any of my research or any of the historical insights I have shared with you, on your honour as gentlemen.' The phrase is so cumbersomely legalistic that Charlie half expects her to pull a sheet of paper from her drawer and require their signatures. Before they are dismissed, she rises to press their hands.

It's Thomas's turn first.

'I regret you are in such a hurry to leave, Mr Argyle. I had high hopes for you.'

'I often disappoint.'

She smiles. 'I imagine so.' She looks over at a letter lying on her desk. 'There is news from Parliament today. I only just received it. They held a special session early this morning. On New Year's Day, would you believe? It's quite unprecedented. The Speaker called for a vote on the proposed amendments to the Purity of the Realm Act. Most of the delegates were out of town, of course. The amendment has been voted down. There will be no changes to the embargo. It's a perfect Tory triumph. I am afraid your good Dr Renfrew will be rather crushed.' She gives them a look of pain and scorn. 'We live at a fateful time, gentlemen. The future of our country hangs in the balance. And you choose to behave like children playing hide-and-seek.'

She lets go of Thomas's hand with a brusqueness bordering on violence. It's Charlie's turn next. Up close her face looks drawn, almost haggard. He has not noticed it before.

'You will, I trust, refrain from mentioning any details about my husband's condition to anyone, even your family. It might be best to suggest you never saw him. He is bedridden. Let that be enough.'

She gives his hand a final squeeze, turns away from them, reclaims her seat.

'That is all. Goodbye, gentlemen. Bon voyage.'

'We won't see you in the morning?'

'I have work to do.'

That is the last they know of her, bent over her desk, dipping her pen into a vat of ink. In her mind they seem to have already ceased to exist.

Φ

Outside Lady Naylor's office, they find Livia lingering. It is obvious she has waited for them, but as they approach she suddenly starts walking, away from them. Charlie runs after her for a few steps, stops, calls.

'We are leaving at dawn,' he calls.

She turns, and at the same time starts running. A twitch cuts a wrinkle through the fine composure of her face. And then the impossible happens: a drop of Smoke, blue-grey and almost liquid, pours from her nose onto her upper lip. The next moment she turns the corner. From far away a word reaches them, muffled, though she must have shouted it.

'Adieu.'

Thomas

I do not sleep. There is another place, of not-sleep, that I can freely enter where one may dream but find no rest. It is like a room with a door that leans open. I try to resist it, but time and again am drawn there, poke open that door, slip my face (only my face!) around its frame. Inside sits another me, an iron ring around his neck, and the wallpaper stages a ball of a thousand *grandes dames* dancing. Gold leaf on mauve. As the Smoke pours out of me (the other me, the one I am watching), I burn my own silhouette into the wall. It discommodes the dancers. When dawn breaks through the open curtains, I am exhausted, my face still swollen like a pumpkin. Outside, the pheasant whose steady patrol was so much a part of our stay here is nowhere to be seen. Perhaps he is no longer with us. We had pheasant soup last night.

The morning does not go to plan. The coach is there, and Thorpe has sent servants to have our luggage loaded, but up on the box sits not Harrington, the coachman who drove us here, but Mr Price, a heavy shotgun thrown across his thighs. When I ask him what he thinks he is doing up there, he spits some phrases into his muffler.

'Lady's orders. A band of Gypsies. Sighted not ten leagues from here. Job calls for someone good with a gun. Just in case.'

He cuts himself a plug of tobacco, sets to chewing it. Thorpe opens the door for us, his face blank of emotion. Charlie climbs in first.

'In a few hours we'll be on the express,' he says.

A jolt of envy runs through me. Charlie's soul is knit for hope. Mine's stuck in the mud of the things that may go wrong.

Nobody waves us off. The moment the door is closed, Thorpe turns away, climbs the stairs to the manor. The sun is coming out, chasing mist along the ground. The crunch of gravel as the wheels start turning. There is a window at the back of the carriage; both Charlie and I press a brow to it, watch us pull away. We leave a pile of horse dung in our wake. Some dogs bark, a rooster hails the morning. Then we pass the gate.

Within two hundred yards of the manor house we stop. Before we can open the door to see what is going on, we hear Price's voice, remonstrating with someone.

'Impossible. I'm not instructed to—' and 'Does your mother know?'

'Drive,' says Livia, entering the coach in a skirt and jacket made of dark wool. 'I am seeing the gentlemen to the station. Quick now, or we will miss the train.'

Reluctantly, Price puts the coach in motion. Livia sits down across from us and stares at us in grim pallor.

If we expect her to explain her actions, we are mistaken. But then, it's obvious, really. She and Charlie haven't said goodbye. They like each other, but she's the type of girl for whom that sort of thing is a big fuss. Only now there's three in the coach, which is one too many for this sort of talk, so she looks at me grimly, while Charlie asks her shyly how does she do, and has she slept soundly and well. I could climb out, leave them to it, but the box only has one seat, and Price is on it, holding a shotgun as thick as my arm. So I settle into my coat and pretend to doze. I find the room without any difficulty. The door is only leaned to. I can feel the wood against my cheek, the handle in my fist. What harm can it do, just to take a peek?

I wake – if that's what I do – when the morning sun falls into the coach window and finds my face. Blinking, I lean out, see a windmill grow out of the long stretch of its shadow and have a sudden sense of déjà vu. I have seen the same windmill in the same sort of light before, on the way to the house; then, too, in the moment of surfacing from the depths of dream, its currents and tides still tugging at my limbs. Then I realise it is not just the sun that has woken me. We have stopped.

There is a muddle to the things that follow, a violation of the laws of sequence that troubles me as much as the events. It starts with the birds, an explosion of birds, spat out of the windmill as though it is a cannon. Starlings. There must be a thousand of them, a spray of ink stains in the sky, clotting, thinning, shrouding the sun.

Then (but how can it be *then* and not *before*?) the whip-crack of a shot, followed – anticipated? – by a scream, a whinny, a sound so poised between the equine and the human tongues that I cannot place the screamer. The coach quivers, buckles; Charlie shouts and my hand can't find the bloody handle of the door. I open it in time to see the second horse shot. The word does not capture it. It's like a hatchet has been taken to its neck. A fist-sized chunk just disappears, is torn out in a spray of meat and bone, then the beast crumples in its harness. I see Price, leaping off the box seat and landing hard in the mud; see rather than hear him screaming to take cover. Behind him the first of the horses that was shot froths in wonder at the dead-weight of its hoof dangling from a thread of skin.

Through all this I am standing half in, half out the coach. I want to ask Price why he stopped, and who's attacking us; whether he has a second gun on him; what sort of trick it is he thinks he is playing. I am so filled with questions at that moment, all of them *there*, present to me all at once, that my head feels light with them, as though thoughts are air, no, lighter than air, are buoyed by the magic of balloon gas, and all the same I cannot get my legs to move, am frozen, rooted, grown into the doorway of the coach at foot and hand.

Then Price is hit. The swing of a bat, an axe, a sledgehammer: invisible, trailing a bang like an afterthought. What sort of gun is this that slams a man into the side of a coach and leaves his chest a hole open for perusal?

Then it's my turn. I feel a punch, then heat, a branding iron plunged into my temple. My last thought is another question of sorts, mute wonder at the fact that neither Price nor I found time to shroud our fall in Smoke.

Then hard hands grab me from behind.

As metaphors of death go, this is one I can believe.

Part Three

Commoners

When one remembers under what conditions the working-people live, when one thinks how crowded their dwellings are, how every nook and corner swarms with human beings, how sick and well sleep in the same room, in the same bed, the only wonder is that a contagious disease like this fever does not spread yet farther.

Friedrich Engels, *The Condition of the Working Class in England* (1845)

In the Woods

Thomas goes down hard. It's Charlie who is pulling him. The force of it surprises Livia: he grabs him at throat and shoulder, kicks his feet out from under him. Anything to get Thomas away from the door. Out of the line of fire. On the way down, Thomas's shoulder collides with the edge of the seat. It twists the body and makes him land facedown, his arms trapped beneath him at odd angles. He may well have broken bones. Then again, what does it matter? He is already dead. Livia saw him being hit. Something dislodged itself, some clump of him, of his face, his head. It flew through the air. She will see it to her dying day. Livia's face is speckled with his blood.

And still it isn't over. Another shot sounds – the fifth, the sixth? – rips a hole in the door the size of a fist. Then the whole coach buckles and leaps. It is as though even the wood and wheels are trying to get away from the shooters. For a breath it stops, gathering strength. Then it leaps again, tilts, topples. The next moment the very ground has given way and they are falling, rolling, her scream drowned out by those of the horses. The impact throws them into a tangle of limbs and breaks open the coach like a conker: sunshine above, the play of sun and cloud.

It is only when she sees the trees that she understands what has happened. She should have thought of it before: she knows this road, has ridden it a hundred times. Across from the old windmill, running parallel to the road, is a sharp dip – almost a ravine – that drops some seven or eight yards, down to the edge of a forest below. In mortal terror, the horses must have dragged them off the path. Three hang dead within the harness now, two bleeding from gunshot wounds, the third with its head twisted backwards atop its broken neck. It's the fourth horse that keeps on screaming. Two of its legs are broken, spilling out of their knee joints like limp flippers. When she starts moving, it is to get away from these screams. Next to her, Charlie is already pulling Thomas's body out of the wreckage. It takes courage to turn and help him lift it up over his shoulder.

She is glad she finds this courage and gladder yet she isn't asked for more. They run for the trees, away from the attack, Thomas's head, chest and arms dangling limp down Charlie's back.

The forest is dense. There is no obvious path and, near the edge, shrubs cut their clothing to shreds. Fifty steps in, their progress improves. There's older growth here, tall trees that throw mighty shadows. They eat too much light for shrubs to grow along the forest floor. Dead leaves swallow their boots up to the ankles; their crackle follows them, the forest's whisper, showing their pursuers the way. Neither she nor Charlie suggests slowing down.

They have to stop eventually. The weight of a second body becomes too much for Charlie. It is astonishing he has borne it for this long. He staggers and drops his burden; falls down next to it. When Livia slides to her knees beside him, she finds Thomas's blood has soaked Charlie's jacket, at the small of his back. It is impossible to think of him now as Mr Cooper.

'Is he alive?' Charlie asks. He has to speak through his panting breath, sneaking the words out in between inhalations. It gives an odd, dispassionate quality to his voice, like he is too exhausted for emotion.

'We must feel his pulse,' she answers. 'It's easiest here. At the throat.'

Without hesitation, Charlie sticks his fingers into the blood that covers Thomas's neck. The wound above is still bleeding. It's the left side that's been hit, near the ear. There is no way of telling how deep the wound is. Leaves have become stuck to it, and clumps of dirt, as though the earth is already claiming him as hers.

'I cannot feel it, Livia. My hands aren't working.'

When she bends to slip her own fingers onto the side of Thomas's throat, she sees what he means. Each of her fingers is drumming, her own pulse shoving blood all the way down to its tips. It is impossible to feel anything. She lets go, bends lower, presses one ear right to Thomas's mouth. *Tell me your secret*, she thinks. *Are you alive?* Charlie bends down with her, lying almost flat on the forest floor, his eyes level with hers, his mouth three inches away. There is something to his face. She studied it all through the coach ride, as they sat there, too awkward to talk. The cast of the mouth, the wide-open eyes. The kind of face saints sometimes have, painted on the glass of church windows. A face so little guarded, so unmarked

146

by Discipline, it taunts her, terrifies her. What sort of creature is he that he can afford to live so naked and not sin?

Something reaches her. Her ear. Not a sound: a sliver of air, like the lick of a tiny tongue.

'He's breathing.' She lets go of Thomas, turns around, lifts her skirt and starts ripping off strips of petticoat. 'He mustn't bleed to death.'

Behind her, Charlie starts praying, his voice light and firm.

Φ

The woman appears like a ghost. One moment she isn't there, then she steps out of the shadow of a tree, four yards away. Charlie does not notice her. He is desperately trying to fashion a bandage out of the strips of cloth Livia has supplied. They have no water, cannot clean the wound.

'Quick,' he keeps berating himself. 'We must keep moving.'

When Livia puts a hand on his shoulder, he does not react.

The woman has no colour. She wears a sort of shift made from patches of leather and cloth. Everything about her – her clothes, her skin, her hair – is uniformly grey, the shade of spent embers. *Ashen.* She stands motionless, her knees bent, back humped, ready to run. It reminds Livia of nothing so much as a cat watching the goings-on of the kitchen. Curious, shy, twitchy; its ears pressed back against its skull. And all the while the woman is smoking, smoking just as steadily as she is breathing, rhythmically, ceaselessly, adding dye to her ashen skin.

Charlie notices her at last. He starts. His movement is answered by the woman's twitch. But she does not run, not even when he rises and shows her his blood-smeared palms.

'Our friend is wounded,' he says, calmly, soothingly, the way Charlie can. Evidently he has decided the woman is not their enemy. Livia agrees with his assessment. Whoever she is, she does not belong to those who shot at them. She is part of the forest. There may be a sharp stone hidden in her fist, even a knife. But not a gun.

'We need help. Water. A doctor. Are there people around?'

The woman does not answer but moves two steps to the side, to gain a better view of Thomas. Livia follows the look. The bandage sits loosely around his head and face. Already it is spotted with red. It will soak through before they have carried him a quarter mile.

Charlie risks taking a step. The woman stares at him from her grey face.

'Help, you understand. Someone who can tend his wounds.' Charlie points to Thomas's head. 'Stop the bleeding.'

She does not react but allows him to approach to within two yards. Charlie folds his hands together, an altar boy's gesture, fingers closed, thumbs resting against the bridge of his nose.

'Please!'

The word does something to her. It is familiar; frightens her, recalls her to a moment in her past. Her head jerks down, her shoulders up, much like a cat's when startled by a noise. Then she tries it, her lips shaping themselves around the sound. Biting it off. Tasting it. Ready to spit.

'Plea-sseh.'

Her expression does not change with the word. It is as though she has unlearned her face's gestures. It convinces Livia once and for all that she is living here, alone in the forest, without human contact. All at once the old servants' stories come back to Livia, about the ghost in the woods. Her father's soul. His reason: gone missing, roaming amongst trees at dawn. But this woman is as blank as he, and smokes with equal abandon.

There is something odd about her Smoke, however, something that sets her apart. It takes Livia several moments to put her finger on it. She smokes with equanimity. Steadily, near-constantly, always the same light-grey Smoke, subtle like a mist. It clothes her more thoroughly than her rags. In summer, Livia catches herself thinking, she will walk the woods naked, dressed only in her Smoke. The thought brings a flush to her cheeks. Anger, embarrassment. Envy? A moan from Thomas cuts short the thought.

The stranger reacts to this moan. She looks over at Thomas, digs in a sort of satchel that seems sewn onto her very garment, draws forth a fistful of something green. Moss. Dry as it is, it retains an eerie emerald sparkle in the grey of her hand. But she won't step closer, not until Charlie withdraws and pulls Livia with him, taking her hand as naturally as though he's held it all his life.

'Please,' he repeats and with a sudden burst of movement the woman sprints over to Thomas's side, falls on her knees, takes off the bandages and scatters them carelessly by his side. She presses the moss into the wound, starts digging between a tree root, finds a fistful of clammy mud, and smears it on top. Livia starts forward but Charlie's hand stops her. They can see the mud caking in the cold of the air. The woman, meanwhile, is digging in her satchel, dismissing a dozen herbs, until she pulls out a dried flower and forces it into Thomas's mouth, slipping it under the tongue. All this takes her barely a minute. As a last step, she knots the strips of soiled petticoat together and quickly slips them into her bag.

When Livia and Charlie walk over to Thomas, the woman withdraws again, crouches in the dead leaves of the forest floor. The poultice looks barbaric and like it will crumble away at the slightest touch. But the bleeding has stopped. Charlie makes to pick Thomas up, then stops.

'We need to get him to safety,' he says to Livia. 'Do you have any idea where we are?'

She closes her eyes, tries to picture the forest and the surrounding land. It is hard to transfer distances from horseback to this stumbling through the woods.

'There is a village somewhere. At the far side of the woods. Near the river. But it's several miles.'

Charlie nods, turns back to the woman, takes a slow step towards her. She does not move. His voice is very gentle when he speaks. Gentle, but not condescending. *How long*, Livia finds herself thinking, *since this woman has been spoken to as a human being not a beast?*

'We need help,' Charlie explains. 'People. A village. But we don't know the way.'

When the woman does not respond, Charlie falls to his knees, clears a patch of forest floor. He uses a stick to draw into the dirt. A house, the way a child would draw it: a box with a roof. A stickman, then another, clothed with the triangle of a skirt. When the woman still does not react he adds a clumsy river, writhing like a worm. This means something to her. She copies the picture with her fingers in the air.

'The river? Do you know where it is?' Livia's words sound hard to her ears after Charlie's gentle whisper.

'Riv-ver.'

'Yes, the river. There are people there. Will you lead us?'

The woman seems to consider the request. She crouches motionless for a moment, cocking her head. In profile, she becomes strange all over again, her features foreign: the jawline strong, the small dark eye almost hidden in its thick fold. When she jerks her head to them and beckons, Charlie gives a sudden start.

'I have seen her before!'

'Where?'

'On a picture of your father's, taken fifteen years ago. But there she had two heads.'

But he does not explain what he means by this, bends down and shoulders Thomas instead, out of whose face mud grows like a dirty tumour.

'Do you think we are being followed?' she asks him as he makes to set off.

'Don't let's wait and find out.'

Φ

They walk for more than an hour. Very quickly Charlie tires of his burden and at Livia's insistence they take Thomas's slumping body between themselves, his arms slung over their shoulders, feet dragging in the leaves. Progress is slow and there is no way of telling how much distance they are putting between themselves and their attackers. The woman walks a good ten paces ahead, melting into the trees seemingly at will, then stepping out a few yards further on and beckoning with her head. At long last they reach the river. They see it first as a wall of brightness cut into the dark mass of the trees: the sun is out and is hitting the water, reflecting up. It's so tranquil it makes no sound. On the other bank the trees cluster thickly. Wherever they are, there are no people here.

But their guide has a reason for choosing this spot. She beckons them on, walking quickly along to the riverbank. Livia knows she cannot carry on much longer. Charlie too is staggering under Thomas's weight, his breathing ragged, the head beetroot red. There isn't far to go: thirty steps on the woman stops and disappears in the shrubs to the side. When they reach the spot, she is gone, somewhere in the shadowy darkness of the woods. The riverbank is steep here. Swollen as the river is by the recent rains, they are walking no more than a yard above the waterline.

'Can you see her?' Charlie pants.

'No. But there is something behind this shrub. Something she wants us to find.'

It's a rowing boat, not six feet long. The forest has very nearly claimed it. Its sides are overgrown with moss and the piece of canvas covering its top is weighed down with leaves and dirt from which grow the grey tendrils of dead weeds. When they slip off this cover, they discover two sculls lying in its bottom, along with a film of rotting water. The smell makes them gag. A bracket of rusted iron is let into each of the boat's sides, to anchor the sculls. As she helps Charlie push the boat out into the open, Livia's fingers unearth a carved crest within the moss at its prow. A boar, basking in the circle of a rising moon. She knows it at once. It's her own crest, her family's, the ancient emblem of the Naylors.

'My father used to disappear for days at a time. Going fishing. It was his one indulgence.' Livia shivers, is transported back to a distant time. Early childhood. Her father's hand stroking her hair. 'But that was many years ago.'

'Do you think it'll float? The wood's half rotten. But it's tarred from underneath and the canvas kept the rain out.'

'Let's hope it does. It's the best chance we have.'

Φ

Getting the boat into the water proves to be hard work. The bank is too high to just drop it in, and they are forced to drag it back a whole ten yards to find a better point of access. Charlie tests it before they heave Thomas in, moving gingerly from prow to stern as though expecting to fall straight through. But the boat holds; turns gently with the slow, even current, ready to run.

There is no way of lifting the wounded boy in without both of them getting soaking wet. Livia's heavy dress clings to her most indecently. Then, too, the boat is too small for three, and sinks low into the water as they clamber in. At last, shivering, they find an arrangement that distributes their weight, with Thomas stretched out along the bottom, prow to stern, and Livia curled next to him, in uncomfortable proximity to his mud-smeared face. Charlie sits above, manning the oars. The smell of rot is strong in the bottom of the boat and it is difficult not to associate it with the wound. Before they set off, she peeks over the side one last time and catches a glimpse of the woman crouching amongst roots two steps from the riverbank. Something connects her to Livia's father, and Livia is afraid she will never learn what. Then she is gone, out of sight, and all there is, is the sound of the river below her, and the heat of Thomas's body far too close. Charlie is nothing but a dark shadow above her: the sun is out overhead and burns her eyes whenever she looks up. It must be right around noon.

Time passes. The boat drifts with the current, then jerks forward with every push of the oars. At some point Livia becomes aware that they are taking on water, that the wet on her legs and back is not just the result of their earlier soaking. There is nothing to be done. She cannot bail the boat, there is nothing to bail it with. Then the sound of the river changes underneath the rotten planks. She looks up, alarmed. The sun has moved enough now that she can watch Charlie's back rocking with the rhythm of his sculling. He is facing upstream, keeping to the centre of the river, too tired perhaps to turn and see what lies ahead. Livia raises herself to her elbow, risks a peek. The river is no longer flat and glassy. There are shallows ahead, rocks peeking through the surface, and the water is speeding up. Just as she thinks this, a scraping sounds from underneath her and fresh water seeps into the boat.

'Ahead, Charlie. Rapids. Quick now. Or we'll sink.'

Φ

There is no way to stop it. As Charlie fights to get them out of the way of a large boulder, one oar snaps and next they know they are in a spin. The back of the boat hits another boulder, loosens a plank, the water rushing in thick and fast. Fortunately, the current has pushed them close to the grassy bank. Without discussing it with Charlie, Livia leaps, sinks to her knees in icy river and mud, takes hold of the prow and pulls it towards solid ground. They have to work fast. Thomas cannot move and the water is rising in the bottom of the boat. As they struggle with his deadweight, the entire side of the boat breaks open in a cloud of rot. They pull him through it, onto the bank, press anxious fingers into his pulse. Downriver, the water accelerates and cascades down a five-foot drop. Upriver, the sun has begun to dip. They may have put three or four miles between themselves and their pursuers.

If they are, in fact, being pursued.

A sound rouses her out of her thought. It is instantly familiar: cloth flapping in a breeze. Livia jumps up, rounds a row of bushes dense enough to be called a hedge. Behind them, she finds a washing line, shirts and sheets rising and falling with the breeze. Half the line is empty: a farmer is collecting clothes in her thick arms. The woman sees her the same moment; walks towards her with a leisurely roll, then catches sight of Thomas and Charlie.

'Three of yous!' she shouts from afar. 'Wet like newborn lambs. But where's your boat?'

Livia walks to intercept her. 'Is there a village here? A doctor?'

'A league that way.' She gestures. And adds, with a habitual weariness: 'My husband, the old blockhead. Says he likes to live apart. So we do, God bless us.'

The next instant she catches sight of Thomas's face. Much of the poultice has washed away. Blood colours the collar of his shirt. The woman's cheerfulness vanishes in an instant. All at once her manner is very brisk.

'Is he alive? Then we better carry him inside.' Without waiting for an answer the woman shoves the laundry into Livia's hands, then lifts up Thomas's head and shoulders.

'Well, jump to it, lad,' she barks at Charlie. 'Take his feet.'

Her cottage is not twenty yards away, but pressed into the side of a hillock in such a manner as to be almost invisible. Inside, a fire is burning in the stove. Kitchen and living room are one, the ceiling low and rutted with beams. They bed Thomas on the kitchen table. The woman fetches a bucket of water and some clean rags.

'Rolled you in mud, did they?' she says to no one in particular as she begins to clean Thomas's wound. 'Moss, too. Well, I suppose it stopped your leaking. Nasty cut this, half the ear clean gone. And a nice deep furrow in yer skull, straight as a die, I could take a ruler to it. Nothing cracked though, not as far as I can see. Funny smell to the wound. Got yourself singed, did you? Played with guns, I take it. And they beat you, too, by the looks of it, a proper thrashing. Lord, will you look at these bruises! Black and blue you are, all the way down to the navel.' She has unbuttoned his shirt and begins wrapping a bandage around Thomas's head. 'Well, here you are, duck. Swaddled tight like a baby. If you have a rest and it don't infect, well, you might just mend. But hello! Here you are yerself, our very own Lazarus. One eye open like a pirate at sea! Good day to you, sir, the pleasure is mine, only don't you try to speak now, just lie back and rest.'

Perhaps it is the pain that has woken him, perhaps it is her voice, deep and pleasant, but as Livia and Charlie bend over him, they do indeed find one eye startlingly open amongst the bandages that crisscross Thomas's face. Removed from the context of his features, it looks less fierce than Livia remembers, and younger. Vulnerable. But then, he has just come back from the dead.

Instantly, both Livia and Charlie start speaking, trying to reassure him.

'You are safe,' Livia says. 'You were shot but all is well now.'

'You are safe,' Charlie says. 'I will go and fetch help. There's a village nearby – I'll have someone ride to Lady Naylor.'

Immediately, Thomas grows agitated, his limbs twitching, his lips moving within his bruises and the bandage.

'Don't, you must rest.'

But Thomas ignores Charlie's advice, keeps trying to raise himself, to speak. No sound will come. Livia accepts a glass of water from the farmer. Something has moved in the woman's face. She has heard the name. *Lady Naylor.* The lady of the manor.

It changes something for her.

Φ

The water helps Thomas. He takes a sip, coughs, licks his lips. They are so bloodless, they lie grey against his teeth. Again Thomas attempts to speak, again he fails. He has to try four, five more times before it bursts out of him, broken and insistent.

'Tell no one.' And then again, louder, spit in his words. 'Tell no one. Don't trust.'

Livia stares at his mutilated face. He's not been awake a full minute. And already he's making her angry.

'Tell no one? He's thinking that Mother—' She turns to Charlie. 'It's absurd!'

Another word breaks out of Thomas, a syllable at a time.

'Labo. Ra. Tree.'

Livia's temper rises in her like a dark cloud. All those years of Discipline, sent packing by a scattering of words.

'He's out of his mind. What – we sneaked into Mother's laboratory and now she's going to kill us? Do you think she put on her riding skirts and a gun and staked us out? Or perhaps she sent Thorpe, the old man.'

'Or Julius.' It is Charlie who says it, beside her, quiet, his face open like a book.

'He wouldn't shoot his own valet. The man is like a father to him!'

Her mouth is bitter with Smoke. Charlie does not respond. On the table, Thomas has slumped back into oblivion, one arm thrust into his open shirt, cradling his own chest. In the silence opened up by his faint, Livia feels herself drawn into Thomas's doubts by her own lack of an explanation. To her side, the farmer stands, folding laundry. She has listened pretending not to listen. When Livia studies her face it is carefully neutral, the intelligence of her eyes locked away behind her half-drawn lids. It strikes Livia that this is a role at which the woman has had practice: acting dull when she's expected to be. By her *betters*. The thought is new to Livia. She has lived around servants all her life but has never been in their quarters. Never in a farmhouse, never in a factory. It has not occurred to her that her whole life she has been watched by hooded eyes. Evaluated.

'Let's go outside,' she says to Charlie.

Φ

They argue quietly, five steps from the door. Her clothes remain wet and Livia shivers with cold.

'It makes no sense,' she says again.

'It might do. What if we saw something? In the laboratory. Something so important that it changes things. Something no one must know. No matter the price.' Charlie is calm, analytical, willing to forgive even his own murder. 'Let's think it through. The attack, I mean. Six shots, I make it. One after the other, but pretty quick. Shot at great distance. One gun or several? A marksman, in any case. If it were bandits, they'd want the horses alive. They are worth a great deal I should think.' He bites his lip. 'If Thomas is right – if someone's after us for what we know . . . then it's best if nobody knows that we are here. No one at all.'

Livia tries to dismiss his words, along with her own doubts. 'Do you really think my mother would endanger her own daughter?'

'No. But you weren't supposed to be there. You climbed on in secret. Outside the gates.' His eyes find hers, hold them, gently and with wonder. 'Why did you?'

She wants to put him off with a non-answer, grow angry even, or prickly at least. But his face makes it difficult. It is open, like a book.

'I wanted to see you off. My mother discouraged my coming to the station with you. We had words about it last night. I decided to ignore her request.' She hesitates before going on. 'I wanted to come to the station and say goodbye to you, Charlie. I even brought a handkerchief to wave.'

'I have been wanting to kiss you.' He says it firmly, like it is simply so, a fact like the sunshine around them and the grass at their feet.

Perhaps it is.

They go inside, and the farmer gives them blankets and sits them near the fire. She has stripped the wet things off Thomas and covered him with a bulky feather bed. Livia wishes she had a chance to change out of her own wet clothes. After some hesitation, she slides down from the hard wooden chair and kneels close to the fire, hoping it will dry her out.

Within minutes she is fast asleep.

Φ

When she wakes the men are there. There are three of them, wearing plain fustian suits. They stand around the kitchen table, looking down at Thomas. A father and two sons. The sons have the same build: tall, high-shouldered, loose-limbed and rangy. Their father is shorter, bigger-boned, holds a pipe clenched between thick, cold-chapped lips. Together, standing elbow to elbow, hip to hip, they make the cottage feel very small.

Livia rises quickly, coming out from beneath the blanket, her hands making sure she is decent. The movement wakes Charlie, slumped over in his chair. He leaps to his feet, sees the men, and immediately steps over to them.

'My name is Charlie Cooper. We thank you for your hospitality.'

He shakes hands in his simple, hearty way. The men seem bemused by the greeting but accept it in silence.

Then their eyes turn to Livia.

She hesitates, aware that it's impossible to repeat Charlie's gesture: it is unsuitable for ladies. The men don't bow and it seems silly to curtsy. She can tell from their faces that they know who she is. The farmer has told them; she is at the stove now, watching the scene in silence. There is no way of putting the men at ease, not with the daughter of the man who owns the very land they stand on.

Livia tries the truth instead.

'I am Livia Naylor. We ran into trouble on the road this morning. Mr Argyle here was wounded. At present we don't know who . . . That is, we think it best if nobody knows where we are.' She pauses, straightens. 'Will you help us?'

The only answer she receives is a nod by the father. It is a thoughtful nod, only given after much contemplation. It seems to take the place of an oath.

Φ

Nobody asks them any questions until after dinner. The men, it seems, don't like to speak. All Livia has learned from them is their names. The father is Bill Mosley. The eldest son, dark-haired, with a thick, drooping moustache, is called Jake. His brother, Francis, is lighter haired and finer featured. He appears to be entirely mute. The farmer herself is called Janet and will not stand for Mrs Mosley, as she thrice repeats. She alone is chatting away, working at the cooker.

'My men,' she explains in passing, 'are miners, all three of them.'

The moment she says it Livia sees the black crescents that mark the fingertips at the edge of their nails; the black dust that has grown into their skin at the knuckles and dyed them blue. Other than that they are scrubbed scrupulously clean.

Dinner is a hearty affair of potato and cabbage soup, some rashers of bacon and a tin-loaf of coarse brown bread. They have shifted Thomas from the table to a bed at the back of the cottage. Charlie gets up every few minutes to check on his friend.

'He's awake. I'll try to feed him some soup.'

Mrs Mosley goes with him. Livia is left alone with the three men. She watches them eat. The father is already done and sits fingering his pipe. The quiet one spoons his soup with an abstracted air, turned inward, smiling to himself. His brother is busy buttering his bread with a haste bordering on anger, as though the loaf is his personal enemy and needs to be cowed. All the while he is looking at Livia. It is not a friendly look.

'Preacher came to the mine today, Mum,' he suddenly starts declaiming, slowly and emphatically, still looking at Livia though it is his mother, behind him, he purports to be addressing. 'Caught us while we were washing. No chance of escape. Always the same song. "Smoking is sin. Don't think because you can't see it, down the mine, that it is less so. God's eyes . . ." And so on and so on.' He

157

snorts, chews, swallows. 'Smoking ain't sin. It's a weapon. Toffs use it to keep us down. Proves everything's just as it should be, with them on top, smug like a bunch of dung beetles rolling their lunch.'

It is his father who answers him, calmly, in his slow thoughtful manner, laying the pipe down next to his plate.

'I don't know, Jake, it ain't as simple as that. Wish that it was. But it ain't. Think of all them regular Smokers over in the village, the ones whose Smoke is full of hate. Collins, for one. Hazard. Lawrence. Old Jimmy Becket. Each of them a right little bugger. Liars, drunks, cheats. Might as well call it sin.'

The son bristles at this, but respects his father too much to contradict him outright.

'It don't matter down below,' is all he says. 'You know it don't.'

'That's true enough,' answers the father. 'It don't matter down below.' And then he turns to Livia, screws up one eye, and asks, firmly but not unkindly, 'What do you think, miss, about all this?'

She hesitates. Truth be told she is surprised: not only by the content of the words but by the fact that these people – farmers, miners – will discuss Smoke so readily, at the dinner table, wondering at its mystery. It had been, in her mind, an inquiry conducted only by her parents and their peers. By well-bred minds, as her teachers might have put it. By those who rule.

'Smoke is the incarnation of sin,' she says at last with all the meekness she has bred in herself through long years of practice. 'It's a dark mark from God. But it may be that we have been too eager to use it as an excuse for the sufferings of sinners.'

The eldest son snorts at this *we*. It excludes him and his whole family besides. But his brother, unspeaking, nods and attempts to spear a pickle. It eludes his knife point, jumps off the plate, rolls over the table leaving a trail of vinegar. On impulse, Livia picks it up and bites on it. It is so sharp it makes her eyes water; she coughs and coughs. Somehow it takes the tension out of the room. In the end even Jake is standing, laughing, slapping her back with the flat of his hand. Ten minutes later, their dinner finished, the men get up to walk to the village, have a pint at the pub.

There is nothing to do but hope that they won't talk about the gentlefolk they are hosting for the night.

Φ

158

They are back inside two hours. Mrs Mosley remains busy in the kitchen, making preparations for the morrow. Livia is at her prayers. She would like to go to bed but does not know where. The cottage seems too small to hold them all. Charlie has nodded off on a chair, his face peaceful in sleep, his mouth fallen open around a half-formed smile. The men's entrance wakes him. His first look darts to her, his second to Thomas. Making sure they are safe. It shouldn't, but the sequence of those looks makes her flush with pleasure.

'Back already?' Mrs Mosley greets her men. 'And sober, like Christian men should be.' But her husband and son do not take up her bantering. 'What's wrong?'

'They're the talk of the town,' Jake announces gruffly, jerking his head at Livia and Charlie. 'Or their coach is, shot up on the high road. Fowler went to town this afternoon. Says it's all everyone's talking about. Rumour says Lady Naylor herself was inside and has been abducted. And then Sutter pipes up that he found a boat, what was left of it, stuck on some rocks a league downriver. Said it had a crest. He didn't give it much thought at the time. Now the whole village is wondering what connects them, coach and boat. And who was inside.'

His father puts a hand on Jake's arm. The gesture quiets him, makes him cede ground.

'You cannot stay here,' Mr Mosley announces after a pause. 'Not if you don't want to be found. The whole village is talking. And management always has its man in the pub. Someone's sure to come and ask questions.' All of a sudden a scrap of Smoke escapes him. He watches it rise, waves to disperse it. 'Excuse me.'

It is like he is apologising for breaking wind at the table. It is the only hint that he is agitated.

'We will go,' says Charlie. 'First thing in the morning.'

The man wags his chin in thought.

'No you won't. That one' – he points to Thomas – 'he can't walk. Not for a while. And he'll need a doctor, or a nurse. He ain't out the woods yet.' He pauses, sets to lighting his pipe. 'There is a place. Somewhere no one will see you. And even if they do, they won't tell. That is, if you are serious. About disappearing for a while.'

He looks to Charlie for an answer, but Charlie looks to her. Livia understands the look. It's her mother who will worry herself sick over her daughter's disappearance. And it's her mother who might have tried to have them killed.

It's her decision.

But if she gets it wrong, it's Charlie and Thomas who will die.

'When do we go?' she asks.

Mr Mosley's expression does not change. He draws at his pipe, exhales. 'Tonight. But not before two or thereabouts. In between shifts.'

Before he can turn away, she walks over to him and looks him in the eye.

'You don't have to do this. Thank you that you do.'

His face darkens. It takes her a second to comprehend it's a blush.

'It was Francis's idea,' he says, pointing at his silent son. 'On the way over. I wasn't sure at first. But now I think he's right.' He pauses, turns to his wife. 'This one will need some woman things, I imagine. And some cutlery for the both of them, a jug or something of the kind, and any blankets we can spare.'

Mrs Mosley looks at him sourly. 'Don't you tell me what to do.'

Her hands are already busy filling a basket. A flask goes in, two cups and a pair of bloomers so large Livia will have to gird them with a belt.

'Where are they taking us?' she asks as she accepts the basket some hours later.

The woman gives her a long, solemn look. Perhaps she thinks her men are making a mistake. Or else that Livia and Charlie are.

'Where?' she repeats at long last. 'Where we all go in the end. Underground.'

Thorpe

The news reaches us at four thirty-three by the tall Comtoise clock in the front parlour. A group of riders bring it, from town, their leader a magistrate, the others good citizens who appear to have nothing better to do. A 'posse', as one of them is heard to say. Keeping the Queen's peace.

There is the news as it is presented to milady; and the news as it knocks on the kitchen door, carried there by a stable hand who talked to one of the townsmen's valets while he rubbed down his horse. Same information, different words. We get the scenic version 'round the kitchen way: get the gore, the smells, words learned from penny dreadfuls. The horses 'butch'red', the coach 'blown all to smithereens'; Mr Price 'slain', his body 'yawning', belly open to the sun, its contents pilfered by crows. They left him there, this posse. Too heavy to carry; too bloody, too, no doubt, too smelly and messy to sling across one's horse. A cart will be sent to pick him up.

There is no trace of either of the boys.

Milady, they say, takes it well. I am not there to see it: as luck will have it I am overseeing the annual cleaning of the silver, keeping the maids honest. Counting coffee spoons. I can picture her though, milady: pale and erect, making the man speak his thoughts in order. She has a serving girl carry refreshments out into the yard. I approve. We don't want the men's dust in our parlour, nor townsmen loitering in our halls.

Livia is sent for, to be apprised of the news. It is thus that it emerges that she is missing. Her maid says she rose before dawn and put on her travelling clothes. She, the maid, thought nothing of it. Now she is in tears. I shall dismiss her in the morning.

A search ensues. It transpires that a stable boy saw her leave the gate when it was still dark. He was relieving himself by the side of the shed. Did he wonder at her departure? The boy only shrugs. The ways of the gentry are a mystery to him. When I order him to be caned, he blanches and smokes. Ten licks of the rod will do him a world of good.

By this time young Spencer has taken charge of the party and ridden out, to hunt down the Gypsies, as he put it. Indeed a band was seen a week ago, albeit ten leagues to the south. He takes his bitch along. It pads out of its kennel, sniffs its master, gives a howl that curdles the blood. When he pets her, a tear is seen in young Spencer's eye and his hand is said to shake. Grief for the valet, the kitchen wench says dreamily. She has romantic notions about the boy, and has spoken before of the 'grace and tightness of his breeches'. When she smokes it holds the aroma of burnt cloves.

Dinnertime comes and passes. I have the cook prepare the meal as planned, but Lady Naylor does not please to come to table. It worries me. I search the house, not seeming to be searching for her. Someone should write a study of the butler's walk: an instruction manual, for those fresh to the profession. A quiet tread, but never inaudible; speculative in its range, but never lacking in direction. A science of walking. I do believe I am its master.

I do not find her at once. There is no light in her study; no movement in the boudoir; no gas lamp flicker from the keyhole of the laboratory. It is after some hesitation that I climb the stairs to the attic.

I find milady with her husband. She has slipped into bed with him, her fuchsia gown a dash of colour in the gloom of the room. There she lies, close by his side, her face nuzzled into his chest. The baron's shackles are fastened, but he is calm, his features slack, the breathing even. I stand in the door for several minutes, watching the scene. I do not know whether milady notices me. When I am certain that she does not require my services, I withdraw. There is wet in my eyes, I will admit. It is not often that we are witness to true love. I have seen it before, when she was younger and the baron the wisest in all the land. I was his valet then, his confidant. Already the guardian of this house.

Since those days, there have been many kinds of work for me. Guard work and spy work. Nurse work and jailor work. Even spade work, once.

I was always willing to serve.

Mr Spencer has his dog. I am the Naylors'. I shall say it with pride when I meet my Maker. There can be little doubt that I am heaven-bound. For a man of my class, I very rarely show.

Then why the dreams that douse me in hot fire?

In Darkness

It's a good mile's walk to the mouth of the pit. They walk by starlight, their faces tapestries of shadow. The air is so cold, each is conscious of walking through the others' exhalations, white like frozen Smoke.

The path leads past fields, then up onto the ridge of a hill, crested by the twisted shape of an oak. Beneath them, in the darkness of a narrow gully, spreads the mining village. Livia is unprepared for its squalor, the long rows of cottages pressed in on one another like the pleats of an accordion, deflated of air. A rubbish heap rises at the end of the gully, patrolled by a pack of curs. The whole village is suffused in the stink of boiled turnips.

Mr Mosley speaks without prompting. Perhaps he has noticed something in her face. Shock. Discomfort. A shudder at the thought of a life lived in the effluvium of yesterday's lunch.

'Newton Village,' he says. 'Six hundred souls, and nine out of every ten work down the mine. Men, women, children. Living hand to mouth; in hock to the grocer, who cheats on his scales. The wife always says we are standoffish. Too good for the village. But it's the village that don't like us living too close. I'm the foreman, see, same as my father was. Posh folk, we are.' Mr Mosley pauses, snorts. 'It's true what the fishwives say. Money makes you lonely.'

It's the longest Livia has heard him speak. But the night is too dark to make out his expression, and his voice too flat to guess at his emotion. He has not stopped while speaking, is striding on, his eyes on the path. Behind them Charlie has his hands full steadying Thomas who walks listing, white as a sheet. Jake and Francis have run ahead, to 'make arrangements'. What these are, Livia does not know. On the horizon, visible against the sky, sits the dark shape of the pit tower, a latticed blackness cut into the glow of the night.

As they draw closer, other objects step out of the shadow of the plain. There are sheds, chimneys, furnaces; a shingled hut leaking yellow light; a copper engine bristling with levers, gauges, ladders; and the roofed holes of the two pit shafts. It is within sight of the latter that Mr Mosley stops them. A pile of timber wood, man-high, provides them with shelter, hiding them from prying eyes. Here, close to the pit, a high, singing whistle, as of blades drawn across mirrors, has displaced all other night sounds. It is a sound calculated to creep into skin and teeth, estrange them from the rest of the body. If one were condemned to live in its presence, Livia thinks, one should go mad. She casts around for its source. At her back, attended by Charlie, Thomas has collapsed to the ground, head and shoulders swaddled in blankets, the mouth distended, gasping for air.

It takes Livia a while to connect the sound to the pit shafts, then to follow it up, along the path of two slender wires, to the whirling of two metal wheels, each crowning the giant scaffold of a pit tower that squats over its hole like a spider made of wood and steel. The wires run taut over these wheels and from there back down, towards two lean-tos at ten yards' remove. Inside, great drums can be seen to spin like giant cloth spools, winding, unwinding wire at speeds that cancel out all sense of motion. Thus, for all the drums' frenzy, there is an eerie stillness to the scene, the wires standing in the black pools of their shafts like fakirs' ropes whose invisible movement carves slivers of sound out of the fabric of the night.

They wait. Mutely, Charlie walks over to stand next to Livia; eases her tension with a quick, shy smile. Side by side they peer into the dark. At long last, a figure steps out of the hut ahead, its door a rectangle of gaslight. It is by the man's movements that she recognises him as Jake. He crosses the thirty or forty yards separating them with long, efficient strides, never breaking into a run but moving just as fast. Already Mr Mosley has pulled them out of the shelter of the timber pile and is marching them towards the pit mouths. The night darkens as they step into the shadow of the bigger of the giant scaffolds. Between its splayed feet, framed by a kind of wooden porch, the pit mouth gapes, a lipless hole, red-bricked and smooth, emitting belly smells like a dyspeptic beast.

Once more the big wheel spins around its axis; once more sounds the eerie song of the wire. Then a cage is spat out of the shaft, hangs flimsy from its thread above the blackness of the pit.

'Quick now, get in.'

Jake swings open the door and one by one they step over the lip of the pit, onto the rough floor of the cage. The contraption quivers under their step, feels insubstantial; its iron frame covered by protective netting, a tin roof above, along with the rusted hook that connects it to the wire. How many men might the cage hold? It feels full enough with just the five of them, Thomas sprawled across the floor, but a picture comes to her, unbidden, of twenty, thirty men, women and children, squeezed shoulder to shoulder, chest to back, their faces pressed against the netting, like bait used to lure whatever lives down in the deep. A sickness rises in Livia. To fight it down, she concentrates on Mr Mosley. The miner has donned a leather cap and hung an oddly shaped lamp from his buttonhole. It isn't lit.

'The operator won't tell anyone?'

Mr Mosley shakes his head. 'No, he's one of us. Besides, he never saw you. Too dark. All it is, is an unscheduled descent.'

He steps closer, makes as though to touch her, pat her on the shoulder. Then he remembers who she is. She wishes he hadn't.

'Hold steady now, miss.'

The shaft swallows them. There is no other word for it. It might as well smack its lips. The light falls away, so fast her stomach rises to her throat, the sickness raging in her. Then the darkness becomes total, the sky a lost memory high above. For a timeless moment total stillness reigns as the cage falls cleanly in its shaft. Livia's fear recedes, pushed aside by something else inhabiting her body, older yet than fear, and at comfort with this blank suspension in the void. Then a screech shakes their bones as the cage touches the guides that line its walls, only to return them to oblivion, a stillness so total it obliterates all thought. An eternity later, they pass a blaze of light. A bricked chamber opens before her, crowded with mine carts. Tied to the wall near the pit shaft, a pale horse stands like a ghost, its dark eyes mirroring her terror. It lasts the blink of an eye.

They keep on falling.

Water starts falling alongside them. Livia hears it before she feels it. First it is a patter against the roofing of the cage. Then it runs freely along the walls of the shaft, is cut up by the protective netting, its spray pinpricks of cold on the skin of her face.

The cage stops. The arrest is so abrupt, she nearly loses her footing, bounces first against Charlie, then against Jake, whose hands, thrown out to steady her, recoil as though bitten no sooner has he touched her. Matches are struck, both he and Mr Mosley light their lamps. Their dull light shows a bricked room, oblong and narrow and closed off by a large metal gate. They swing open the cage door.

A moment after Livia steps out, the cage is yanked away, upward, like a marionette banished from the stage. Behind them, the hole looms, too dark to offer any sense of depth. It might as well be filled with Soot.

Charlie, pale, eyes torn open in the gloom, lingers longest at its lip.

'How far does it go down?' Livia hears him ask of Jake who is helping Charlie with Thomas.

'All the way? Don't know. It's a game we play, counting on the way down. One lad will sing out four, another six minutes forty-five. There's no man here rich enough to own a watch.'

He spits, pulls Charlie away from the lift shaft, points him inwards, towards the metal gate. 'But this level here, we know the measure. Eight hundred and seventy feet. Quiet now, we must hurry. Here, help me with your friend.'

Φ

The metal gate functions as a sort of air lock. Beyond lies the mine proper. Here, a different climate reigns, the air cold and clammy, tasting of mould. Only now and again a gust of warmer air catches them at intersections, furnace-hot, a relief to skin and lungs, but itself dead and heavy as lead.

They walk along rail tracks. It takes a while for this to register with Livia, and then to grow into an image: the iron bulk of a steam engine bearing down at them from out of the dark. But as they continue walking in a drawn-out procession, nothing emerges from the tunnel ahead of them, no train, no colliers, no beam of light. The tunnel itself is man-high and sloping. Steel supports bend into Gothic arches at every fourth step: cathedral cloisters built from brick and rust. Low tunnels branch off from time to time, dark gates leading into further darkness. Strange sounds carry along these shafts, the groan of steel and timber, the rhythmic whistle of moving air. They walk steadily, their heads in a stoop: gallows birds with broken necks, patrolling the warren of their afterlives to the stench of cold rot. Eight hundred and seventy feet of rock pressing down on them.

The train tracks end. Beyond, the tunnel narrows, the ceiling lowers. The steel supports give way to crooked timbers, the brick of the walls is replaced by sheer rock. And still they carry on, bent double now, humbled by the deadweight of the earth.

At long last they reach a destination, or at any rate, an ending. The tunnel widens into a long chamber, then is blocked abruptly by a pile of boulders that fills it floor to ceiling. To their right, a deep alcove yawns, not four feet in height, but some thirty feet wide and ten or so deep. Its far wall is so black it swallows the light. With a start, Livia realises this is the face of the coal seam that has been hewn away by men who must have worked it lying on their sides. Now there is no sign of recent work. Instead, the beam of Mr Mosley's lamp catches a series of sheets that have been hung from the supporting timbers and divide the space into narrow niches, each furnished with some dirty straw. A strange noise permeates the collapsed room, a sort of slurping, as of air sucked greedily through a half-closed ventilation trap. The mine's breathing has grown laboured, the air heavier. It sticks to the skin like Soot.

'What happened to this place?' Livia asks.

It's Jake who answers. 'What does it look like? Gas explosion. This whole area has been closed down. The seam runs into a fault line there.' He gestures at the rock. 'Not worth the trouble.'

'And that?' She points to the makeshift beds, each in its cubicle, filthy with coal dust. 'Who comes here?'

'Young couples. Sneaking an hour during their shift. For privacy.' He shines his lamp in her face. 'In winter mostly, when the woods are too cold.'

She feels her skin blush in the lamplight.

'That's sordid.'

'Is it now, miss? It's hard, waiting, when you're in love and don't have the money to set up a house. But you wouldn't know about that.' He snorts, turns the light away from her, and walks over to where rockslide meets wall at the opposite end of the grotto. 'You'll have to be quiet, in any case. You'll be staying within forty feet of them.'

She wants to ask what he means, when he suddenly disappears, swallowed up by the rock. Only his light remains visible, oddly refracted, painting shards of light onto the floor.

'Go,' Mr Mosley encourages her. 'I will help Mr Cooper with the sick lad. This will be hard going, this part.'

Φ

There is a path that leads through the wall of rubble. No, not a path: a cut, so narrow she has to squeeze through sideways, and twisting in ways that suggest that the way forward is blocked off. But somehow it never is, each twist opening to another wedge of space, in between the fallen rock. The lamp ahead gives so little light that Livia has to feel herself forward with hands and feet. Her touch is slight. She fears dislodging the rubble, causing a rockslide. It is hard to shed the feeling that she is walking to her own grave.

Then, abruptly, the rock maze ends and spills them into a low tunnel. Jake's lamp finds a row of wooden crossbeams disappearing into the darkness, like railway sleepers in a topsy-turvy world. They don't follow the tunnel, however, but rather branch off left, where a narrow doorway opens on a large, square room, its low ceiling held aloft by twin rows of wooden supports. Livia's eyes take in the tables and benches, the shelves with provisions and tools, and marvels at the sudden abundance of space. Fifty people could assemble here without feeling cramped. To one side stands a hulking structure not unlike a shelf but deeper and segmented into long rectangular boxes, coffin-sized. It takes her a moment to decipher its purpose.

'What's that for then? Don't tell me it too is for trysts. Lovers don't require bunk beds.' She is surprised at how cold her voice sounds. Unsympathetic. In judgement. 'You are up to something. What is it?'

When Jake does not answer at once, she walks over to the wall where a small wire cage has been screwed into the wall. It houses a group of limp canaries that press their beaks against the mesh. Beneath it stands a box, neatly stacked with a score of wooden clubs, each handle wrapped with rope for a better grip. A newspaper article comes to Livia's mind, something she has read in the county circular, written by an Oxford don, worried for the body politic.

'This is a meeting hall. You are organising the malcontents, is that it? A "workers' union", that's what you call it. A gang of thieves.'

A look at Jake's face tells her she is right. There is anger there, at the ease with which she has guessed his secret as much as at her tone. He walks over to her, holds up a hand, spreads out his fingers in front of her face like he wants to smother her. But the hand remains where it is, a five-spoked fan spread out thickly in the gloom.

'By itself, each of these can be broken by a child.' He wriggles his fingers, then crumples the hand into a fist, the knuckles standing out white in the half-light. 'Try breaking this, Miss Naylor!'

A fist the size of a ham hock. Black, casting a shadow over her face. But Livia feels outrage rather than fear.

'It's illegal, that's what it is. It'll land you in jail.' The newspaper's warnings come back to her, well-wrought phrases, warnings for the custodians of land and Crown. 'What does it want, your union? Riots in the street, I suppose. Burnt manor houses, looted granaries and free gin for every man, woman and child. Anarchy! There'll be famine before you know it.'

Jake drops his fist.

'We are fighting for proper insurance,' he answers with an odd sort of dignity. 'When there's an accident. Last month a man got cut by a snapped cable. Lost both hands. Manager wouldn't give him a penny.'

He lifts up the lamp, opens it, blows out the flame.

'You must keep it off. There is shale gas in the area. Besides, the next shift will start soon. Light travels a long way down here, and colliers' eyes are sharp.'

The darkness is so total the words are disconnected from their speaker. Jake no longer exists. Her own body has disappeared. All of a sudden, Livia is to herself just the breath of her lungs, the taste of her tongue between her teeth.

'No light?' she asks, her voice spilling out of her then evaporating in the dark. 'How will we live?'

Jake's answer has the simplicity of truth.

'You'll get used to it.'

Φ

Very soon she is alone.

It isn't true, of course, but it feels like it. *Abandonment.* As though she has been left here to rot.

'Listen for the canaries' movements. If they die, there's gas in the room. But don't worry, you'll be just fine. I'll send someone down to look after Thomas. At the start of the shift after next.'

It was Mr Mosley who said it and why would he lie? But it was dark already when he spoke, and his voice had no body, no presence, sprang from no source. Like God's, when He spoke on the day He made the world. But that's blasphemy. No wonder though that the first thing He made was light. The dark is a lonely place. Livia has been here for no more than a thousand breaths. And already she knows it.

Of course, she is *not* alone. There is Thomas whom she heard being bundled into one of the beds. And Charlie, not five steps away. The wound has reopened, he has announced. Now he is busy at Thomas's bedside, muttering to himself, trying to stem the bleeding in the dark. She fights with herself not to speak to him, distract him from his work. And so she waits, listens, drowns in the black.

The disorientation is total. She is, to her own senses, only her breath, the gurgling of her stomach. Her outside has dissolved, can be made present only by running her palms down the length of her skin, her face and neck and (bashfully this) down the front of her dress, all the way to its hem, touching her sides, her knees, her calves, making herself real to herself and preserving her image, assembled through a hundred run-ins with a looking glass.

She bites her lip, and savours the reality of flesh and pain.

Time slips by, moves through the dark in slippered feet. In the absence of sight, other senses become vivid, fill the void with meanings true or false. At times it seems to Livia as though there are other people in the room, creeping around in silence, just inches from her, brushing her clothes, pulling faces in her sightless face. Sounds tug at her, have no origins other than the dark. It might be Thomas moaning, or Charlie's mutter. Lovers embracing in the cave next door. A miner screaming far away as his hands are burnt by shale gas. The canaries' brittle talons raking at the cage as they slowly suffocate.

For suffocate they must, since there is no air down here, just a cold, leaden thickness that presses on her along with the weight of the rock, hundreds upon hundreds of yards of rock, held up by some mouldy timbers, like matchsticks holding aloft the slab of a giant grave. Livia shudders, grows angry at her fear; forces herself to move, explore. She does not trust her feet, slides to the ground, needs to feel the floor with her bare hands to know it is there. On all fours then, like an animal, she crawls about, finds a wall, a shelf, a tin filled with something that might be food. Shortbread, oatcakes, hardtack? Her fingers feel stupid in the dark, unable to interpret texture, and her nose cannot make out the scent. She grabs a piece, too hard, feels it crumble and scatter on the floor. It is now that she starts crying. There is no one to see it, each sob silent, hidden, swallowed down. And yet Charlie finds her. She is alone, distraught, crumbs on her palm, sweat running down her back. The next moment his voice is in her ear.

'It's eerie down here,' he says as though he's sitting at the breakfast table, commenting on the porridge and toast. 'Like being in a strange kind of church. One daren't even speak.' He pauses but his voice does not change. 'Are you afraid, Livia?'

'No.'

'Well, I am.'

She pictures his face as he says it, eyebrows arched in wonder at himself. Something touches her between her throat and her chest, reaches, searches, then hastily withdraws as though stung. Too late she realises it was his hand. Looking for hers. Embarrassed by what it found: the softness of her body.

It almost makes her laugh.

A moment later she reaches out herself, touches some part of him, clothed, his hip, perhaps, his knee, the narrow strip of his flank. The possibilities taunt her: how easy it would be to linger, in this absence of all sight. But she, too, withdraws her hand. They settle on a subtler sort of touch, sit leaning one against the other, shoulder digging into shoulder, until her legs fall asleep beneath her and she has lost all sense of where his body ends and hers begins.

'How long have we been here?' she asks.

'Ten minutes,' he answers. 'Ten weeks. But shorter than a miner's shift.'

A miner's shift. How long is that? Eight hours? Ten? Twelve?

Help won't be coming until it ends.

Φ

When help does come, it bears a familiar voice. Familiar, but hard to place: calling quietly in the darkness and rousing her from sleep, Charlie's jacket underneath her cheek and serving as her pillow. It is only when a match is lit – feeble, flickering, shielded by a glowing hand; and all the same blinding, radiant, a beacon from another world – that a face attaches itself to the voice. Immediately, all of Livia's relief turns sour.

'You? What are you doing here?'

The voice that answers is as surprised as hers. And sulky.

'This is my home village! Half your servants hail from here.' Then: 'If I'd known it was you I wouldn't have come.'

It's Lizzy, the scullery maid they let go for thieving on Christmas Eve. She is dressed in collier's breeches and jacket, and is carrying a

172

safety lamp; opens the glass and lights the wick, turns it down to a faint glow, sends it sweeping through the room.

'You are the talk of the village, you are. Ravished by Gypsies. Only some say that it was an elopement of sorts.' She sneers, is unguarded in her anger. 'Who's sick then? You look just fine to me.'

Her manner changes when the beam finds Thomas. The bandage is drenched, blood sitting on his face like a crab, red-black and many-legged, dredged up from the sea.

'It's him! Mr Mosley didn't say. Just that they needed a nurse. I thought it was a collier. Or someone on the run. Hiding from the law.'

The last word is chased by a shadow: Smoke in the lamplight, falling through its beam like dust. It has no smell.

And just like that Lizzy's anger leaves her again. She kneels by the bunk bed, begins to peel off Thomas's bandages; wets a cloth from the mouth of a water bottle she has brought and sets to cleaning the wound. She beckons to Charlie to sit with her, asks him to hold her bag open for her.

'Quick now, Mr Cooper. I promised I'd keep the light off as much as possible. It's against our rules.'

Livia hovers behind them, watches Lizzy work.

'What do you know about nursing?' she asks, unable to reconcile what she is seeing with her knowledge of the girl. 'You're a maid.'

'I help out when a miner gets injured. Cuts, burns, smashed limbs. Got 'prenticed to it when my pa was brought in one night. Broken spine.'

'What happened to him?'

Lizzy's shoulders stiffen.

'What do you think happens to a man with a broken spine?'

Again Smoke leaps from her mouth. Again it carries no smell. As it turns to Soot it joins the coal dust on the floor, the walls, their skin and clothing. Lizzy takes no notice. She turns to Charlie, and gives him instruction to fetch a bucket of water from a barrel further down the tunnel outside; a rope is fastened to the tunnel wall and will guide his way. The moment Charlie is gone, Lizzy returns her attention to Thomas, never once looking at Livia. It is as though she has wished her out of existence. So marked is the reversal of their former relationship that Livia finds herself intrigued rather than vexed.

'Why are you angry with me? Because I caught you stealing?'

'I wasn't stealing.'

'You were. I caught you red-handed, rifling through the pile of presents.'

'I wasn't stealing,' Lizzy repeats. 'I was wanting to add a present. Hide it in the pile.' After a moment she adds, 'For him,' and points at Thomas with her chin. 'And then you came in and called me a thief.'

'You are lying. I saw you smoke: thick green shrouds. It was as good as admitting it.'

Now Lizzy does look at her. It's a hard look. Coal has caught in her lashes and lends a startling beauty to her eyes.

'I was angry, that's all. I could've scratched out your eyes.'

Still Livia does not believe her. 'You never said any of this. And you didn't hold any present. Nothing of your own.'

'I shoved it down my blouse. Oh, I know, I could've showed it to you, and explained. But I couldn't stand it. You'd have laughed at it, it was so pitiful next to all your splendour. And of course you would've read my note, and made fun of it.' Her voice drops to a hiss. 'It was for *him*, not you.'

Livia is taken aback by the force behind Lizzy's words.

'And *he*?' she asks. 'Would he not have laughed? At your pitiful present and your note?'

'Perhaps not.'

At last Livia understands.

'You *like* him.'

Lizzy's chin rises with the answer. Back in the manor house, Thorpe would have slapped a servant for such a show of pride.

'He looks at everyone the same. You, your mother, the servants. Not friendly, like, but the same. High and low.'

Livia considers this, remembers her own encounters with Thomas's eyes. 'He looks at one as though he means to search one. Down to one's petticoats. Strip one of all secrets. It isn't a pleasant look.'

But Lizzy only shrugs. 'I don't mind. I haven't got nothing to hide.' She sighs, bends over him. 'He was handsome then. He'll be ugly now for ever.'

'Hush! He might hear you.'

Again anger returns to Lizzy like the gust of a draft. 'So? This one, he's not afraid of the truth.'

She falls silent, turns back to her patient, her fingers stained with coal and blood.

As she watches Lizzy get on with her work, Livia marvels at how much the girl has seen and understood. And from what? Three or four moments of interaction. No, not interaction: less than that. Proximity. A greeting or two, a look exchanged as she passed Thomas in the corridor. And yet she has seen him more clearly than Livia ever did.

She takes a step to the side, for a clearer view, and studies Thomas. His face is laid bare. The girl is using a razor to shave the hair around the wound. Despite her efforts with the washcloth, the coal dust is everywhere and has already seeped into the open skin. It will be there for ever, an ink stain blooming in his hairline and eating into the upper portion of the cheek. The top part of the ear is gone, the stump swollen and knotty. *Ugly.* Yes, no doubt. But for the first time Livia sees something in Thomas she has missed before. Nobility: something quite separate from bloodlines and the lottery of birth. His eyes are open, unseeing. Soon a bandage covers one of them and his head is swathed in layers of cotton, quickly turning from white to grey.

Charlie returns, laden with a six-gallon bucket, black water slopping over its rim. When Livia steps over to help him, an urgent whisper rises up from the sickbed, like the hiss of a kettle.

'Fever,' Lizzy says, dowsing the lamp. 'He is talking in his sleep.'

The next instant they have returned to a darkness given texture by the ravings of the sick.

Φ

As Livia soon discovers, there are no days in the dark, no nights. They eat when they are hungry, relearning the sense of taste disassociated from sight; sleep on the bunk beds when they tire; walk the dark tunnel beyond their door when they require exercise. There are other rooms down here, connected by a system of rope handrails that assist navigation. Some are filled to the bursting with food, clothes, furniture, tools, as though the miners are preparing for a siege. Two rooms hold giant water barrels; one is a communal latrine. Beyond that the tunnel leads to the sheer wall of a coal face, oddly soft to the touch.

People come and go. Lizzy does not live with them, but looks in periodically, changing the bandages and searching the wound for signs of rot. Mr Mosley also stops by at irregular intervals, as does Jake, blandly inquiring after Thomas's condition. At times they are accompanied by other men, known to Livia only by their voices, or by their outlines when Lizzy briefly lights a lamp. These do not introduce themselves. Nor do they ask any questions; avoid the use of names even amongst themselves. If the men are curious what they are doing there, these three scions of the gentry, not one of them puts it into words.

Listening in to their conversation, Livia gathers that they are all part of the inner circle of whatever revolution is brewing here, down in the depths of the earth. Her sole interaction with one of these 'Union Men' occurs when she feels her way into the latrine and, with outstretched hands, suddenly comes into contact with a man's face and wiry whiskers, hanging waist-high in the darkness. It comes to her that he is squatting there, trousers around his ankles. She gives a cry and recoils.

'I am sorry! I didn't know—'

The man answers with a husky laugh.

'Sorry about what, lassie? Dark as a badger's bum down here. We could all be running around with no clothes on for all anyone would know about it.'

She hears him rise, pull up his trousers.

'Don't ya worry, now, I'll leave you in peace. Guard the door if you like, make sure you've got yer privacy. You young ones are shy about this sort of thing.'

She hears him walk off, stamping his feet loudly, so she knows where he is. It is just as well she would not know him from Adam if they met in the light.

Φ

In this sightless, featureless world in which she finds herself, the one thing that remains to her is talk: whispered conversations in the void, sitting on the floor, more often than not, her shoulders leaned back against the wall, and speaking as one does in one's own head, with a newly found abandon. Most of the time she talks to Charlie. To her surprise, their talk often drifts into argument.

'What did you think of me when we first met?' she will ask, careless in this darkness of the vanity unmasked by her question.

'That you were stiff.'

'Stiff?'

'Yes. Stuck-up, I suppose. And pretty.'

'I suppose now that you can't see me, I am merely stuck-up.'

'You are trying to be holy, that's all. But it doesn't suit you.'

'Doesn't suit? You are saying I am bad at heart.'

He pauses over this, for longer than is comfortable. 'Not bad, no. You are just yourself.'

And later: 'We don't choose how we are made.'

She moves away then, to be alone with her thoughts.

Φ

Next time they speak, she finds herself punishing him for this 'doesn't suit'. It's Charlie himself who gives her the opening. He wants to know about Thomas's father: the details of his crime.

She does not immediately satisfy him with an answer.

'You don't know?' she asks instead, as though overcome by wonder. 'You are his best friend and you don't know?'

'All he told me is that his father killed someone. I thought he would explain it, sooner or later. But he never did.'

It is only when she hears the hurt in Charlie's voice that Livia realises what she is doing. And feels ashamed.

'I will tell you what Mother told me,' she offers. They are lying side by side on a blanket in one corner of the room. Their forearms very nearly touch; she can feel his hairs caress her skin. They have been doing this a lot lately: almost touch. If there were light by which to inspect, to judge herself, she would have condemned such licence. But in the dark their closeness has no censor.

'It's like this. Thomas's father got into a fight with one of his tenants who claimed Mr Argyle had taken liberties with his wife. Apparently, he stormed into the public house in broad daylight and bashed in the man's skull. He was arrested and tried, but then he died in prison before the sentencing could take place. 'Flu, Mother said. Thomas had just turned eleven.

'When the news reached her, Thomas's mother was already sick. A growth on her chest. They were impoverished, the estate heavily in debt, but she refused all offers of help. It was thought that she had sent her son to a local school. Somewhere up north: a provincial establishment, for the children of the minor gentry. But she must have kept him instead, to look after her. He comes from an isolated place: no visitors, the closest neighbour twenty miles away. Nobody took any notice – nobody who mattered – not until she died. But when she did, lawyers got involved. Mother says they always do. The custody of the estate went to Thomas's uncle – his father's brother – until Thomas turns twenty-one. A Lord Wesley, of Pembrokeshire.

'Apparently Lord Wesley never went up himself. He sent a steward instead, to look after the estate. Mother says the steward found Thomas living alone on the grounds, holding court over a gaggle of village urchins. All the servants were gone. So the steward wrote to Lord Wesley who in turn wrote to Mother, and she arranged to have him bundled off to school.'

Charlie's voice is incredulous. 'I never heard a word about any of this.'

'You wouldn't have. It was all carefully hushed up. A nobleman committing murder – impossible! Imagine the scandal, the implications if the story spread. So they bought off the witnesses and forbade all mention of the affair. Even the trial was held in secret. Mother only found out because, somewhere along the line, Thomas's mother broke her vow of silence and sent her a letter.'

'Trout must know. Our headmaster. But he hasn't told the other teachers. If he had, they'd have used it against Thomas.'

They are speaking in whispers, too low to be overheard. All the same, a cry issues from Thomas's bed. When they run to his bedside, they find his face wet with blood or tears.

Φ

Lizzy comes and goes. She makes little attempt to speak to Livia, and Livia finds herself avoiding her, avoiding Thomas. Moving away from them, sitting in darkness. Lizzy is the only one who always lights a lamp.

On occasion, though, Livia will linger and watch Lizzy tend to her patient, draw infection from the wound, spoon soup into the feverish boy. There is something more to Lizzy's movements than solicitude. Even when she's wiping off his pus. It worries, fascinates Livia.

Periodically, too, she forces herself to lend a hand in turning Thomas, or in changing his sweat-drenched bedding. When they are done, still squatting at his bedside, Lizzy makes a comb of her fingers, and runs it through Thomas's tangled hair. Her eyes are on Livia. She speaks abruptly.

'You really don't like him, eh? Well, can't help your heart.' Lizzy spits, unselfconsciously, not intending any insult, merely clearing her throat. 'How about Mr Cooper, though? You're sweet on *him*, ain't you?'

'Sweet?'

The moment Livia says it she knows the tone is wrong, mistress speaking to servant. But here she is, a beggar in this house. Livia tries to summon the meekness she has spent years growing in herself. It never came naturally.

It doesn't come now.

'He is a fine young man,' is all she manages.

Lizzy snorts and for a moment Livia feels it, the commoner's derision for a life where one does not dare put feelings into words.

Φ

Thomas's fever begins to ease. He remains weak, withdrawn, sleeping through three hours out of every four. But he's on the mend. It forces Charlie and Livia to discuss the future. They have shied away from it thus far. Part of it is that Charlie reproaches himself. He says, 'I should have stayed on top. Found out what was going on. Or made my way back to school and talked to Trout.'

Livia does not answer, hugs herself standing invisible in the blackness of the cave, a step from him, thinking: *We would not know one another if you had stayed on top.*

But Charlie's thoughts remain far away.

'I could write to Ireland,' he says. 'To my parents. Explain the situation, ask them for their help. The miners will post the letter.'

'Will they? Mr Mosley would have to go to the post office in town. I doubt he keeps much correspondence. Somebody would notice. Better to keep quiet for a little longer. Lie low. Disappear.'

'Now you sound like Thomas. *Suspicious.*'

She wants to tell him that it is more than that. That she has found something here, in the darkness, something she does not understand yet. But what she says is: 'That's because Thomas is right. He is in danger. They shot off half his face.'

But Charlie is too honest to let it go at that.

179

'If he's wrong,' he says, 'your mother will be going mad with worry. For all of us, but above all for you.'

Her reply is curt. 'Mother won't miss me. I'm a disappointment to her.'

'Why?'

'I don't really know.'

She feels an anger burn in her so rich and thick it must coat her skin in suds. The feeling is quickly smothered by confusion when she feels something soft brushing her cheek, searching it, finding her mouth. Charlie's lips are dry on hers. She moistens them with her tongue. Livia does not realise how close they are standing until she feels her chest pressed into his. It unlocks something in her that makes itself heard in a sigh, a whelp, the sound of a pup when you touch its belly while it's sleeping. The sound scares her. She recoils, sniffing the air; feels a greed rise through her body, up the ladder of her rib cage; finds him once more, explores him with her face, her mouth, and for the first time in her life feels the need to nip, to bite another's skin, cram his breath into her lungs. It lasts a moment. Then she remembers herself, walks away, licking her lips, her teeth, hunting for the taste of sin and finding only Charlie: the taste of sweat and coal dust, with a hint of the cold cabbage soup they ate for lunch.

It leaves her with another riddle.

Φ

It is Francis who helps her solve it. The silent son. She hears his voice for the first time when he comes to look in on Thomas and stands whispering to Lizzy. She herself is sitting some yards away, near the doorway of the sick chamber, leaning her back against the tunnel wall. She does not try to follow the conversation. Her ears are latched on to a different sound, issuing from the cracks and crevices of the rockslide that separates them from the mine proper. Beyond lies the lovers' cave. Of late it has drawn her. Its sounds are distant; soft. Talk, sighs. Quiet laughter. And, once in a while, a smothered moan that tugs at her very skin. It takes her a while to put a name to it. *The sound of letting yourself go.* It is not a sound she can imagine herself ever making.

Francis approaches. His step is near-silent but she hears him all the same, can gauge the distance at which he comes to a stop. She is like a bat now, attuned to the dark.

The comparison makes her smile.

'Are you getting on all right?' he asks.

'I thought you were mute.'

'Only on top. Down here I'm a regular chatterbox.' They are speaking in whispers, are barely audible to themselves. And yet she can sense purpose underneath his banter. 'I want to show you something. Out there, in the mine. But you'll have to change into miner's clothing.'

'Now?'

'Soon. At the end of the shift. It'll be safest then.'

On his instructions, she locates a shirt, jacket, cap and breeches in one of the storerooms, then changes in the dark. How odd that she can do so, not even closing the door: strip half naked, with no thought to her modesty. Francis remains where she left him, out in the tunnel near the rockslide. He asks whether she is ready and instructs her to tuck her hair beneath the cap. The next moment he has taken hold of her hand. It's so intimate a gesture, she feels herself stiffen.

'You don't need to be afraid of me,' he reassures her. 'It's nothing like that. I already have a girl. A real talker, just like me. Hush now. It isn't far.'

Without further explanation he tugs her after him, first through the twisting path between the fallen rocks, then out into the lovers' cave and the corridor beyond. Nothing stirs.

He lights his lamp, rushes almost to the point of running, tugging her down a series of corridors. Once he stops short, smothering their light, and waits for a group of haulage women to pass in the distance, each bent double and pushing their loads. Not one of them shoots them a glance.

'They shouldn't be here,' Francis rasps. 'Their shift is over. And Father tweaked the work rosters for the next shift, to make sure nobody'd be around.'

'Did they see us?'

'Let's hope not. Management has its people in every work crew. They spy on us, make sure we don't slack off. No politics allowed, no talking, a quarter hour for lunch.' He curses softly, rekindles the light. 'Never mind. We are almost there.'

Soon after, they arrive: a long, narrow room, well supported by timbers. A dank animal smell hangs in the air; the sound of

181

breathing, oddly heavy and many-mouthed. Much of the space is given over to a row of wooden pens. As the lamplight strafes them, it picks out the outline of a snout. Tender pink flesh frames the flared holes of two nostrils. A whinny sounds.

'Horses?' Livia asks, uncertain.

'Pit ponies. Here, let's give them a treat.'

Francis digs in his pocket, retrieves a few carrots. He passes one to Livia. When she lifts it up to the window of the first pen, a pony's head emerges out of the shadow, teeth bared. Its lips brush her fingers as the animal tears the carrot from her grasp. It turns to eat, like a dog protecting its bone. In the pen next door, its neighbour kicks its hoofs against the wooden gate. It has sniffed the carrots and wants its share.

'What do you think of them?' Francis asks, as he goes along, distributing treats.

'They are stunted and dirty. Their legs are bandy.'

'Mam says it's because they get no sun.'

'You don't take them up?'

'Rarely. The lift terrifies them. Some literally die of fright. And when they get outside, well, some of them go mad. They will run till they drop with exhaustion. Others just stand there, shivering, closing their eyes against the sun.'

She searches his face while he says it. He, in turn, is looking at her very closely, as though waiting for her verdict.

'It's sad,' she says at length.

The young man nods. 'Yes.' His eyes are expectant, waiting for her to say something more.

'Why take me here, Francis? It's an awful risk to take, just to show me some sick animals.'

He nods, shrugs, keeps his eyes on her.

'What do you think of it?' he asks obliquely. 'Our life in the mine?'

She starts answering, falters, feels herself back away from the light of his lamp. There's a thought that has grown in her, almost without her noticing. Now it wants out.

'You're free,' she says. 'I did not understand it at first. Your love of total darkness, the reluctance to light any lamps – it's not just fear of gas, or of discovery. It's a way of life. Almost a religion. You are building a kingdom. Beyond the rule of Smoke.' She pauses, eyes the ponies. 'And yet, it is doomed.'

He nods, keeps the lamplight on her face across the three-step gap she has opened up.

'Yes, we are free down here,' he says at last. 'But man is not meant to live in the dark.'

He reaches forward suddenly, encircles with his left hand the glass of his lamp, keeps it there. Shadows fill the room, swallowing her; his hand glowing red, leaking pink at the fingers; beyond it the light sits white in his twisted face.

It's hot, she realises, *the glass is burning his skin. But why . . . ?*

As though in answer a cloud of dark rises out of Francis, his pain converted to sin. He lets go of the lamp, steps over to her, wafting Smoke threads at her like incense. She sees it but cannot smell it; remains unmoved in her blood. All at once she is back with Charlie, mouth locked to mouth, her body tingling with Smoke.

'It does not smell, nor infect,' she whispers. 'It's as though it's dead. But how can that be?'

'We think it's the coal dust. It filters it somehow. So it's everyone smoking for themselves. Unseen, unheeded. Miners dying, fighting, making love. All alone.'

'But that's good, surely. Better than on top.' She looks for the word, finds it. 'Tidier.'

'Tidier? Yes, perhaps. My brother, Jake, he has a word for our life down here. He calls it "democracy".'

Democracy. She knows the term, has read its definition in one of her father's translations from the Greek. Democracy, Aristotle says, is the rule of the many: hence of the poor. It leads to chaos, greed and desolation.

'Will you take arms?' she asks suddenly. 'Rise up?'

'How can we? Yours is a race of angels. Fair cheeks, hands like marble; linen as white as the day it was spun.' He shakes his head, in wonder not anger. 'Down here we can curse you and plot revolt. But up in the sun? Oh, there too we have our jokes. We laugh and mock. But who is so coarse not to be shamed by your skin? God chose you, made you special. You rule us not by force but through this simple fact.' He leans closer, eager now that she understand him; a quiet man talking. 'We must cower underground, just to learn boldness.'

His voice is so earnest, his words so carefully chosen, he reminds her of one of her schoolmasters, Professor Lloyd, who teaches philosophical theology. But Francis is a commoner, a miner's son, unschooled in Discipline. He has never studied Leibniz's theodicy or Kant's *Three Discourses on Smoke*.

'How long did you go to school?' she asks in wonder.

'Four years. Got my numbers and letters. They aren't good for much, though. There's no money for books.'

'And yet today you had a lesson for me.'

He smiles at that. 'A time may come when we will need to understand one another. Your people and mine.'

He does not explain who these are, his people and hers. There is no need. The poor and the rich. A week ago she would have said: the corrupt and the righteous.

'I am only a schoolgirl,' she says quietly. 'What can I do?'

'You are the next Baroness Naylor,' Francis answers. And then he bows to her. She did not know a bow could combine mockery and admiration. Before she can respond, he has turned around to lead her back.

Φ

They don't speak again until they have entered the lovers' cave. It remains empty of people. She knows this from its sounds; the quality of the air: Francis has once again doused the lamp. Livia finds she does not mind. It is oddly comforting to have returned to the dark.

'How long have we been down here?' she asks.

'Six days.'

The number gives her a shudder. Six days buried under the earth. And yet it seems much longer to her. She must have lain down to sleep a dozen times. Catnaps; her natural rhythm when divorced from the sun.

'Is anyone looking for us?'

He answers slowly, picking his words with great care.

'Yes. There is a rumour you've been in the village. Someone's spending an awful lot of money to find you. The men who know you are here, they have given us their promise. A holy oath. But it's an awful lot of money, and some have more mouths at home than they can feed, and others have a child that wants the doctor.' A moment later he adds: 'Lizzy says your friend is better. Able to stand. To walk.'

'So that's why you came to me today! We are placing you in danger. We will go, of course.'

He presses her hand at that, lifts it up, touches his forehead with it as though receiving her benediction.

'My father will fetch you.'

She hears him walk away. Even his gait has a certain elegance to it, a gentle purpose. It makes her smile. Were he a few years younger, and a little more handsome, she might grow to like him almost as much as Charlie.

'Do you ever take her down here?' she whispers after him, gesturing sightlessly into the cavern. 'Your girl. The one who won't stop talking.'

His voice reaches back to her, so soft she might be imagining it.

'No. When the time comes . . . on our wedding night – I want to share her Smoke.' Then: 'There is life in Smoke, Miss Naylor. Communion. What people do down here, that's something else.'

He says no more. And leaves her wondering what it would do to her, kissing Charlie out in the sun.

Φ

She seeks him out soon after and tells him that they have to leave.

'As soon as possible, Charlie. We are endangering the miners.'

If Charlie is surprised, he does not show it.

'Thomas is better,' is all he says. And: 'We'll have to think about where we want to go next.'

They are sitting on the floor, in a storeroom beyond the main hideaway, where they can talk without disturbing Thomas's sleep. Their hips and shoulders are touching, get in each other's way. It would be more comfortable if she threw an arm around his shoulder, leaned her head into his neck. She is about to, when he speaks again.

'You have changed,' he says, 'down here.'

'Have I? How?'

He does not have to think about the answer: 'You're happy here.'

'I was happy before.'

'No, you weren't. You thought of happiness as a kind of Smoke.'

It isn't until later – after she's gotten up and walked away in a huff – that she realises Charlie is right. And that he's worried.

Worried she'll change back in the light.

Φ

185

She takes the thought for a walk, back to the edge of the lovers' cave, still empty but for that laboured, slurping whistle peculiar to the space. The breath of the mine. When she re-enters the sickroom some time later, it too seems emptied of people. Before she can confirm her intuition, she hears Thomas's voice cut the quiet with his whisper.

He is not talking to her.

'Well, go on then,' he says. 'After all, I owe you my life.'

There is no answer, only a sound, soft and spongy. It is followed by a giggle, then the sound of flat feet running out the door. Lizzy. At once Livia realises she's been witness to a kiss. She does something then she has not done in all the time she has been in the room: light a lamp. Her hands are unaccustomed to it. When she finally manages to put match to wick, she sees that Thomas has sat up, hunching forward on the bunk bed. A bandage still covers his head, but it is a simple wrapping rather than the thick layers he was swaddled in before. His face is sunken, haggard; the features overlarge, as though pasted on. It makes it hard to tell a smile from a smirk.

'Listening in, Miss Naylor? How naughty of you.'

She grows angry at once: a trickle of Smoke seeping from her nostrils. Down here, she lacks the will to drown it in meekness.

'You are a cad, Mr Argyle.'

He shrugs at that, blinks into the lamplight, raises his chin, for her to better see him.

'And tell me – have I grown very ugly?'

She locates her scorn, finds it like a garment she hasn't worn since summer. It belongs to the world of light.

'No need to worry. The scar will make you look tough. Like a dog that's had a good scrap. Half the ear missing. All the boys will love it.'

'Oh,' he says, 'I wasn't really thinking of the boys.'

Six days she has barely talked to him, has avoided his eyes. Now they are looking at her hard and level. She bends down to blow out the lamp.

'Better get ready, Mr Argyle. We are leaving. Soon.'

'Good. I have said my goodbyes. And I know where we go next.'

It irks Livia then that he – wounded, feeble, risen from the dead – so naturally presumes to take charge.

And even more that she is willing to follow.

186

Lizzy

Lord Spencer comes to the village the same day they ask me to go down the mine. They need me to look after an injured comrade, Mr Mosley tells me. I know Mr Mosley well. He's one of the Union Men, a Voice in the Dark: the one who asked me will I join when I was only fourteen. They had use for a nurse and my father, dying, vouched for me. But then Mother sent me away before the year was out.

When we stand near the mine shaft waiting for the cage to arrive, I see a rider on the hillside, sitting tall in his saddle, looking down. Dark hair, that's all I can see. I remember thinking: that's what Mr Argyle would look like, riding a horse. *Thomas.* It's first names for us, now that I have washed him and sewn up his head. It wouldn't do to kiss a 'Mister'.

By the time I returned from the pit, it was the talk of every kitchen. Lord Julius Spencer, Lady Naylor's son, come to visit us. Asking questions. And bringing news: that the lady's coach has been attacked, and the lady's daughter kidnapped, along with two young gentlemen. Only it might be that they've escaped their attackers and were wounded, lost in the wilds. Did we know anything?

They told him about the rowing boat they found smashed at the bottom of the rapids and he asked to see it; walked both sides of the riverbank, heading upstream, his dog digging its nose in the grass. It found something, near the cottage of the Mosleys. He questioned Mrs Mosley most patiently, they said in the village pub that night. Spent a full hour in her cottage. And left her with a good bit of money. *For her trouble.* She put it all in the village alms box on the Sunday.

Lord Spencer returned to us the next morning. And the morning after that, and the one after that; came at dawn, alone on his horse. He liked the village's 'prospect', he said; was interested in the mining business. Each day, he spread more money about. Talked to the drunks, the urchins, the village roughs. Tuppence for anyone who had a tale to spare; a pint of bitter at the pub. In his purse, a more precious kind of coin for anyone who had any real information. He'd make sure to flash it wherever he went, let people hold it, to see how heavy it was. Everyone was very impressed. We had none of us handled gold before.

I doubt the young lord learned much that was of any use. He heard hints, no doubt, about the union. That's what he'd come for, most villagers assumed. To check up on us. Though from the smile on his face, you'd think he'd come to woo the village beauties. And they came out for him, too, in their Sunday frocks, hitching their skirts up when they passed him in the street, flashing their plump calves. He doffed his hat at them, Lord Spencer did. They all talked about it for days on end.

But as to the three people we were hiding, down in the blackness of the mine, nobody said a word. Only the Union Men knew, and of them only the inner circle. I didn't tell a soul myself; sneaked down the mine, night after night, with Mr Mosley's help. It weighed on us though, our secret, all the more because we didn't know what we'd got ourselves involved in. Nobody dared ask why they were hiding from the girl's own mother. It wasn't done to ask questions. Not down there. Against our rules and the union's spirit. Besides, it was safer that way. The less we knew, the less we could be held to account.

All the same there were theories about our charges. There always are. An elopement, an estrangement, a fight amongst nobles. The one I heard most often (whispered, in the darkness, far from Lord Spencer's ears) was this: that the three were running from the law. That they had committed a mighty crime, the worst crime of all. *Treason Against the Crown*. Now it was the noose for them. If they were found. The way these whispers made it sound, they were as good as dead already.

The thing is: sooner or later, everyone gets found. There's not one miscreant in the village who ever gave the bailiff the slip. You can hide for a week, a month, a year. But the law don't forget. Or so my mum always says. She would know. She has a brother in jail somewhere and an uncle that was hanged.

One thing's for sure. If Lord Spencer was trying to find *me*, I would be hiding too. There is something crazed about his endless ream of questions, something forced about his constant smile. The third day he came to the village, the butcher slaughtered a pig in his honour. Lord Spencer went to watch. We have all of us done it, every child in the village, from curiosity, or on a dare, or because the screams drew us there: climbed the fence and taken a peek. And we all of us smoked; got good and filthy and went home to a hiding, for ruining our clothes. There is something about blood and offal freshly raised that sets it off. It takes many months to get used to it, till you can put down a sow with the same calm you tuck in a babe. That's what Mr Dillon told me, who is the village butcher and once had his eye on me, though he is fifty years old and I was fourteen then and still given to blushes. It's why Mother sent me off into service. To protect my innocence. Well, the manor house took care of my innocence soon enough.

Lord Spencer, in any case, held to village custom; showed up at the slaughterhouse in his shirtsleeves and was hastily ushered to a stool; sat, pale and sweating, a quiver in his cheek; and was seen to swallow deep when the blood poured out into the bucket. But he did not smoke, his shirtsleeves stiff with starch and lily-white.

There are other oddities, other reports. Little Beth, the Kendricks' daughter, says she saw him crying, walking hatless down the bridle path. And old Todd swears blind he saw him out riding after dusk, wearing a devil's face made of rubber and steel. I myself watched him whip his dog with its leather leash for straying after a squirrel or rat: his mouth moving as though in admonition, but not a sound passing his lips. He did not smoke even then.

Lord Spencer has not always been like this. I first saw him a month or two after I had been taken into service. The Naylors' cook came from our village. She was a childhood friend of my mother's and recommended me. I arrived in May, a six-mile walk, my good clothes folded in a basket that got sodden with rain. Milord came in his summer vacation. They made a big fuss before he arrived: the servants, I mean, not his kin. Baron Naylor was already 'unwell'. I didn't know what they meant by that word just then. When the coach pulled up, we all assembled outside, with much giggling.

I liked him, in a way. He was dark and skulking and wore tan leather gloves, even around the house. Ate a lot, especially pudding. Slept in, went hunting. Blackened his sheets more than he should've done, considering his station. He was very full of himself even then, but so what? He was the future Lord of the Manor. Handsome. Rakish. Always teasing us girls.

Then he started changing. It was towards the end of the summer.

Talk in the servants' kitchen was, Lady Naylor had started paying *attention* to him. Called him to her chambers; kept him locked in with her for hours at a time. Nobody could quite work it out: what they were to each other, how they felt. I mean, he is the fruit of her womb. But he'd been raised by her first husband's parents, people she would not consent to see even once a year. As Mother would put it: a proper rich people's shambles.

In the course of the summer, Lady Naylor did for Lord Spencer whatever those schools of theirs are supposed to do to all them noble-born: she chilled his blood. Beat the Smoke out of him, and put it on a leash. The few gentryfolk I have seen in my time at the manor, they always looked a little sickly. Like they had their bowels full and didn't have no prune juice. Though, of course, the vicar says it's the only way to get to heaven.

With Lord Spencer it was different, though. Not one of us ever saw him smoke again. Not a mark on his linen. But whatever was dark in him only kept on growin'. You could almost feel it, when he walked past you in the hallway; the way a girl knows a man's looking at her, Smoke curling out of his skin, even if he's ten steps behind and walkin' against the wind. The horses felt it too, grew skittish around him, unless he'd ridden them before. Broken them in. Same with the dogs in the kennels. Only his own bitch could abide him. It's a smell, some of the stable hands said, too fine for our human noses. It's like his Smoke has become invisible. Scratch him, though, and I swear he'll bleed Soot.

Φ

Six days in, our charges announce they want to leave. Quickly. Just as soon as we can get them out.

I go down with Mr Mosley when he goes to fetch them, deep in the night, no shift due for another four hours. I asked to come, so I can change the bandages one last time. Only they don't need changing. The bleeding's long stopped. I just want to see him one more time. Thomas. For six days I have nursed him. And got a kiss for my trouble. I know myself he does not like me the same as I like him: it's there in his eyes when we light the lamp. But it was a good kiss all the same. He squeezes my shoulder when we part, and I wag a finger. Sister and brother then. I can live with it. It's better than naught.

Before they set off, the others, too, wish to say their goodbyes. They line up like they are waiting for service at the grocer's. We are still in Thomas's sick chamber, what we so grandly call our Union Hall. I shan't be taking the lift with them, will stay behind to destroy any trace they was ever here. Mr Cooper goes first. He steps close to me and shakes my hand. 'Thank you,' he says. He even gives a little bow. If he'd kissed my hand on top of it, I would have died laughing. Despite my best attempts, I have grown fond of Mr Cooper. He is hard to dislike. The trouble though is that he is awfully posh. Well-bred, down to the vowels of his 'Thank you'. It's not his fault, mind, but he can't open his mouth without it reminding me what he is. And what I am. *Not of his class.* A servant, a miner's daughter. Common as sin. He tried to wash his clothes one day, in a bucket, and it was so pathetic I did it for him in the end. But only when Miss Naylor was out. The young milady.

I wouldn't piss on her if she was on fire.

But she too tries to say goodbye. Tries to pay me, in fact, taking a silver cross off her neck and holding it out on her open palm.

'For your trouble,' she says.

I suppose she's trying to be gracious. In the dark, I might have taken it and worn it against my breast. But in the beam of the lamp I can see the stiffness of her bearing, those meek, I'm-a-saint-because-I-know-I'm-a-sinner eyes. Like she's standing portrait for a bust of Jesus.

'Please accept it as a token of our gratitude.'

I hiss my answer.

'Can't,' I say. 'People will see and assume I'm a thief. The Justice of the Peace will have me flogged.'

Miss Naylor looks aggrieved at that. And also a little cross. But she fights it down, takes off the collier's jacket she's sporting, tears off the whole of the sleeve of the dirty blouse she wears underneath, and hands it over to me.

'It's French lace. You can resew it. Turn it into a handkerchief, or a baptismal wrap. When you have children, I mean.'

The coal-streaked rag hangs limp from my hand. I suppose she can see what I am thinking, because she grows embarrassed, tugs it out of my grasp.

'Forgive me. I'm sorry.'

And just for a moment she sounds real. Almost a little desperate.

Trying in earnest to reach across the chasm between us. God knows who's dug it.

It makes me feel sorry for her.

'I'll keep it,' I say. 'It's very nice.'

We share a smile. Then she quickly slips back into her jacket, so the boys cannot see her, in her state of undress. And just like that she is her old self again. Distant. Cold as the dew.

'Mr Argyle owes you his life,' she says, to close our transaction. 'We are all in your debt.'

I nod, wave the rag in front of her face.

'That you are. But look here, you've already paid.'

The Liberal

Dawn breaks and Charlie thinks his heart will break for joy.

They have been walking for several hours already, tottering along in the dark, taking breaks every few minutes when Thomas grows dizzy and can no longer keep pace. Then a ribbon of predawn light appears on the horizon, hazy and pale. But what miracles are revealed by this pallid smear! They are walking on a muddy path: rectangles of fields stretch on both sides, parcelled up by enclosure walls and dotted with barren trees. Above them sits a leaden sky, so overcast that the clouds have no contours. It is a world of browns and greys. But what greys! How many shades of brown!

Charlie cannot believe his eyes; stops in his tracks, blinking tears from his eyes. Then, rising from the knolls of lowly hills, a smear of orange paints itself across the east. Theirs is not a picture-book sunrise, a fire-red balloon slowly mounting the world's edge; sitting on it; then lightly bouncing up, to scale the sky. And yet it is the most beautiful thing Charlie has ever seen. By increments the world gains in contour. And when the cloud cover breaks, momentarily, he feels the light on his face like a physical touch, searching his features. He stares down, at himself, his hands, his legs, and laughs from pure joy, marvelling at how even the sound is different under an open sky.

Only then does he turn to his friends.

It has been, for Charlie, a lonely week, stuck in a hole in the earth. He spent many hours sitting with Thomas, unable for much of the time to reach him through his fever, listening to his dark ravings, cut off even from his Smoke that appeared to have no smell in the dark, nor any power to infect, and danced aimlessly before the timid light on the few occasions when they dared to light a lamp. He talked to Lizzy, of course, but the girl was taciturn with him, jealous of sharing her time with Thomas. And Charlie talked to Livia: touched her, kissed her, took her breath in his. But even this was an adulterated joy in a world without sight; a love affair conducted by shades. In the dark, Charlie felt, they could not be fully *present* to one another. It was a world without smiles. Without beauty. He would wake from sleep and be beset by the fear of not having woken; would reach around himself and find no one; or a stranger; or a friend – a lover? – whose emotion he could not read.

The dark did something for Livia, though. Something important, a kind of tempering, something smiths do to their steel. Charlie looks at her now, his first look since their kiss, and finds her changed. Thinner. Dirtier, of course. Holding herself differently. It makes him shy and awkward with her, and shyer yet, more awkward, when she looks back at him and does not mirror his smile.

If Livia is thin, Thomas is emaciated. Cleaner than the rest of them (Lizzy saw to that, with the constant application of bucket and sponge) and pale underneath the speckling of coal dust. Out of the lip of his bandage crawl the tendrils of a dark blue tattoo, touch his eyebrow and the corner of his eye, where coal has grown into fresh scar tissue. His face is a mask of concentration: on the muddy path, on each step, keeping himself going by a sheer act of will.

By the time dawn has given way to midmorning they see it before them: not so much a village as a train supply station. Freight trains stop here to take on goods. Apparently, one can hop on a freight train for pennies, and ride with pigs or chickens or black mounds of coal. Mr Mosley advised them to come here; it would attract less notice, he said, than going to town. It is a place tramps come, in the hope of transport. Tramps. Well, thinks Charlie, we certainly look the part. His trousers and jacket are stiff with filth. A drizzle has started and is leaving patterns on his dirty skin. As though on command, they stop in the shelter of a hill. It is time to make decisions.

Φ

And yet the words won't come right away. Overwhelmed by a world without a roof, they have spoken little all morning and an odd timidity clings to them yet, as though words will put in motion something irrevocable; will put a close to one part of their lives and commit them to a new one.

It's Charlie who accepts it first.

'Do you want to go home?' he asks Livia. 'To your mother?'

The girl shakes her head. She has come this far, assuming her mother's complicity in the attack. Now she will see it out. Charlie knows better than to argue with her.

'To London, then.'

As Charlie says it, he hears the question in his own voice. It is directed at Thomas. He is their leader. They did not vote on it, nobody picked him and yet it is true, even now – especially now – that he is wounded and weak.

'I mean, if we can't go back to Lady Naylor's and want to do more than just sit around, it's the only real option. "The Tobacco Dock, midnight, the twelfth of January." That's what the ledger said in the laboratory. "Collect in person": Lady Naylor will be there. She is working on something, something important, and she paid a fortune just for this one item.'

Thomas has clearly been thinking the same thing. Nevertheless there is a hesitation to his response.

'What day is it today? We were attacked on the second, and went down the mine on the third. Six days down the mine. The morning of the ninth?'

Both Charlie and Livia confirm his calculation.

'Then we have four whole days. Time enough.' He shudders slightly, squats down on his heels, steadying himself with one hand. It comes to Charlie that Thomas is very close to fainting. That he does not have the strength even to stand.

But his voice is firm.

'What we need is to talk to someone who can shed light on everything. The laboratory, the experiments, Lady Naylor's theory of Smoke. Fresh information; some other perspective. Without it, we will continue tapping in the dark.' He juts his chin out, his mind made up. 'You two go to London. I will go and see Renfrew.'

'Renfrew! But how do you know we can trust him?'

'I don't. But he was Baron Naylor's student. And he is the one who told me that I was sick with Smoke. If we are right – if that cage in the laboratory is meant for me because of what is growing in me – then, Charlie, I need to know what it is *for*. Otherwise, I am making choices in the dark. And I am sick of doing that.'

Charlie wishes he could tell his friend that he is wrong. That Renfrew won't know a thing; that he will treat him as the errant schoolboy he is, scold him, lock him in a schoolroom, and make him scrub the floors in penance. But in his mind's eye he sees him again, the Master of Smoke and Ethics, sitting in the coach back from Oxford, quietly talking to Thomas. Renfrew knows. *Something*. Many things.

Perhaps he can be persuaded to tell them.

'In that case,' Charlie says, looking calmly at his friend. 'We will all go.'

But Thomas won't have it.

'Too risky. After all, we don't know whose side he is on. For all we know he is mixed up in this and working with Lady Naylor. If she is, in fact, our enemy. We need to split up. To make sure someone is there, in London. In case Renfrew detains me. Someone who *knows*, and can act as a witness.'

Again Thomas's reasoning is sound. And again, Charlie draws a different conclusion.

'Then I will go.' He goes on speaking over Thomas's murmur of protest. 'If you are right – about the cage, about the Smoke in you, all of it – then it's *you* who is important. Not me. So I will go.'

Still Thomas tries to argue, rises from the ground, anger in his voice, his whole body shaking with exhaustion.

It's Livia who shuts him up.

'You can't go,' she says to him. 'Not by yourself. You'd never make it. Someone would have to come and be your nurse. So no matter what you do, you will put one of us at risk.' She speaks very calmly, dispassionately, reciting the facts.

'I don't know this Master Renfrew, nor would I easily be able to find him. And you require an attendant. So either we all go and risk our hides. Or none of us goes. Or Charlie goes, and bears the consequences of your decision.'

She looks from one boy to the other as though weighing them up. It is, to Charlie, an uncomfortable glance.

'You have to make up your mind, Mr Argyle.'

She adds it quietly, sadly, as though she knows he already has.

Φ

They say goodbye once they have arranged a meeting place and time. It's easy. There is only one place in London both boys are sure they will find. Execution square; at the foot of the scaffold. Three meeting times a day, dawn, noon and dusk: starting lunchtime tomorrow. It's the earliest they can imagine Charlie can make it to London. He will have to sleep at the school. Or on the road.

It is best if they don't enter the train depot together. Whoever is looking for them, is looking for three scions of their gentry, two youths and a girl. There may be leaflets out for all they know, eyes at every train station. But they won't be interested in a dirty tramp in stolen clothes; nor in a pit girl and her companion. Or so they hope. Charlie is to go first. A head start of three hours. Enough time not to connect the one stranger with the other two. And for Thomas to rest.

Before he goes, Charlie steps over to Livia. Thomas looks away, immerses himself in the study of his boots. Giving them privacy. Even so, saying goodbye is not easy. They don't know how to. They have never touched each other in daylight.

In the end it is Charlie who extends his hand. Livia takes it shyly. They may have been strangers, meeting at a dinner party, only they don't let go at once but stand there, her hand small between his fingers. Charlie considers kissing her palm. But she pulls it away before he has raised it even halfway to his mouth.

'Too dirty,' she whispers, staring at her black little hand in disgust. 'Be careful, Charlie.'

'And you.'

Then it's Thomas's turn. Charlie walks over to him, crouches down where he is sitting on the ground.

'Look after her, will you? For me.'

Thomas nods but his look is gaunt. There is a fear there Charlie cannot fathom.

'It's I who should be going,' Thomas says after a while.

'We decided. It makes sense.'

Thomas shrugs. 'Be careful what you say to Renfrew. Don't give away too much.'

'I will only say what I can. We gave Lady Naylor our word. Not to speak of certain things. She may be a rebel, or a villain. But our word is our word.'

Then he hugs his friend, turns, and leaves.

Φ

Charlie need not have worried that he would stand out in the little hamlet that serves as a loading station. There are plenty of strange men milling in the street, dressed in a wide variety of costumes and rarely very clean. Women, too, young and old, and a gaggle of urchins pelting one another with rocks. Workers, traders, unemployed miners. A dandy without boots dragging a donkey by its bridle. A hulking Scot in a greatcoat shouting drunken swear words at the sky, his accent bending every vowel. A consumptive woman, thin as a rail, selling charred, bone-studded meats from a grill she has set up by the side of the road. A beggar dressed in little more than a shift, flashing the stumps of his legs at every passerby.

Where there are people, there is sin. Charlie is shocked when he catches the first whiff of Smoke. It's been a week since he has smelled it. As he draws closer to the train station, clouds of Smoke become more obvious, drift on the wind, dusting the buildings in Soot. He breathes it in and feels himself grow irritable. It is hard, in this world, not to walk around with clenched fists.

Securing passage to Oxford is surprisingly simple. A man on the platform has made a business of it: selling tickets for a berth on the freight train. He operates out in the open, from behind a little table, just like a normal ticket seller. A group of men are in his employ, one more disreputable-looking than the next. They walk up and down the platform, discouraging customers who think they can just leap on a train without paying. 'We're conductors,' one of them keeps shouting. 'No tick't and you pays yer fare in teeth.' He himself is missing most of the latter item along with the better part of the lower jaw. It looks like it has been sliced off with a knife.

Like Thomas, Charlie lost his portmanteau along with the rest of his luggage when they ran from the ambush. Livia never brought a purse in the first place. Consequently, the only money they have between them are the few pennies Mr Mosley gave them early that morning, counting them out into Charlie's dirty hands.

'Won't get far without,' he told them when they tried to refuse.

They divided the money evenly before splitting up, reasoning that Charlie had two trains to catch to Thomas and Livia's one. Now that he faces the ticket seller, Charlie worries that it won't be enough and holds the coins on his open palm.

'How much . . . ?'

The man looks at him, snorts, and swipes the lot. Only then does he ask, 'Where to?'

'Oxford.'

'"Ohx-fjord",' the man imitates his accent. 'Posh boy, eh? Runaway son of a burgher, is that it? Didn't take to the cane. Or fell in love, what, with a lass that wasn't suitable. Suited *you* though, eh?' He makes a gesture of such obscenity that Charlie finds himself blushing to the roots of his hair. 'Ah, you should've left with fuller pockets, son. Never mind, you're in luck. Train due in an hour. Any of the last five wagons. The doors'll be open. If the stationmaster catches you, in Oxford like, say you're travelling express. Won't give you any trouble, he won't, the man's well paid.'

'Thank you.'

'Ah, no bother. It tickles me. Being friendly with a toff. Now off with you, I have business to conduct.'

Φ

It takes Charlie until dusk to get to Oxford. The train is steady but very slow, huffing and puffing up every hill. Charlie spends the hours squeezed in between a row of other tramps, one of whom un-ceremoniously dips his hand in his pocket to search it for money, all the time smoking like a chimney from both mouth and ears. When they stop, Charlie does not recognise the station at once: they are far from the public platform, their view obstructed by a dirty brick wall. Further up the train, he sees a number of shadows leap out of carriages and clamber over the wall. He follows their example and is spilled into a warren of backstreets and courtyards, alive with smells and noise and people. Navigating by the setting sun, Charlie heads to the western edge of town, looking for the road that will lead him to the school. A league out of town a cart driver rolls past and offers Charlie a ride in exchange for his coat, dirty though it is.

'Where you headin'?' the driver asks him.

When Charlie, too honest to lie, names the school, the man eyes him narrowly.

'Going there to beg? I shouldn't bother. It's half-term. No one around. Besides, they are skinflints they are. Tight as a trout's arse. You're better off tryin' your luck in the village.'

Is Charlie going there to beg? Well, in a manner of speaking he is. But Charlie merely mumbles something about knowing one of the porters, speaking indistinctly, hiding his accent. The thought of Cruikshank, sour and stupid, puts a stitch in his heart.

The man lets him off near the village, an hour's walk from school. It must be nearing ten at night. The sky is clear now and it is growing colder. None of the snow that marked December remains on the ground, but there is a smell to the wind that promises more.

Charlie hurries along until he sees the dark shadow of the school ahead. He has seen it before from this angle, in similar light: the

199

night they returned from London. A single window is lit, high up, where Trout has his chambers. He asked Charlie to spy on the Naylors and would be keen to hear his report. But it is not to Trout that Charlie is heading.

Instead he takes a path that leads past the rugby field across the little creek, to a cottage that stands alone there, surrounded by a picket fence. Most of the teachers live in, inside the main school building itself, and leave for the holidays, to see their wives and children at home or go up to their alma maters, to stay in chambers there. But a handful of the masters – the poorer it is sometimes said, not without derision; those without good family ties or their own estates – have houses at the edge of the grounds that are rented to them year-round. This one is Renfrew's. A lamp is lit above the narrow door, and another light shines dimly through drawn curtains. Charlie stops by the creek before he enters, dips his hands in the black and icy water, washes his face. There is not much he can do without a bar of soap, but at least he can face his teacher wide awake. The door knocker has the shape of a silver owl. Minerva, goddess of wisdom.

It may be childish, but Charlie crosses himself, before engaging its taloned feet to knock on the door.

Φ

The knock is answered with an alacrity Charlie does not expect. It is almost as though someone had been waiting for him by the door. Indeed there is a stool in the plain little hallway that opens up to him. But no person. Charlie has to adjust his gaze, downward, to understand who worked the doorknob. Dressed in a plain grey shift, the fair hair braided into pigtails, the girl can't be any older than eight or nine. Her face is narrow, the eyes large and scared. Her shoulders and upper body are encased in a strange metal harness. Two spokes run upwards, at both sides of the neck before they stop just under the point where the chinbone bends and charges up to the ears. At the harness's front, at the centre of the sternum, rides a little brass wheel. She stands in the hallway, quivering, like a rabbit caught out in the open by a fox.

'Hullo,' Charlie greets the girl, and then once more, softer now, crouching down on the threshold as he does so. 'Hullo there. Don't be scared.'

The girl does not move, shivers, looks across at him, then reaches to her chest and turns the wheel on her contraption with a quick jerky movement. Next Charlie knows, her eyes have filled with tears. But she does not start crying.

'My name is Charlie,' he says, still crouching in the open door. 'I am looking for Master Renfrew. I am one of his students, see. Is he at home?'

The girl shakes her head: stiffly, the chin pushed very high, avoiding the spokes of her harness.

'Then you are waiting for him.' Charlie points to the stool. 'Are you his daughter? I did not know Master Renfrew was married.'

But the strange, half-mechanical girl only shakes her head again, with that same stiff gesture.

'Well, perhaps you help him keep house.' Charlie rises, pats the top of the stool. 'Here, please, sit down. Perhaps I can keep you company while you wait? Yes? That's kind of you. It's cold outside. Do you think we should close the door? We are letting all the heat out, and you'll catch your death, standing there in the draught.'

Φ

Renfrew returns within the hour. They have not moved, Charlie and the little girl, are standing in the hallway, two paces apart, the stool she is too scared to use standing between them. At several points Charlie considers leaving and waiting outside. But it disturbs him, the thought of this young child alone in the house. Even though he has no success in drawing her into conversation – even though he cannot rouse from her even a single smile – he is aware that his presence soothes her; that he is not the cause of her fear but something else, some weight on her childish heart so heavy that she hardly dares breathe.

Then they hear the sounds of steps crunching on the gravel path. Charlie opens the door long before his teacher can reach the house, wishing to reveal himself to him and apologise for intruding. Dr Renfrew wears dark leather riding gear, mud-splattered and steaming with the heat of his exertion. The horse is nowhere in sight, and must have been left with the school's groundsman. When he catches sight of Charlie, the teacher stops in his tracks, his features registering surprise, even alarm. Then he collects himself, strides on, and shifts his riding crop from right hand to left. It frees the former for a handshake.

'Mr Cooper. This is most unexpected! Most unexpected indeed. Do come in.'

Renfrew passes his hat and gloves over to the stiff little girl, sits down on the stool, and peels himself out of his boots.

'If you will excuse me. I have just returned from Parliament. I was asked to speak on issues pertinent to the future of the realm.'

He winces as his feet leave the long shafts of his boots and accepts the slippers the girl hastily brings out for him, each movement made oddly formal by the bulk of her contraption.

'A wretched session. Rows and rows of perfect blockheads, jabbering away about "tradition" and drowning out the few beacons of science and reason in the room. It is enough to drive a man out of his mind.' Renfrew frowns. 'But listen to me prattle on, when it is you who should be talking. You have a tale to tell, Mr Cooper! Half of England is looking for you – including your father who has rushed back from Ireland and is calling for a closure of the borders! Last anyone heard you were abducted by Gypsies. Though there are other rumours even more outlandish than that! It is good to see you are safe. But out with it: what on earth happened to you?'

Charlie looks at the square, grave face of his teacher and does not know how to answer. So he does what he always does. Charlie smiles.

'I am hungry, Master Renfrew.'

Renfrew laughs. 'So am I. Well, I suppose it can wait until after dinner. To table then. I see you have met my niece. Eleanor, please set another place, there's a good girl. And here, let me have a wash. You, too, might benefit from the application of soap, Mr Cooper. Please tell me, my good boy, that you are not covered in Soot.'

Φ

Dinner is a rather frugal affair of bread, cheese and pickles. The bread is a few days old and there is no butter, nor any dessert. Renfrew has sat Charlie across from him and his niece by his arm. The Master of Smoke and Ethics says a short grace before he cuts the bread, and eats in almost ritual silence. Charlie finds himself working hard not to make any noises with knife and fork. The little girl, too, eats with extravagant care and never raises her eyes from her plate. At one point she stops eating abruptly, puts down the slice of bread in her hand, and reaches to her chest to once again engage the little wheel that rises out of the harness like a growth. The action is followed by a strange, jerky shudder. Again, the girl's eyes fill with tears. Her uncle watches all this nonplussed; he turns to her and asks her quite gently, 'Did you smoke, my dear?'

The girl whispers her answer rather than speaking it, her eyes on the table.

'I thought I felt the seed of it.'

'You did well. You may go now and retire. It is well past your bedtime.'

Obediently, the girl pushes her chair back very carefully, rises, collects her plate and cutlery, and leaves the room: each action performed with an exaggerated slowness as though fighting the temptation for haste. When she has left, Renfrew, too, puts down his knife and fork and turns to Charlie.

'A lovely child. My brother's daughter. Her parents died when she was but an infant. I have come to be very fond of her. How old would you say she was?'

Charlie thinks about it. 'Nine?'

Renfrew smiles. It's a proud smile and sits strangely on his self-denying face. For a moment the smile puzzles Charlie. Then he understands.

'She does not smoke.'

'Quite.' There is, to Renfrew, something of the glow that he had after London. 'They say it is impossible to achieve self-mastery before the age of fourteen or fifteen, and even then imperfectly. But the girl is eight and has not visibly smoked in more than six months. You see, I have a pedagogic system.'

'The harness?'

'Is a small if important part of it, yes. An invention of mine as a matter of fact, modelled on something I saw during my travels. In Italy. Initially, I used it to correct her posture. But it proved more useful in correcting the soul. The wheel contracts the harness, you see, albeit very slightly. It causes a modicum of pain. Over time, she has learned to use it herself, warning her body against temptation. It will revolutionise child-rearing before too long. Assuming the government changes and permits the introduction of such innovations.'

Renfrew studies Charlie's reaction to his explanation with detached amusement.

'There is no need to pity Eleanor, Mr Cooper. She is quite used to the contraption. And with the progress she has made in the past two years, she is now allowed to take it off at night. Though she chooses not to, much of the time.'

He rises, walks Charlie over to the armchairs by the window, and pours out two glasses of water from a simple earthenware jug.

'But enough of this. It's time you reveal your great mystery. Here you come to me late one evening a week after you have disappeared. Dirty as a sparrow. And looking, if you will excuse the phrase, rather shifty. What happened to you? And why are you here?'

Φ

Charlie tells him the easy parts first: how they were attacked, their coachman killed and Thomas shot; how they ran away through the woods and were hidden by 'good people'. He does not explain why they did not contact anyone after the attack; nor does he mention the wild woman who helped them staunch the bleeding; nor yet the miners and the week they spent hidden in the mine. Charlie grows even more evasive when Renfrew asks him about his time at the Naylors' and inquires particularly after the baron's health. His skin feels itchy where he scrubbed it with Renfrew's soap and he feels oddly naked, sitting under the bright glare of the gas lamp, without the protective covering of coal dust. When Renfrew presses him for further details in his calm, systematic manner, Charlie pushes forward in his chair and looks him square in the eye.

'There is much I cannot tell you, Master Renfrew. I promised I would not.'

His teacher narrows his eyes, hesitates, purses his lips. 'Then why are you here, Mr Cooper?'

Now it is Charlie's turn to hesitate, uncertain how to broach the topic. He finds refuge in a question.

'You said there were other rumours. Before, when you first saw me. A Gypsy attack, you said, only there were other rumours, too. What did you mean?'

Renfrew gets up, puts a kettle on the fireplace. Charlie is conscious of his thinking it over, calculating how much to reveal: just the same as Charlie. *Another game of chess.* Thomas would play it aggressively, threaten with his queen. But Charlie knows the value of positional play. And of patience.

By the time Renfrew has resettled himself in his chair, he has evidently made up his mind to be frank with Charlie.

'The rumours concern the bullets recovered from the horse carcasses,' he begins, his voice clear and firm, unadulterated by emotion. 'An enterprising magistrate insisted on having them cut out. It's quite unusual, as procedures go, and raised some eyebrows, amongst the Conservatives, you understand. An English magistrate, commanding the scalpel! It smelled of Continental methods.' Renfrew allows himself a smile. 'Now, the bullets that were recovered are quite unusual. They are not of domestic manufacture and were shot by a rifle that must not exist on these shores, by the rules of the embargo. A very powerful rifle. Of course, all this is hard to discuss out in the open. Officially, after all, we are not to know such weapons even exist. The report was circulated privately, which is to say it entered the world of whispers. I daresay half of England's lords are kept awake at night, longing to own such a rifle.'

'You are saying it's not the sort of gun a poor person would carry.'

'Precisely. Gypsies carry blunderbusses or something similarly crude. And you really did not see any trace of your attackers?'

Charlie shakes his head, thinking. Then he takes a risk.

'I have heard things,' he says. 'About Smoke. I came here tonight to find out if they are true.'

'Ah,' says Master Renfrew. 'I rather thought it might be something of that kind.'

Behind him, the kettle starts whistling and summons them to tea.

Φ

It's Charlie's move. He cradles the teacup between both hands, lets the warmth spread through his fingers. He says, 'There was a time before Smoke.'

Renfrew smiles, counters. 'I see you spoke to Baron Naylor. How is he? He no longer answers my letters, not for many a year. It is most vexing. Suspicious, even.

'"There was a time before Smoke." Yes, I remember his whispering those very words to me, and how shaken I was. Like a lightning bolt hitting me out of the clear blue sky. For three whole years I could think of nothing else.

'And the lengths the baron went to prove it! Hunting for paintings, letters, diaries. It was quite an obsession with him. "None of these accounts mention snow," he whispered to me once. "It's changed our climate: all the Smoke in the atmosphere, it's blocking out the sun."

At times I feared he had gone mad. Before long I believed it as surely as he. We would sit together and discuss it, night after night.'

Renfrew chuckles at the memory, fondly, Charlie thinks, a man remembering his mentor and friend.

'What if there was, though, Mr Cooper? A time before Smoke. If it came to us in the seventeenth century, as Baron Naylor posits, by land or by sea, from some far-flung corner of this world? What difference does it make?'

Charlie surprises himself by the intensity of his answer. 'It means we can fight Smoke. Defeat it.'

Renfrew smiles. It's a friendly smile but also condescending.

'That's just what the baron thought. He declared a war on Smoke. A crusade! And threw himself into a frenzy of research, on all manner of fronts: history, archaeology, anatomy. Travelled the world, collecting evidence. Cut open a dozen carcasses, pickling their livers.

'And to what end? To defeat a symptom. The one thing that tells us we are sick. Foolishness. It's the one thing he never understood. Yes, very well: Smoke has a history. But so does sin! Oh, it did not come to us two hundred and fifty years ago. It's older than that! Much older. But *not*' – here Renfrew rises, stands towering over Charlie, steam rising from his china cup – 'eternal!'

Charlie looks up at him, takes refuge in ignorance, only half feigned.

'I don't understand,' he says.

It sets Renfrew to pacing: three steps one way, three steps back. It's a small cottage, really, and mould blooms richly on one white-washed wall.

'Remember your Bible, Mr Cooper. The holy books of the Jews, what we call the Old Testament. Genesis: the tree, the snake, expulsion from Eden. What is this book if not the record of a memory, very ancient, preserved in the form of story? A primitive people making sense of a momentous event in their past. The memory of the coming of sin!

'Sin is a *disease*. A germ, as some of the Continental scientists would say. Through time, it transformed, became visible to the plain eye, materialised externally. A startling event, no doubt, but one of no consequence; merely a change of symptomology. What we must work on – scientifically, that is, pooling all our knowledge, and not hiding behind an artificial wall like the embargo – is the eradication of the actual disease. I have a scheme, you see. We need to breed it out of society. First out of the gentry. And then ... Until at last, we are all the same.'

He stops in his tracks, looks at Charlie almost frightened, whether by the greatness of his vision or by his revealing too much to a pupil it is hard to say. But a shake of his head dispels his doubts and his pacing resumes.

'Did you know, Mr Cooper, that there is a scholar languishing in Her Majesty's dungeons who posits human beings have developed – *evolved* – from more primitive organisms? In the course of the generations, we change, according to our environment, and the habits of our lives. Thus, over time, new species form out of old ones.

'Have you seen pictures of giraffes, Mr Cooper? No, of course not, it's not allowed. Well, I have seen the real thing. In the African savannah, Baron Naylor at my side. They are animals, not unlike tall deer, but patterned in brown and yellow, with necks that are five or six feet long. Quite astonishing, really. Well, the theory posits that it comes from stretching: to eat the leaves in the trees. Generations of stretching. Like doing gymnastics. And each generation passes on a little of its strength. It is a slow process, of course, taking thousands of years. What, however, if we slaughter the weakest animals? The ones with the shortest necks? Those who lack the will to change? And devise a systematic programme of stretches for all the young, a programme that starts even while they are still in the cradle, so to speak? Imagine the acceleration, the speed of progress! And then transfer this to the moral theatre.' Renfrew pauses, lowers himself back into his chair, careful not to spill tea. 'God is a scientist, Mr Cooper. We are promised a Second Coming. A Republic of the Virtuous. But we have to work for it!'

Above them, the ceiling creaks and Charlie pictures the little girl, bending awkwardly over a washbasin, trying to clean her body underneath the contraption of steel and leather that keeps her safe from herself. But perhaps it is merely the old wood, shifting in the cold of the night.

When Charlie returns his attention to Renfrew, the man is watching him expectantly. It is almost as though their roles were reversed, Charlie the teacher and Renfrew the pupil, awaiting a verdict on his essay on political ethics. Another boy may have taken pleasure in the situation. For Charlie, it causes a sort of ache; proof that the world has fallen into disorder.

'Then you have travelled far?' He sidesteps the look, along with its expectation. 'We saw a picture, at the Naylors' house, of you and the baron, standing on a foreign plain. I did not recognise the landscape. Flat, open, devoid of features. With a mile-high sky.'

If Renfrew is put out of temper by Charlie's change of topic he does not show it. There is no frown, no pursing of the lips. But whatever was boyish in his face dies away, leaves a harder man behind. *Not hard,* Charlie thinks. *Righteous. Rational.*

It amounts to the same thing.

'Yes, we travelled far and wide – it was still legal then. The Continent. All the colonies. And beyond. Beyond the pale of civilisation.'

'I think I know what you were looking for. The birthplace of Smoke. Where it came from originally. The source.'

Renfrew shakes his head. 'An intelligent surmise, Mr Cooper, but wrong. It's what I thought when Baron Naylor first explained his theories to me, and asked me to travel with him. It was the summer after my first year at Cambridge. I was only a little older than yourself. The baron had invited me to stay with him in the splendour of his manor. We read, went out riding, hunting, boxed. Oh, he picked me well! A scholarship student. Poor; risen above my station. In thrall to his title as much as his intellect.'

There is something scornful to the way he says it, something rigid about Renfrew's posture. It takes Charlie a moment to understand it. Here he is, the scholarship student, instructing the English elites at the finest school in the country. No, not instructing. Sitting in judgement. He is not in thrall to titles any more.

'Our first journey was to Bulgaria. Gathering evidence, in old monastery libraries. But by the next summer the baron had a new idea. Something rather more daring. If Smoke only came to Europe in the seventeenth century, he reasoned, there might be places in the world it had not yet reached. Remote places, at the very edge of things. You see, he was looking for an *innocent*.'

Charlie remembers the picture. A girl chained to a wall: twisting her head away from the camera. A girl that grew up to save Thomas's life.

'You found one.'

'We found a whole people. Or at least we heard about them. A

208

people without *Smoke*. Living in tiny tribes in a land of eternal ice. Hunting whales from boats no bigger than a dinghy. Eating raw seal. The tribes to the south thought of them as demons. When they saw them, they turned and ran away.

'We had a problem then. It wasn't just that none of our guides would take us to them. There was also the question whether contact with us would infect the tribe. Imagine destroying the very specimen we had travelled so far to collect! We spent weeks debating the problem.

'In the end fate decided the issue for us. A local hunter caught one in his trap. By accident, mind. He was hunting for bears. God knows what had driven her so far south. A girl of fourteen. He wouldn't go near her, but he sold us her whereabouts. Twenty pounds sterling he wanted, in gold. The baron never even haggled.

'Her leg was in a bad state by the time we reached her. Broken ankle, a thousand flies laying their eggs in the wound. But she was alive, awake. We watched her for a good hour: shouting, wailing, screaming at us. Not a hint of Smoke. It wasn't just caution that kept us away. The absence of Smoke: we were not prepared for it. We were afraid to touch her.

'But in the end we realised she would die if we didn't. So we brought her to the camp. Most of our native guides fled at once, terrified by this monster in our midst. They took most of our provisions along. We set up a hospital in our only tent and slept outside.

'The leg healed well. We ministered to the girl's needs and otherwise kept our distance. She withdrew into herself, didn't speak, hardly ate. Without guides or food there was no way of prolonging the expedition, so we took her home. To Baron Naylor's manor. To observe her, and to conduct experiments.'

'And then?'

'Within three weeks of our return, she started to smoke. All through the journey we had isolated her. Nobody apart from the baron and I ever came closer than five yards to her, and we only approached her with the purest of intentions. And all the same she started showing.' Renfrew's smile still carries the pain of their disappointment. 'In any case, it was all a mistake. Chasing the Smoke. We should have realised right away that there was no virtue to the girl.' He pauses. 'Baron Naylor wrote to me a few months later that the tests had been terminated. The girl had died.'

'From lack of love,' Charlie murmurs.

'Love is not a scientific entity.'

Charlie ponders Renfrew's answer and decides not to tell him that the girl is alive and roaming the woods of Nottinghamshire. She might have escaped. But in his heart Charlie wants to believe that it was Baron Naylor who released her.

Renfrew, in any case, has run out of interest in the past. His focus is on the future.

'I note you elected not to comment on my vision. *A Republic of the Virtuous.* I must admit that I had hoped for more enthusism from you. If there is to be reform, it will have to be carried by the young. People like yourself. But perhaps you are thinking of your family interest. And share your father's Tory politics. Change does not come easily to the powerful.'

Renfrew rises, steps close to Charlie, and pulls him up gently by his shoulder. Standing close, the man still smells of leather and horse.

'There will come a time to choose between virtue and vice, Mr Cooper. There will be an *accounting.* Ask yourself where all the money comes from. The rich of the land. Your own family, too, Mr Cooper. An audit, before the eyes of God and men. Our currency needs to be as virtuous as our thoughts.'

Charlie, unsure how to respond, simply nods. Renfrew appears to accept it as a sort of promise.

'Very well. And now, Mr Cooper, I must ask you to lay aside your bashfulness and provide me with a full account of everything that has happened to you since you left school for the holidays. Everything the baron told you. What you have seen of his latest experiments. Or his wife's, if the rumours about his ill health are true. I will also need to know where you were the past week, including a full list of names of the people you spoke to. Above all you must tell me what you saw that made you hide from the Naylors – oh, don't bother denying it, why else did you not alert them to your whereabouts, you must think them implicated in the attack! You must also tell me where Miss Naylor is, and Mr Argyle. That boy is very vulnerable. And a potential danger to those around him. In short, I have to insist on the truth. As your teacher. And as a servant of England.'

Charlie looks Renfrew in the eye. For all his insistence, there is no anger, no threat to him. He is stating Charlie's duty, as he sees it. For a moment Charlie is tempted to oblige him. Pass on responsibility to this man who is so eminently responsible. Who watched a girl scream with pain for an hour. Who thought her a 'specimen' that must be collected, and chained her to a wall.

'I am sorry, Master Renfrew. I cannot. I gave my word. As a gentleman.'

Renfrew appears saddened by his answer.

'Very well, Mr Cooper. We must all follow our conscience.'

He turns, fetches a lamp from the table, nods towards the stairs.

'I suggest we retire. I will appeal to you again in the morning. Perhaps I can change your mind.'

Φ

The guest room is small and plain but after a week of sleeping wrapped in filthy blankets the white feather bedding looks deliciously comfortable to Charlie. Master Renfrew puts out a nightshirt for him, and fills the washbowl with clean water, before leaving him to retire in peace. For the briefest moment Charlie considers refusing the offer of hospitality and returning to the road. But it is snowing outside and even in the room the cold creeps into his bones. When he slips under the down duvet, such is the wave of well-being washing over him, he almost feels ashamed.

Charlie is about to extinguish the lamp, when the door opens once more and Renfrew walks in, still in his travelling clothes, carrying a tray with a steaming mug of what proves to be hot milk and honey.

'Here, Mr Cooper, you look like you could use it. You must have lost half a stone since I saw you last.'

He sits at Charlie's bedside and watches him drink it before carrying the tray back out. There is to his solicitude something so touchingly maternal that Charlie drifts into sleep with the image of his mother in his head, singing softly, tucking his eiderdown up under his chin.

Caesar

The man who tips me off wants to tell me about a workers' union the miners have set up. The gold sits heavy in his hand. He can't take his eyes off the coin. Already he has bitten it three times. I should have shoved it up my dog's arse before I gave it to him. See whether he'd like the taste then. I am sure he would not mind.

He is like so many of his class. Crude, greedy and stupid. Smoke drifts out of his hairline in thin, greasy streaks; he's hunching his shoulders, in apology, or fear.

'They be a rebellious lot,' he says for the fourth or fifth time, squinting at me. 'Crim'nels in my book.'

He sounds West Country to me. An outsider here. Living his life by a handful of lies that have become true through ceaseless repetition.

'I'm a good man, I am. Salt of the earth.'

He bites the gold again, wipes snot across his beard with the heel of his palm, farts. Nervous wind, Mr Price used to call it. He caused it in a good many people, would stand there sniffing and flash me a wink. The thought of Price lends fresh focus to my task.

Again I ask about the two boys and the girl. 'Posh folk,' I say. 'Gentry. One of them is badly wounded.' It is hard to explain to the man that I don't give a toss about their dwarf insurrection. It's not like the Spencers own the mine.

He remembers something at last. A girl has been seen, down the mine. A stranger. In the company of one Francis Mosley. A haulage woman passed them in the dark.

'Can't have been gentry though,' he muses. 'Dirty like an Arab, see. Wearing breeches. Most likely a whore. And then, a-course,' he adds after much frowning, 'there was three figures on the path. Stevie Milner says he saw 'em pass. But gentry, no, that they wasn't.' He looks at me wearily, worried he'll lose his gold.

'Let me guess. They were dirty, too.'

'Like they was dunked in mud.'

'Take me to the place where they were seen.'

My bitch growls when he moves. Nótt: named for the Norse mistress of the night. She has taken a liking to the greasy little man, sniffs his crotch like it is made of bacon. He nearly drops his coin.

Φ

I have been at it for six days now. Each morning, I get up before dawn and saddle the horse. Each evening, a supper with Mother, pale and fretting, in her eyes a question she's afraid to ask. We have a simple relationship, Mother and I. We have replaced emotion with economics. Recently we have added crime to the ties of debt and blood.

'Are you assisting the magistrate's search?' Mother asks the second morning I set off.

'No. I have my own ideas.'

'You have found a trace then?'

'Perhaps.'

'Please. Be careful,' she says and for a moment I think she means for myself. I look at her, my breakfast in my throat, hoping, dreading that she will force a talk.

But she says nothing further.

As I ride off her hand brushes the saddlebag bulging by my thigh.

Φ

I never thought they might be hiding down the mine. But that's where Nótt leads me, once she puts her nose to the narrow bridleway where the strangers have been sighted. The colliers stop in their tracks when I enter the work yard. The smell of snow is in the air, but nothing has fallen yet. The sky sits low against the hills. It would make a wonderful painting, Nótt crouching, long tail cocked, her ears pressed high against her head. I ride over to the pit shaft, watch it spit up a cage. A union, forming down the bottom of this hole. Talking revolution through mouthfuls of bread and dripping. All you'd need to do is cut the cable. Trap them like rats. Grandfather is right. This is a world of idiots. I wait until Nótt has emptied her bladder and then we turn, back to the bridleway. They must have left before dawn. Six hours head start. But I have a horse.

Φ

213

They split up once they reached the train depot. It takes me a while to establish this. The men here are close-mouthed, suspicious. But no pauper can resist gold.

They remember a boy with a bandage, of course. He travelled with a girl. Heading south I am told. London-way. Cooped up with a wagonload of chickens, and some fellow cutthroats, heading home.

It's the other boy no one can tell me about. Not until I find a man who spoke to him, the boss of a racket selling passenger tickets to freight trains. He has a band of degenerates on staff who will break your legs if you think you can catch a ride for free.

We talk at length. An enterprising man. He reminds me of my grandfather. Affable, given to whimsy. Happiest when making a profit without breaking a sweat.

'What's he to you?' he asks once we have established he knows the boy I am looking for.

'I'm his elder brother.'

'You don't look alike.'

'Ah, well. You'd have to talk to Mother about that.'

The man laughs. I slip him money.

'He ran away, did he? This brother of yours.'

'He is guilty of that particular folly.'

The man jingles coins within a meaty fist.

'Awful dirty for gentry,' he muses.

I smile and add one more coin to his stack. Then I call Nótt to my side. The man studies her weight, her teeth.

'Big dog.'

'Enough of this.'

He shrugs, counts up the money. 'He was heading for Oxford. Got family there perhaps?'

'A kindly uncle.'

'Those are the best sort.'

Φ

I am left with a choice then. London or Oxford. My inclination lies with the city. Thomas is there. He tasks me, Thomas, tender like an abscess in my throat. How deftly has he slipped into Mother's regard, where I could only wheedle with my money. How artfully has he contrived to set a mark against my name at school, so that I have to endure Renfrew's insolent probing. And how similar is our

214

Smoke once woken; how seductive in its kinship; how intolerable in its rivalry. But it'll be hard, I imagine, tracking someone in London. Too many people, too many scents, even for Nótt. Oxford will be easier. Charlie Cooper must be heading back to school. To do what, I wonder; talk to whom? How much has he seen? It is this simple question that decides me. I want Thomas. But there must not be any talk.

There are no trains to Oxford until the following day, not from this depot. I resolve to make my way by horse. It won't be any faster that way, but after a week of waiting it feels good to be on the move.

Darkness falls early. And just like that unease descends upon me, half childish fear, half longing, my hand dipping in the saddlebag. The feeling has grown familiar in the week since Price's death; resembles the tangle of shame and excitement that attends the first discovery of self-abuse.

In confusion then, fretting, unsure whether it is to indulge or to distract myself, I look for company and shelter; make out a farmhouse by its chimney in the distance then see the glow of a fire in a field much closer by. When I approach, I find two men sitting around a pot of boiling potatoes. Two rabbits, crudely skinned, hang skewered over the fire. The men rise, alarmed: crooked figures, thin as rails, the clothes mere rags. Underneath the dirt and Soot their complexions are fair and ruddy. Tinkers, not Gypsies. All the same, unwelcome on these shores.

'A pastoral scene,' I greet them, resolving relief into swagger. 'Two Irishmen poaching rabbits in another man's field.' I dismount. 'Not my field though, so please don't fret. I am just another traveller. Weary. Now my friends, might I share some of your rabbit, seeing that you stole it and are eating for free?'

Φ

They are drinking men. I don't usually partake in alcohol, but as I lie there, listening to their talk and laughter, I accept the bottle and take a swig, and later another, then another. It heats the stomach, and gives an odd sharpness to the night. At length I slip a sweet under my tongue and taste the liquor through its herbal tang.

As for the Paddies, they are quite at ease with me now. I am prey to them: a rich fool waiting to be robbed. I for my part am too preoccupied to disabuse them of the notion. When one of them sidles over

215

to the pile I made of saddle and bags, it is Nótt that jumps up and pushes her maw into the soft of his tummy. I trained her to do it and hence know the feeling, of her hot wet breath soaking through one's shirt. It feels as though one's skin grows paper-thin. The man starts smoking, very faintly, and my bitch, she wags her tail.

'Sure meant nothing by it,' he says almost sulkily though he holds his body very still. 'Just admiring the rifle. An unusual piece. Foreign design, is it?'

'And what do you know about guns?'

'Father was a gunsmith. Never learned the trade myself, mind.'

An artisan's son, fallen on hard times. And for a moment it rises in me, the urge to tell him about this rifle and its telescopic sight, accurate at four hundred yards. A German design. Illegal. *Cursed.*

I am aware that it is not the desire to show off that tempts me but the lure of confession, boyish and weak; am aware, too, that within this weakness, buried like a thorn, sits some other longing yet, darker in temperament and stronger by far, which has long sketched its own outcome to the night.

'Best leave it alone, my friend.'

But the man has sensed my hesitation. As has Nótt, who has stepped back and eyes me in confusion while the vagrant, slowly but brazenly enough, kneels down next to my saddlebag and studies its bulge. Again the urge takes hold of me to self-betray.

'Go on,' I say, sucking weakly at my sweet. 'Pull it out if you must.'

What emerges looks (even to me, after days of familiarity) like nothing so much as a man's face, denuded of bone and cured by a tanner. The eyes are brass-rimmed disks of glass. Where nose and mouth are to be expected, the face grows a proboscis, long and limp like a wet sock. At the far end, this snout is weighted down with something very much like the head of a watering can. For a moment a gust of wind catches the mask and fills its features with volume; then the rubber inverts and the thing hangs dead from the man's fingers.

'What is it? Some kind of mask?'

I find the semblance of my normal voice, brittle at its edges.

'A respirator. Chap called György came up with it. A Hungarian inventor. He wished to design something that would protect soldiers from the madness of battle. It filters out Smoke. Trouble is, you can hardly breathe in it. And who ever said soldiers should be sane?' I hesitate, watch the mask watch me from brass-rimmed goggles; each breath of breeze a hint of life within its rubber cheeks. 'But, you see, it works differently now. A family friend made alterations.'

The Irishman, however, has already lost interest in my explanation and picked up the drinks bladder that was stashed alongside the mask. It's heavier than he expected, the bladder's neck hanging flaccid from his fist; the bottom swollen like a woman's rump. He unscrews the nozzle, sniffs at the contents, squirts a drop into the palm of his hand.

'What's this? Tar? Soot?'

Pain, I say. Rage. Shreds of childhood. Infancy, the years unremembered. Bottled and raw.

I am no longer sure whether I am speaking aloud.

He stares, shrugs, replaces the bladder then returns his eyes to the gun, keeps looking at its angular butt, shod in finest silver. The leather sheath alone is worth five guineas.

'We aren't thieves,' he mutters, either to convince me or to convince himself, turns on his heels and returns to the campfire to offer me another pull of his jug. 'No, that we are not.'

And without further ado, kicking off his shoes and picking through his toes for clods of dirt, he launches into a song, high-pitched and morose. When he is done, his companion, silent till now, looks over to me, a blade of grass in his mouth.

'Begging your pardon, sir,' he smiles, 'but you mustn't let my brother here spoil the night with his sorry old bleating. Tell us a tale, then, something that'll pass the time while there's still liquor in the jug. Please do, sir, or this one, he'll never shut up.'

'A tale?' I say, gazing over to where the mask, carelessly repacked, winks one eye-glass at the moon.

Why not?

They have seen the gun. Our fates are already decided.

And I – drunk, heartsick, on the threshold of my future – I am needful of some talk.

Φ

'He set out to shoot horses.

'Imagine a young man, lying naked on a blanket high up on the dust floor of a derelict mill. Not me, mind, but someone like me: a well-born, handsome youth, the heir to a large fortune. Like a prince in a tale. He is freezing, our prince. A January morning, dawn just broken. Above him are the rusted gears once powered by the wind-sails. Beyond them vaults a hole-punctured roof. A streak of pale light cuts across his shoulders, another separates his hand from his arm. The window in front of him points west. All around him, in the mill's old timbers, there nest a thousand starlings. They scattered when he first climbed up. Now, an hour later, they have returned to their home. A rifle stretches from the young man's hand. His clothes are tied into a bundle near his feet.

'There is a bar of soap in the bundle, too, and a rough cotton towel. By his left shoulder sits a box of sweets. (You know what sweets are, my dears? Oh, I think you do!) You see, our prince, he is expecting to show, that morning. Not much – he pops a sweet in his mouth just as he thinks it – but a little. Shooting horses, it's a different business than dropping a deer. Especially when they are in harness: dressed for work. His fingers are moist on his gun.

'It is a long wait. Time for a thousand thoughts. He smokes a cig-arette. To settle himself. To get in the mood. Cigarettes and sweets: he's been indulging himself of late. It's changing him, little by little, on the inside. It's as though his skin has become a soft cocoon. A new self, straining against it, denting it, stretching it taut. It is a pro-cess not without pain.

'Soon the worry grows in him. That he's not up to it. That his hackles lie flat and his spirit is cowed. That he will fail, will miss his shot, be humiliated. A fortune in cigarette butts, stubbed out on the mill floor: and yet he can find no edge, no fire in him, feels like a match that will not catch. His teeth are aching with the sweets. He gets up, reaches for his bundle. He fetches his mask.

'It's a new toy, this. Borrowed rather than stolen; paid for, if you want to be petty about it, by his grandfather's coin. It's like the cig-arettes, he has been told, but also different. He has yet to try it out. It is, he understands, a simple chemical reaction. You fill up a tin-like container, then screw it onto the front of the respirator. And then, when you are ready, you inject it with a syringe. The science behind it, well now, that's a well-guarded secret. The basis for his family's wealth. But none of this matters to our friend. He lies, naked, a rubber mask over his head. Gooseflesh on his back and buttocks; sweat beading on the inside of the mask.

'He waits until they come into sight. A team of four, dragging a four-wheeled coach: slow on the muddy road. Two horses, they agreed, he and his man; when the coach stops. An easy target, with a gun of this precision. The telescope sits awkward against the goggles of the mask. As for our friend: he's scared, the coward. Liquid bubbling through his bowels like he's eaten rotten meat. It's all he can do to press down on the syringe.

'Now all he has to do is breathe, and drown.

'In the first moment, all he feels is panic. It should be like cigarettes, the best and the strongest, dark as tar; just the same, only more so, a new kind of kick.

'But what he inhales is not like cigarettes at all, is overwhelming in its purity, wilful and alive. Dying men's sins: handpicked and distilled. His own rise feebly to their summons, childhood pranks called to muster before Satan. The sweets in his mouth have long turned into lumps of coal.

'Their plan is simple. It's a bad plan, really; hastily drawn up and lacking in logic, but a plan all the same. He is to aim for the front two horses. His man on the box will cut them loose; turn the coach with the remaining two; flog them half to death as he races them home while more shots are fired at the fleeing coach. An investigation will follow, a curfew, a national hunt. All this, just to convince two schoolboys to stay put. You have heard of unwelcome guests. Well, these guests are very welcome indeed. One will not hear of their going home.

'The first bullet passes clean through the horse. It is so simple. Our young man pulls the trigger *here*, and over *there* a ribbon of red flies through the air. The shot is bad, a full yard low, shatters the shin and sends a shudder through the horse's torso, so present in the crosshairs, he could reach out his hand and feel the dance of muscles underneath the fur.

'He pauses for a moment, looks up. All around him the air is alive with the flight of birds. A thousand wings beat patterns into his rising Smoke. Little vortexes forming; sculptures of shadow, writ on the air. A moment, that's all: the double thud of his heart. Then he takes aim at the second horse and shoots it through the neck.

'There: he has done it. The horses are down, his mission is completed. But already he's pushed back the bolt, put another bullet in the rifle's chamber. He is not himself, you see. He is wearing a new face.

'The telescopic sight finds the coachman. He is the young man's servant, his confidant, his surrogate father. It may be said that the young man loves him. And yet the word beats in his ears. *Father.* How close have they been; how many years has the older man protected him; how many times has he offered him comfort, how many tears wiped away?

'How many humiliations has he witnessed?

'*Father.* A poor surrogate this: stupid, coarse, clumsy like a fool. A caricature bought to mock him; kept in service as an admonition, as a joke. The thought thickens the Smoke in his mask, flavours it with childhood. Our friend's an orphan, you see, or something very like. His parents were a picture framed on the table by his boyhood bed. "This one's a snake," his grandfather explained, "and that one was a sissy. It's a wonder he sired you at all." No goodnight kisses, just the heavy touch of the old man's hand. A boy not bred for weakness. Crosshairs drawn on his father's chest. A curl of the finger. The smoke of the gun swallowed by the billows of his personal pyre.

'Parricide. You might think it'd be enough, the wages paid, the mask satisfied. But the lad has already worked the bolt. He sights another target; a young man standing in the open door of the coach. The telescope brings him ever so close. Fun-house mirror: like a twin born to different loins. Gawking, not yet in fear; the mouth an arching O. Three shots. The third one hits him, right in the head. The whiplash of impact. By rights he should be dead.

'Then the coach tilts and is swallowed by a hole. Our prince does not understand it, thinks the earth has opened for his prey. Birds in the sky. The chamber empty; the hammer falling useless; fingers too Soot-slick to reload.

'By now the mask owns him, has grown into his skin. It is also suffocating him. It's in his struggle for air that he manages to rip it off. Dry heaves and tears: the wind has turned, his own Smoke is stinging in his eyes. On the floor, the barrel of his rifle trips up his feet.

'How does he get down? It might be said that he's gone mad. Only a madman would risk the windmill's ladder while his body is shivering with cold and shock; would walk the hundred yards clothed only in a coat of Soot; would crouch, naked, over the broken body of his man and christen it, gape-mouthed, with his snot. Our friend loses his balance when he tries to blow his nose; he falls in the dirt, face-up, and watches starlings dance dark clouds into the sky.

'The coach, meanwhile, lies at the bottom of a steep ravine. He looks down at it, sees a threesome of figures disappear into the woods. They may have seen him, recognised him. Hence he must follow. But how? He is naked and dirty and left his horse in the stable so no one knows he ever left. Something else holds him back, a discovery. He finds that, without the mask, he is once again a schoolboy, a coward. There's a creek on the way home where he washes his hands, his neck and face with soap of lavender and lye. Only then does he step into his clothes, the Soot so thick on his thighs and knees that it chafes raw his skin on the three-mile jog home. He slips inside through a back gate and then makes sure he is seen to emerge from his room late-morning, his usual time. Kippers for breakfast, and a potful of strong tea.

'Do you know something? Tea tastes better, the thinner the cup. The china is so fine in this house, if you hold it up into the light it shines right through. And so she finds him, distracted, his empty cup raised into the morning sun: a servant girl, replenishing the toast.

'"Is everything all right, sir?" she asks in her simple way.

'*Is everything all right?* Have you ever tried to picture the moment, my friends, when a moth first slips the confines of its pupal prison and wonders at the colour of its new-grown wings? Sitting wet and sticky in the wind, waiting to take flight. I imagine it is terrified at first. It is only later that it begins to see itself reborn.

'"Never better," I say, and surprise the girl with the shy twitch of a smile.'

Φ

And so it passes, our evening, the jug making its rounds, the liquor churning in me till I get up and vomit half-cooked rabbit. They tell me about leaving Ireland. The father who gambled; the sister they buried; the Englishman who cheated them out of shop and land. Talk is like Smoke, I discover: once in the air, it breeds with abandon. I tell them many things. My plans and secrets; my life and dreams. I talk and talk.

It does me the world of good.

Φ

221

I wake before them, with the first hazy light. I have heard about the price of consuming alcohol, but my head is clear and my blood oddly eager, embracing its fate. I do not get dressed at once. The two Irishmen made no attempt to rob me: Nótt kept watch. Besides, we are friends now. Daniel and Stephen. From Donegal.

The knife cuts Daniel's throat like butter. The blood spurts up, onto the mask: smears against the eyeglass, seeing red. What's in my lungs, what's rising up the insect's snout and coating my mouth, has no need for sight. It guides my hands by touch. As for the boy beneath the mask, he has no wish to see.

Stephen I beat with the barrel of my gun. He wakes on the second blow and is dead on the third. Pale green eyes; the eyelashes sticky with sleep.

I leave them with ten silver guineas. The rifle I also leave behind, slip it loosely into Daniel's hands so that his fingers rest on the silver butt he so admired. Two dead Irishmen with money in their pockets and a foreign gun. Show me a magistrate in England who can't close an inquest based on evidence as good as this.

By the time dawn proper breaks I am two miles west. Snow is coming down in thick, wet flakes. It will be rough going today. There is not a soul to be seen. It is mid-morning by the time I realise I am still wearing the mask. Its buckles are stiff under my frozen fingers.

'Abomination,' I rage as I wrestle to take it off. 'Freak, monster, elephant man.'

Soon it will own me, body and soul.

Perhaps Mother would help me. I could still turn around.

But there is no time.

Charlie Cooper is spreading stories about me down the road.

Questions and Answers

When Charlie wakes the room is flooded with daylight. He senses rather than sees it, has trouble opening his eyes. His body does not follow orders, lies leaden under the down bedding, a stranger to his will. He mutters in surprise and finds his tongue sitting dry and heavy in his mouth, so swollen he has to breathe around it. No sound will come. As he struggles against his eyelids' weight, a soothing voice sounds close by.

'Easy now, Mr Cooper, take your time. There was a sleeping draught in the milk. You were in need of rest. Here, I will help you sit up.'

The dark shadow of Renfrew bends over him, slips a second pillow behind Charlie's back, then sits down again on the stool he has drawn up to Charlie's bedside.

'There, that's better.'

Renfrew reaches forward with a washcloth and wets Charlie's lips.

'You must be quite parched. It is one of the draught's side effects.'

Embarrassed at being the subject of such mothering, Charlie once again attempts to shake off his drowsiness or at any rate take charge of his limbs. It is then he realises his wrists are manacled to the bed frame with leather restraints. A vision of Baron Naylor shoots through him, strapped onto his bed, smoking darkly in the attic. It helps in its way.

Fear bids Charlie wake.

'Ah, I think you are coming round now. Very good. I was starting to be afraid I had given you too much. It's gone ten o'clock. Not that it would have been a day for travelling. The snow has been coming down thick and fast. I imagine the road is quite impassable.'

Renfrew places a hand onto Charlie's forehead, checking his temperature, then slips a finger between Charlie's wrists and the restraints, making sure they are not cutting into Charlie's skin. The finger lingers a moment, takes Charlie's pulse. Throughout, Renfrew's movements are unhurried, efficient. He would have made a

223

good doctor, or better yet, a surgeon, excising rotten flesh with a steady hand. His task accomplished, Renfrew straightens, smoothes his necktie and collar, and looks Charlie straight in the eye.

'I must ask you again, Mr Cooper, to relate to me all the events that led to your being attacked in a coach heading from Lady Naylor's estate on the morning after New Year's Day, and all events that have transpired since. We need a full accounting. It is, I'm afraid, a matter of national significance.'

Charlie attempts to answer, but his tongue is not working.

'Water,' he croaks, 'water.'

Renfrew sadly shakes his head.

'Let us talk first, Mr Cooper. Here, I will moisten your lips again. It might be small consolation, but I drank a measure of salt water this morning and have not taken anything since. There, on the windowsill: I have poured us two glasses. Let us drink together, Mr Cooper, and quench this infernal thirst. Once we have finished our conversation. What do you say?'

But Charlie can only stare at him and struggle against the restraints.

'You've gone mad,' he manages at last, his mouth so raw it comes out as a whisper.

'If you need to perform your ablutions,' Renfrew answers stiffly, 'I can offer a bedpan for your use.'

Φ

The hours creep past. The room's window looks directly south and Charlie can track the journey of the sun. The window itself is frozen solid, and the sun a matt disk of orange that is being pulled across its frosted pane. Renfrew is sitting two feet from him, a pen in his hand and a lacquered lap desk perched on his knees. He has explained it all very patiently.

'Please don't think I intend to hide my actions. I even considered informing Mr Trout this morning, but his political allegiances are somewhat unclear. It would be easy to use this situation to discredit my party. Unconscionable, of course, but very easy indeed. The facts of the matter are these. The baron is planning something – or, if the rumours are true and he has gone mad, his wife is. There is some evidence of their purchasing laboratory equipment from abroad. Don't misunderstand me. I am a scientist myself and regard the embargo as a folly beyond measure. The old order is moribund. Under the masquerade of virtue it is trying to stop the march of science – of truth! – simply to protect its own interests and prolong its life. All the same a change is coming, a mighty change, one can smell it on the wind these days. But here is the thing, Mr Cooper. This change – this revolution – it can take many forms. We can have order, or we can have chaos. I – my party, the men concerned for the moral future of the realm – we need to know whether to protect Baron and Baroness Naylor and their projects, or to stop them.

'Did you know that there was a motion not long ago to have the Naylor estate placed under surveillance? Not in Parliament, of course, but in one of the parliamentary committees, the ones that dare to think outside the conventional norms. It was debated very seriously. The trouble is, we are lacking in an executive. A police force. It is said England has secret government agents, but if so, who do they work for? Who gives the orders? Oh no, Mr Cooper! If we want virtue, it will take ordinary good men to step up and make the business of the country their own. Whatever the risk.

'Don't imagine then that I will not take full responsibility for my actions, Mr Cooper. Here, I am writing a report even as we speak. I will send it with the evening mail, along with your statement. Oh, I know, you think what I am doing is a great crime. No doubt your parents will insist on my dismissal once they learn that I have detained you. They may even press criminal charges.'

He pauses, closes his eyes, opens them again. His gaze is serene.

'The Smoke would warn me, Mr Cooper. If I was doing wrong.'

A curl of grey drifts out of Charlie in response. Renfrew takes no notice. Instead, he takes hold of Charlie's hand, helpless in its restraint, and speaks quietly at him in tender appeal.

'I was never a utilitarian, Charlie, but for the first time I feel the force of Mr Bentham's argument. The happiness of the many outweighs the happiness of the few. Who are we to spare ourselves when a million souls are at stake?

'But enough of this sulking, Mr Cooper. It is time for you to speak. I have always known you for a boy who has a good heart. Or have your father's interests poisoned you?'

And Charlie looks past him, watching the slow movement of the sun across the frost-bound pane, like the fog lamp of a distant ship. In front of it stand the water jug and two filled glasses, alight with its glow.

As the day wears on, Charlie finds it increasingly difficult to take his eyes off the water. It stands four feet from the foot of the bed. The more Charlie stares at it, the more details he sees. The two glasses are filled to precisely the same level. One has a chink in the glass that refracts the light across the water's surface and adds texture to its shadow. The laws of optics bend the window cross directly behind: at times it is the glasses that appear flat and the window behind that bulges with volume. When Charlie struggles hard enough against his manacles to agitate the whole of the bed, the old floorboards pass on the movement to wall and windowsill and conjure a ripple: trembling water; a speck of dust suspended in the left glass sent dancing until it glues itself to the inner wall and adds its shadow to the pattern. Charlie swallows past his drug-thickened tongue, hunts his mouth for spit, finds Soot sown like grit amongst his gums, and realises he must have been smoking. When he glances over at Renfrew, he catches him, too, eyeing the water with the intensity of longing. The schoolmaster rises abruptly, walks in stiff long strides to the window and lifts one glass up to his eyes.

'The human organism can live without water for four or five days. Longer, perhaps, in our humid climate. And yet, it isn't dusk yet, and we are both struggling with our fast. Ah, the flesh is weak.' He chuckles softly and replaces the glass in precisely the same position. 'A good lesson, this.'

When he bends over Charlie to look him in the eye, his breath is sour with his thirst.

'Will you tell me what I need to know, Mr Cooper? For the good of the realm?'

'No,' says Charlie, his dry lips hurting with the word.

'Then we must continue to suffer, in our modest little way.'

Renfrew leaves him. For a moment Charlie has a vision of him, sitting in his kitchen, downing pint after pint of fresh water. But at once he knows this is not true. Renfrew is a man of his word. It's what makes him so terrifying.

Soon Charlie can hear the scrape of a spade against stone. The schoolmaster is clearing a path from door to fence. Charlie pictures him working with brisk, efficient movements, a scarf knotted high, unfurling his long, gaunt shadow away from the dipping sun. It will be dark before long.

As the room grows gloomy and while the spade is still separating snow from stone in long, scraping shovelfuls, Eleanor steps into the doorway. She does not enter but stands with her feet level with the threshold and leans in her head. Her harness gives an odd bulk to her shoulders, as of a knight in armour. A wind-up knight, a round little key sticking out of her chest. It is easy to believe that, in the depths past her sternum, this key connects to a complex clockwork mechanism of interlocking wheels, weights and lead bearings; that the whole spare body of hers is a machine. Her face, however, is pure little girl, flushed and shy. Charlie smiles at her. She recoils as though stung, pulls her nose back past the invisible line marked by the tips of her toes.

A minute or two later, however, her head and upper chest once again invade the room. This time, Charlie's smile does not immediately chase her away.

'Hullo, Eleanor,' he whispers.

She mouths rather than speaks her response.

'Hullo, Charlie.'

His name sits prettily on her childish lips.

'Did your uncle tell you that you are not to enter the room?'

She nods, gravely, checks the line of her toes. They have not passed the threshold.

'What else did he say?'

'I must not speak to you.'

As she says it she mechanically reaches for the little brass wheel sticking out of her harness and gives it a crank. A shudder follows, a spasm of the cheek.

'I see. I am sorry. The truth is, I need help. Do you want to help me, Eleanor?'

The girl does not respond but holds herself very rigid, as though afraid that any motion may betray her wish. Charlie, meanwhile, struggles to keep his thirst out of his voice; each word dry and graceless as it falls from his parched lips.

'I'm afraid if you do want to help me, you will have to disobey your uncle. I wish there was another way.'

Again Eleanor does not respond in words but simply looks at him with clear, honest eyes. He does not rush her but simply returns her gaze. When he starts chewing on his lip in nervous need, he finds her mirroring the movement, her incisors forming bunny teeth across the pink of her chin. He screws shut one eye and finds a girlish eye screwed shut in response; slips out the end of his swollen tongue and is graced with a flash of Eleanor's rose tip, rolling itself into a graceful little straw. He laughs then, and she laughs with him. The next instant she stops, jumps back in sudden terror and runs away, down the corridor and the cottage's naked flight of stairs, a clatter of tiny feet.

It is only when she reaches the silence of the carpet below that Charlie realises the scraping of the spade has ceased.

Φ

Renfrew returns. He appears to be thoughtful, walks to the window, stares out into the gloom. It is almost dark now, though the snow retains a pallid glow and sends it up into his stern and thoughtful face.

'I saw a rider. Out by the school gates.' He turns to Charlie. 'Someone to see Headmaster Trout, perhaps. But he did not enter the premises. Or is it someone looking for you, I wonder? A man with a dog.'

'Julius.'

Charlie mouths the name rather than saying it. All the same, Renfrew reads it off his lips.

'Mr Spencer? Yes, I suppose it could have been him.' He scratches his chin. His fingers remain encased in gloves: a black hand in a white-blond beard. 'Did you know he is Lady Naylor's son from a previous marriage? Yes, I imagine she will have told you. A most unhappy association. I must confess I have my suspicions about the boy. His serenity feels *artificial*. Have you heard about *sweets*? They absorb Smoke at the moment of its genesis.' He frowns. 'They will need to be banned entirely. Their present proliferation, even beyond the nobility – it is like building the kingdom of heaven out of cardboard.'

Renfrew steps over to the bed, slips his hands out of the gloves, folds them neatly on the bedside table. Charlie flinches when his teacher sits down at his bedside, but it is only to better see him. Renfrew has yet to light a candle. His face, in the failing light, is grave and marked by earnest concern. He might be sitting at Charlie's sickbed, exhausted from the long hours of his vigil. Involuntarily, Charlie feels a pang of sympathy rise in him. Renfrew is following the commands of his conscience. It gives him no joy.

'I must ask you again, Mr Cooper,' he says now, his own voice strained by thirst, 'to pass on the information so vital for the future of our polity.

'Please, Charlie,' he adds, as gently as his dry tongue will allow, 'put an end to this silly game.'

Charlie considers it. It is difficult to say whether his words would result in harm or in good. But he gave a promise. Not just to Lady Naylor but to Thomas. To Livia.

'I can't.'

Renfrew nods.

'You do not lack in courage.'

He slips a hand into his coat pocket, pulls out a flask followed by what looks like a short, wide belt with a stiff piece of tubing sewn into its leather front.

'Don't struggle now.'

With utmost calm, Renfrew takes Charlie's jaw into a vicelike grip and slips the belt around his head, forcing the tubing between his lips and teeth. Charlie kicks, screams, gags on the tubing; feels a buckle dig into the back of his skull. Beyond Renfrew's shoulder he becomes aware of Eleanor's figure standing in the doorway. He wants to make eye contact, tell her not to be afraid, but all he can see is her feet, agitated, rubbing heel on heel. Charlie ceases in his struggles. They are hopeless, and he does not want the child to endure the sight.

'There,' Renfrew says, 'that's better.'

He unscrews the flask, upends the cap, and uses it as a measure.

'Don't choke, Charlie. You have to swallow. All it is is salt water. Keep it down, though. If you vomit, you will suffocate.'

Without the slightest hesitation the Master of Smoke and Ethics pours a measure of liquid down the tubing. An instant later it is in Charlie's mouth, his whole body rebelling against the shock of salt, stomach heaving, dank brown Smoke drifting from his lips.

Renfrew removes the gag, disperses the Smoke with the back of his hand, then pours out another measure and quickly drinks it himself, sealing his lips against the spasm of his gag. They stare at one another, teacher and pupil, each mirroring the desperation of the other's thirst. Beyond his shoulder, Charlie is dimly aware of soundless movement. Eleanor has slipped away.

At last Renfrew rises from the bed and walks over to the water jug and glasses. He picks up the glasses and carries them over to the bedside table. The water quivers as he sets it down.

'Perhaps,' Renfrew croaks, speaking against the rawness of his mouth, 'perhaps I have not explained myself sufficiently. Baron Naylor and I, we were once like father and son. We made a pact, long ago, to change the world. But he won't see me any more and does not answer my letters. I am fighting for change, Charlie, for virtue. All I need to know is that the Naylors are doing the same.'

Charlie stares up at his tormentor.

'I don't know,' he whispers.

'Tell me everything,' Renfrew answers, 'and we will work it out together.' And then, mournfully, his cracked lips twitching with a hint of bitterness: 'Why won't you trust me, Charlie?

'Help me,' Renfrew pleads. 'Help me, Charlie, to breed out sin.'

Φ

There is a knock at the front door, loud and insistent, three sharp raps that echo through the house. Charlie is grateful to these raps: they save him from the need to answer. It is quite dark now but for the few rays of light that creep up the stairwell from the downstairs lamp. The room's floorboards, too, prove porous and are outlined by the faint glow of their cracks.

When a second set of raps rings through the house, Renfrew rises, straightens his jacket, then turns back before he has reached the door. In the dark Charlie cannot see what he is doing until he feels the smooth circle of the tubing force itself back into his mouth. He is too exhausted to struggle.

'It is better,' Renfrew says quietly, 'if your presence here remains a secret until we have finished our conversation. I will see who it is.'

A third set of raps hurries him out. The staircase groans under his quick step. A moment later he can be heard opening the door. The floor is so little insulated, each sound carries up with total clarity. It is as though Renfrew and his guest were standing in the darkness, at the far end of the room.

'Mr Spencer! This is a surprise. What brings you here, my boy?'

If Renfrew's voice is polite though strained, the voice that answers is rich with the practised insolence of master talking to servant. Even behind his gag, salt burning in every cranny of his gums, Charlie flinches at the tone.

'Master Renfrew! What a perfectly charming cottage this is. Cosy. But won't you ask me in?'

'If you wish.'

'Oh, I do!'

Two sets of steps, and a dog's hard-clawed paws: they pass under Charlie's bed and walk on to the living room, on the other side of the house. From there the voices carry more dully. It's Julius who does most of the talking.

'Ah, that's better. Build up the fire, won't you, Master Renfrew? The roads have been filthy today, and I am soaked to the bone. And help me out of these boots, if you will.' A moment later he adds: 'Tell me, master, is there anybody else in the house? A visitor perhaps?'

Renfrew does something unprecedented then.

He lies.

'No. I am by myself. What brings you here, Mr Spencer? I must confess it is not the most convenient of times.'

Julius sees fit to ignore the question.

'I heard you were living with your niece.'

'Yes. She is spending the holidays with her grandparents, in Herefordshire. I assure you we have the cottage to ourselves.'

'No servants, eh? Not even a valet. How awfully squalid. But never mind, it suits us, doesn't it, this tête-à-tête? Here is the thing, Master Renfrew. I want to talk about Charlie Cooper. He came to you last night. A groundsman saw a "beggar" walk up to your door. I happen to know that beggar was no such thing. Did he rush off right away or did he spend the night?'

'He left at dawn.'

The voice is confident, unhesitating, impossible to doubt. At the same time Renfrew is speaking loudly, making sure his voice will carry through the floorboards. Charlie wonders what it is about Julius's appearance that has made such a liar out of the schoolmaster.

'But tell me, what is all this about, Mr Spencer? Julius. You are most unlike yourself!'

'Am I? Well, all it is, I ran out of sweets. Ah, watch you blush with indignation! My family holds the monopoly now. We *make* the bloody things. Did you really think I would be ignorant of my own affairs?'

'By rights you should be! You are a minor.'

'I am nineteen next month and my grandfather's sole heir. He's been ailing of late, a growth in his bowels. He won't see the spring. I think you will see me take my role as head of the household sooner rather than later.'

There is a pause into which Renfrew interjects something inaudible, the tone low and warning. Julius's voice, by contrast, is rich with the volume of his arrogance.

'I believe you are mistaking the situation, Master Renfrew. I am not here as a schoolboy who can be ordered about. I need to know what Cooper has told you; what he has *seen*. And where he is headed.

'Have I introduced you to Nótt, Master Renfrew? Isn't she a beauty? She is out of sorts, I'm afraid. Grouchy. Hasn't eaten a bite since yesterday. Look at her sniffing around. It's Cooper's stink, she's been primed to it. There, it must be on you, too. Hold still, will you? I'd hate for there to be an accident.

'Ah, Master Renfrew, don't clamp up now. You don't look well, if you don't mind my saying. All dried up somehow. And don't worry about your shirt – what of it, a bit of drool amongst friends, it'll wash out. She has a good nose, though. I bet you she can smell what you had for lunch, all the way through your skin and your intestines. Meat pie, was it? Or perhaps something more frugal. Porridge? God, you really are the most disgusting prude.

'Cooper, Master Renfrew. Charlie Cooper. What did he tell you, and whom have *you* told? I warn you. I am not myself these days. Look here, I have acquired a second face. I swear just now, as I was coming in, I could not remember whether I was wearing it or not.

'You see, Master Renfrew, I find myself at a threshold. No longer one thing, nor yet another. A door has been opened in me, a hole, an abyss. It scared me at first, but I have been sneaking up to its ledge, taking peeks. And what horror, what wonder waits in its depth!

'But all the same I am afraid, Master Renfrew. Afraid of what lies in wait. Help me tonight. Help me remain myself. For another hour, another day. Of all your grim-faced talk of charity, this might prove your one good deed.'

As Charlie lies there, listening to Julius's words, it is as though they surround him, standing in the darkness, not a yard away: *here*,

232

the great bulk of the dog, its snout pressed into the schoolmaster's waistcoat, a wet spot spreading from button to pocket; *there*, the head boy, first sprawling insolently in the armchair, then leaping up to march his strange disquiet back and forth between fireplace and door. And, superimposed on this scene, Charlie sees once again the tall, rigid form of his teacher, bending down over him, feeding him salt water.

Talk to me.

Help me.

Why won't you trust me?

The hole in the gag affords Charlie but a spoonful of air with every breath. He lies in darkness and breathes hard through the nose.

Φ

There is a change of light. The room is so dark now that its only features are the window, the door, the subtle leakage of the floor. Even so, Charlie's senses register the change long before he can actually see her, standing by the side of the bed. Eleanor. The only part of her that has any colour is one eye, the right, which catches the night glow from the window and soaks it up into its green-and-white. She is not looking at him but into the distance. It comes to Charlie that she, too, is listening, straining to understand what is happening beneath their feet. A moment later, her hand slips into his. It happens very naturally, she simply moves forward, and searches the bedding for his palm. Manacled as he is, all Charlie can do is squeeze Eleanor's fingers with his own. The girl does not respond.

Again the voice draws them into its spell, softer now, oddly suspended between heckling and wheedling as though two voices were speaking in unison, their timbres matching but their moods at odds.

'I know what you are thinking, Master Renfrew. "This cannot be happening." Or: "I will report him to my friends in New Westminster. We shall put him on trial." I can just see it! A week of debating the principles of liberalism. And then you put a rope around my neck. From reason, naturally, with regret. You might not even show. Do you know, Master Renfrew, that I have lain awake many a night, there in my dormitory bed, wondering what it would take to get you to smoke?

'But talk, Master Renfrew, talk, I beg you. If you keep to your silence, I must don this mask. We will both smoke then. Is that how it must be? You, my Judas, my Gethsemane? Oh, I love a metaphor these days. It's the Smoke, speaking in pictures. Look at you frown! I bet you've never used a good metaphor in all your life.

'Please, Master Renfrew! You mustn't be shy. I am your husband, you are my bride. There can be no secrets between us tonight. Tell me about Charlie Cooper. Tell me what he told you. Tell me your dreams and fears. Please, Master Renfrew, tell me.

'Tell me, or I must set fire to our souls.'

Eleanor starts shaking. Charlie feels it between his fingers first, then sees the whole of her bulky shadow, quivering in the darkness above him. At the same time, there begin to issue from her little hiccups of Smoke, one by one, clouding her teeth at every breath. And each time a pellet of Smoke breaks free from her, he can hear rather than see her free hand reaching for her harness, turning the screw upon her chest. After five such turns she staggers. She might squeeze herself to death.

Charlie tugs at her hand.

'Don't,' he attempts to say, 'don't,' through the gag of his mouth, his own smoke shooting through the little pipe in a narrow concentrated jet. A second later he can no longer see her.

It is then he realises he has begun to cry.

'You must free me,' he shouts into his gag, 'we have to run away,' and all that comes out is the sound of a man chewing his own tongue.

The girl by his side gives her screw another turn.

Φ

She undoes the manacles. He is not sure how she has come by the decision, or what it is he might have done to sway her, but all of a sudden, without any announcement or change in her aspect, she bends down to his wrists and works open the restraints, her little hands moving with the dexterity of one familiar with the interaction of buckle and strap. When he is free and has ripped out the feeding tube, the first thing he does is hug her, draw her little body tight into his own, so that the brass wheel of her harness digs itself into his chest and bruises him. She is still smoking and crying, is limp in his arms, soundless, her lips clamped shut against her sin, the Smoke seeping straight from her skin now, from her throat and cheeks and eyeballs, dying her black.

The second thing Charlie does (holding on to the girl, her

stockinged legs dangling freely at his waist) is reach for the water glass and drink. His stomach heaves when the water hits it, but he keeps it down, and a voice drifts through the floor, manic and needling, 'Tell me, God damn you, tell me!' answered by a silence more chilling than a scream.

He must get her out of the house. This is all Charlie knows. He must get Eleanor out of the house and do so quickly, while Julius is distracted and his dog focused on another task. The window opens easily enough in the room that was his prison, but beneath lies an eight-foot drop onto a ground bumpy with flower pots that he cannot risk, not with the girl clinging to him, fighting for breath against the grip of the harness and her fear. Snow enters the room before he can shut the window again, carried on a gust, along with the cold of the air.

He turns, walks quietly, his whole body stiff from lying still all day, out into the hallway and the room across. The light shining up from underneath is brighter here, and Charlie makes sure his feet do not stray from the dark squares of two rugs. Renfrew's bedroom is spartan, holds a bed, a wardrobe, a washbasin and little else. The living room is close under their feet. The sounds that issue from there have moved into a realm beyond speech. They mingle with the blood pounding in his ears. Charlie tiptoes and times his steps to his heartbeat; to the moans of a man in pain and the low growl of a dog. A snowflake has caught in Eleanor's eyelash, melts as Charlie's breath fans across her face.

The window is veiled in frost, disclosing nothing, but when he lifts it, carefully, quietly, it opens up over the flat roof of a shed cushioned with a foot of snow. He slides the child out first, dives after her. They swim to the edge of the roof, spilling snow. The cold is intense on his face, the roof's edge draped in ice: it drops them onto a mound of snow at its back. From there they reach the back fence and a row of trees. Two steps bring them around the corner of the house, where a window stands brightly lit, the curtain open. Through the frost-thickened pane little can be seen other than a bit of wall across, the movement of a shadow at its utmost edge; the glow of the fire split into four tidy rectangles by the window's wooden cross. Then it is as though someone has dumped ink into a water tank: the dark swirl of a viscous cloud takes possession of the room, drowning out the light and covering the pane until it appears to be dripping with darkness.

The sound that accompanies the cloud serves to drown Eleanor's shriek: a single protracted note so shrill it sounds as though it has been cut from Renfrew's lungs.

Before Eleanor can shriek again, Charlie has picked her up and fights his way through trees.

Φ

Perhaps he should go and find Trout. But Charlie's wrists are sore from being tied, and his throat still raw from thirst. He won't risk his freedom again, won't trust another grown man's judgement about what is right and wrong. And yet the little girl needs shelter, and her uncle needs help; the world a warning about a monster walking in its midst.

The porter's lodge has a hut attached to it, too squalid to be called a cottage. It is tucked away at its back, out of view from student eyes, behind a thorn hedge four feet deep. Inside – his feet nearly in the fire, a kettle hanging from a chain by his side, his head tied into a rough scarf against the draft – sits Cruikshank, the porter. He has not drawn the curtain and sheltered as it is by the hedge, his hut's window remains clear: one can see his dirty bed and the stacks of dishes by his sink; the crumbling dart board that hangs on one wall next to a shard of black slate that lets you mark the score. They draw close enough to touch the window and study the knotty little figure of the man, immersed in darning his socks. Charlie tries to put Eleanor down, but the girl is clinging to him awkwardly, her harness pressing into his face. Her breathing continues to be laboured. He has tugged at the contraption but has been unable to get it off.

'Go and knock on the door, Eleanor,' Charlie whispers to the little girl. 'That there is Mr Cruikshank. You must tell him who you are and that your uncle needs help. Tell him Spencer has gone mad. It's very important that you remember. Julius Spencer. Tell him to tell the headmaster, and to fetch a club or a knife. Can you remember all that?'

But the girl won't answer and just keeps clinging to him, each breath a struggle, her lips blue with cold and fear. He wrests her hands free, puts her down gently, walks with her to the door.

Again Charlie tries to tell her that she must knock and talk to Cruikshank, that he cannot go with her. Again she huddles back into his chest, buries her face there, shivers.

'Go on,' Charlie pleads with her. 'Please. I beg you.'

She says something in response. To catch it, he has to put his ear to her lips, so close he can feel her breath against its skin.

'I'm bad,' she says. 'I'm bad. That's why the devil came to our house.'

Her hand reaches for the wheel on her chest. Charlie has to force it away.

'You are the best little girl I have ever met,' says Charlie.

Then he slips off his belt, loops it quickly through her harness and ties her to the door knob before knocking hard against its wood. The girl starts crying as he stumbles away through the bushes, but she does not shout. She may not have the breath to do it.

Φ

Charlie lingers on the far side of the hedge for far too long, lying flat against its base, hiding in the dark. Julius might have left Renfrew's cottage by now. He might have seen their tracks (how much has it snowed?) or gone upstairs and realised someone was staying there. His dog might have taken Charlie's scent. It is madness to linger. He needs to run, lose himself in the snowstorm. Go to London to report to his friends.

What Charlie does do is lie flat on the ground, count the minutes. Crawl back through the bushes, back to the window. Raise his head above the window ledge and take a peek.

Eleanor is sitting on a chair, tears rolling down her cheeks, her skin glowing red from the cold. Other than the sobs that rack her frame, she is not moving at all. Her hands are wrapped around a mug of tea, demurely, in an attitude oddly like prayer. By her side, crouching and hence shorter than her by half a head, is Cruikshank, holding a big pair of scissors and moving them about her torso like a bird picking berries from a thorny shrub. Each sharp little snip cuts a leather belt on Eleanor's harness. When one side gapes open like a burst valise, the knotty old porter moves around to the other side, facing the window. Charlie is not quick enough to duck and for a full second they stare at each other while the girl sits unmoving, warming her hands on the hot tea.

Then Cruikshank looks away and resumes his labours, and Charlie turns to run into the frozen night.

Headmaster

There is something objectionable about Swinburne. It goes beyond his overbearing boorishness; the wheeze of his voice; his massive, hulking, clumsy body, so much like a dead man's brought back to life. I think it is his eyes, small, too-round eyes, tucked piglike under too many wrinkles. They are fixed on me now, studying me past the rim of the teacup he has lifted to his lips and then forgotten. His thoughts are easy to surmise. He is wondering why I asked him up here, at an unconventional hour, too hard on supper to call for tea. Other questions are churning in him, close to the surface. In the end he cannot help himself: it spills out without subtlety, the thing that bothers him most. It never ceases to surprise one how much like a schoolboy this old man really is, underneath the fire-and-brimstone bluster: a schoolboy in a cassock and with a licence to spank. It is little wonder the pupils fear him so.

'It is impossible,' he says. 'Out of the question. Absurd.'

I make him wait until I have dunked, bitten off, and chewed my mince pie, brushed crumbs from my lips and chin. The regret in my voice is sweetened by cinnamon and sugar.

'Cruishank tells me the girl spoke the name quite distinctly, and repeated it twice. There cannot be any mistake.'

'Then she is lying!' Swinburne scowls, looks around the room, then at the door that leads to my bedroom. 'Is she here?'

'Yes. Sleeping. The poor thing is exhausted. We mustn't wake her up.'

'Is it true she does not smoke?'

'Oh, she smokes a little. But no more than our sixteen-year-olds. Less than some. It is really quite remarkable. Renfrew ought to be congratulated.'

'Then you do believe her.'

I am amused to see how crushed Swinburne is by this notion: that his favourite pupil should be thought of as a killer. It would be touching if his concern wasn't born entirely of vanity.

'It really does not matter what I believe. Young Spencer has been named, so he will need to be found and questioned. But there is a larger point to this. Julius is Lady Naylor's son. He was staying with her when Argyle and Cooper were abducted. It gives the government an excuse to place Lady Naylor under investigation. And her husband, the baron. Officials will be arriving at their house this very night, with a warrant authorising a search.'

I pause, lean forward a little, making sure Swinburne takes note of what I am saying. The man has a thick skull. One has to be emphatic with him.

'You see, we had cause for suspicion before. A letter of Lady Naylor's was intercepted some weeks ago. She was writing on behalf of the baron, communicating with a scientist on the Continent. As it turns out you know the man in question. I understand he was one of your pupils, what, twenty, thirty years ago?'

Swinburne blanches. 'The apostate!'

I do my best not to laugh out loud at the word.

'No more than an errant sheep, surely? Should you not be trying to save him? Return him to the flock? As I understand he was a favourite of yours, once upon a time. You taught him Greek, I believe, at his special request.'

Swinburne's face is bitter with rancour. 'We should never have admitted a foreigner. He fooled me, fooled us all.' He adds, when his slow brain works its way from past to present: 'What does the baron want with him?'

'Who can say? The letter was rather cryptic. And we have not been successful in placing a spy in the Naylor household, to provide us with information by other means.'

Swinburne seems unmoved by the idea of spies infiltrating the bosom of the families that rule the land. All he wants to know is: 'How hard can it be?'

I shrug. 'They have a good butler. Attentive chap.'

'Surely you could have bribed a chambermaid.'

'We would not dream of trusting anyone quite so common.' I ignore Swinburne's wince. It is said his mother was a tanner's daughter. There are words in his vocabulary that make the other teachers blush. 'In any case, we will know more soon. The warrant was sent by special courier. The Crown is taking an interest, you see.'

At the mention of the Crown, Swinburne grows ponderous. Again it is almost comically easy to follow his train of thought.

What does fat Mr Trout have to do with the Crown?

It nearly breaks his thick little head to puzzle it out.

'Headmaster Trout,' he ventures at last, almost shyly, 'is it true that you used to be some sort of magistrate?'

'A Justice of the Peace.'

'A *witchfinder*, is what Master Barlow once told me, when he was in his cups. An *inquisitor* of crime.' He uses the words without reproach.

I laugh, pat my stomach. 'Merely a servant of the state. I was more slender then.'

I think I have done enough to ensure that Swinburne will pass on whatever information his wooden skull can retain to his patron. He has long been the Tory Party's ears within the school, just as Renfrew is the Liberals'. There is an interest, on the side of the Crown, in keeping the factions in balance.

'Now, if you will excuse me.'

'Of course, Headmaster.'

It is only now when he rises to leave that the thought occurs to Swinburne that he should have inquired about the victim of the assault, whatever his feelings about the man. It behoves him, as a Christian. Nonetheless, it comes out rather coarsely.

'Is Renfrew dead, then?'

'Not at all. On the contrary, there is hope yet that he may live, though if he does he will be much changed. The surgeon had to remove several feet of his intestines. An Oxford man, he is, one of Renfrew's party. I had him fetched.'

Swinburne frowns, wets his lips with the thick-veined tip of his tongue, lowers his voice to the whisper of insinuation.

'It's unnatural. By rights he should be dead.'

'You are a suspicious man, Swinburne. We have no reason to believe that the man used any techniques or technologies he acquired illegally. And no reason to inquire. Surely you are pleased Dr Renfrew is still with us.'

As I see the old churchman to the door, I catch a whiff of his breath. Atop the rotting smell of his dentures there sits another, cleaner smell, almost medicinal and carrying the sweetness of turpentine. My guess is that he never leaves his chambers without a sweet tucked into the pocket of his mouth. I wonder briefly how he justifies his consumption theologically. But then I realise that a man like Swinburne does not bother with justifications. Churchmen and teachers are allowed to use sweets. Other men are not.

For him, it is as simple as that.

Φ

The girl is asleep when I enter the bedroom. There are some marks on the pillow and the bed-sheet, but they are light and grey, bad dreams become manifest. It would be churlish to call them sins. Slowly, not wishing to wake her, I lower myself onto the chair next to her, and tuck the quilt back up to her chin. She mutters something, and – still asleep – her little hand comes up to her chest and performs an odd, turning movement, as if she were placing her heart into a loosely formed fist and giving it a twist. It is a disturbing gesture, made by a mind that is disturbed. One can only guess at what the girl must have witnessed.

I did not enter Renfrew's cottage until after he had been removed from the premises. Cruikshank had found him, he and the two stable hands he had roused in response to the girl's warning. He'd armed them with stout clubs, he told me, and himself with an axe. They had found the door unlocked.

All three of the men had walked through Renfrew's blood. That's the first thing I saw coming to the cottage, bloody footprints leading away from the front door, growing fainter with every step until only their heels and bootnails showed pink upon the path from cottage to school. It had been snowing through much of the night. No other prints showed in the blanket of white.

In the squalid little hallway, the same three sets of footprints were visible on the floorboards, along with a fourth, wearing narrow riding boots and attended by a large-pawed dog. Near the door to the living room, one of the stable hands had dropped his club. He had not stooped to pick it up.

Beyond this point, the prints no longer showed. Indeed, one had to squint to make out the shadow of blood upon the blackened floorboards. It was as though a great fire had raged in the room, a fire that consumed only people and left the furnishings untouched. There had been two centres to the fire: the first an armchair, whose worn leather was covered in an oily layer of Soot, a finger deep; the

241

second on the floor, two steps away, where a body had written a sickle of deepest black into the dark flooring. The blood had pooled there and mixed with the Soot; it formed a sort of treacle, stringy to the touch.

When people burn to death, their bodies fold into themselves, into the posture of unborn children: the knees tucked up to the chest, the fists raised high in front of the face like pugilists taking cover, the skin a black tissue above bone. It was tempting to ascribe this position to the man who had lain there on the floor, bleeding from an abdominal wound which, Cruikshank assures me, 'had his innerds pokin' through'. I have rarely seen him this upset.

I made, during my initial visit, only the most perfunctory search of the doctor's private papers. There were a number of incriminating manuscripts, suggesting research into illegal matters, as well as a wealth of foreign correspondence, which I made sure to take along lest they fall into the wrong hands. It was only on a second visit, some hours later, that I found, tucked inside a handsome portable desk of mahogany and rosewood, a very interesting if incomplete report pertaining to Charlie Cooper, and discovered a room upstairs whose bed frame was fitted with leather manacles at either side.

One need not have been a Justice of the Peace to string these facts together to a narrative of sorts and endow it with a plot. All the same, Cruikshank insists that the girl came to his door alone; that he looked outside and found no other tracks leading up to his home. I suppose he has a soft spot for Cooper and imagines he is doing him a favour. When we lie from sympathy, I have found, the Smoke seems fit to spare us. It is the sort of fact that keeps Swinburne up at night; runs counter to his view of things.

The girl mutters something, deep in her sleep, and summons me back from my reverie. I bend my ear down to her lips until my cheek nearly touches her nose. She makes me wait for several minutes until she speaks again, and I stand there, awkward, my fundament pushed back for balance and bending double at the waist, looking for wisdom from the mouth of babes. When it comes, the word that travels across the gap of air is fragile, foreign, unexpected.

'Asch-en-stedt.'

I wonder what it was about living with Renfrew that made her snoop around his private papers, and what it was she did to punish herself for so obvious a sin.

Φ

A noise runs through my chambers. I know at once what it is, and yet I have never heard it before, not here, in my rooms, atop the kingdom that is my school. It cuts me to the marrow. It is a noise that must not exist. There it comes again, the shrill bleating of a bell. It jerks me upright, sees me race to the door. I lock her in, the girl, just as the third ring sounds; am by the custom-built cupboard at the fourth. It takes me three more rings to find the key; insert it (how clumsy my fingers are, how sweaty my palm!), turn it and open the cupboard door. The ringing only stops when I take the receiver off the hook.

'Hullo,' I say, unsure of the procedure. 'Samuel Trout here.' And then, blustery in my confusion, whispering hoarsely into the funnel jutting out of the wooden box: 'This had better be an emergency!'

The voice that answers is so immediate, it seems to stand in the room with me. Its words pour out from the shell of the receiver straight into my ear; they have a crackle to them, as though someone were talking to you in a storm. I listen carefully, find myself nodding, before realising that it is sound that is transmitted, not motion.

When I replace the receiver, I lock the cupboard very carefully, place the key in my pocketbook, and change into my travelling clothes. Half an hour later sees me leave the school in our fastest trap. In my carpetbag, clutched against the soft of my chest, are thirty pounds sterling, two changes of undergarments, my razor, my hairbrush, ten illegal cigarettes and a box of sweets.

The Colt I wear in its holster. It rides high up my flank, the butt turned outward, like a doorknob growing out of the hollow of my armpit. Outside, the land lies dark under a sickle moon.

Part Four

Angel

I asked him whether there was a great fire anywhere? For the streets were so full of dense brown smoke that scarcely anything was to be seen.

'Oh, dear no, miss,' he said. 'This is a London particular.'

I had never heard of such a thing.

'A fog, miss,' said the young gentleman.

'Oh, indeed!' said I.

Charles Dickens, *Bleak House* (1853)

The Country and the City

It is hard to say when exactly it starts. Thomas is tired, busy with his fatigue and his wound, his thoughts about Charlie. He is lying in the corner of the train wagon, the squawk of chickens by his ear. Two steps from him the door to the wagon remains wide open. A savage wind whips at them whenever they gather speed, then relents when the train labours up a hill. There are other men in the wagon, other vagrants, a group of two and a third, a solitary man. Livia is sitting far from them, her knees tucked into her chest. It is only later that Thomas realises that she is trying to hide her breasts.

The men sniff her out all the same. It begins without rancour, witless banter about what a pretty boy she is, how creamy her skin.

'Short for 'is age,' one man ventures, shouting against the wind. 'A little scrawny. But nice 'ealthy thighs.' When she gets up to shift closer to Thomas, his mate calls after her: 'Don't you worry, pet, we're just having a bit of fun.' The little Smoke that wafts over from them is playful and oddly inclusive, as though inviting them to join their game.

It is the solitary man who changes the equation. He climbed on later, hours into their journey, running alongside the train at the steepest side of a hill. This man is not interested in Livia. It's lunch he wants. The chickens are packed into two massive crates, sturdy enough to discourage thievery but perforated at the side to let in air. All one sees of them is a mass of feathers; the occasional blood-red beak sticking out of a perforation; a dozen unblinking eyes. They are packed in willy-nilly, literally stacked on top of each other, are restless, squawking, fighting for floor space and air. The man has hooked two fingers through one of the holes. His face is weather-beaten, the creases caked with Soot. Light, deep-set eyes. It is as though their colour has run.

He catches something, pulls back his arms, holds a chicken foot hooked between his fingers. The man continues tugging until pale pink cartilage broadens to a wedge of fine white feather. Then he gets stuck: the hole just isn't big enough.

At first Thomas thinks the man means to cut off the leg. But it appears he has no knife. Rather he just continues pulling, his dark face growing darker with the effort. A riot of chicken squawks plays chorus to his effort.

When the blood starts flowing, the man starts smoking, and when his Smoke reaches the other two men, all that is dark in them rises up like a dog called to its master. Again they turn to Livia, and again they begin teasing her, but there is a different quality now to their taunts, something dangerous and needy, and the language soon grows coarse.

'Won't you come over here, pet?' one of them keeps saying. 'We've got things to show you.'

'That your sweetheart there?' the other one jumps in. 'Looks in real bad shape, 'e does. No joy cuddlin' the sick.'

Livia looks over at Thomas. It is a closed, a haughty look. It must mean she is scared. She does not ask him for his help. But Thomas is already on his feet. The Smoke wafting through the carriage helps him, gives him strength. He breathes it in with a sense of recognition; watches his body exhale a fine blue mist in response. All the same he is careful not to inhale too much. He must not get too angry to think.

'Ah, look at the pup! Chival'russ, 'e is, a proper little knight. Forgot 'is armer though, didn't 'e?'

'Nah,' says his mate, 'he's got his lass there to protect him. What you say, bonny lad? Sit yourself down again and we'll help you break her in.'

Thomas ignores them, steadies himself against Livia's shoulders. From the corner of one eye he is aware of the third man, plucking feathers off a bloody lump of chicken. Ahead, the land shifts from flat to the slight incline of a hill. Livia's ear is right in front of him, its outside clean, the inside glowing black with coal dust. Her body is shaking under his hands, or perhaps he is shaking and passing it on into her slender frame. He whispers to her.

'I'm too weak to fight them,' he whispers. 'But if we stay here, I must.'

Her eye flicks back momentarily. It communicates a question. *Why?*

'The Smoke,' he explains. 'I'm not like Charlie. It makes a home in me.'

As he says it, he realises he is afraid to fight these men not because he will lose. He is afraid he will disappear, disappear into the Smoke, as he did when he fought Julius. One day, he thinks, he won't find his way back.

But there is no need to explain all this to Livia. She has already understood the most important thing. They must get off the train.

'When?' she asks.

'Now.'

He has been listening for it, the moment the train's engine clears the crest of the hill. The moment it is at its slowest, its rump tethered to a dozen wagons, gravity tugging at its nose. It is a sound the body hears, not the ears, a change in vibrations racing through the chain of wagons like a rumour: steel wheel to axle to coupling to wood.

Now.

Thomas pushes Livia with both hands, afraid that she will miss the moment; pushes too hard, perhaps, and sees her stumble awkwardly across the threshold of the door. The wind whips at her hair. Then she is gone from sight.

Him, the vagrants try to stop before he can follow. It is a clumsy charge. Thomas ducks one man's arm, sidesteps the other's leg, and throws himself forward. He feels himself falling through the sharp twigs of a shrub. Then the ground jumps up at him. He hits it shoulder first, feels the air pushed out of his lungs; goes head over heels, then starts rolling down a slope of unkempt grass, the world a carousel, hips, elbows, knees pummelled by the impact of each revolution.

Φ

They are lucky, in a sense. The hill slopes gently where they leapt, and the hedgerow that parallels the tracks is free of thorns. All the same, the twigs have torn clothes and skin. They each come to rest some six or seven yards down, where a ditch welcomes them with its bed of hard-caked mud. He looks around winded, and sees Livia sitting up not far from him, her face dark with dirt, and blood seeping from a cut lip. She gets to her feet and stands over him, rubbing her upper arms and neck. He thinks she will ask him whether he is all right; whether his wound has reopened or he has broken any limbs.

'Stupid,' she says. 'We should have waited for a steeper hill.'

He tries to speak but doesn't have enough air.

'How far to London?' she asks.

He gasps, spits.

'Don't know,' he manages. 'Can't be far.'

'Get up then.' She brushes at her clothes, her face. 'We need to find water. I want to wash.'

Φ

She won't be talked out of it. What does it matter, he tries to explain to her, if they are dirty? In London everyone is dirty. It will help them blend in. She could wet her handkerchief with some spit, rub off the blood if it bothers her. But she won't be swayed, glowers at his words. Something about him makes her angry. He understands this well enough. Something about her makes him angry too.

Half an hour later she finds a creek. They are walking south, keeping the tracks in sight, on an unmarked path. Already the sun is sitting low in the sky. The day has cleared, its light bright and pure, carving shades of colour out of every blade of grass. It is hard to believe that they emerged from darkness only that morning. Seven hours of daylight and already Thomas's wonder at the world has worn thin. His head is hurting, his back, the bruises on his hips and knees. A lone crow sits in empty fields and watches him hobble past.

The creek is three feet wide and a foot deep. There is no bridge, but a fallen tree has been placed across from bank to bank. Livia climbs down to it, crouches, then looks at him expectantly.

'What?' he asks, uncomprehending.

'Some privacy, if you will.'

'You are going to strip? Just dunk a hankie in and mop your face. Be done with it.'

It's like talking at a stone. He curses, turns away from her, shuffles ten steps down the path. The crow is still there in its field, caws hoarsely at him, picks an insect out of the dirt. While he waits, impatient, Thomas makes an inventory of his pockets. There is a penknife and a handkerchief so stained with coal dust it is a featureless black. A length of yarn; a spent and broken match. A stone he picked up in some childish moment because it impressed him by its smoothness. Then he finds the cigarettes. There are four of them, each bent like an old man's fingers. He has a memory of forcing open Julius's little box and stuffing them in his coat. The smell leaps up to him, sticks to his fingertips even after he scatters the cigarettes on the ground. An invitation to sin. Renfrew would have been pleased to witness his fear.

When Livia finally emerges, her hair is streaming wet. She has no towel and has put on her shirt over her still-wet frame, is using the miner's coat like a blanket thrown about her shoulders. Her face is flushed with cold. Beneath it shivers her young body, more naked than dressed. Thomas sees it and quickly turns away.

A silence descends. Behind him he can hear her wring out her hair then climb into the shoes she has been holding in her hand.

'There,' she announces at last. 'Nearly dry. I needed to . . . Those men made me feel dirty.'

Thomas hardly hears her. He wonders whether she saw him look. Whether he showed. He needs to say something; warn her; apologise. Her belly button showed dark through the wet cotton of her shirt; he saw the slender arches of her rib cage. *You have to be careful*, he wants to say. There is a curve, a hollow where her arm runs into torso, so much softer than a boy's. *I am no different than those who rode the train.*

'Livia,' he says instead, his eyes on dirt and crow. It sounds sulky rather than apologetic. 'What sort of name is Livia?'

Instantly, her voice turns cold.

'What do you care?'

But his mind has already moved on, slides from thought to thought without finding traction.

'I wish Charlie was here,' he mutters. And then: 'He's in love with you.'

'And you disapprove.'

He listens into himself and discovers she is right.

'Charlie is the best,' he tries to explain. 'The most honest, the bravest person I have ever met.'

'While I'm a stuck-up little madam pretending to be a saint.'

'You are like me. Flawed and angry. Only you hide it better. Some day you will let him down.'

'I won't.'

He startles himself with the sadness that rises up in him. 'Who can say for sure, Livia?'

251

Then he adds, turning now, looking boldly in her eye. 'You are pretty. I did not notice it before.'

In answer, she wraps her arms tight around her slender frame.

They resume walking. As they set off, Livia quickly, furtively crouches down to the cigarettes he has discarded and picks them off the ground one by one. She does not offer an explanation.

Thomas does not ask for one.

Φ

She tells him later. They are walking single file, Thomas in front, Livia behind, straining to adjust her pace to his slow stumble. Her explanation has no face, therefore: just a voice, measured and even, reciting the facts.

'The name is Roman,' she says. 'Livia Orestilla. An empress: Caligula's wife. She was to marry someone else, but Caligula stole her on her wedding night. Then he divorced her after only a few days.'

'A funny thing to put into your cradle. In lieu of frankincense and myrrh.'

'That's just what Julius said. Not the words but the sentiment. It was he who told me. About Caligula.'

Stung, Thomas turns around to her, careful to place his eyes on her face, her jacket closed now, swallowing her body.

'It is good that you hate me. I'm dangerous. I have tainted blood.'

He is surprised to see she holds his gaze. Thus far, she has always avoided it. It must be something she brought up with her, from the depth of the mine.

'So you are,' she replies, serious and not. '"Tainted". "Dangerous". Why is it you think I'm walking three paces at your back?'

It shouldn't, but it makes Thomas laugh. When they start walking, her steps fall into rhythm with his.

One pace, he thinks. *Two paces at the most.*

Φ

They reach the border at dusk. The transition is gradual but also distinct. On their side, the dipping sun finds the earth rich and brown; trees tall and proud even in hibernation; hollies growing in green vigour. On the other side all growth is stunted, the soil barren, mixed with Soot, the puddles greasy with sin's residue, the air pregnant with its stink.

The other side. The city. London.

The day has grown colder and snow is in the air. Thomas wonders whether it will fall black, *over there.* They stop under the shadow of a tree. It is a species Thomas does not recognise, a conifer nearly as broad as it is high, its branches growing sideways and forming a series of platforms, filtering the last of the sun. On the London side, the tree stands black, smeared in Soot, and threadbare in its canopy. He walks up to the trunk and touches the bark. Livia watches him, puzzled.

'What is it?'

'Nothing. It's just – I like this tree.' He talks with his back to her, so she won't see his face. There is a catch to his voice, a hint of a younger Thomas, gentler in pitch. 'What kind is it? I have never seen it before.'

'A cedar of Lebanon,' she answers without hesitation. 'There is a grove of them on the grounds of my school, along with a plaque. It says an explorer brought back a handful of seeds, in the early 1600s. All British cedars descend from that handful. There was a debate in Parliament not long ago over whether they should all be cut down.'

'Why? No, I know. Because they are foreign. An outside thing.'

'Well, it's true, isn't it?' she says reasonably. 'They do not belong here.'

'It's beautiful.'

He touches the bark, both hands flat on the tree, lets it take his weight. There is a high, light humming in his chest. Bone music. Singing of home. Home? A tree transplanted from its native soil, planted at the edge of purgatory. The early 1600s. It came with the Smoke. Its bark warm and rough under his spread-out palms.

'Come,' Livia urges, not unkindly. 'We cannot stay here. We'll freeze to death.'

Indeed a deep chill has started to rise out of the land and pinpricks of snowflakes stand in the air, catching the sunset. Only the breeze blowing in from the south is a little warmer. It carries London to them, sewage and sin and the dank stink of boiling cabbage.

They walk towards it side by side.

Φ

Darkness falls just as the muddy little path they follow feeds into a cobbled road. All of a sudden there are people, dwellings, mangy dogs hunting for offal in the ditch. They are still far from the centre, in a no-man's-land of pig farms and factories, vegetable plots, lean-tos made from wood and sackcloth. The closer they draw the less certain they become of the way, encounter sinkholes, dead ends, intersections that split the street in confusing ways. Then also, with every step Thomas's fatigue is mounting, the ache of fever returning to his joints. It isn't long before Livia stops him.

'We have walked all day. You need rest. There, we can find shelter in that doorway.'

Thomas is too tired to argue. The doorway is ripe with smells but deep enough to allow them to disappear into its shadow, even to lie down, using their arms for pillows. For a moment the muck that seeps through his coat and shirt makes Thomas gag. Then exhaustion wipes the feeling from his mind. What remains is the cold. Even out of the wind, heated though it is by the furnace of London's sin, the night is near-freezing. Against their will, they are forced to huddle close, back pressed against back, each keeping the other awake with their shiver. The floor of the doorway is uneven from use. It dips at the centre. Late at night, not explaining himself, Thomas turns around to take Livia in his arms and mould his chest, knees and legs against her frame. It is warmer this way. Her hair smells of coal, sweat and peaches. It is the peaches that trouble him as he drifts off to sleep. Dawn brings noise and the acrid smell of fresh Smoke. They roll apart like disgruntled puppies and stiffly resume the road. Behind them, their doorway remains empty, the door locked, the house unmarked and ordinary but for the lopsided contour of a cross that declares it a chapel.

Φ

They walk in comfort with each other, two steps apart. Some truce appears to have been struck between them in the course of the night, almost a friendship, dispelling the tension of the previous day. It fills Thomas with hope. In a few hours – the next morning at the latest – Charlie will rejoin them and all danger will have passed, this strange, dimly sensed trap laid for them by the road. In the meantime Thomas gives himself to London. In the thin light of morning it seems different to him than it was when he first came here. Or rather, *he* is different, has shed both school and uniform, become one of the crowd. Already the streets are choked with wagons and people: farmers bringing sheep to market, costermongers, morning drunks, factory workers marching to their shift. The Smoke is light yet, dissolved in yellow fog, tugs at Thomas in ways not entirely unpleasant, gives rise to unruly feelings he does little to suppress. Next to him, Livia walks more guardedly, suspicious of this haze, yet gawking, too, at this sea of people whose steady current carries them along.

They find the square by midmorning. There is no scaffold there today, no soldiers, no hangman, no rabid mob. Even so the square is crowded enough that all movement becomes a matter of negotiation, of space claimed and yielded, shoulders brushed, weights gently shifted. *London is a place where people touch.* It strikes Thomas as a succinct definition of its sin.

Despite the press of people, however, the square feels different today. During the execution, there had been but one crowd, focused on a single spectacle. Today there are many centres of attention. A group of farmers have set up stalls and are selling produce to a jostling throng, their boys armed with cudgels to discourage thieves. Behind these stalls, a ring has formed around two fighting dogs; a crone with a chalkboard is accepting bets. Right next to her a man has mounted a crate and is screaming at the score of people who form his congregation. Beyond, a small tent has been set up, and a gaudily dressed youth is selling tickets to a show that, judging by the sign dangling from his neck, appears to involve a woman undressing to reveal her scorpion's tail. Each of these groups is knit together by a mist of Smoke, light and volatile in the air, if thickening in places into dark swirls. At the borders these mists mingle or rain down in flakes of Soot soon absorbed by the ground's black grit.

'It's not like it was down the mine,' Livia says, disappointed. 'I had started to hope that Smoke was benign.'

'And now you are shocked.'

'Well, look at it,' Livia answers. 'It's a disgrace.'

'I was just thinking the opposite. That it's not really that bad.'

Just as Thomas says it, two women at the far end of the square start fighting, the shorter, stockier woman wrestling the other to the ground then pelting her with insults.

Φ

They choose a perch atop a set of shallow stairs that lead up to a church. *Church* does not capture the building's scale; it is very nearly a cathedral. A row of marble columns rise behind them, holding aloft a portico high above their heads. Beyond it a single tower spikes two hundred feet into the heavens, where the Smoke thins and a cloudy sky spews snowflakes that reach the earth as dirty drizzle. For all its grandeur, the building is dilapidated, its great doors leaning burnt within their frames, held aloft by a crude patchwork of timber. The windows, too, have long lost their glass and are similarly boarded shut. High up, the brickwork that peels itself out of the city's sooty varnish shines with the pallor of limestone. The long, angular lines of the 1720s: built a hundred years into the time of Smoke. Thomas stares at the church and imagines a time when, despite it all, a decision was taken to build it here, at the heart of vice.

Morning turns to afternoon and Charlie does not come. Dawn, noon, dusk: these are the meeting times they have agreed. They shall have to leave soon, to look for food and shelter for the night. There is a water pump on the market square and though the water is grey and tastes of tin they have gone down to it repeatedly, to slacken their thirst and fill up their stomachs with something other than air. To obtain food, they will need to raise money. Or else they will have to steal. It is a problem, Thomas imagines, faced by a great many Londoners.

A man approaches the stairs. It takes Thomas some time to understand why he notices him. There have been others walking past, some openly staring at them, assessing their wealth, their station. Others yet have sought out the stairs as they have: as a place to rest. One old woman sat to feed the pigeons from a tin of dug-up grubs, cooing sweet nothings and all the while gently smoking from the shafts of her high boots.

This man is different. He moves briskly without wishing to disclose his haste, as though he is straining at the lead of his own discretion. A man in his fifties, bald, a crick in his neck that tilts chin to shoulder. But it is not this that draws Thomas's eye. He only makes sense of it after the man has turned and darted down the alley by the side of the church. Everyone else who walked towards them, past the various islands of spectacle that dot the square, veered off

256

somewhere, even if only for a moment. The Smoke made sure of it: it called to them as they passed, pulled them towards its centre, as though they were celestial bodies passing the weight of the sun. In his repressed hurry, walking through the siren song of sin, this man alone – the man with the bent neck – never once veered.

He is eating sweets.

There can be no other explanation. But something else tugs at Thomas, a memory older than the discovery of sweets, if not by much.

'Charlie,' he says abruptly, startling Livia out of her doze. 'He once told me he saw an angel. Right here on the market square. An angel with a crooked neck.'

Livia stares after Thomas when he jumps up and runs to the alley. But the man is long gone.

'Is he important?'

'Charlie thought so,' Thomas replies. 'In any case, it's more than just chance. Two sightings on the very same square. He must have business here.'

Φ

Soon after, Thomas and Livia are spooked off the perch by a group of respectably dressed men traversing the market in an open landau marked with bold lettering and the symbol of the Crown. There are four of them, plus a driver in livery; each so obviously a gentleman with soft white skin and brushed moustaches, they might as well belong to a different breed of human altogether.

'Who are they?' Livia whispers in the alley to which they have fled. 'Magistrates? Are they looking for us?'

Thomas reads the lettering on the side of the coach. TAYLOR, ASHTON AND SONS, ENGINEERING. His relief is immediate.

'No. They are sewage men.' He repeats to her the gist of Renfrew's explanation, given in Oxford some weeks ago. 'Liberals. Social pioneers. They want to clean up London, starting with the cesspits.' He shrugs. 'That's what Renfrew was preaching to us. That we should join their ranks. He did not tell us that they're here because they'd like to have a go at corruption and can't afford any cigarettes.'

'Perhaps we are doing them an injustice.' Livia watches the carriage disappear at the far end of the square. 'They looked like honest men.'

'They looked clean, Livia. That's all.' He shrugs, tugs at her elbow, walks back out into the street. 'I'm famished. Let's go and find some food.'

Φ

For the second time in two days Thomas makes an inventory of his belongings and tallies up what he might sell. His penknife. His jacket, only he'll freeze to death if they don't find better shelter for the night. The cigarettes Livia picked out of the dirt. They are said to be worth a fortune. But who needs to buy sin in London? It's as free as the air they breathe.

The row of market stalls on the square only sells raw meat and vegetables, and fish so malodorous even the locals seem to avoid it. They choose a street at random, follow a pair of chimney sweeps who are either the most vicious of men or are simply trailing the dirt of their trade. A bakery draws them with its smell. The penknife buys them two loaves of coarse white bread and a dozen penny rolls. They gulp down the rolls while huddled into a doorway, until a gang of urchins sets on them, begging a loaf with such dirty-palmed insistence that they have no choice but to flee.

And so they drift, strangers in a strange place. Around them the city is working, talking, seeking pleasures. It is not, in some ways, unlike the bustle of a school corridor or of a holiday fair in a respectable village. Only here, every interaction – every word spoken, every coin that changes hands – hovers at the precipice of danger, and moods can shift with the gust of the wind. They walk through arguments; through drunkenness; through laughter; skirt a billow of raw lust, a couple kissing, her hands buried in his jacket, one naked hip bone sticking out into the cold. And at every step, Smoke calls to Thomas, a dozen shades of vice.

It happens like all accidents, suddenly and without warning. Perhaps it is no accident at all but an ambush, well-rehearsed and executed with aplomb. A group of running urchins splits them (the same group as before? another?), shoves Thomas up against the wall and Livia into the kissing couple. She loses her balance and all three fall hard into the street. And even as they fall the man's hands slip into Livia's pockets, searching them for coin. He discovers what Thomas did a day before; that the shapeless coat hides something softer than a boy's frame; grins, his fallen lover's skirts tangling

258

around his legs, licks the length of Livia's face, jumps up, is gone, dragging his woman behind him, her cheeks painted crimson in imitation of health. All this in a breath or two, while Thomas swims against the crowd, the last of their bread spoiling in a puddle by his feet. He reaches Livia, drops to his knees, finds her head twisted into dirt, the neck strangely tilted; scoops up her chin with outstretched palms, afraid. The moment they touch a jet of Smoke breaks out of her, dark green and dense. His own skin answers. They freeze, their faces conjoined by a twist of Smoke so dense they cannot see each other. It is Livia who recoils, shaking off his touch, kicking his legs in her haste to get away.

'Don't ever touch me!' she shouts, her Smoke still oozing out of her in stark betrayal.

Then she runs down the street and out of sight.

Φ

Thomas searches for her, afraid he will find her, afraid he will not. The streets all seem to smell of her, peaches and Smoke; he sees her face in every girl who rushes past on her business. At dusk he returns to the church steps. Livia is already there, sitting on the topmost step, her arms wrapped around her knees, exhaustion, shame marking her wan features. She scrubbed them raw to rid them of his Soot. Spasms of Smoke keep darting out of her mouth, sudden retchings of black, each abrupt and violent, shaking her frame from head to toe. He climbs past her and sits upwind, his skin bumpy with fresh squalls of fever. A cold drizzle is falling, taunting them with the kind of proximity they resorted to during the night, shoulder to shoulder, thigh to thigh. They ignore it and sit yards apart. Even so he is conscious of her Smoke; feels it reach across the gap and tug at his very bones. It is as though he were built to drink her sin.

London is a place where people touch.

Before, he had not understood the implications of this simple truth.

They sit and wait. Thomas's fever has returned, makes a home within his joints; knuckles and knees tender with its ache. Down on the square, the market vendors are slowly packing up their wares, all but a dentist who remains at his stall, bent low over a lock-jawed patient, his tools a bucket and pliers scabby with old rust and paint. The tooth finally gives amongst an eruption of black savoured by both dentist and patient. Then blood is spat into the bucket and the dentist paid; the tooth thrown to a pack of passing dogs who fight over it with bristling furs.

Φ

Half an hour later, Charlie's angel reappears. It is very nearly dark. The man acts on Thomas like a magnet, drawing his anger, his confusion, his hope. He enters from the far side and walks the length of the market square. The last of the light catches him from the front and right, his shadow thrown behind and tilted at the top, where his chin dips to his shoulder. The longer Thomas watches him, the less he is certain that there is anything special about the man. He is as dirt- and Soot-stained as any other; more downtrodden than most. No halo illuminates his bluff and common features. Only: once again the man avoids all groups and conflagrations, walks solitary, never swayed by any cluster of people nor any cloud of drifting Smoke.

As the man draws nearer, Thomas makes a point of turning away, watching him only from the corner of his eyes. Livia, four steps to his side, has slumped into exhaustion; is listing sideways and forward, her head drooping to mirror the angel's. At the bottom of the stairs, the man swerves and disappears into the alleyway by the side of the church. For a fraction of a moment Thomas hesitates, unwilling to rouse Livia, struck by the blankness of her resting features, the thinness of her sloping neck. Then he jumps over and taps her awake with a flick of his shoe.

'The angel's back. Let's follow him.'

She makes to rise then drops back onto the step. 'You go. Someone has to be here. For Charlie.'

It strikes Thomas that Livia fears him more than she fears being left defenceless and alone.

Φ

There is a second entrance to the church. Halfway down the alley a narrow staircase of some four or five steep steps climbs the church wall. At its top is a door so small one has to duck through. Thomas does not actually see the stranger go in. All he sees is the door close, four feet above the ground. A moment later he himself is pulling the crude handle. Inside, a deep gloom reigns, taking little heed of the

260

cluster of candles that burns at one end of the nave. The church is in a dismal state. Its pews are gone, robbed for their wood perhaps, and the stone floor littered with mud and rubbish. A great wooden cross rises above the altar, plain unadorned lumber, painted white.

A figure is sitting on a little stool in a side chapel. The folding table next to him holds a candle, a jug and a cup of wine. Thomas has stepped over to him before realising the figure is not the one he followed. The priest is a smaller man, weasel-faced, his hair a patch of stubble. He looks up at Thomas and fills a second cup. Thomas ignores the gesture that invites him to sit.

'I'm looking for the man who just came in here.'

It comes out gruff, commanding. He has no patience left, no interest in this stranger. The stranger, for his part, is looking closely at Thomas, as if measuring his intent. A pale face, his; Soot-rouged at the cheeks. Broken veins thread the nose.

'Is that so?'

'Where did he go? I want to talk to him.'

'Talk to me instead. That's what I am here for.'

Thomas frowns at this, looks about himself, suspicious of the man's collar, his jug of wine, the long smock of his office.

'Your church is a mess,' he says at length.

The priest shrugs. 'What use does the Lord have for pretty windows?'

'And you are drunk.'

'It *is* a failing. But I am a kindly drunk, and it does not interfere with my faith.' He smiles. 'How is it that it's always laymen who are the biggest puritans? But sit, please, I beg you. Looking up at you is like talking to the bishop, when he's in a mood.'

Thomas reluctantly lowers himself onto a stool.

'So you really are a priest?'

'Yes, my son.'

'And this church, it's . . . open? I mean, people come here?'

'Oh yes. Do they fill the pews on Sunday? No. No pews, for one thing. Do I celebrate mass in shining vestments? No. They were stolen, actually, some months ago. But they come. Largely for that.' He points to the wine jar, then a few steps beyond it, to the plain cupboard of the confessional. 'Are you that way inclined?'

Thomas shakes his head. 'No, I only came in to . . . But I must go now, someone's waiting outside.' He rises, keen now to get away from this priest. 'I only came because I saw a man go in. An unusual man. He has a crick in his neck.'

'And what do you want with him, this unusual man?'

'Nothing. A friend saw him. Weeks ago. He saw him and decided he was an angel.' Thomas's voice wavers between resentment and hope. 'I suppose I just wanted to make sure that he was wrong.'

'An angel? What an odd idea. Wherever did he get it from?'

'The man does not smoke.'

'Ah! He's a gentleman.'

'No. What my friend meant: the man does not smoke at all. It's a trick, I think.'

'A trick?'

Thomas snorts, sudden anger in his breast. 'You're a churchman. I have been told you get issued sweets. A monthly ration, so you can lie to your congregation and pretend you are a decent man.'

The man smiles. It sits surprisingly well on his narrow, weasely face.

'Ah, sweets! Yes, the church sends me two every Christmas. Two! I don't know by what method they assess the needs of every parish. I sell them for drink. A sin, though I have never smoked during the sale. Your angel is a fraud then, and you want to unmask him.'

'I don't know what I want. He might be a spy. Someone pretending to be an ordinary citizen.'

It sounds stupid the moment it leaves his lips. The priest takes no heed.

'Yes, a fraud,' he mutters. 'Or else, a miracle. You know what most people do with miracles? Shit on them. Burn them at the stake.' He looks up at Thomas again, a sober look, the narrow face dirty and shrewd. 'Are you like that, my lad?'

Thomas shudders, light-headed with fever. Talking to this man feels dangerous and liberating all at once. It is the first time in months he has spoken to a stranger – an adult – and not immediately felt judged.

'My father killed a man,' he says hoarsely and is appalled at the note of pride. 'I was told I'd end up doing the same.'

The priest drains his glass. 'Ah. Well. In that case, let me talk to your angel. See whether he wants to be introduced.'

Φ

They find him in the bell tower, cleaning the mildewed brass of the great bell.

'We ring it on holidays,' the priest explains as they labour up the narrow stairwell, 'but it's started to sound off-key. Constipated. It's all the dirt clogging up the bell.

'He does odd jobs for me,' he carries on as they step onto a minuscule landing. 'Grendel's the name. Tobias Grendel. Gren, here's a lad to meet you. Violent, he says. But I think he's got a good enough soul. Anyway, I will leave you to it. Have a chat. Shout if you need refreshments. Cheerio.'

The priest's steps retreat back down the stairwell. It leaves Thomas alone with the stranger. He finds himself at a loss for words.

The man called Grendel has continued working, rubbing the side of the great bell with a dirty cloth, all the while watching Thomas shyly, from behind lowered lids. The crick in his neck lends something abject to him. It forever condemns him to cower before his peers.

'What is it?' Grendel says after the silence has stretched to several seconds, his voice quiet and gentle, inflected with a slight, pleasant lilt. 'Some sort of trouble?'

Thomas shakes his head, steps closer to him.

'You were there at the hanging,' he says at last, unsure where to start. 'At the end of November. A woman was killed. The whole square was painted black.'

The man nods, a vague fear showing in his eyes.

'Yet you did not smoke.'

Thomas reaches out with his fingers, grabs hold of the man's collar, turns it back, aware of his imposition, of the brutal rudeness of the act. The shirt is discoloured, Soot-stained, more black than white. But the inside is grey rather than black. All the shirt's Soot clings to the fabric's outside: city sin, absorbed from walls and air.

'Where do you get your sweets from?'

'Sweets,' the man repeats, shaking a little.

'Don't play stupid now.'

'The priest gives them to me.'

'The priest told me he has two a year, and sells them for wine.'

'I found them,' the man cringes.

'Enough to keep you smokeless while a woman dangles from a rope?'

Thomas shakes his head, feels an emotion fill him that he fails to recognise. Something very close to fear. Awe perhaps: a vice around the heart. It releases some Smoke in him, an iodine plume that he does his best to spit in the stranger's face. It drifts past his cheeks, flakes as Soot onto his shoulders and neck, and draws no change from his bluff and honest features.

Φ

Livia finds them. The priest must have fetched her off her stoop. She is upset, angered, frightened by Thomas's failure to return. But even so she does not step too close to him.

'Charlie didn't come,' she hisses. 'A beggar pestered me for money.' And then: 'What are you doing to this man?'

As she says it, Thomas realises that his hand is still clutching the man's collar. The fingers of his other hand are wet. He has just finished shoving them in the man's mouth, hunting his cheeks for hidden objects.

'He does not smoke,' he says, shaken. He tries to explain it to Livia. A part of him wants to kneel before this man. Another is angry that he seems such a fool.

Livia listens to his account without moving a muscle. At last she says, speaking to the angel not Thomas, 'You are afraid.'

Then she does something for which Thomas is unprepared. He did not suspect her capable of such grace; not here, not at this moment, her lips still jet-black with her Soot.

She steps past him and embraces the angel.

The man giggles nervously. And then he starts crying.

Φ

He takes them home. Grendel. 'Just like the monster,' he says. He says it happily because Livia is holding his hand.

It's her doing, this hospitality of his. She has taken to him in a way Thomas cannot quite explain; has stepped into his presence as though into a shelter. One of the first things she has said to the man is: 'I wish my father had met you. When he was younger.' And also: 'He tried to be like you, just like you.'

But Grendel had only flapped his hands in agitated denial until she desisted and started talking about their journey here and how they are waiting for a friend.

'Charlie,' she explains. 'You will like Charlie. Everybody does.'

Her eyes are on Thomas as she says it, showing the only sign of anguish that will pass through them all evening.

Grendel lives a half an hour's walk away, close by the river. Dark has long fallen and the road is treacherous. They are beset by beggars and prostitutes, by lamplighters with smoking torches, asking for tuppence, offering to see them home.

As they draw closer to the angel's neighbourhood, the city smells grow worse, offal and mud, the stale, rotten waters of the Thames. The house he leads them to has burnt and adds cold ash to the stink. It looks uninhabitable, but Grendel leads them through the gateway to a crooked, triangular courtyard, then beyond to a sagging building overhanging the riverbank. There are a whole series of low-beamed rooms, but two hold no glass in their windows, and one has a collapsed wall that is growing a thick layer of moss. For all that it is cosy enough, with a gaily painted kitchen table and an ancient stone hearth that Grendel immediately sets to lighting.

Before they have had a chance to throw off their awkwardness and begin a conversation, steps can be heard labouring up the staircase behind them. Grendel jumps to open the door, and in comes a woman in mud-smeared boots, carrying a bucket heavy with water so dirty it resembles mud. Her arms, too, are smeared with greenish-brown filth. She is a tall woman, so thin as to appear haggard, her fine bones framed by thinning grey hair. As she stares at them, unmoved by Grendel's explanations, the bucket begins to boil, and dark claws break the surface, along with the spasmodic twitch of an armoured tail.

'What do you know,' says Thomas. 'The angel has a wife. And she's been fishing.'

She smiles at that, an unpractised, awkward, bashful smile, rinses a fistful of crayfish in a deep, lead-lined sink, and sets to cooking them for dinner.

That night, Grendel sits up with them and tells them he is sick.

Φ

'It started when I was nine. I had smoked as an infant, though never very much. An easy child they called me, good-humoured and docile, perhaps a little dull. Then the Smoke ceased. I was sick, I remember, German measles, spots up and down my body and a

265

terrible fever. When the sickness went, the Smoke went with it. I've never shown since.'

They are still sitting at the dinner table, each on a stool of a different height, their fingers vivid with the smell of crayfish. From time to time, Mrs Grendel rises and busies herself at the stove, where she is boiling up the empty shells for stock. She is humming something, listening to her husband talk; contentment in the hum, but also worry about these strangers who have burst in upon her life. Grendel, for his part, speaks simply, trustingly, as eager to shed his story as a child is to slip out of its Sunday clothes. Thomas listens to him with the heightened intensity of fever. He sits far from Livia, out of her sight; has picked a fallen crayfish leg from off the floor, black and spindly, spikey at the joints; sits rolling it within his palm, digging its edges into his skin.

'Nobody really noticed it at first. I was placid before and was more placid after. It was my clothes that gave it away, my bed linen. No stains. Not by day and not by night, for weeks on end. But it was more than that. I didn't fight any more. Didn't argue. I would watch my sisters do it, get into a proper scrap, clouds rising out of them like steam from a mangle, and feel left out. It was as though I was watching them walk on their hands, or speak a foreign tongue. As though sin were a knack, and I had lost it.

'Before long the whole village realised something was wrong. The children noticed it first. They started teasing me, trying to get me to lose my temper, get into trouble, smoke. But I couldn't. It's not that I didn't try. I'd go to bed thinking about it, planning out some piece of mischief: how I would take a swing at someone, or steal Granny's hat and feed it to the pigs. Sometimes I even went through with my plan, hit a boy over the head with a log, or ripped the sleeve on the blouse of an aunt. But my heart wasn't in it. I did it like I did my chores. The Smoke never rose.

'By the time I was eleven, the children in the village had started avoiding me. The adults too. A rumour got around that I was sick somehow, gone funny in the head. My parents tried to quench it. I was just like a gentleman, they said, an angel, a proper little lord. The village should be proud. It calmed things down for a while, but the suspicion did not cease. I was different. *Separate.* Not part of the fabric of life. An angel, maybe. But who wants to go fishing with an angel?

266

'One day, they took me to the vicar. Our village was small and isolated; we had a church but no priest of our own. He came on Sunday mornings to read us our sermon, good and salty, as the villagers liked to say, to last us the week. A thickset man with a marvellous head of curly red hair.

'He examined me in the little shed at the back of the church that served as a sort of office. I have a memory of standing before him, stripped to the waist, and his counting up the moles on my chest. "Dost the devil live in thee?" he asked. I told him I did not know. One of the moles, he told me, looked like a cloven hoof. A witch's mark, a most evil omen.

'He wrote a report, they say, and even sent it to the bishop. There was no answer. Perhaps he decided against posting it in the end. The vicar was a simple man. He did not want to invite trouble.

'In any case, it got out, the thing about the mole. The whole village took against me then. It was said that I was cursed. The Wandering Jew, they started calling me. Bearing the mark of Cain. I did not even know what a Jew was then, but I'd heard about Cain. I left the village the day I turned fourteen.

'I had learned no trade but found work at an inn, some twenty miles from home. Three weeks I lasted, then the innkeeper sent me on my way. "You are scaring away the customers," he said. "One cannot trust a man who does not sin." His wife packed me lunch and gave me a pair of socks in parting. When I walked out of their gate, I saw her cross herself against my curse.

'By the time I was twenty, I had learned that it was best to hide my condition. I kept to myself, moved from town to town every few months. The Wandering Jew. Condemned to be good. Though not good, not really. Lukewarm. There is a line in the Bible, in Revelation, about God spitting out the lukewarm. He loves the hot, the cold. I am not welcome at his hearth.'

He frowns, but then his wife is there, resting her hands on Grendel's shoulders. Her eyes are on Thomas and Livia, daring them to add to her husband's woes. But this is not the time to be bashful. Grendel is a miracle, or else a man with a crippled soul. It is important to understand which.

'So you don't *feel* anything?' Thomas asks.

'Oh, I feel,' Grendel says quietly, mournfully, reaching up to brush his wife's arm. 'I feel sadness and irritation; feel grateful to have steady work and fearful every morning when I set out across the city; relieved when the day is over and my good wife welcomes me at home. But my heart does not boil with it, and I do not forget myself. It's as though my blood runs thinner than other men's.'

'Don't you listen to him,' Mrs Grendel interjects, her face flushed dark and a hint of a shadow darting from her nostrils. 'He is the best man that's ever lived.'

'I believe you,' Livia says into her anger. She is different now that they are with Grendel, hopeful and composed, the afternoon's terror banished from her face. 'If my father weren't ill, he would make him famous up and down the land.'

It's only Thomas who fails to chime in but simply sits there, twirling a crayfish leg, the stump of his ear itchy with fever and sweat.

Farmer

The boy comes to my door. A young man really, ginger fluff on his cheeks. You don't see many of his colour. Deep copper red, with copper skin. Like a ginger Tartar, but prone to blushes, hale cheeks filling with a darker hue.

Somehow it isn't a surprise to hear his accent. His clothes are dirty but there is something to his bearing. I'm no friend of toffs but you have to like the way they hold themselves. No slouching, shoulders squared, the eye resting comfortable on yours. And for a rich sod, he's awfully polite.

'My name is Charlie,' he says. 'I am heading to London. Might I beg some food and water?'

'Beg,' he says, calling it what it is. A good clear gaze on him. Puts a man in a mind to regret he does not have a son.

'You can have water at any rate.'

I draw him a measure from my well. He drinks straight from the ladle.

'As for food,' I say, 'I've got the rot.'

I show him to my storeroom, where my potatoes lie riddled with black; break one in half and show him the deep veining, clammy to the touch.

'You're welcome to a plateful, if you can stomach them' – I point to the stove, where I am heating my lunch – 'but they may do you more harm than good, not being used to such fare.'

He wavers, clutches the broken spud I have shoved in his fist, too tired to think. When I offer him a stool, he sinks down exhausted.

'Maybe I'll try a bite.'

Once they are boiled, I fry the potatoes in some dripping. The smell that rises from the pan is frightful, even to me, but the hole in the boy's stomach proves bigger than his disgust. I don't offer him seconds. I don't have enough to be generous, and it won't do him any good once the food hits his guts. We each have a thimble of

269

liquor afterwards. 'Calms the brewing storm,' my Mary used to say. A better use for the potatoes perhaps.

'You are dead tired, son,' I say when he rises to leave. 'I can offer you shelter. A place in the barn. You won't make London tonight.'

'I can't,' he answers, giving it thought. 'I have friends ahead, waiting for me. They'll be worried.' And then he adds, firmly, with a simplicity I did not know existed amongst the gentry: 'You are a good man.'

'Ah,' I say, embarrassed, 'I smoke as much as the next sinner. But the sun is out today, and my knee's finally on the mend. Small blessings, eh, son?'

'Are you married?'

'Was,' I say, pointing to the row of crosses that mark my wife's and daughters' graves. 'It's a hard life.'

'A hard life,' he repeats like it is news to him, and weighty information. 'Thank you for your kindness. Goodbye. Beware of dogs.'

Φ

I chew on this all through the night – *Beware of dogs* – my stomach queasy with the rotten food. At dawn the second gentleman comes calling. He is a dark one, head to toe, fine clothes shiny with Soot, as though they have been lacquered by an enterprising tailor. A young one, too, not much older than the copperhead. His dog is an odd thing: red, drooping eyes in a dark, drooping face. A beaten cur, slavish and vicious. It steps close and smells me like I am a steak.

'I am looking for a young man who passed this way,' the dark one says to me. His face lacks colour underneath the Soot. It is pale and papery, as though it has been powdered with chalk.

'You wouldn't have seen him? Well-born, dirty, reddish hair.'

The words are well-tuned, clear, emphatic. And yet there is something odd to his delivery, as though they are strange things, found at random in a pamphlet and performed.

'Mind,' he adds, 'don't lie to me. It will throw me in a rage.'

I hesitate, a breath, two breaths, before telling him that yes, a youth that answers his description called here the previous afternoon. He drank some water and was on his way.

'Heading where?'

'To London, I suppose.' I gesture to the road.

'He did not stay?'

270

'He did not want to.'

The dark youth nods, then bends forward and sniffs me. If his dog's nose, wet on my leg, is an imposition, his own, dry against my cheek, is a violation. And yet I let him, do not move. No face has been this close to mine since I kissed my wife farewell.

'It's a chore, tracking someone who doesn't much smoke.' He shakes his head, moves his head back, takes me in. 'You though! A cowardly sort. Twice the weight as I and yet you stand here like a post. And your Smoke' – he sniffs, *sampling* me, the pale green haze now rising from my breath – 'is limp. Weak. Boring. A defeated man.'

I do not argue with him. Indeed it is true. I should have grabbed an axe handle and kicked him off my yard. But he scares me, this youth. No man's ready for pain, not even I, my wife and daughters buried out the back.

He has one more request before he leaves. He explains it so calmly, so sanely, that I fail to understand him until he pushes me into my kitchen and fetches the knife. He does not threaten me, never says what will happen if I decline to do what he asks.

'But why?' I ask, already seated at the table, the knife shaking in my hand. My Smoke is all around us now, thin and pale as poor man's gruel. 'It makes no sense.'

He does not answer, sits there, watching; his dog flinching whenever he moves.

'Go on,' he says. 'Here, let me fetch your liquor. For courage, what do you say?'

He himself drains the last of the bottle.

'Do it. I haven't got all day.'

All the time watching me, a mouse in a trap, tugging weakly at its stuck and broken limb.

'Go on!'

The voice lighter now, impatient and gleeful; his hand raised and stroking the air before his chin as though searching it for something no longer there, a beard, a mask, a second face.

'Go on!'

Φ

I do in the end; take measure and chop. A man can live without a finger. He discards it in the bushes not five steps from my gateposts,

271

a child already weary of its toy; his dog following, whimpering, as angry and lost as I. By the time the wound stops bleeding they are both long out of sight.

Somewhere ahead of him, the boy with the copper hair will be walking. I want to wish him well. But the dark gentleman hurt me, wounded something that goes beyond the flesh. My hand looks like it might infect. So I sit there, boiling potatoes, and curse all those who are gentle-born.

Bone Music

They stay the night with Grendel. Livia is glad when he asks them to, and smiles when he shows her around proudly, leading her from room to room, a tallow candle in his hand, dripping wax on the stone flooring.

'Please,' Grendel says for the umpteenth time when they return to the kitchen where Thomas has not moved from his stool. 'You must.' It is as though it is he who is the supplicant and they the ones owning warmth and shelter.

For a while Livia is afraid that Thomas will decline the offer; that she will be thrust again into his company without the protection offered by a witness. But there is after all no choice. Thomas is weak, the night cold and alive with the shouts of strangers. For her own part, Livia is free of fear as she lies down on a wooden pallet and passes over into sleep. She trusts Grendel. She has known him for four hours, and she trusts him as much as any man or woman she has ever known. It is more than a feeling; it is a matter of fact. Grendel does not, *cannot* smoke. There is no malice in his heart.

Φ

When Livia rises the next morning, she finds Thomas still in the room assigned to him, curled into a blanket and radiating a clammy heat. He has not even taken off his boots. Livia watches Thomas, for longer perhaps than is decent, then accepts Grendel's invitation to walk with him to the church. It is early, dawn not quite broken, the streets near-empty and free of Smoke. In the quiet, Livia notices how run-down the city is, how badly in need of repair. There is hardly a building untouched by decay. Walls have caved, window frames fallen, ceilings and floors collapsed; holes stoppered with rags, paper, rubbish. And yet every house seems teeming with life, each cellar hole vivid with the movement of bodies, clothed and not. Through the broken windows and doorless doorways a hundred lives stand open to perusal. A woman stripped to the waist, feeding her newborn. A gaggle of boys ringing a chamber pot, relieving themselves with the unselfconsciousness of a litter. An old man in heavy boots picking his way through the dozen sleepers, leaving between them a trail of dark mud. Grendel notices Livia's staring and the ensuing blush.

'Too many people,' he explains. 'Living on top of one another. And everyone's always hungry. It darkens their Smoke.'

'Don't they have work?'

'Why yes. Factory work, most of them. But the factory doesn't pay for housing.'

'Then why don't they leave this filth? Move into the country?'

Grendel's voice is gentle when he answers as though he's afraid that his words will embarrass Livia with her ignorance. It deepens her blush.

'It's difficult, you see. When they go to a parish, looking dirty and hungry and full of sin, they get "pushed on". Concerned neighbours, rounding them up at dawn and marching them to the parish border.' Grendel grimaces as one familiar with the experience. 'Of course there's no law against going where you wish. But you can't live without work. And there's no work for strangers.'

Livia muses on this. 'Then it's the factories' fault,' she concludes. 'They should provide housing for the workers. Spread them out across the land. Who owns them?'

'Who owns the factories?' Grendel's face is free of accusation. 'People like your parents, I suppose. The gentry. But look, here's our church. I better get going on that bell.'

Φ

Charlie does not come, not at dawn, nor at noon, nor yet at dusk, when she waits for him on the steps of the church until London has sunk into darkness and people bar their houses against the night. Grendel walks home with her, the streets full now and misty with Smoke. Back in his room, Thomas lies as she has left him. Mrs Grendel tells Livia he woke long enough to struggle into his coat and insist on heading out to meet Charlie. When she assured him that Livia and her husband were fetching Charlie even as they spoke, he collapsed back on his blankets and fell asleep at once.

'Let him rest,' Mrs Grendel says. 'He is healing. Gathering strength. It's the last stage of illness. Two more days and he'll be

274

right as rain.' She speaks as one familiar with the sick. At their feet Thomas lies like a dead thing, rancid in his sweat.

Livia draws up a stool and sits with him. It is, she tells herself, an act of duty, towards Charlie as much as Thomas. And yet there is more to her gaze as she studies his curled-up form, the bold lines of his face, the blue-black mark that crawls out of the crater of his wound and insinuates itself into his cheek. She sits, feet planted a yard from his chest, the room still around her, cooking smells drifting from the kitchen. Sits, half-conscious of a question. Her hands in little fists. When she shifts, minutely, her back is stiff with tension.

The silence weighs on her, is like a blockage in her thoughts. She needs to speak to learn what she is thinking; finds comfort in the fact that he cannot hear.

'Charlie did not come today,' she says, so quietly it sounds only within her, the words a movement of her jaw. 'I'm worried about him.'

She crosses her legs, uncrosses them, disconcerted by the warmth of thigh on thigh.

'And yet I was scared of his coming. Isn't that strange?'

Scared, she thinks now, because he will bring something. The memory of the mine. The taste of his skin: two tongues at odds, sparring, breaching the guard of the other's lips. They shook hands when they last parted.

'But I was scared of something else too. Scared that he would know.'

She holds her breath, listens to Thomas's breath, deep if uneven, the hint of a whistle marbling each exhalation.

'Something happened, did it not, Thomas? Between us? Yesterday. In the muck of that street.'

As she says it, she knows it is true. Something *did* happen – not just in the alley where she lay beneath that stranger's grope but before, on the road, at the creek, perhaps, while she was cold and wet, off guard, or later, in the night shelter of a chapel doorway, when he breathed his warmth into the nape of her neck.

Thomas noticed her.

It was an accident, unsought, irreversible. Livia has watched him struggling against it ever since, cheeks bunched, fingers picking at the scab that runs past his temple, resting his eyes on her only in moments of distraction, dark, unflinching eyes, taking her in. When his Smoke rises, as in London it must, *she* is there amongst its flavours, dissolved in fear and want and spite. He cannot spit, it seems, without her presence being written in the bile.

She frowns, lingers over the thought, shies at the threshold of another. For there is more to it yet. Thomas has noticed her.

She has noticed him too.

It is odd that this truth should come with so much anger.

'I am in love with Charlie,' she whispers, defiantly, and watches a skein of Smoke crawl out of Thomas's sleeping form and hover above him like a second blanket. A boy with a dirty soul. He will spoil your dress if you step too close.

But Livia is no longer wearing dresses.

She slips off the stool, slides onto her knees, the miner's trousers so dirty that they cushion the knees like felt patches. Thomas is a foot away, is hateful to her, a trial to which she must submit. She leans forward, stretches her neck, seeking to understand him and, in understanding, dismiss him; purge him from her thoughts. She slurps his Smoke like soup. Inhales him, tastes him, and learns nothing she did not already know. This is he: anger and strength. It's her own Smoke that shocks her. It leaps unbidden, a little pink plume that forms a whirlpool in front of her breath, then spirals up, towards the ceiling. It's like picking up your diary and finding you wrote a name in it over and over while you were not looking. Thomas's name; thick and ragged, like she was punishing the quill. She recoils, jumps to her feet, disperses her Smoke with dismayed hands.

'Dinner, my dear,' Grendel's voice calls from the kitchen. 'Try to wake your friend. It'll do him good.'

Φ

They eat in anger. When Thomas learns that Charlie did not come at the appointed hour – and that Livia neglected to wake him – his mood sours and soon colours the mash he is shovelling into his mouth. Livia, too, tastes Smoke with each spoonful, though she does not visibly show. Between them, Grendel sits, unperturbed, imperturbable, a crooked-necked Jesus at supper, sharing out their meagre loaf of bread.

'You woke with an appetite!' he keeps praising Thomas. 'Tomorrow you will be strong enough to meet your friend yourself.'

Despite these words, Thomas is visibly worn out by the time the last spoonful has passed his mouth and has soon retreated back to the blanket in his room. Mrs Grendel too is soon to retire. It leaves Livia alone with Grendel. She is glad for it. She is in need of distraction, of hope. Grendel, she knows, will offer her both.

Φ

They talk without strain, sitting at the kitchen table, tea in the pot. It's Livia who picks the topic; something safe, simple, far from her fears.

'How about that name?' she asks. 'It must have been a burden.'

Grendel answers plainly, directly, the way he told his story; unworried by truth.

'Not at all,' he says. 'Growing up, you see, I simply never realised. Not until much later, here in London, when I heard someone sing the song. Have you heard it? Apparently it is very old. There are many versions. But in each of them there is a monster. Grendel. "It filled the great hall with its Smoke / And tore the men / Gristle from bone."' He snarls playfully; smiles. 'I doubt my father ever gave it a second thought; nor Granddad. Perhaps though, ten generations back, there was a monster in the family. Or perhaps' – his smile fades, and a frown grows into his forehead, more of wonder than of grief – 'the name is like a seed, planted in my bloodline a thousand years ago, waiting to sprout in the one for whom it was intended.'

Livia reaches over and lays her hand in his. How simple, how natural it is to touch him.

'What sort of villain are you? Do you steal away at night to feast on swordsmen in their sleep?'

'What is an angel,' he answers, 'if not a monster of some kind?' But he giggles as he says it and seems almost happy. 'What about "Livia" though? It's a beautiful name but I've never heard it before.'

'A family name. It was my grandmother's.'

Grendel nods and smiles and holds Livia's hand.

Φ

That same evening she tells Grendel how her father went mad. She shouldn't, of course, it is a family secret, all their servants are sworn to it and only two of them are trusted to tend to his needs. But she wants Grendel to know about him. Perhaps they can visit him some day, stand by his bedside and hold his hands. Grendel is the miracle Father prayed for all his life.

277

'He wanted to be like you,' she says. 'Sinless. Pure. But he wasn't. When I was a child, I remember, he had a quick temper. I found him once, shouting at a stable boy, Smoke coming out of his ears. Two mighty plumes, thick as candyfloss.'

She cannot help laughing. It is a happy memory, despite the sin.

'And then he conquered his Smoke. Conquered it completely, for more than two years. We were all in awe of him: the servants, Mother, and I above all. He was like a holy man. Only he grew very thin. And then he started talking to himself. Little things, not always in English. When I returned home after the next school term, he was chained to his bed.

'I'll tell you another secret: for the past year and more, I've wanted to be like him. Like he was, before he went mad. Holy.' She surprises herself by being able to laugh. 'But Charlie thinks I have no talent for it.'

'Tell me about Charlie.'

'Charlie is the one we are waiting for. Thomas's friend.' She feels herself blushing. 'My friend, too.'

Soon thereafter, they each retire to bed.

Φ

Thomas is up early the next day. His sickness has left him at last. Now he stands, itching for action. He is that hateful word found in cheap novels. Virility. It's in his every stride and glower. No other word will do.

And yet he cannot meet her eye.

'I'm off,' he announces after breakfast and does not wait to see whether she will follow. His impatience only increases once – five steps apart, him rushing, her chasing – they reach the foot of the church. Dawn is breaking; a smear of colours in the fog.

There is no Charlie.

'Something has happened to him.'

'You don't know that,' Livia replies, though she, too, is bowed by the same thought. Charlie is alone: detained in Oxford, or lost on the road to London; in a train compartment, on the back of a wagon, lying wounded in a ditch. They were shot upon before. When Livia closes her eyes she can hear the screaming of the horses dragging her mother's coach over the precipice.

Charlie does not arrive at noon. She does not need to wait for

Thomas to tell her what he is thinking. He wants to go find Charlie; trace him all the way to Oxford if need be. She can feel it in her pores, on the hairs of her arms. And yet, Thomas is not smoking. There must exist, then, another type of Smoke: invisible, clinging to them as surely as their shadows. The breath of their needs and worries; the truths each must assert and impose upon all others. The potentiality of sin. If so, they are all in each other's mouths every time they speak. How dangerous then proximity, those hours and days spent shoulder to shoulder until the other's being begins to grow into one's own and sows its hunger in one's furrows. How blissful, conversely, solitude, and how miraculous Grendel's isolation. Of all the men and women in London, he alone is an island, unadulterated, himself.

'You go,' she says as much to release Thomas as to be rid of him. 'See whether you can find him. I will wait.'

'It isn't safe for you here,' he barks back, protective, resentful.

'There's Grendel. And the priest. I will be all right.'

He thinks, nods, hesitates over how to say goodbye, then simply turns and strides off.

'I shan't be long.'

Thomas walks as though he is leaning into wind.

Φ

It's well past dinner by the time Thomas returns. When Grendel dons his coat and goes to look for him out on the street, Mrs Grendel turns from where she stands scrubbing dishes.

'Boys, eh? Hard to keep track of them. Always running off on some adventure.'

Livia cannot tell whether she is taunting her or trying to soothe her worries. Mrs Grendel's face does not take easily to emotion, and her interactions with Livia have been guarded and stiff.

'Here he is now.' Grendel returns, a grim-looking Thomas in tow. 'Let's find you some food, my lad. You must be starving.'

Thomas accounts for his day over a bowl of cold fish stew, eating with a crudeness, Livia notes, which speaks of a childhood running wild.

'I took the main road west. Asking whoever I could for news. A red-headed youth in dirty clothes. Well-spoken; good boots. I thought maybe somebody had met him up the road.' He grimaces, slurps stew, picks fish bones from pursed lips.

'I walked for miles out of town and talked to dozens of people. But nothing: no sign of Charlie, no word. Then I met a tinker hailing from Oxford and he told me about rumours concerning the school. He said that one of the schoolmasters had been attacked by a gang of robbers. "They fed him to their dogs," he said. "Can you believe it? They literally ate him up, crown to sole."' Thomas shakes his head as though wishing to rid himself of the image. 'The tinker also told me that someone came and rescued the schoolmaster's daughter. "A ginger knight dressed as a beggar," he said. "Whisked the girl to safety right under the robbers' noses. But listen to this: what the lad didn't realise, not until he'd got her to safety, was that the school-master had done surgery on her. On his own daughter! Turned her into half machine. I swear by all the popish saints."'

Thomas pauses, pulls a face.

'But that's nonsense. Gibberish.'

'Gibberish, Livia? I suppose so. I also met a man who told me there was a devil on the loose on the London road. A devil with a necklace made of human fingers.' Thomas stabs his spoon at the last morsel of fish. 'That "ginger knight" of the tinker's story, though, that must be Charlie. And if so, something happened at Renfrew's, something bad. And now he is lost, in between Oxford and here.'

'So what do we do? Charlie could be anywhere. And Mother's delivery is tomorrow night.'

'We should never have split up.' Thomas curses, rises, his face flushing dark with more than blood. 'What can we do? We wait.

'If Charlie's hurt,' he adds, storming out, 'I will make them pay. Your mother. The school. Everyone.'

But even here there is to the train of Smoke he leaves behind something other than his anger, something guilty, whispering her name.

Φ

Livia sits up late, talking to Grendel. It's that or going to bed. Wor-rying about Charlie. Listening to Thomas shift on the blankets in his room. It is the first night since leaving her father's house that she wishes she had never met the two boys.

So she sits and asks questions. About Grendel's youth. About London. About his work at the church. Then she asks Grendel about his neck. It is the only thing that's twisted about him. One side of his

280

throat appears shorter than the other. It bears the puckered line of a scar.

'How did this happen?'

'I did it myself. I was sitting shaving one morning. The razor in my hand. You know that sound it makes when it scrapes off the bristle. I heard it and felt lonely. Not just lonely. Alone in the world. A creature all to itself. So I thought to myself, why not end it? Or rather my hands thought it. It's like they had reasoned it out.' He shrugs, lopsided. 'I cut the muscle, largely. Missed the artery. The surgeon patched me up, only he was drunk and botched it, or so another surgeon told me when he had a look at his work. All the same, he saved my life. My wife, you see, she was the surgeon's daughter. She looked after me while I was lying sick.' His eyes grow warm. 'She figured out what I was, and she cared for me all the same.'

Livia sits still, trying to square this account with the woman whose house she has been sharing. Her life is not an easy one. She trawls the river mud each day, picks shellfish, mussels, rags and bone, then trades her findings against meat and money at the market; a cudgel dangling from her belt to ward off rivals. Mrs Grendel stood washing kidneys that evening, preparing them for the morrow, complaining about their price. 'Two extra mouths,' she kept saying, 'it is a strain on the purse.' All the while looking at Livia; the tang of urine rising from the sink.

What Livia says to Grendel is: 'You must love her very much.'

He heaves a sigh. 'I do. But I love her with my head. There are moments in married life when it is important that one love with other parts. That one forgets oneself and smokes.'

He stops abruptly, in doubt whether Livia is too young for such truths, and too nobly born.

'*Passion*,' she whispers, not looking at his face. 'You are talking about passion.'

He hesitates before he nods. 'I have seen it in others. It's a kind of greed.'

'You are saying you can't – in married life, I mean. And of course you have no children.'

He smiles shyly, looks about himself, furtive with the weight of his insight. 'Oh, I can, I can. But not with that greed. It makes a difference to one's wife.'

Φ

It is a small step from there, in conversational terms, and yet Livia is flustered by it, feels primness return to her bearing, bland modesty to her face. All Grendel does is point into the depths of the flat.

'Is that one your sweetheart then?'

'No.'

He seems surprised by her denial.

'You like him though.'

'He's a bully and a brute.'

He weighs her words, his gentle face grown gentler yet, speaking to her as though to a child.

'Then there is someone else. This Charlie, perhaps?'

Livia chews on this, not looking at him, struggling to turn away the lies that rise to her tongue.

'You can't like two people,' she says at last and flinches at the fear in her voice. 'Not like that.'

'Can't you, Livia? I wouldn't know.'

He gets up, his knees creaking, finds a bottle of port, almost empty, and pours them each a finger's depth of wine.

Φ

They sit and drink. Her mind has become stuck on the earlier word. 'Passion'. *Lust*, really, if one looks it in the eye. There is something so illicit to the word, Livia finds it hard to let it go. Grendel's questions have unsettled her. There is, on her lips, that strange tingling that presages Smoke. She is literally a breath away from sinning.

It makes her look at Grendel in renewed awe.

'So you really never feel it?' she asks him. 'Not even a hint? That moment just before the Smoke takes hold of you? Like a drug injected into your blood?'

He starts shaking his head, stops.

'Well, perhaps. There are times, you know, quite ordinary moments, when I stumble on the stairs in the belfry, say, and I bump my head, or the neighbourhood children pelt me with garbage for sport, when I think there's *something*. Just a hint, see, a buzzing in the skin.' He smiles and blushes, with pleasure. Then his smile wilts. 'But of course, I cannot be sure.'

'And you would like to smoke so very much? Even though it's evil?'

282

He nods, thoughtfully. 'It isn't evil. It's *human*. I'd give everything. For just an hour in the Smoke.'

'Then I have something for you.'

On impulse, before her better judgement can intervene, Livia reaches into her pocket. Collier's trousers, too large for her, her hand disappearing past its wrist. Three twigs, bent and brittle. She picks one at random and straightens it between her palms.

'Here, Grendel. Smell it.'

'What is it?'

'Sin. Packaged sin. You only have to light it. Who knows, it might just work.'

He nods, dumbfounded, then gets up to search the kitchen for matches. His fingers fail him when he tries to strike a match. Livia can see that he is shaking. She takes the box from his hand and lights the cigarette for him. His inhalation brings a blood-red glow to its tip. He holds the smoke down for as long as he can. The exhalation is a stream of grey, unspent; it curls around Livia's face and calls to her skin. Her own Smoke is there before she knows it, white like steam. It fills her with something, light and seductive, the feeling a gambler might have the moment he turns over the cards.

'Do you feel it, Grendel?'

A shy smile creeps over his face.

'I do feel a little wicked. Do I look it?'

'Oh, very much.' Emboldened, her skin steaming, Livia proffers the curve of her cheek. 'Do you want to kiss me? Go on. Your wife will never know.'

He does, quickly, shyly like a child.

'Oh, you rake!'

Through the open doorway they can hear Thomas groan in his sleep.

'It'll be our secret,' Livia says, pulling her legs up onto the stool while Grendel continues sucking on the cigarette, staring out of the crooked little kitchen window, and not a wisp of Smoke jumps from the pallor of his skin.

Φ

Later that night, Livia goes and stands over Thomas's sleeping body. He is agitated in his sleep, has kicked off the blanket, his rib cage rising and falling underneath his linen shirt.

'I picked up your cigarettes,' she confesses to him, a rustle in the silence of the room, 'because I thought there might come a moment when I'd like to sin. I was thinking of Charlie. I was not sure I would know how to touch him, out in the light.'

She lights a second cigarette, crouches down next to him, studies the stain of coal that mars his skin, the stump of ear sticking out of his shorn patch of hair like a mouldy potato.

'Lizzy said it, down in the mine,' she whispers. 'You will always be ugly.'

And then, just to try it, the cigarette curling in the corner of her mouth, she lies down next to Thomas and presses her cheek into his shoulder, and thinks of the doorway where he held her and warmed her with his shivering chest.

Φ

He wakes long after the cigarette is spent. She herself must have fallen asleep, for he has turned and is facing her now, his eyes aglitter in the dark. Livia finds that she is crying.

'I hate you. I hate everything you stand for. I hate what I find of you in myself.'

He is unmoved by her words, knows it all already, has read it in her Smoke.

'Hold me,' he says and she does, cheek flush with cheek, and the stump of his ear level with her mouth.

In the morning they roll apart without words and get ready to meet Charlie.

Φ

It is their fourth morning in London. The twelfth of January, the day of her mother's delivery. A day wet and raw. Charlie does not come. They stand on the market square morning to dusk, stamping their feet, cold, guilty, calling his name.

'The Tobacco Dock at midnight,' Livia says when she can no longer bear their silence. 'Charlie knows we will go. He might meet us there.'

Thomas does not answer. He flinches when she reaches for his arm.

What frightens her most is just how easy it is to picture Charlie dead.

284

Sailor

He hires us in La Rochelle. A whole ship's crew, right off the deck of our previous berth, the *Lorelei*, which is going into dry dock for repairs. Captain van Huysmans: a Dutchman of good repute. He comes personally, a fisherman rows him over; shakes hands with our own captain then explains his terms. There isn't much to it, a Channel crossing, there and back. Good money for a few days' work. There's only one condition: no landfall for us, we are to transfer straight onto the *Haarlem*. The men mutter, more than half of them decline. After weeks at sea we are all weary, longing for a bath, a drink, a woman, and it seems churlish somehow, secretive, to whisk us away within sight of the harbour. Those of us who agree transfer to the *Haarlem* in dinghies that very night. Herring rise all around us, feeding in the light of the three-quarter moon.

The *Haarlem* is a big steamer, built for the open ocean and its generous swell. The icy, crabby water of the Channel seems to suit it less. She lies twitchy in the waters. At dawn we run into a freezing mist and slow to a crawl. We can't see a thing. The hands squat in corners, play cards and dice, then quickly put the games away when the captain draws near.

He is everywhere. If I was captain with a nice, cosy cabin, I would stay there the whole journey. Lie in bed in my fancy uniform and holler for the cabin boy to fetch more food. Not so Captain van Huysmans. All night, he has haunted the deck. Going by his complexion, he must have spent time in the tropics: the pallor of freshly peeled skin, still sunburnt in the hairline. No doubt his arse is lily-white.

An odd duck, our captain. Restless, prone to nightmares when he sleeps. Fond of music, it would seem, of singing, but in some strange sour-toned manner that is hard to credit as joy. A well-behaved man, fastidious even. Most captains have one sort of manner when they deal with shipowners and quite another once they are at sea: a swear word here, a gust of Smoke there, a dirty joke. Not so van Huysmans. Stiff as a plank. A chubby man, but his heart is starched.

I complain to the cabin boy about it. Poppy. God knows how he came by the name. Poppy is a fellow of fourteen; this is his third voyage. A wide-eyed sort. The whole world is new to him. Looks up to all the sailors. I am a hero to him because at the age of forty-three I have managed to be promoted to the dizzying height of first mate.

'Our captain wants to be a gentleman,' I say to Poppy, watching van Huysmans mince around the deck.

'A gentleman!' Poppy replies enthusiastically, not catching my tone. 'Imagine it! Clean sheets, nobody cussing you out or even raising their voices. No pushing and shoving. A soft world.'

I snort. 'Always thinking before you speak. Inspecting your bedding in the morning. Keeping your farts in, lest they trigger something. A life lived with your arsehole clamped. Never letting rip.'

But the boy is adamant, forgets for a moment that I am his senior and prophet, his shipside god.

'What's so great about coarseness and dirt?' he asks.

And when I don't answer (for he's hit upon a point, I suppose) he adds, angry now, wet in his eye: 'They'll go to heaven, sir. And you and I shan't.'

Φ

The first set of customs officials boards us two full leagues off the coast. His Majesty's servants! And how thorough they are, how prim, fine gentlemen in worsted suits. Always in twos, watching each other's virtue like hawks. They must submit reports, it is said, about each other's behaviour. And all the same I would bet my pecker they are just as bent as that one-eyed thief that runs the port at La Rochelle. This is Britain, though. Here crookery has had a haircut, and its shirt cuffs are freshly ironed.

There are four checks in total. Each time the cargo is examined and re-examined. Seals are applied, paperwork lodged, fees paid. Each time our captain fawns and twitters; attempts small talk; offers drinks and is rebuffed. All captains are like this when it comes to customs.

But our captain is dripping with sweat.

'What are we smuggling, then?' I ask when yet another pair has left the ship and we are steaming down the mouth of the Thames.

Captain van Huysmans starts.

'A joke, Captain, a joke. What's our cargo? Spices? Flowers? Opium?'

He shakes his head, dries his forehead on a handkerchief.

'Machine parts.'

I whistle. 'Special permits?'

'Of course.' Then he blanches, as though in aftershock to my comments, cocks his head like he's heard the rumble of an approaching storm.

'If you will excuse me.'

And I swear he starts singing, shrilly and out of tune, hurrying to his cabin and trailing his handkerchief like a little white flag.

Φ

In good weather, you can see London all the way from the mouth of the Thames. Not a plume, exactly, more like a dark mist. Some of it is the factory chimneys, though the mist is darkest near the ground. Poppy stands next to me at the railing, staring at the mist ahead. I can see him make the sign of the cross.

He blushes when I laugh.

'Is it like they say it is?' he asks me shyly. 'Gomorrah? A den of thieves?'

'It's a city. The biggest in Europe.'

'But the Smoke.'

'It's where the sinners live. The workers, the paupers. Good people live in the country. Bad people there.

'It's like everywhere else,' I add a little later. 'Only more so.'

Φ

We head for the Tobacco Dock. There are cheers when the captain announces that the men are to take the night off. Even the cabin boy looks happy at the news. He is afraid of this Gomorrah, this den of thieves. But he wants to explore it too. I look forward to showing him around, talking some of his fear out of him, showing him that people are people, even here, when the captain takes me aside.

'Stay. I have special orders for you,' he announces quietly.

We haggle over it for the better part of an hour. Then the sum he names gets so large I begin to worry he will withdraw the offer. I am pleased, of course, but also afraid.

What grave felony must the man be up to if he is willing to pay a dozen gulden just for my standing around?

Delivery

'Do you think it's midnight yet?'

'How would I know? I haven't seen a single working clock in the entire city.' Thomas adds, thoughtfully: 'They'll have the time on the ship though, and nobody's stirred.'

'Are you sure about that?'

'This is a steamer, built for the open sea. They need a clock to take readings. Otherwise it'd be impossible to navigate. And there is no way on and off other than that plank.'

'You know about boats.'

'Ships. I grew up near the sea. Hush now, the watchman is coming back.'

They fall silent and watch the man approach. His movements are easy to follow, even at a distance. He has lit a pipe and with every puff the tobacco glows red in the darkness of the dock and reveals a fragment of his face, deep-lined, whiskered, a clean-shaven chin. He passes half a dozen steps from them, then turns and leaves behind the sweet smell of burnt vanilla. At his turn his heels squeak on the cobbles.

Rubber soles, thinks Thomas. *He is from the ship.*

At the far side of his round, the man stops, his pipe momentarily obscured by the back of his head. A moment later a sound can be heard, water hitting water. The dock lies so still that the noise travels through the dark. Then, his bladder empty, the man starts humming past the stem of his pipe. The melody that reaches them is unknown to Thomas; is lovelorn and sweet. After the second chorus, the man breaks off and resumes his round. The pool next to him lies flat, black, glassy: an absence of space, too Soot-soaked to reflect the occasional fragment of moonlight peeking through the clouds.

There are three such pools, rectangular in shape and connected to the Thames by deep, iron-gated locks. All three are gigantic. The largest might fit a score of cricket fields. The Tobacco Dock holds the smallest of the three basins, though it is still large enough to berth an East India steamer. All around the basin's rim rises a city of ware-houses, of workshops, cranes, ship parts, barrels and bollards. It is a landscape built for machines, towering husks of metal, sweating rust. A propeller stands by the side of the dock, each blade bigger than a man and twisting around itself like a broken-necked shovel. If machines had religion, this should be their cross. It is not hard to imagine a creature nailed onto its blades.

On all sides the quay is secured by a high brick wall. There is only one gate. Approaching it – passing through the crowded piers of the Western Dock just as work was winding down, then hiding behind a row of barrels until all the stevedores were gone – Thomas and Livia had found its doors unlocked, the guard booths empty, their entry witnessed only by the hinges' squeak. Thomas suspects that this is more than an oversight. The Western Dock does not admit foreign ships and security is light. But at the Tobacco Dock foreign custom is expected. Signs warn of trespass, and dense loops of a peculiarly spiky wire crown all the walls. Nonetheless the whole site stands abandoned, as though waiting for thieves. Someone has been paid off, the guards sent home, the dog kennels emptied for the night. All that remains is this one lone watchman. A careless fellow: thanks to the pipe, they spotted him as soon as they had passed through the gate. They have been playing hide-and-seek ever since.

It had been easy to identify the *Haarlem*. While the two other vessels tied up at the short end of the dock are little more than river barges, the ship by whose side they are cowering must be a hundred and fifty feet stern to prow. It reeks of the open sea. There are no waves in the basin but there must be a current of some sort, down deep. Periodically the ship will either tug at the ropes that secure it to the pier or lean on the padded barrels that ride between its flank and the wall: two types of groan, one taut and creaking, the other a patient grinding. They give texture to the night.

Close up to its side, it is hard to make out the ship's details: a confusion of masts and chimneys; the angular contours of an iron hull, sitting low in the water. They made their way there running from cover to cover, the dock a plane of overlapping shadows, deep as wells; then hid by a cluster of crates stacked man-high on the quay. The edge of the basin is five feet from their hiding place, the hull another three feet beyond. Above their heads droops a flag it is too dark to identify. Beneath, the water is viscous with the oily weight of undissolved Soot.

The watchman finishes another round. When he turns, Livia rises from her crouch and stretches. The night is raw and the wait has invited the cold into their limbs.

'Is it possible they've unloaded it already?' she whispers. 'It could be sitting right here, stacked on the quay.'

Thomas has asked himself the same question.

'Can't be,' he decides at last. 'If it is really all that valuable there would be a cordon of guards standing right next to it. Something else – have you noticed there isn't any crew? The captain must have sent them all ashore. Apart from that one, unless that's the captain himself. Whatever your mother is buying, it's so secret even the sailors mustn't know.'

Livia appears to consider this. It is so dark he cannot even guess at her features. And yet he would know her, just by the pattern of her breath.

'Tell me again what we know about this delivery.'

Thomas shrugs. 'I never even saw the ledger. Charlie read it. Midnight, the twelfth of January. The *Haarlem* out of La Rochelle, under a Captain van Huysmans. "Collect in person and arrange for transport." Whatever it is, it cost a fortune. Your mother must have wagered her entire estate.'

'So she will come.'

'Yes.'

'And then?'

'I don't know. Depends what it is, I suppose. All we can do is wait.'

But as the minutes creep by, measured only by the watchman's regular steps, waiting becomes more and more impossible. The cold is everywhere now, has crept through the ground and the soles of his shoes, up the inside of his thighs, and from there into his chest and back, his skin so goose-bumped it shies from contact with his clothes. Then, too, doubt has begun to tug at Thomas: that Lady Naylor won't come after all or that they have the wrong ship; that a bargain is being struck right now, deep in the hold, and a rowing boat will paddle all answers away across the stillness of the inky pool.

He speaks only after he has made his decision. Anything else would be a waste of words.

'I'll go the next time he turns away,' he says. 'See, when he passes the hut over there. You wait here and observe.'

Immediately she reaches over to detain him. Her hand on his arm. How normal it seems today for her to touch him. The thought makes him angry.

He shakes himself loose.

'*Where* are you going?' she hisses, too loud for the silence of the dock, though the guard does not appear to hear.

'Aboard. See what I can find out.'

She does something with her head, forgetting that he cannot see her, not here in the shadows of the cargo. A shake, a frown? That little gesture she makes sometimes – the lower lip pushed forward, a shrug of the chin, moving right to left, her eyes narrowing to almonds, tan and hard? Perhaps she is worried for him. But her objection is reasoned, matter-of-fact.

'You don't even know what you are looking for.'

'I do. "Arrange for transport." That means it's big. And at the same time squirrelled away someplace where it didn't attract notice. Not from the sailors and not from customs.' He touches one of the wax seals that marks the boxes they are hiding behind. 'I will know it when I see it.'

He withdraws his attention from her, counts the steps of the sailor. Not the captain, he has decided. It's too cold for that, too mindless a task, the man too bored, too unconcerned with his duty. A mate, a trusted man, or one too well-paid to simply skip out. Trailing the smell of burnt vanilla. One hundred and three steps for a full round. Nineteen while he is behind the customs booth, if that's what it is: hidden from sight. Nineteen leisurely steps. Thomas can reach the gangway in eight, cross it in three. All he will need to do is crouch behind the railing. A darkness melting into darkness. Theirs is a world of infinite depth.

He times it well and starts moving the moment the man disappears behind the booth. Halfway there he realises that his steps have an echo. He almost turns to shout at her, then reaches back and grabs her wrist. The plank has a spongy feel, creaks and vibrates underfoot. Passing this close, the hull comes into relief: rivets like pockmarks, adorned with barnacles, seaweed, rust. A tangy smell, thick in his mouth, not unlike blood.

They hit the floor as soon as they are across. Ice-cold iron against his cheek. The plank is still moving, a regular quiver, up and down, just audible in the still of the night. Wave physics, they learned about them in school: with pencil and paper, he could work out its amplitude. Pencil and paper – and a sliver of light. Beside him Livia is the sound of her breath.

Thomas counts to fifty and nobody raises the alarm. One hundred and three steps. He counts to fifty more.

They crawl forward, reach the cabin wall, then the narrow space between two cabins, fore and aft. Two stairwells, each pointing downward, felt rather than seen. He picks aft on instinct. At the bottom, silence stretching ahead, Thomas can no longer contain his anger.

'You were supposed to wait!'

She inhales his Smoke like she is drinking him, spits back his anger.

'I am not yours to order around.'

There is something else in her breath, something roughly tender. It frightens Thomas, how well they speak without words.

Φ

They make their way by touch. Thomas has a sense that the main holds should be down and aft, so down and aft they head. The corridors that lead them there are narrow enough to touch both walls with angled elbows. As they descend a second staircase, the quiet around them changes into something else, duller and heavier than before. They must have stepped below the waterline. At intervals a creak runs the length of the ship, urgent and pitiful, metal shifting in the cold.

They find a door. He recognises it by the heavy bar of its bolt. His hands locate the handle, the hinges, then, on a little shelf by the door's side, a lamp and matches. Once they are through and have waited out the darkness with a dozen breaths, he dares light the lamp, the door shut and bolted behind his back. The eye flinches from the sudden light, then feasts on it. Steel engines, man-high, the swell of their sides hung with pressure meters as though with medals. A mound of coal ready for the shovelling. Levers, valves, some pairs of heavy leather gloves with greaves, dark with sweat and coal. Livia is about to speak but he shushes her, points to a cluster of pipes descending from the ceiling, each ending, face-high, in a fluted metal bell; a bouquet of trumpets.

'Speaking tubes,' he whispers, his mouth close to her ear. 'To the bridge, the captain's cabin, up to the deck.'

He bends his ear to the flaring bells. One carries a sound, rhythmic, as of fingers snapping at a distance. Confused, Thomas gestures to it. Livia's ear proves better than his.

'Steps,' she mouths.

Now he hears it, too: someone pacing, back and forth, a pause where he turns tightly on his heels. A confined space, but bigger than most on a ship. The captain's cabin.

Then the steps cease and, after a minute, are replaced by an eerie crackling, from which, as from a sack of gravel, emerges a voice. A woman, singing, her pitch near-perfect but subject to odd wavers, soft ululations half stuck in her throat. She is joined by an instrument, a violin, sweet, note-perfect, but similarly wayward as though time ebbs and flows for its player against the pulse of his beat. He looks to Livia for explanation but she merely shakes her head. The captain's cabin. A singer, a fiddle, a pair of boots measuring the cabin, side to side. A copper pipe speaking through the mouth of a bell. It is like a missive from the realm of ghosts, disembodied and obscure. They smother the gas lamp before exiting the door.

A few steps from the engine room, Thomas's hands find another bolt and, beneath it, an icy metal wheel, five turns of which open the room ahead. Only the drip of water disturbs its silence, echoes coolly in the air. A large room, then, a hold. Livia has held on to the gas lamp and now lights its wick. A scramble of shadows, then the room comes into focus, an iron-walled hall supported by girders, only half full with cargo. Crates and barrels mostly and, beyond them, an array of metal parts: articulated pipes, gear wheels, fan blades and giant perforated disks, like overgrown pieces of plumbing, stacked into a mound and secured to the floor by heavy chains. Not waiting for Thomas, Livia walks the lamp down the length of the hold and takes an inventory, placing a palm on each item, one by one. As she walks deeper into the space, the lamp dislodges movement at the edge of its shine. A hard bony clicking, claws on steel. Livia's movements are flushing the sounds towards him. She is walking boldly in her circle of light, her eyes on the cargo, never looking about. He supposes this means she has heard the rats, too. Her return causes a second wave of scrambling, inverted now, back into the far reaches of the hold.

'Whatever we are looking for, it isn't here,' she reports. 'All items have customs stamps. Some of them have several. Brazil, Portugal, France. England.'

'And it would be hard to hide anything down here.' Thomas scans the room again. His eyes are drawn to the giant metal parts. 'Machinery. You wouldn't think they'd be allowed to import it. Not with the embargo in place.'

'The seal on them is a different colour. A special licence, perhaps. What do you think they are for?'

'Don't know. Come, it must surely be midnight now.'

As he says it a sound carries to them from the quay, a whistle. It reaches them faint and tinny, down here under the waterline.

'The watchman. Something's happening.'

Without needing to discuss it, they rush to the door and re-enter the corridor outside.

Φ

A light has been lit. It is far away, broken up by stairwells and corridors. But as they scramble their way back down the corridor by touch – their own lamp long extinguished – and reach the first sets of stairs, they catch a hint of it, enough to suggest a direction. It seems at once foolish and inevitable that they should follow it, making haste, hungry for answers. A moment later – a corridor, a bend – and it is gone, leaving them stranded, disoriented.

Then a voice sounds. Another voice answers. They are too far away to make out either words or speaker.

'Above.' Livia whispers it, close to his ear. She must be standing on tiptoe. 'They are on deck.'

'Your mother?'

'Not sure. What now?'

The light makes the decision for them. There it is again, moving purposefully now, towards them, trailing the sounds of steps. Unwilling to be caught out, they back away from it. A junction forces a decision: left or right. They choose badly, the light following and their path cut off by a door. It stands ajar. They slip through, into a room cluttered with shadows, conscious that they will be caught. There are not enough yards between them and their pursuers to find a likely hiding space. Then the light relents; pauses; slips a wedge through the half-open door, like an angular toe. It finds a carpet, and a sliver of wood-panelled wall. At the same time a voice can be heard, distinct now and foreign.

'Look now,' it says, its accent thick, tilting the vowels and giving an odd sharpness to the *k*, 'before we go in, we must talk about the money.'

'You have been paid, and generously.'

In other circumstances it would be a shock to hear it again. Lady Naylor's voice. A wonder of a voice, actually: composed and reasonable; at once amiable and aloof. But Thomas is busy, scanning the room for a hiding place. Shapes peel themselves from shadows. A bed, a desk, some chairs. The bed is built into the wall, the chairs too small to cower behind. At one side, two portholes glow with a lighter shade of dark. The clouds must have lifted and the moon come out.

'There have been complications. I had all sorts of problems getting past the authorities. And then the refitting costs! Do you have any idea how difficult it was to find a suitable carpenter in La Rochelle?'

'We can discuss all that once we have seen the merchandise. After you, Captain.'

A new voice this, also accented, if differently. Shy and precise. A man used to talking, but not about himself. Thomas pictures him to himself even as he finds the wardrobe, built into the wood panelling in such a manner that only its key protrudes. Livia sees it at the same time. It's deeper than expected, but low. They cower amongst shirt-sleeves, their limbs entangled, her hair in his mouth. A fingertip inserted into the keyhole, a sharp little pull, and the wardrobe door closes behind them just as the cabin door is pushed wide open and light floods the room.

Φ

They take turns at the keyhole. The door is not locked and hangs open a tiny crack: they must not lean their face against it, lest it move. Then, too, the key is in the keyhole: does not quite block it but leaves to them only a curved sliver through which to observe.

Three people. The captain is plump, soft-faced, balding beneath light blond curls. He is turning away now, bending, lighting an additional lamp. White trousers underneath a short-cut pea coat. A picture-book sailor, with a wide, fleshy rear.

Lady Naylor stands close to him, looking pale and thin; handsome, thinks Thomas, a stretched, pinched version of her daughter.

The third man is at the edge of Thomas's field of vision: not old, fine-boned. An umbrella in his gloved hand. Both he and milady cast about the room. *They have seen us*, it comes to Thomas. Her face – backlit now, the lamp a halo at the back of her head – is taut with impatience. Somewhere behind Thomas and Livia, as though in the wood itself, a rat is scraping, digging channels into the wardrobe's back.

'Where—' Lady Naylor begins to ask but is interrupted by the captain's eagerness.

'This is just what I mean. It took the carpenter a month to get it right. It had to be *seamless*. And just like the old cabin, in case one of the customs people remembered. Some men have a surprising memory for that sort of thing. The same cabin, exactly. Only we shrank it by forty cubic feet.'

He paces nervously as he speaks. Thomas recognises the sequence of steps. Four steps, four steps. Then he stops at a machine, a little box with a fluted bell, like the head of a lily made of brass.

'I had to hire a whole new crew. Just to be safe! The old ones might have noticed something. Good men, too, hard to replace! And then the journey. Days at sea, lying here in my bunk, and the devil restless behind the wall. Played music through the nights, just to drown out the sounds. I aged twenty years, I swear.'

'You followed my instructions minutely?'

It is the man with the umbrella who asks. He has stepped closer to the wardrobe, as though sensing them there. Livia pushes Thomas's head aside, takes charge of the keyhole. He leans back, hears again that scratching at his back, pictures the rodent squatting in the dark, its claws an inch from him, fanned out and eager.

'Yes, of course. We used the lead lining, just as instructed. And I kept a sweet in my mouth, even at night. Nearly choked on it more than once. And feeding times . . .'

Thomas hears a crash and, pressing his cheek into Livia's, catches a glimpse of the captain retrieving a stick he has dislodged from its perch. It is stout, the length of a broom handle, and has an oddly shaped metal hook at one end.

'I got quite adept with this, fending it off while pouring your concoction down its throat.'

'*Him*,' says the man with the umbrella. 'It is a he.'

Behind Thomas, the rat scratches the wall. Then it starts screaming, a sound high-pitched, inarticulate, feral. And also: human. Thomas's body knows it before his head has finished the thought. He and Livia react as one. They jerk away from the noise.

It pushes open the wardrobe door.

Φ

It is not that they spill out and tumble to the floor like potatoes from a bust sack. But all the same the door is open and a foot is sticking out into the open. The man with the umbrella reacts first. He steps up and pulls them out, by an ankle and a shoulder. They are so conjoined that they drop to the ground together, a muddle of limbs. For all the shock their presence must cause him, the man is not interested in them. He steps over, sticks his head into the wardrobe, stands there sniffing.

'Did you smoke?' he asks them, clipped and measured, not shouting. 'In the wardrobe, did you smoke?

When they don't answer, he gestures to the captain. 'Take them out of here. Quick now. You, too, Katie, if you will?' This last part to Lady Naylor who is staring at them in pale silence.

By the time Thomas has recovered his wits, the captain is holding him and Livia by their arms and is pushing them out of the cabin, all the while muttering excuses, curses, his head drawn into his body, a dog expecting to be whipped. Outside, his grip relents a little. Thomas might be able to wrench free. What then, however? Run away? Hide? They have come too far to leave without answers.

Lady Naylor saves him the decision.

'Let go of them,' she instructs the captain. Then, taking the lamp out of the Dutchman's hand: 'You may go now. Wait for us on deck.'

Captain van Huysmans hesitates only a moment before walking away, red-faced and shaking his head. He must be honest enough a man to know he has lost command of his ship. Lady Naylor shines the lamp after him until she is sure he is gone. Only then does she turn to Livia.

'You are alive!' The relief on her face is unmistakable.

All the same Livia evades the hand her mother stretches out towards her.

'You tried to kill us!' she rages, and a curl of Smoke fills the space between them.

They both stare at it, mother and daughter, while it settles as Soot on one side of the lamp and colours the light. Livia's face shows defiance, Lady Naylor's a mixture of puzzlement, relief and pride.

'So you learned to sin.'

'No jests, Mother, no clever talk, no evasions. You tried to kill us. We have a right to know why!'

'Is that what you think? Why you went into hiding? That I sat in that windmill and took potshots at my own child? It makes sense, I suppose. No, I did not try to kill you, my love. I believe Julius did.'

'Because you ordered him to!'

'I didn't.' A frown appears on Lady Naylor's forehead, fine-etched, scrupulous. 'I merely asked him to scare the boys into returning.'

Her palm rises to halt any further questions and she looks back over her shoulder, to the door of the captain's cabin.

'Hush now, I beg you. There are more pressing things to discuss. How long were you in there? You may have done terrible, irreversible harm. And yet I am glad to see you! Strange, isn't it? Foolish! Our one and only chance and here you may have dashed it all. When did you slip into the captain's wardrobe?'

'We came just before you did.'

It is Thomas who answers and for the first time her gaze jumps from her daughter to him. She takes in his ear; his dirty, Soot-starched clothes.

'What's behind the wardrobe, Lady Naylor?'

'Change,' she answers. 'Revolution.' Her voice shakes with the word, as does her hand and with her hand the lamp: the corridor spinning, skirmishes of light and dark. 'But I am a fugitive now. The manor has been searched, and my London house is being watched. Trout's after me.'

'The headmaster?'

'Headmaster? Why yes! I forgot that you know him. See, your headmaster is like the rest of us: he has a past. Master Trout has returned to his old profession.'

Before she can explain further, the door of the cabin swings open and the gentleman with the umbrella steps out. Thomas has a clearer view of him now. The man is small, slight, doe-eyed; elegant in a brown wool suit and fawn-coloured gloves. Unusually for a man of his station, he does not appear to have brought a hat. He speaks to Lady Naylor, not to them.

'I think it is all right, Katie. Significant weight loss and anaemia, but no sign of infection. I have put on his respirator now. We will know for sure once I have taken some blood tests.'

Thomas notes again the familiar use of the first name. *Katie*. Lady Naylor's name, he believes, is Catherine. These two know each other well. From the Continent; in a different tongue, perhaps. The man's accent is slight if distinct, the words overly clipped.

'This must be your daughter. And one of the boys you told me about. Thomas, is it? The Smoker.' He looks at them with interest. *Gently*, if such a thing is possible. There is no harshness to the man. 'We must leave the ship now. Will they pose an obstruction to our plans?'

He turns without waiting for an answer, back into the room, closing the door behind him. His question remains with them, a problem he expects them to figure out by themselves. For a long minute, not one of them has the heart to take it on. Then Thomas speaks.

'What is he talking about, this man?' Thomas is not smoking yet, but he can feel it close, the edge of rage. At what exactly, he does not know. 'Who is he? What plans?'

Lady Naylor watches him intently. He is reminded of the night when he confronted her in her study: he held a letter opener then, and searched her skin for a likely place to bury its point. He might have killed her that night. But is this true? The Smoke – visible now, curling from his nostrils, from the stump of his ear – may be darkening his memories. Even the past bristles with his anger. It must take courage for her to step close to it, lay a hand on his chest. He does not flinch.

'I promise I will tell you, Thomas. On my husband's life. But right now we need to leave the ship before Trout catches up with us. Or all is lost.'

She waits until his Smoke dissipates before phrasing a question of her own.

'Was it you who set Trout on me?'

'No.'

'I am not accusing you,' Lady Naylor smiles. 'I am just wondering what set him off.'

'Charlie,' Livia says.

Thomas has the same thought. A stab of fear in his guts, down low, beneath the navel. *People talk about hearts too much*, he thinks. And reaches out, Lady Naylor's eyes following the gesture, to squeeze Livia's hand.

Φ

The man with the umbrella emerges. He is followed by a monster. Four feet high and livid with the smells of the chamber pot, its hands cuffed to a belt. Where the face should be something else reigns, not quite a blank. Smooth, hairless skin, more black than brown: taut on top then hanging slack around the cheeks and neck. Twin lenses for eyes, palm-sized, ringed in metal. A leather trunk for a mouth, trailing to its chest.

A mask, Thomas realises. *A child in a mask.*

The man has attached a leash to his belt and walks the boy past them in precise, urgent steps. The child himself shuffles as though drugged; shoulders stooping; hopeless. They are past before Thomas can demand an explanation. All he can do is fall in step behind.

Up on deck the captain stands quietly near the stairwell. It is too dark to see his face. The man with the umbrella passes him a purse, then turns away without a word, marching the child across the plank. On the quay he stops, takes off his long woollen coat, and carefully wraps the child in it head to toe. The next moment he has gathered him up, is cradling the boy against his body: a shapeless mass, four feet long and sagging at the centre.

'Wait here,' the man orders, then walks briskly down the quay. After five steps he is no more than a shadow. After ten, he is lost in the night.

Lady Naylor rushes to the shelter of a tollbooth, beckons to them. Thomas hesitates. 'I did not try to kill you,' she told them. Thomas finds that he believes her. Does that mean she is their friend? Her steps are hasty at any rate, the boot heels loud on the empty quay. *She is nervous*, it comes to Thomas. *Impatient. Afraid.* But perhaps he is simply projecting his own feelings, his heart too large in his chest, clenching, unclenching like a swollen fist.

Again she beckons, and still he remains out in the open, Livia by his side.

'So it's all about this child,' he calls over, taking pleasure in the noise. 'Where are you taking him?' Then it dawns on him. 'The cage. The cage in your laboratory. It is meant for him.' He shudders. 'I thought it was for me.'

'For you?' Her surprise seems genuine. 'Yes, of course. It's Renfrew's fault. He told you that you had murder in your heart. He scared you, did he? And true enough, your Smoke has a certain quality. It is *attuned* to Julius's in quite a startling manner. A phenomenon worthy of further study. Once upon a time I might have found a use for you.'

In the dark, across the distance, all he can see is the pale oval of her face. The eyes are deep pools, devoid of expression.

'Poor Thomas. All this time you thought you were special. At the centre of events: your Smoke the key to all the secrets in the world.' The words are mocking. But her voice carries sympathy. 'Here is the coach. You have a decision to make. Are you coming or not?'

Thomas and Livia look at one another. There is no need to discuss it. They can stay and remain ignorant. Or they can go along and get answers. One after the other they squeeze into the little fly that has pulled up in front of them, an unknown coachman on the box. If they had wanted to leave, they would have done so already.

The next moment they race off, down the quayside and through the metal gate, still unmanned. A quarter mile on, they slow to a less conspicuous speed. The clip-clop of hooves half drowns their conversation.

Φ

'Talk! Explain yourself. Who are you? Who is the child?'

The stranger is unfazed by Thomas's anger. He is sitting across from him, holding the child in his lap, his umbrella hooked into his elbow and tangling up their feet.

'Patience. Call me Sebastian. Here is my hand. How do you do? Mr Argyle. Miss Naylor. You take after your mother, my dear, if you don't mind my saying. Exquisite bones. Lady Naylor has told me all about you two, and about Mr Cooper, too, of course. Now first things first, if you don't mind. We have to make an adjustment to our plans.' He turns to Lady Naylor, his voice precise, even, confident. 'Where are we going, Katie?'

Lady Naylor hesitates over the answer. 'Are your lodgings being watched, too?'

'No, they don't know about me yet. But it will be noticed if I bring guests. And there is no easy way of smuggling in the child. You do not have another apartment in town?'

'I have two more. But Trout will be onto them already.'

'Very well, we have no choice then. All the inns in the city will be searched, and we need shelter fast. We must leave the city and go to my country cottage. We shall leave via Moorgate.' He pauses long enough to close his eyes then open them again: a gesture more deliberate than a blink. 'What about these two?'

The man's voice and eyes remain soft. And yet there is a threat to the statement.

We know too much. Witnesses, that's all we are to him. Peripheral. Disposable. The thought startles Thomas, recalls his earlier humiliation. *All this time you thought that you were special. At the centre of events.*

So perhaps he is nobody after all. An angry youth: his father's child. But Livia's with him, and he must protect her. There could be a blade in the shaft of that umbrella, a gun hidden in those trouser pockets. Lady Naylor appears to sense Thomas's thought. She speaks to him rather than her daughter.

'It's like this,' she says. 'Either you betray us, and everything stays just as it is. The lies, the sweets and cigarettes, the whole hypocrisy of power. Or we end it all. Send it crumbling into dust.'

'An end to Smoke.' Livia's voice is thick with something. Hard to say whether it is suspicion or hope. 'Is that what you have been working on? A new world of virtue?'

Lady Naylor nods then gathers her daughter's hands in hers, a scooping gesture, like pushing together the crumbs scattered on a table.

'Yes! A new world of virtue. Of justice. I am doing this for your father.'

Justice. The word is like a call to arms. It triggers a yearning in Thomas. He struggles to contain it.

'What about the child?' he asks gruffly. 'Will he come to harm?'

His eyes seek out the shapeless lump of limbs and coat on the stranger's lap; he thinks of the scratching in the wardrobe and the captain brandishing his twisted hook. It is hard not to see that the child has come to harm already.

The man who calls himself Sebastian follows his gaze.

'The child will come to further inconvenience. But not to harm.'

'Then where are his parents? You stole him. And here he is alone and frightened.'

'We had him stolen. But the place he comes from . . . Please understand that his life was not a good one.'

'Would you have stolen him if it had been?'

'Naturally, yes. All the same, we saved him from deprivation. Though you will say that we imposed starvation on him all over again.'

There is something disarming about Sebastian. He appears to have no capacity for hiding behind self-deception. At the same time there is to him a calculation that reminds Thomas of Renfrew. He too has made a god of reason. Just now Sebastian's mind is moving seamlessly from the ethics of child theft to the layout of London.

'Ah, I see we have passed Spitalfields Market. Time to alert the coachman to our new destination. Alas there are grave risks in leaving the city. The gates may already be watched. It may prove difficult to return.'

Sebastian is about to rap at the little window that separates them from the box, when Livia stops him. Her hands are still in her mother's fists.

'We know a place. You won't be found there.'

She hesitates, her eyes fierce with a kind of angry hope.

Don't, Thomas thinks. *We have no right.*

But Livia does not seek his advice.

'We are staying with some people. A man and his wife. We met them by chance. You can trust them.' A beat, a twitch of the mouth. 'If we can trust you, Mother.'

'But of course. I swore it, did I not?' Lady Naylor looks at Livia in pleasure. 'These people you met – they are poor?'

'Yes, very.'

'Good. Then we can pay them. Tell us the way.'

Φ

When they pull up at a corner not far from Grendel's house, Thomas is still trying to figure it out. They set off that evening to spy on an enemy. Now they are leading her *home*: the only place in the world where, for the moment, they have reason to consider themselves safe. And so, in the course of a few hours they appear to have changed sides. There wasn't even a great deal of talk to it. All Lady Naylor has told them is that she bears them no ill will. She is fighting the Smoke. And has kidnapped a child, with the help of a stranger with doe-like eyes.

It is not much to build one's faith on.

And yet: here they are, abusing the trust of a man who suffers from kindness as though from the flu. They wait until the coach has disappeared out of sight, then rush through the dark streets, Sebastian carrying the child wrapped in his coat and slung over one shoulder. The child is unnaturally still. Drugged, Thomas surmises. Their new friends are not picky about their methods.

For all that it is a relief to step into the little courtyard behind the house's burnt front and ascend the narrow staircase to the top floor. Livia looks tense when she knocks on the door. Perhaps she regrets her eagerness to volunteer a hideaway. Neither she nor Thomas have mentioned Grendel's condition. If he is found out – well, what then? Thomas still has not decided whether he pities the man or admires him. Grendel is an ox in a world of irate bulls: a kind creature, given to melancholy and fond of his food. If Lady Naylor's future is to be a world of Grendels, Thomas can think of worse.

It is their host himself who opens the door. He sees Livia first, gets excited, flaps his hands, almost extinguishing the stub of candle he is holding.

'You are back! Come quick. You will never believe—'

Then he spies Sebastian and Lady Naylor in the dim of the stairwell.

'Friends of yours?' A step backward as he says it. Behind Grendel, someone else is rushing to the door.

'My mother,' Livia replies. 'I'm afraid we will have to impose.'

Grendel nods, distracted, not moving. His eyes are on Sebastian and the bundle he is holding, wriggling now, waking up. At Grendel's side a new face pushes itself into the sparse glow of the candle. It takes Thomas a heartbeat to recognise him. It's not just that Charlie is thin. Something has happened to him, a loss weightier than pounds. Still he is smiling. Then the smile freezes on his lips. It might be the sight of Lady Naylor that saps his joy. But Charlie's eyes are on Livia and Thomas, not on the threesome they have brought.

We are not even touching, Thomas thinks. *It must show then, like Smoke.*

A moment later Thomas has pushed past Grendel and wrapped Charlie in a hug. His friend hangs limp in his arms, a sack of bones.

Captain

They pick me up at four twenty-five, ship time. Perhaps it is chance that determines the hour, but if they want to scare a man, find him at his most vulnerable, his weakest, they could hardly have picked a better moment. The crew has not returned yet and there is no one to warn me before the hammering on the door. They refuse to let me dress. A man in his nightshirt marched down the gangplank to a coach; his bare legs flashing in the wind: what more ridiculous spectacle can there be?

The stranger in the coach is kindly and stupendously fat. We sit on the same side, and he makes such a depression in the seat cushion that I am forever tumbling towards him. The last I see of my ship is a squadron of men, swarming over its decks. Not one of them wears a uniform. Whatever they are, they wish to appear other. Gentlemen. A gentleman would have allowed me to pull on my drawers. I shiver and fret and feel ashamed for the pools of Soot that glue my nightshirt to my belly and thighs.

I rage at my captor, of course: tell him that I am a subject of Her Majesty, the Queen of the Netherlands; that this is an outrage, an outrage; that I demand to be released at once. But the fat man merely pats my shoulder and never answers, as though agreeing with me that these words need to be said, that they are part of the form of things, and that it is best to get them all out at once. The only time he interrupts me is when my protestations take on the pitch of a shout. Then he lays a finger across his lips. He is wearing gloves. It quiets me down, precisely this part, his wearing gloves. Of course, it is cold, and no gentleman is fully dressed without. Still, it brings something home. The potential for violence. It is easy to picture these gloves, bunched into fists. And all the time he is cheerfully silent.

When we have travelled some half an hour, the man reaches into the darkness at his feet, retrieves a hood, and pulls it over my head. He might be putting blinkers on a horse. I could struggle, but his touch is so deft, so simple, neither rough nor gentle, that I don't have the heart.

At first I find I do not mind the hood. It absolves me in a way. I no longer need to shout and protest, or pay attention to the road we are taking; need not muster courage for resistance or escape. It is only when we alight and I am ushered into a building that the blindness begins to transform into fear, then abject panic. There are sounds around me, you see, sounds I cannot place. Typewriters, I think, and once a shrill little peal. Men talking at a distance in a serious manner, never laughing, nor raising their voices. A place of business. Large, it seems to me, subterranean. We keep descending stairs. A scream, not far from us, like a cat with its tail caught in a slamming door. But this is no place for cats. I am weak in the legs when they push me down upon a stool and pull off the hood.

An office. A carpet, a bookshelf, a desk at the centre, the fat man behind. No windows. A smell to the place like boiled dish towels. A coiled beast of a radiator dispensing too much heat. There are no guards in the room. My captor offers me a glass of water that he decants from a large pewter jug.

For the longest time he does not ask any question but simply sits there, reading various letters arranged on his desk. The stool I am sitting on turns out to be very uncomfortable. It is an inch or two shorter than a regular stool, and my knees jut up awkwardly when I plant my soles. I consider re-rehearsing my protestations, or at least requesting a different chair, but despite the glass of water my throat is very dry.

At long last a younger man enters the office without knocking. He is impeccably dressed, rounds the desk without looking at me, bends down to the fat man, and whispers something in his ear. Then he passes over a folder full of papers, before retracing his steps and leaving the room. His boots were muddy and he has left prints on the floorboards (he avoided stepping on the carpet). I keep looking at these prints while my captor studies his papers. From my vantage point, lower than his, he appears cut in half: the top half leaning forward on his elbows, the lower, beneath the desk, impassive. He has crossed his legs. Oxford shoes. Unlike his clerk's boots they are unsullied by dirt.

When he has read and turned over the last of the papers, he closes the folder, takes a fountain pen out of his jacket pocket, makes a note in a booklet lying on his desk. For a moment he looks like a teacher. No, a headmaster. Disciplining a delinquent. I shift my weight on the stool.

Then he finally speaks.

'Here we are, Captain van Huysmans. Only, you must be wondering where "here" is. What criminal enterprise is this, operating in the heart of London? What sort of robbers are these that have taken hold of you? What can you do to set yourself free?

'And then, you heard the typewriters, as we passed them in the corridor. I saw your head tilt. Typewriters, in England! Even on the Continent, I understand, only a small number of bureaucracies have adopted them wholesale. Always, always, there is resistance to innovation – even without any embargo. I find this reassuring. Human nature at its best. Afraid of the new. And yet, I approve of our typewriters. Our reports, see, they become easier to read, and by putting special paper between the pages, we can create copies even as we type the original. It is miraculous, really.

'So who are these men, who can abduct you with impunity, who have access to foreign technology, and who have use for records and reports? I will let you in on a secret, a terrible secret. *England has a police force.* Not officially, mind. Three times the issue has been debated in Parliament and three times it has been rejected. A police force is something for the French, the Germans! For godless countries in which the government spies on its citizens. For what is a police force if not an army of spies and meddlers? People invading the privacy of our homes! Our gentry are partial to their homes, you see. They like to be able to lock the door.

'And yet, all the same, here it is. A *secret* police force, created by a subcommittee for public welfare. A very tiny committee it is. Five permanent members. Not aligned with either of the parties but neutral. A pure organ of the state, if you will. One of the first things they did was to have strands of wire drawn across the land. In secret of course, underground where possible, a thin, fragile network. Seven telephones: that is all we have, after a decade of work. I took my first call a few days ago, and how foolish I felt, shouting words into the ether.

'So here we both are, at headquarters. I am not even a regular officer! Past my youth too: too old – too fat! – to go trundling after bad people. But there are so few of us with any experience, and the matter is so very sensitive and at the same time so very important. All hands on deck, and those with experience, well, one likes to do what one can, doesn't one? For Queen and country; for the good of the state. I am sure you will understand. My remit, I am afraid, is near-absolute. I can quite literally do to you whatever I wish. Ghastly, when one thinks about it. I prefer not to.'

All this the man recites quite fluently and without any menace, his chubby hands folded together high on his chest. For the first time I see that he is wearing sleeve protectors that run black from wrist to elbow. For some reason, this detail bothers me just as his gloves did before. How different is it, I wonder, from a butcher donning his apron before stepping into the abattoir?

'We had your ship searched, Captain. The cargo, it appears, is entirely in order. None of the custom seals have been meddled with and all the contents match up to the inventory you filed with the authorities. There are a number of pieces of illegal technology on board, but all these are listed and licensed: as long as they remain on board, there can be no objection. The logbooks are in order and chart your ship's recent voyages without any obvious anomaly. Your private ledger is similarly unremarkable, though it contains a receipt for a very sizeable amount of money made out to you by the Behrens Bank of Rotterdam. Now this would be entirely your business, if it were not suspected that the money in question originates in England and was, in fact, paid to you by Lady Catherine Naylor acting as the legal signatory of her husband, Baron Archibald Naylor, and with the Behrens Bank acting only as middleman. One may well say, however, that a man may accept money no matter where it comes from. It is noted that it was paid into your private accounts rather than the company who has ownership of the ship. You are a rich man, Captain van Huysmans. I congratulate you.

'On the ship itself, there is but one anomaly. It took my men a while to see it, it has been very well masked. Somewhere along your journey you had your cabin altered. It was very cleverly done. The proportions and look of the cabin were left entirely unchanged, but a narrow, L-shaped compartment was created behind the wood-panelling at the bow and starboard sides. A foot and a half in width, if this hasty drawing my men made is to scale, and perhaps five feet long in all. Not one of the crewmen we have located on shore knows a thing about this secret compartment, Captain van Huysmans, not even your first mate whom you had performing guard duty between the hours of ten and ten to one tonight, and who was dismissed by you the moment a certain coach pulled up at the end of the quay. You will understand that we are curious about this compartment. What in God's name were you smuggling onto our shore, Captain?'

Of course it occurs to me to lie. An animal, I want to say, a tiger. Brought from furthest Sumatra, for a collector of exotic beasts.

But I am afraid to lie.

No, not just afraid. I recognise his authority. Not as a police officer but as a gentleman. His complexion is clear, his moral imperative beyond doubt.

So I ask instead: 'What will you do to me?'

'For smuggling?' He weighs it, puffing out his cheeks, then letting out the air in a silent whistle. 'Technically, it *is* a felony. A judge would have to hear the case. He might very well condemn you to the rope.

'Then again, we don't really want to involve a judge. Who knows what you might tell him about this, our amiable chat? Square with me, Captain. Tell me all. If you do, we won't touch a hair on your head. You can keep your money. Of course you are done doing business in this country. All travel privileges will be revoked. You will never clap eyes on fair England again. But then, this may be inevitable. There is a bill up for vote that will mark the end of foreign trade. One of our nobility, an illustrious earl, has lost his son to Irish hoodlums. He wants the borders shut for good.'

I consider his proposition. It is a damp country, this, no more beautiful than most. I shall not miss it. And I am, as he said just now, a rich man. It would be foolish to ask for guarantees. Or have him spell out the alternative. They are the secret police. They will do with me as they please.

'What,' he resumes, 'did you transport in your secret compartment, Captain? Mind now, I won't ask again.'

'The devil,' I answer. It feels good to say it. It has lain heavy on my heart. 'The devil in the body of a child.'

Φ

I tell him almost everything. The letter I received by private courier more than a year ago, the meeting with an agent in Rotterdam, then the dealings with the explorer in Belém. A rough man, I try

310

to explain, used to living in the jungle. Instructions reaching me in the New World by telegraph, terse little missives that I read in the mildewed foyer of a self-styled Grand Hotel. How well I recall them when my captor prompts me, almost word for word! On the telegrams' instruction, I ordered repairs when they weren't needed and had the ship brought into dock for twenty-three days. A dreary seaport, the sailors drunk and whoring, the heat of the jungle rotting the clothes off our backs.

When they finally brought it, it came in a crate. The lid nailed shut and reinforced with ropes, like they were transporting a tiger. They loaded the crate at night: a group of natives, twigs through their noses, looking scared. And all the time, there was an invisible hand behind it all, some master strategist who, telegram by unsigned telegram, pushed us around a giant draughtsboard of his own design.

I had no contact with the cargo until we arrived in Europe. We'd emptied a hold for it and there it remained for the whole of the voyage: one crate, chained to the wall, and its guardian, the scar-faced explorer. A Boer he was, speaking with the awful dialect of the settlers there; always chewing on a native leaf. I did not see him more than a handful of times during three weeks at sea. Each time he had grown thinner, sallow, hollow-cheeked. We had difficult seas.

The paperwork proved to be no problem: a bag of money changed hands, and all stamps were issued. The New World is corrupt. So is the old, only more expensively so; one pays extra for the customs officials' sweets. It was after our arrival in La Rochelle that I finally met the man I had corresponded with all these months. I try to describe him to the policeman. Slight, clean-shaven, well-mannered. Like a bookish manager, I say, at the best hotel in town. Only later it turns out he is the owner, returning your tip without malice.

My captor is amused by this description.

'What language did you speak in?' he asks.

'German.'

'He spoke it like a native?'

'Yes.' I hesitate. 'But there was something foreign to it all the same. He gave me blueprints for the secret chamber in my cabin, worked out in detail, to the tenth of an inch. And made me sole custodian of the child.'

I explain the feeding instructions I was given, the pole I hooked into his harness to keep the creature at bay whenever I cleaned out its sty. There was special food, liquid food, like sloppy porridge, I had to mix it twice a day. There was a drug in it, I reckon. A sedative. It kept it asleep, much of the time. At others, I played the gramophone, or sang at the top of my voice. Once, it bit through its gag. I had to pretend to the crew the screams were mine.

The policeman nods, takes down a note, rings a little bell on his desk. It must be an agreed signal, for a clerk appears carrying a plate with some bread and two boiled eggs. A reward, I understand. We both eat hastily, sharing the plate, left hungry by the interrogation. When we are finished, the fat man licks his fingers one by one, uncaps his pen again, leans forward.

'What name did he use, this man in La Rochelle?'

I note the phrasing of the question. As though he already knows who the man is.

'He never gave his name,' I answer truthfully. 'I am sorry.'

The policeman's face looks placid. If he is keen for this particular piece of information, only his legs show it, uncrossing themselves under the table. His weight sits low, below the belly. Like he has crammed a cushion into his crotch.

'Think, Captain. I beseech you.'

But, faced with his need, I find myself reluctant to speak.

Φ

It takes me two days to answer the policeman's question. I spend them in a cell. The room is clean and heated. Nobody mistreats me. And yet a steady feeling of dread is growing in me. It is as though the world has forgotten me. I try to pray but there is no God in this nameless place, only the clattering of typewriters, the bustling steps of clerks. Every few hours my interrogator stops by.

'Did you think of anything else?' he keeps asking.

'I've told you all I know.'

'Perhaps.'

He has explained to me that he regards torture to be distasteful and contrary to the tenets of British Law. But after that little snack of bread and hard-boiled egg, there is no further food.

Two days. The length of the interval is not chosen at random. If my business partner keeps to the terms of our contract, he will have instructed his bank in Rotterdam to transfer the final instalment within forty-eight hours of delivery. I hope I can trust to his honesty as he has been able to trust to mine. I am a Dutch trader, after all. We do not cheat.

When two days have passed and the hunger starts eating into my guts, I decide that the time has come to reveal my final piece of information. Perhaps the policeman will be satisfied and permit me to leave.

'I remember now,' I tell him when he next makes his visit. 'He received a telegram once, the man in La Rochelle. The porter called him over. We were having lunch at the hotel.'

'So you heard his name.'

'Not clearly. In any case, I must have misheard. You see the name was English. But Englishmen are no longer allowed to travel abroad, are they not?'

'Just tell me what you heard.'

'Ashton,' I say. 'Mr Sebastian Ashton.'

The fat man's eyes light up. 'Sebastian Ashton! Ah, very funny.'

He turns to one of his clerks who always seem to be hovering in some corner, just within earshot.

'Find out everything you can about the sewer project in the city. Check on the immigration paperwork for the whole company. And set up surveillance.'

'Am I free to go?' I call after him, as he makes to leave.

'Soon.'

Φ

There is a commotion some hours later. Two men bring in a yelping dog. It is a big beast, a bloodhound. Both its hind legs appear to be broken. In between its howls, the dog tries to snap at the men. They throw it in the cell next to me, where it cowers, sniffing at the air, staring at me with blood-rimmed eyes.

The fat man appears in order to have a look at it.

'Make sure you don't smoke,' he says to me. 'It goes wild over Smoke.'

'What is it?'

He shrugs. 'A related inquiry.' He reaches through the bars with a stick, touches its side. The dog whimpers, then sinks its teeth in the wood. 'My men say they did not see the owner. But I think they saw him and were afraid. Of a schoolboy! There's a rumour on the loose . . . But of course, you already believe in the devil, Captain.'

'What will you do with the dog?'

He looks at me in good humour. 'What we do with all our prisoners. Tame it, or kill it.'

'Am I free to go?' I ask again.

'Soon.'

At least they have started feeding me again.

Scar Tissue

'Do you still pray?'

The words are small things, fragile: the hush of the church soaking up Charlie's voice.

Thomas does not need to think about the answer.

'No,' he says. 'It's all a lie.'

'It is. And yet I do. Despite myself. Late at night: hands folded under the blanket, where even I can't see them.'

'Why?'

'Habit, I suppose. There could be, you know. Something *real* behind all this bloody mess – but look at you flinch!'

'You swore,' Thomas complains. 'Charlie Cooper swears. In church. Where God can hear.' Then adds, lightly, looking down the length of the nave. 'So it appears I also still believe.'

It's the first smile they have shared since their reunion. Perhaps they came here just for that. A night and a day cooped up at Grendel's house. Watching Lady Naylor bustling about; Sebastian coming and going. The child in the mask. They needed air. And to see whether Lady Naylor would let them go; whether they were prisoners or free.

They found their way back to the market square almost mechanically. This is where they were meant to have met. But when Charlie arrived here, long after nightfall the previous day, there had been no one to greet him. Cold and hungry, he had sought shelter in the church. The door had been locked but the priest had heard him; had listened to his explanations; and had realised that this dirty, shivering lad was the very Charlie for whom Grendel's newfound friends were looking. Next came Charlie's introduction to the man without Smoke. It made him happy somehow: that such a thing could be. Happy – until Thomas and Livia returned, her mother in tow.

Now he casts around for words to say what he feels.

'My cousin gave me some naughty books last Christmas,' Charlie states abruptly. 'Not naughty, really. Risqué. Five volumes that he found in his late grandmother's study. All five of them romances, translated from the French. They all have the same plot: two men love the same girl. They all end in a duel.'

Thomas does not deny what Charlie is implying. His features are gaunt in the pale light. They have all lost weight these past ten days. It makes them look old. 'It may be an illusion, Charlie. A lie. Borrowed emotion. Round here, it drifts on the air.' Thomas frowns, clearly worried by the thought. 'In any case, she does not even *like* me. She hates me.'

'No, not quite hate.'

Their words sound hard in the cold, pewless nave. Suddenly, scared by this coldness, they reach out and grab each other's hand, fiercely, like two children lost in the woods. They race out of the church, still clutching each other, back out into the square. The sun is low in the sky, and for a moment it is beautiful, London's haze of sin, soaking up the slanting rays and unfurling in orange Smoke rings high above their heads.

Φ

They walk back slowly, recounting to each other the days spent apart. They have done this before, but then there were other listeners and the tales tailored to another purpose. Charlie does not linger on Renfrew; the day he spent chained to the schoolmaster's bed. He does tell Thomas how he got sick on the way back.

'From the stomach. Rotten potatoes and all the snow I ate tramping through the night. They never write about that in stories. Getting the runs.'

Before long the cramps got so bad that Charlie found himself unable to continue. A farming couple put him up when he knocked on their door, doubled over with pain.

'Imagine it, waking under a stranger's roof, flailing about every time, my heart pounding, thinking I'd been chained again. Scrambling for the chamber pot, wondering whether Julius was there, watching me, lurking in the shadows. The pain passed within twenty-four hours. Then the farmer made me work off the cost of my lodgings.' Charlie shakes his head, turns up his palms, displaying blisters. 'A coarse man, always swearing, complaining about rich people, the chickens, his wife.'

They reach Grendel's house but linger outside, the breeze carrying the river to them, smelling of refuse and rotting fish.

'And after all that,' Charlie finishes, gesturing behind them and meaning the ambush, the mines, the long road to London, 'here we are, back with Lady Naylor.'

'We can leave if you want. Just say the word.'

But Charlie can see that Thomas does not mean it. He knows why.

'We have to stay and protect the child.'

'You think so too, then!'

Charlie has only seen the boy for a moment. The first thing Sebastian did was commandeer a room for him, one whose door could be locked. Next thing they knew he had nailed shut the window shutters. Then he left, taking the key. When he returned in the morning, he brought a metal bolt and reinforced the door.

Later Charlie spent an hour at the keyhole, but the boy was outside his field of vision. Only his feet showed from time to time, the tips of his boots, man-sized, too large for him, nobody had thought to help him take them off. A boy of six perhaps. Younger than Eleanor. Alone, confused, slurping air as though through a straw. Once, he rose and raced to the window, his non-face pressed against the slatted shutters, drinking light.

'He does not smoke,' Charlie says to Thomas. 'That's why he is so precious to them. The mask is a respirator. Keeping him from infection.' It is a surmise, but Charlie is sure of it. He repeats to Thomas Renfrew's account of Baron Naylor's expedition, how they scoured the world for an 'innocent'.

'They needn't have gone to all that trouble,' Thomas observes. 'Here we've brought them to Grendel, free of charge.'

'It's different. The boy must be like the wild woman we met in the woods. After we were attacked in the coach. If so, the boy will smoke soon enough. He just has not caught it yet.' Charlie smiles at the memory of the shy creature who stopped Thomas's bleeding, her Smoke seeping out of her with the unselfconsciousness of breath. 'Do you think they will notice, about Grendel?'

Thomas spits. 'If they haven't already, they will before long. They are too attuned to Smoke. It's all they think about. I suppose they must hate it.'

'Don't you?'

'I don't know, Charlie. Lately I think it's not the Smoke that's bad but the people underneath.' Thomas turns towards the stairs that lead up to Grendel's rooms. 'Let's go, eh? They'll be waiting for us.'

Φ

They stop one more time before they reach the top of the stairs. They both know why. Livia. It is as though they can sense her, moving around above their heads.

'They end with a duel do they, those French novels of yours?'

'Always,' says Charlie. 'The handsome one wins. Or sometimes the girl comes, stops them, and picks.'

'Know this,' Thomas replies with all the bluntness of his nature. 'If she was asked. She'd have you ten times out of ten.'

'That's just it, Thomas. One does not get to choose. Not like that.'

Φ

Inside, the stink of the river is replaced by the smell of cooking. Butter-fried fish and boiled turnips: Mrs Grendel stiff-backed at the stove. She was curt and surly when the priest brought Charlie. Another foundling. Another mouth to feed. The first thing Lady Naylor did was give her a purse.

'Here's money,' she told the woman. 'There'll be more, much more, before the week is out.'

Mrs Grendel took the purse quickly. But it did not improve her mood.

They find Livia sitting at the dinner table with her mother. Neither is saying a word. Before he joins them, Charlie crouches down again before the locked door of their prisoner. The keyhole is dark, as though blocked. It takes Charlie a second to understand what he is looking at. A glassy surface throwing back the door's reflection; the shadow of a masked head, blocking out the light. There, at the centre, imprisoned by the goggle's glass, one might imagine an eye, a pupil. Grown big against the darkness, crowding out the iris.

Scared.

Charlie scratches the door, quietly, so Lady Naylor won't hear. The boy on the other side scratches back. Then the door jolts in its frame. At the same time a crash sounds, is repeated, two drumbeats. The child is hammering against the door. Lady Naylor comes running.

'You better get away from there. It agitates him.'

'How long will you keep him like that?'

'Not long now. Sebastian says the mask will come off tonight. He will be more at ease then.'

318

'Does *he* have a name?'

Lady Naylor does not censure his anger. 'I do not know it, Charlie. He comes from a small, isolated tribe. I don't think any outsiders speak its language, not even the man who found him and took him away.'

The child hits the door again, with his feet this time.

'Come away,' Lady Naylor says again. 'He might end up hurting himself. It is best if he is calm.'

Indeed the hammering stops as soon as Charlie rises and moves away. The dinner table has been laid with an old but pretty tablecloth. A candle stands in the middle. Stools have been found and arranged around it. A family dinner. Grendel joins them, fussing over a bottle of wine he has been sent to buy, then realising they have no glasses, just chipped old cups. Livia avoids Charlie's eyes when he sits down next to her. It isn't anger, he reminds himself, but confusion, embarrassment. But it is hard to read anything in her features other than the stony-faced humility she perfected in her family home.

Dinner is a restrained affair. Nobody is in the mood for talking, not with the Grendels here, seeing to their food like hired servants, awkward in their own house. The rest of them resemble a family that waits for the help to leave the room so it can argue in peace. At long last Mrs Grendel does them the favour.

'I will do the dishes on the morrow,' she declares sourly, then pushes her husband out of the door. 'We will turn in early.'

Their movements in the back of the house are studiedly noisy: they wish to convey they are not lingering to eavesdrop. It is disturbing what money will buy you, Charlie thinks, discretion and resentment both paid for with the same coin.

The moment the Grendels have settled themselves for the night, Thomas leans across to Lady Naylor.

'Tell us again,' he says, fingering the edges of his missing ear, 'why Julius shot at us when we left your house.'

Lady Naylor rehearses the same answer she gave them over breakfast. That she was afraid when they announced their departure, the very morning Julius informed her they had broken into the laboratory. Afraid of what they had seen. Afraid they would talk. That Julius, in a rage with the boys and keen to protect his investment in Lady Naylor's project, offered to waylay them and send them running back to the manor. All she needed from them was a week of silence.

Two dead horses: it seemed a cheap enough price for revolution. It was a weak plan, really. She should, Lady Naylor now says, not have been surprised that Julius decided to alter it.

Thomas wrinkles his nose at this. 'What was it we saw, exactly? That had you running scared? The ledger? The cage?'

But Charlie knows different. 'We saw the blueprints. London's new sewer system, though we did not recognise it for what it was. There was a name on it: Aschenstedt. I thought it was the name of a city. But it is a man. Aschen-Stadt. Ash-town. Taylor, Ashton and Sons. Renfrew would have seen it in a heartbeat.'

Lady Naylor sighs. 'Stupid, isn't it, this play on names? Dangerous. But he's a silly man sometimes. There is a child in every genius.'

As she says it, a key turns in the flat's front door and Sebastian Aschenstedt steps through, cheeks ruddy from the cold.

Φ

They talk in the hallway, Sebastian and Lady Naylor. It appears he is too excited to sit down. Charlie watches him closely while he listens in on their conversation. A clean-shaven man, the skin young and chafed where the razor has touched it. When he smiles, dimples dig themselves into the corners of his mouth.

'I did the tests. Three separate blood samples, all negative. He's unspoiled.'

'When do we start, then?'

'The sooner the better. I'll go in to him now.'

It's Thomas who blocks Sebastian's path. Always Thomas: the one amongst them least afraid to start a fight. Livia draws close to him, chin drooping, false-meek, edgy, small hands curling into fists.

But it's Charlie who speaks.

'What are you going to do to the child?'

Sebastian turns to him, answers frankly, guilelessly, his hands busy sorting through the contents of his doctor's bag.

'We will take off his György respirator. The mask. He needs to breathe freely and to eat. He has had a rough voyage. No sunlight, liquid food, sedated for much of the time. Now he is anaemic and showing early signs of scurvy. We can fix all that once the respirator is off.'

'It'll infect him.'

320

'Why yes. In fact, we'll make very sure he's infected before we take it off. You object? He was bound for infection the moment he left his jungle tribe. It took severe precautions to preclude it until now.'

'Once he's infected – he won't be able to go back.'

Sebastian seems surprised by the comment, as though Charlie has said something he has failed to consider. But before he can answer, Lady Naylor intervenes.

'Before the week is out, the world will have changed. Not just London, or England, but the world! None of our truths will hold any more.'

'Then he *will* be able to go back?'

Her answer is raw with emotion. 'We will all be free for the first time in our lives.'

Without saying a word, Livia pulls Thomas out of Sebastian's way. He lets her do it, his eyes on Charlie, soliciting his thoughts.

Sebastian is through the door and has locked it long before Charlie has puzzled out what his thoughts may be.

Φ

One glimpse is all they get before the door closes: a little creature with an outsize head, the mask bulbous up front and smooth around the back, rubber-coating his skull. A proboscis dangling from the jawline. Eyes ringed in metal, portholes to the child within. He is sitting on the ground not on the bed, squatting really, bum on heels. His fingers are busy with an insect, pinning one of its legs to the floor, watching the bug's body march itself around this pivot. The boy looks up when Sebastian's shadow intrudes upon him. Then the door falls shut; the lock snaps, the key is removed. Is pocketed, Charlie imagines, the doctor's bag put down. Thomas takes up position at the keyhole without hesitation, almost shouldering Lady Naylor aside. His report is terse. Charlie and Livia stand close behind him, Charlie conscious of her smell, her presence, and careful not to touch.

'Sebastian is talking to the boy. I cannot hear what he is saying. Now he is tying his hands. No struggle. He is attaching something to the end of the mask, to the breathing tube or whatever it is. A metal disk of some sort, like a tin of boot polish. It screws onto the end. Now he reaches for his doctor's bag, pulling out a syringe. Big needle. It goes into the tin, not the boy. And now . . .'

Thomas falters, pales, stands up abruptly and starts hammering on the door. Charlie and Livia both start forward, to the keyhole. He captures it first, greedy for the horror beyond, and afraid, too, wishing to protect Livia from it, his heart beating from the warmth of her cheek next to his.

What he sees is hard to describe. The child is shaking, convulsing. Sebastian's hands are steadying him, pressing him down to the floor. The mask appears changed, the eyeholes jet black, the rubber tube jerking as though alive. Then, around the edges of the mask, the boy appears to start bleeding: black, sticky Smoke seeping out like oil. Minutes of this, Thomas pounding the door. Then Sebastian takes off the mask, a buckle at a time; takes a handkerchief out of his pocket, dabs it with a liquid from a bottle, wipes down the exhausted child's face, removing a glossy layer of near-liquid Soot. The boy that emerges is thin, sallow underneath his dark skin, the hair black and vigorous, if cropped very short. Crooked teeth and small crinkly eyes. The moment he has regained some strength he starts pummelling Sebastian, biting and kicking. Charlie looks away in anguish. Livia takes his place. They are all speechless. Thomas has stopped attacking the door, his fists swollen. Beyond it the sounds of struggle reach them dimly.

Then Livia says, 'He is not smoking. He's angry and scared, and you've infected him, but he isn't smoking.'

'He won't,' Lady Naylor says. 'There is an incubation period.'

'How long?'

Her mother hesitates. 'Several weeks before he starts showing. But in seventy-two hours his blood will begin to change.'

The door opens and Sebastian emerges. Behind him the child is a crumpled figure on the bed; his head lost in its linen, exhausted and still. For a moment Charlie has the urge to hit Sebastian, Smoke black and bitter in his mouth.

But the man's eyes dispel his anger.

'Poor child. He is exhausted. Best let him rest now. *To-ka*. He keeps saying *To-ka*. Perhaps it means Mother.'

When Sebastian locks the door it seems a mercy, not punishment. Though, of course: it also suits his plans.

'What was in the tin?' Thomas asks hoarsely.

'Soot. Very black Soot.'

'Then you found a way to bring it to life.'

'Yes, of course. Soot can be quickened: turned back into Smoke. Temporarily, partially, at great cost. It's an inefficient process.'

'Like cigarettes.'

'Yes. The technology is decades old.'

Φ

It is hard to sleep after what they have seen, hard to talk even, compare notes. They sit around uneasily, Charlie, Thomas and Livia, on the floor of the room shared by the two boys, each of them caught in their own thoughts. Livia has pulled a bent cigarette from her pocket, one of Julius's, and is cutting it open with the edge of a fingernail. After some minutes she stands to get closer to the lamp.

'It's a mix of Soot and tobacco. But it's sticky somehow, like it has been treated with some goo.'

'That's what does it then,' Thomas suggests. '*Quickens* it. Makes it revert to Smoke.'

'It has a peculiar smell. And the Soot is very dark.' Livia runs her finger through it, raises it up to the eye. 'And look: each little particle is different, some black, some grey.' She turns, catches Charlie's eye, looks back at her finger. 'I have never done this before. Study Soot. In school they just told us it was dead. *Inert.*'

She rerolls the cigarette, sticks it in her mouth, bends to the lamp. At once Charlie is on his feet. His hand is near her shoulder before it occurs to him that he no longer has a right to touch.

'Don't,' he says.

'Why? Will it turn me bad?' She hides her face by lowering it to the gas lamp, sticks the end of the cigarette into its flame. 'One puff, Charlie. We live in London. We are all inhaling fifty puffs a day.'

Charlie retreats a step, sees Thomas rise in expectation. *He likes her smoking*, it shoots through him before he buries the thought. Livia inhales, exhales, her cheeks flushing dark after some delay. It takes her a moment to collect herself.

'Nasty but weak,' she says. 'A tingle of filth. It made me feel angry, imperious. And also a little—' She breaks off, biting her lip. 'Animal functions. That's what it speaks to. A whisper in the blood.

'But look,' she adds, stroking the cigarette's ashes onto her palm as soon as they have cooled. 'There's no trace of the tobacco. But the Soot remains.'

'Not all of it,' says Thomas, stepping up to her, taking hold of her

323

hand and bringing it up to his eyes. 'Look, all this Soot is light. The dark stuff is gone.'

Livia starts, compares the smudge on her fingertip with the base of the cigarette that remains unlit.

'You are right. What does it mean?'

'It means that only black sin can be activated,' Charlie whispers from the sidelines. 'Temporarily. Partially. At great cost. The small sins,' he says, taken aback by his own anger, 'are as dead as dust.'

Thomas and Livia are still holding hands when he storms out of the room.

Φ

It proves hard to find a place in which to be alone. Charlie is too restless to sit still in some corner; too haunted by the thought of Julius to take to the streets of London at night. So he wanders the flat, its hallway and landing, back and forth past the boy-prisoner's cell. His fingers brush the walls, the doors, the windowsills, collect specks of London's Soot grown into the paint and plaster, some chalky grey and coarse, others fine as paint pigments, the soft greys of photography. Irritation, appetite, illicit joy; the sting of want. Everyday vice: the humdrum of life. Once infectious, now sour and dead. He wipes it off against his trouser leg and continues on his rounds; brushes the walls again, searching for something, the side of his leg soon shiny with grey.

It is during these restless rounds that he catches sight of the sewer map. Sebastian and Lady Naylor have spread it on the kitchen table, are poring over it. Or rather there are two maps, one marked 'Ashton', the other 'Aschenstedt'. It is hard to tell from a distance, but the second seems a denser web: a replica of the first with added lines. Lady Naylor turns it over when Charlie draws close. He feigns disinterest and fetches the pitcher from the sideboard.

'One word to the authorities,' Lady Naylor calls after him, worried. 'That's all it would take. And nothing about the world changes.'

'How do you know I care?' Charlie replies. And: 'You are like Renfrew, then. He too wants change.'

'No, he only thinks he does. But all he can imagine is more of the same.'

Φ

Half an hour later Charlie hears her arguing with Thomas. His friend has barged into the kitchen and is demanding answers.

'Talk straight. You swore it to me! On your husband's life.'

His voice rises further when she does not give him what he wants.

Within an hour of their shouting, milady comes to find Charlie, sitting alone outside the child's door, listening to the silence beyond.

'I cannot talk to that one,' she says softly, then surprises him by easing herself onto the floor next to him. Baroness Naylor, Dowager Countess of Essex, Marchioness of Thomond, her bottom in the dust. She looks dignified even here.

'He is always angry. Just like my Julius. I suppose that's the problem. He reminds me of my son.'

Her words take Charlie back to Renfrew's. Julius's voice rising from below the floorboards. The schoolmaster's scream.

'Your son has changed,' he says hoarsely, his head light, chest heavy with his heartbeat. 'He's lost in Smoke. He killed Dr Renfrew.'

'Killed him?' Lady Naylor is silent for a moment, digesting this. 'Poor Julius,' she says at last. 'He has been imbibing quickened Soot. Not your ordinary cigarettes but something infinitely stronger. Something he stole from me while you were playing truant.' She smiles a hard little smile. 'But it's my own fault. I introduced him to it. To cigarettes and to sweets. In the summer when he turned fifteen. Wooing him. Like a knowing bride.'

Charlie looks at her, aghast. 'But why?'

For the fraction of a second she leans her head against his shoulder. Like a sister. Pleading with him. Winning him over to her side.

'He looks just like his father. My first husband. A weak man. God, how I hated him!' She jerks upright, away from him. 'Our fathers had arranged the betrothal. It was good politics; two old bloodlines conjoined. My husband left for the Indies within four months of the wedding and was dead of a fever six weeks after that. Julius's grandfather took him away from me the day he was born. He raised him to be my enemy. But I *needed* him.'

'You needed his money!'

'The Spencers are very rich. And I have been running up debts. So I presented Julius with an investment opportunity.'

'You mean you lied to him.'

'Naturally. The Spencers are England's most prominent family.

They have no need for revolution. Still, it's a fair bargain. If I fail, he will own every scrap of Naylor land.'

She stands up abruptly, then walks away from him, towards the room she has selected as her bedroom. Up until yesterday the Grendels slept in there. It holds the apartment's only proper bed.

'I should have spoken to you earlier, Charlie. You have a generous soul. One might find forgiveness there. My own children have very little of that.' She stops at the door, looks back. 'Perhaps it would be best if we understood one another. Do you want to know where Smoke comes from? How the body generates it?'

'Yes.'

'Then follow me.'

Φ

She makes him close the door. Immediately the room feels too small, the big lumpy bed filling it wall to wall. She sits down on it, smoothing out her skirts in front of her, puts her hands onto a particular place on her right flank. Underneath the fabric of her dress, Charlie can make out the skeleton of her corset, shaping her waist.

'Do you know what organ resides here?' she asks.

He swallows. 'The liver.'

'Indeed. A vile thing really, though it makes good enough eating. Do you know what they used to say about sour-faced old women who smoked all day long? "She's got an evil liver." This was back when I was young, in Brittany, where we went for the summers. The children used to chant it as a taunt. Many years ago I told Baron Naylor about it – in passing, really, sharing a memory, nothing more. But my husband thought there was more to the phrase than superstition. Before the week was out he had purchased surgeon's knives. And cadavers. He got to be quite an expert at excision.'

The words sink into Charlie and transport him back to Lady Naylor's laboratory. A glass vitrine filled with large, lidded jars. Spongy tissue floating in thick liquid, its edges overgrown by something hard and black. Next thing he knows Lady Naylor has started unbuttoning her bodice, her hands working behind her back, wrestling with hooks. Charlie turns to the door.

'Stay, Mr Cooper. I have no designs on your virtue. Unlike my daughter, perhaps. Here, give me your hand. You may close your eyes if you like.'

He returns to her, both staring and trying not to look. She has not taken off any clothes, but simply loosened them, creating a gap near her spine. Gently, she takes his hand in hers and guides it through this gap, slipping it underneath the corset then forward towards her front.

'Smoke is produced by a gland in the liver. From there it connects to our blood and lymphatic system and, ultimately, to the sweat glands and lungs. Our whole bodies are calibrated for Smoke. Unless, that is, you are like that child next door. But even as we speak his body is starting to transform.'

Charlie can hardly listen. All his senses are in his hand. He feels the smooth warmth of silk, then her skin, hot to his touch. They follow the ridge of a rib, then down, towards her stomach. Then they stop, her fingers stroking his across a long, raised, puckered line, tough like gristle.

'For a while my husband came to believe that the answer to Smoke was surgical. That Smoke could be cut off at the root. Not by excising the whole liver, naturally, merely the gland itself. But there was no way he could operate on himself.'

Sick now, Charlie wrestles with Lady Naylor, trying to withdraw his hand. But her grip is firm, pressing his fingers into the scar.

'Please understand that I accepted willingly. You see, I love my husband. More than life itself.' At last she lets Charlie go, watches him jump back and cradle his hand as though it were cut. 'And *he* loved me. Which is to say, he did not go through with it in the end. He opened me up and sewed me shut again. In any case, it would not have worked. Aschenstedt sent us a study. From Romania. A lord there made extensive experiments on his peasants. They either died or continued smoking. All twenty-seven of them.'

Charlie watches her button up her dress again. This time he does not fight his staring. His sense of modesty is gone. All he can think of is the ridge of her scar. His breathing is loud, as though he's been running; pins and needles down his back.

'Why show me?' he manages at last.

'I need you to understand, Mr Cooper. What people are willing to do, in the cause of virtue. So you will help us, when the time comes.'

He grapples with this, finds it too large, her revolution, unfathomable. The stakes he understands are smaller. They dwell next door.

327

'Do you promise that the child will be unharmed?' Charlie asks and surprises himself by the firmness of his voice.

'I can if you like. It is the truth. But you won't believe me. Why would you? Adults have been lying to you all your life.'

She rises, reaches past him, opens the door, standing so close he sees each tired wrinkle round her eyes.

'And tell me this, Mr Cooper: what is he to you, this boy next door? How many boys like him have suffered and perished throughout your life without your taking the slightest notice? Back in his jungle, or on one of our royal plantations, picking precious flowers that we import by the ton?'

Before Charlie can answer, she has bent forward, put her lips to his ear.

'Talk to my Livia, Charlie. I cannot reach her. Tell her about our conversation. Tell her I am glad she is ... But you will know what to say.'

'I'm afraid your daughter and I no longer speak.'

'Don't you? Oh, what a child you are, Mr Cooper! What a perfectly charming child.'

Φ

Charlie tells the others about his conversation later, sitting once again in the draughty room he shares with Thomas. It is cold in there, cold enough that his hands and feet grow numb, and their only light is a sliver of silvery sky that outlines the broken shutters. As he tells them of the scar, of his hands on Lady Naylor's body, he is glad of the dark, glad he cannot see Livia's expression nor she the rush of blood that momentarily heats his face.

'Smoke is grown in the dark of our livers,' Thomas sums it up drily once Charlie is finished. 'Swinburne would not like it. His lot would be done if it were known.'

Livia disagrees. 'Why? It does not change anything. Smoke is what it always was: the visible manifestation of vice. How stupid to cover up a truth that does not matter.'

Charlie can hear Thomas shift in response. A shrug, a wave of the arm. How well they know each other, precisely in the dark. For a split second they are back in the dormitory, swapping confidences.

'In any case we learned one thing today,' Thomas says after a while. 'Seventy-two hours. That's when something starts changing in the boy. Whatever it is, they want it to happen, they need it. Which means we have three days to learn the truth. It's got to do with the sewers. We must go and have a look.'

Charlie looks into himself and finds he agrees. Only: 'We don't know where to go. The sewers, yes. But we don't even know how to get in.'

'We need the blueprint.'

'She will notice if we steal it. And the plan is too large to copy.'

'Not if we only mark the entrances. And the bits where the two plans differ. The secret passages. The bits Sebastian must have built on the sly.'

'That's clever!'

'It was Livia's idea.'

In the dark Charlie can hear her rise. It's like he has caught them at something: putting their heads together. Plotting the future.

'Goodnight,' she calls from the door, sounding agitated, enraged.

'Goodnight,' they answer, then huddle close against the cold.

When sleep comes, it comes with dreams. A black-clad figure, shadowed by a dog.

Charlie never learns whether it is Julius or Renfrew.

Lady Naylor

Livia storms in as I am getting ready for bed. I have loosened my hair and sit, on the room's one rickety chair, combing it. Our hosts have no mirror and it is odd that I should feel the loss of my reflection so keenly. The hair is tangled, greasy with city Soot; the brush soon bristling like a cat in a storm. It would be nice to take a bath before Sebastian and I set off to change the world.

Livia, I am pleased to say, is in a temper. Oh, there remain signs of the nun poking through her demeanour. My long-suffering daughter shouldering the burden of her needling mother. Mostly though she is fuming, stands with her fists buried in her hips.

'You look,' I say into the breathlessness of her anger, 'ridiculous in trousers. Here, I had Sebastian buy me some dresses. You can have the green one. It is a little short on me.'

She ignores my words entirely, snorts back the Smoke that's crept out of one nostril.

'You talked to Charlie,' she manages at last. 'You took your clothes off!'

'Is it that which brings you here? You are upset about my lack of decorum. But there is more to it, isn't there? You are jealous. Jealous of your poor spent mother. It is as bad as that, then.'

'I don't know what you are talking about.'

I study her, feel the urge to touch her, offer peace. But it does not belong to the vocabulary of our relationship, and at any rate I am rather enjoying her loss of control. She has been prim with me for far too long.

'Poor Livia,' I say. 'I saw it the moment Charlie greeted you and Thomas at the door: your whole little romance. You had convinced yourself that you had betrayed him, or some such thing. That you had shifted allegiances, once and for all, to your eternal shame. And how you scowled at him: like a fishwife at a customer. But all the same your heart leapt at the sight. Charlie – alive and in one piece! Or perhaps it wasn't your heart so much as another organ.'

My daughter flushes, underlines her words with Smoke.

'Don't be common, Mother!'

'Common? What do you think love is? Sonnets and a wedding ring? Perhaps it is time we had a conversation about flowers and bees.'

She flinches, seems ready to launch herself at me, this jeering heckler of her heartache. It shames me, her pain, and it occurs to me that I am afraid of my daughter, afraid of her disapproval of my choices and plans; that I'd rather have her hate me for my coldness than judge my motives and find them wanting. 'I have lost my conscience,' I once wrote to Sebastian in one of those letters that prepared the way to our partnership. But it appears I have merely sent it off to boarding school. Now it has come to call in dirty trousers.

I try an approach. Rise from the chair, take a step, careful and measured, and watch her withdraw. Another pair of steps – first mine, then hers – press her up against the wall. She has changed during the week and a half I have feared for her, grown prettier, both more confident and more vulnerable. I see my own face in hers, just a few years older, the day my father told me that I was to wed. It softens me.

'Poor Livia,' I say, no longer mocking. 'Do you think you are the first girl to ask herself whether she should be happy with a nice boy or unhappy with a cad? It is perfectly natural.'

For a moment she seems ready to accept my wisdom; to sit with me atop my bed and share her heartache. Then she remembers herself and slips on that mask of meekness that has separated us ever since my husband lost his wits. She speaks calmly, her face a foot away from mine, the voice demure.

'Charlie says that Father cut you open. From the hip to the ribs. It must be quite a scar.'

And just like that our roles are inverted and heckler has become heckled. She is ready to continue, twist the knife. But I do what she found impossible to do. I start crying.

It takes her a minute before she wraps me in her arms.

Φ

So we end up on the bed after all. Her clothes are so dirty she leaves stains on the bedding. She smells, too, of sweat and the street. I cling to her all the same, elbow hooked into elbow. It is well when emotion aligns with strategy. I wish to secure her loyalty. Her cheek rests an inch from mine. She is scrupulous about avoiding its touch.

'How is Father?' she asks, not shifting. 'How is his health?'

'As ever, I hope. Thorpe is looking after him. You see, a search was made of our house. By now, the whole of England will be talking about him, poor soul. "Mad Baron Naylor." How he would have detested such gossip!' I pause, allow my emotions to sweep me from anger to nostalgia. 'Do you remember, Livia? How he used to be?'

'Of course I do. He was righteous and gentle. Almost a holy man. Like that famous count in Russia, the one who walks around in a peasant smock.'

'Tolstoy? What a funny thing to say! But no. I mean before all that. When you were young.'

'Before? He was – busy. Frantic, even. I remember him sitting in his study with so many papers around him they covered the floor. Always reading and scribbling. Talking over dinner. One month it was the Greeks, then a trip he was planning to the Antipodes. He got so very excited, I thought he would start smoking, right in front of the servants.'

'He never made that trip. The Antipodes.' It is funny that it should make me smile. 'He went to the Argentine instead. Four months and one letter home. The vagabond!'

Livia is quiet at this, caught up in the past. Her head slides towards mine. She remembers herself just in time.

'Why did he go mad, Mother?'

'You know why he did.'

'The Smoke overcame him, and he got lost.'

'No. He had given up smoking. Quite successfully it must be said.'

'Why then?'

'Just that. He had given up and decided to become a saint. It put a strain on him, a terrible strain.'

I want to say more, explain it to her: how he foreswore his experiments and tried to conquer Smoke through a sheer act of will; how he changed week by week until it was too late, driven mad by the effort to be sinless; how he abandoned me and our love. But there are things too private for one's child. Livia sees my hesitation, slides her feet off the bed and sits up.

'I don't know when you are lying, Mother, and when you are telling the truth. That's the whole problem.'

It's her sadness that impresses me, the sense of loss.

'You won't tell us what you are up to, will you?' she continues. 'This grand plan of yours.'

I shake my head. 'I am just like you, Livia. I don't know if I can trust you.'

She bristles at this. 'I brought you here, Mother. I found you shelter! I pulled Thomas aside when he wanted to stop you from infecting the child. I did all this because you promised me answers.'

'Yes, you did all this. But will you tell me who hid you after Julius shot at you? Where those clothes come from?'

My daughter stands silent, head bowed.

'You see, my dear, we really are much the same.'

Φ

I don't want to let her go. She has turned around twice now, and each time I have called her back with a question, something stupid, aimless, asked only to force another moment of her time. It is the first time in years we have attempted any sort of exchange, beyond trading hurtful nothings across the dinner table. But in this specialised skill of talking to one's daughter I feel utterly inept.

'Tell me,' I try again, inching forward onto more treacherous conversational ground. 'What do *you* want out of all this?'

When she looks at me in puzzlement, I make a gesture that is meant to encompass the enterprise in which we find ourselves grudging partners, but largely seems directed at the bed. It is fitting enough: not an hour ago found me flat on my knees and fumbling underneath the bed frame, hiding my secrets like some old woman afraid of being robbed. There is not a piece of furniture in the whole room that could be locked.

'Sebastian and I are changing the world,' I add. 'There must be something that you want.'

To her credit I see her struggle with it. She is about to give me something pat and worthy, a nunnish answer long-rehearsed. But I have asked her earnestly and earnestness is one thing she finds hard to resist.

'I want to be certain again,' she says at length, 'of who I am and what is truth. I want to be inscrutable, immovable, safe in myself. Can you do this, Mother?'

She says it softly, because she knows the answer.

'No, I cannot.'

'What, then, will you do?'

I repeat what I told her before. 'I will give the world justice.'

'Virtue?'

'Justice is virtue,' I say, quoting someone my husband was fond of, one of his Greeks.

My daughter wrinkles her nose at this, turns around and leaves.

I retrieve the brush and finish with my hair.

Φ

I am about to extinguish the lamp when there is a knock on my door. A soft knock, one that is careful not to be heard throughout the flat. Bemused by this string of visitors, half hoping for, half dreading Livia's return, I open the door. Mr Grendel is in his nightshirt and flustered; he wrings his cotton sleeping cap between work-hard hands. A strange man, shy and cringing in his movements; so diffident that I have yet to see him smoke. There are not many who would have stood at the threshold of my boudoir without giving my figure a passing glance.

'Mr Grendel. This is hardly appropriate.'

'I am sorry,' he says, abject and whispering, his head tilted to one side. 'May I . . . ? I saw your light was on and there is something . . . You see, it's rather important.'

'Oh, out with it!' I laugh, usher him in by his elbow, and sit him down on his own rickety chair. 'Go on, speak, Mr Grendel. It is late and I am in need of my sleep.'

Φ

We talk for a full hour. As it turns out, I was wrong about Grendel. He is not diffident nor shy but that rarest of creatures: a man touched by fate who lacks a purpose. His wife has sent him to me to provide him with one.

I do my best to oblige.

Pencil and Paper

Livia sleeps late, her mother's words refracting in her dreams. By the time she emerges from her room, Sebastian is in the house and there is a new arrangement. Grendel has been made nursemaid to the child. The smokeless man smiles when he emerges from the nursery-prison, and continues smiling when, under Sebastian's watchful eye, he turns the key in the lock. Then he notices Livia – and starts.

'Caught in the act!' He blushes then adds, as though in apology: 'Mrs Grendel and I, we were not blessed ourselves, you see.'

Grendel flashes her a smile, habitual and fleeting, and runs to do the dishes in the kitchen.

Sebastian stays, studying Livia.

'You disapprove, Miss Naylor.'

Livia shakes her head, wondering what emotion her face has betrayed.

'It's a good idea. Grendel is a kind man.'

'You know yourself he's quite a lot more than that! He's a scientific wonder. At another time . . . but, alas, it isn't possible just now.' He sighs, points at his prisoner's door. 'As it is, Mr Grendel can make himself useful. I believe he reminds the child of his people at home. Though the resemblance is superficial. In any case, he will help calm the child. The boy is bewildered by Smoke, and I am afraid we smell of it, even when we are not showing.'

Livia's heart sinks. 'So you know.'

'About Grendel's condition? Oh, yes. He told your mother last night.' Sebastian nods enthusiastically, a man delighted about every scientific riddle on this earth and frustrated only by his own lack of time. 'We have given the boy a name. Mowgli. After a recent book, set in the Raj.'

'Mowgli.' Livia too has read it. A boy raised by wolves. The animals decide to send him to the human village so he will learn to control his Smoke. Her mother had dismissed the book. She thought it sentimental; a lie. 'How old is he?'

'Hard to say. I should think he was malnourished even before he embarked on his journey. Physically he could be as young as six. Eight, nine? A sullen child. Though his disposition is irrelevant for our purpose.'

Livia takes in the man's smooth face and clever little hands playing with his umbrella; weighs his accent, the fact that he stole a child and condemned him to live encoffined in a mask. The question comes out before she can think better of it, artless and direct.

'Who are you exactly, Dr Aschenstedt?'

This brings a grin to Sebastian's face, boyish.

'Who am I? A scientist.'

'Mother says you are a genius.'

'I suppose I am.' He says it lightly, almost modestly. 'I am also a criminal. False papers in my pocket, hiding behind an English name. Under my real name I am wanted in much of Europe. A threat to social order! They are not wrong. I'm a revolutionary, Miss Naylor. A terrorist! But I dislike bombs.' He laughs, boyish still, steps closer to Livia, and confides: 'Your two gentlemen friends and I have something in common. Our alma mater. For all we know we have slept in the same beds. And listened to the same sermons. I must ask them some time, trade stories, don't you think?'

Livia fights being drawn in by this man. A lifetime of being lied to by her elders. Charlie, chained to his teacher's bed. A little boy stolen in the name of Theory. Emphatic lessons in suspicion.

And yet it isn't easy.

'What are you up to, Dr Aschenstedt? Why are you here?'

'Officially? Officially, I am Sebastian Herbert Ashton, engineer, overseeing the building of the sewers. My papers are British. Of course there is the matter of my accent. But then, the English refuse to believe that anyone can learn their tongue, not fluently, you see, so I must be a native after all, reared in some far-flung colony perhaps.' He gives a giggle, quite literally a giggle, the sort of sound some of the girls at school might make after someone has made a chancy remark. 'And of course, half my men are foreign. The beauty of the embargo is that nobody receives adequate training here. It is hard to instruct engineers when the books are all censored. "Forbidden science", "immoral physics" – it really is quite funny! So we have Poles and Italians and Czechs and Russians. And Germans, of course.

Grand engineers! Without them, London would sink in its stink. The English gentlemen on the project are largely there to supervise their morals and to make sure they finish on time. Good, earnest Liberals these gentlemen are, one and all. A great deal rides on the project, the whole of the Liberal Party's reputation. A clean London, a moral London. Oh, it's very ambitious in its way.' Again he giggles. 'There you are. For a decade I was not allowed to enter on threat of death; now I get paid to come. But you must excuse me now, Miss Naylor. I am expected at work. Goodbye. Or rather: *Au revoir. Auf Wiedersehen.*'

Φ

Livia watches Sebastian leave and goes looking for Thomas. But it is Charlie she finds, standing by the open window of the room the boys share. She is tempted to leave at once. In the past few days she has come to terms with Thomas's darkness. It's Charlie's kindness, his forgiveness, that are difficult to accept.

'*Auf Wiedersehen*,' he says, his eyes on the rain outside.

'You heard us talk.'

'Yes. "Until I see you again." Not "goodbye".' He puts a hand into the downpour outside. '*Hundewetter*, the Germans call this. Dog weather. That's about all I remember from class. Isn't it funny that they make us learn French and German but nobody's allowed to travel? Nor to read any foreign books.'

He turns his face and she sees his earnest, honest face. It cuts her, not with guilt but with something more complex that has its own flavour of Smoke. *Your heart leapt*, she hears her mother's words. *Or perhaps some other organ.*

'*Dog* weather,' she says and annoys herself by the cool primness of her pronunciation. '"Until I see you again." You are worried about Julius!' The realisation helps her move past her emotion. She looks out into the street. 'Have you seen him?'

'Seen him? No. Only in a dream.' He hesitates, tilts his head with the thought. 'I sometimes wonder whether I dreamed him even at Renfrew's. The stuff of nightmares. And how he pleaded to be saved!' The next moment his eyes are back on hers. A naked gaze.

'You are looking for Thomas, aren't you?'

It is she who blushes.

'Has he gone out?'

337

'He realised he needs a pencil and paper. To copy your mother's plans. Would you believe the Grendels do not have a single pencil in the house? So he borrowed some money from Mrs Grendel. Or stole it, maybe. When he gets back I am to distract your mother while he searches her room. He thinks she and I have rapport.' He hesitates, swallows the trace of accusation that surfaced in his last phrase. 'She tried to seduce me last night, didn't she? To her cause. I knew it but was seduced all the same. She is very clever.'

'Yes. She tried to seduce me, too.'

'Livia,' he continues, without transition. 'Please. You and I, we need to—'

She turns to flee. 'Not now, Charlie. Later,' she whispers. 'I promise.'

But by this time she is already out of the door.

When she walks past the room a little later she sees him standing by the window, his hands shoved out into the rain.

Φ

The rain falls hard and perpendicular, unharried by wind. Thomas is soaking wet before he finds a stationer's. It appears London is in little need of paper. He stops at a butcher's to ask for some wrapping paper and a stub of pencil, but the man is so suspicious of his request and accent that he won't sell him anything, not for all the money in the world. Annoyed, but happy too to be out and about, alone with his thoughts, Thomas ventures beyond the familiar streets between Grendel's flat and the church into a part of town unknown to him. Everywhere there is the bustle of people: noise and mud, the air oddly clean, London's emotion picked off by the rain.

Before long he reaches a complex of old, dilapidated buildings of such enormous size that they form a hamlet unto themselves. Like the house Grendel has made his home, more than half the structure appears to have burnt down, though here the smell of ashes has long been absorbed into the city's stink. Despite the fire, a thousand people appear to be living in its medieval shell; have improvised walls with timber and plaster-stiffened cloth; have opened stalls, a tailor, a carpenter, a quack selling tonics of laudanum and fermented bitters. Thomas walks the length of the building before realising what it used to house. WESTMINSTER CLOTHES AND RAGS, a painted sign proudly announces above the narrow entrance of a shop. A Jew is tending to it, wearing a fur hat, his sidelocks swinging limply in the rain.

The post office is not ten yards from the building that used to be his nation's Parliament. It surprises Thomas that such a thing exists at all. A guard in postal uniform is positioned outside, billy club in hand. Thomas is worried he will ask for some sort of identification papers, but all he requires of those who present themselves to him is proof of their solvency. Thomas holds up his palmful of coppers and goes inside.

Beyond the door there lies a little pocket of another world. The floors here are made from polished marble, the ceiling recently painted if no longer clean. Gentlemen in well-cut suits are reading newspapers or are queuing to see the postal clerk. Two ladies stand in hushed conversation, their expensive dresses as of yet unmarked by Soot; both wear veils to hide their faces and have footmen in attendance, their liveries hidden under bulky coats. A few dirty messenger boys scurry around but are careful not to address their betters. It's like Thomas has stepped through a barn door and found a ballroom inside. For a moment he stands dead in his tracks, unsure what to do. Then he shrugs and joins the queue.

It is four deep and well-behaved. It startles him, this good behaviour, like silence after a protracted shout. Nobody grumbles, pushes, swears. They are like an unknown breed, peaceful, inoffensive: people who do not smell. Each shut up within his own intention, isolated and pure. Thomas stands amongst them and feels a pang of longing for this world of manners, the parlour-room peace of Discipline, predictable and without life. Just then a gloved hand touches his shoulder, firmly if without violence. It's the doorman who has trailed him inside.

'Trade goes over there,' he says, turning the touch into a push, and moving Thomas towards a different clerk, in a separate cubbyhole, hidden far away to one side. Some workmen are queuing there, or rather are jostling, laughing, trading jokes.

Thomas moves over, listens to the men ahead and watches the gentry in their line, the well-drilled silence of the respectable. How many of them are in London on business, braving the city to look after their factories; how many for a holiday in the murk of sin? There must exist a tribe of locals earning a good living by acting as tour guides to the city's charms.

'Next,' barks the clerk behind the counter.

An urchin, no older than seven, jumps the queue and gets into a shoving match with the man at the front.

Φ

It's Thomas's turn. He has been skipped over twice, defended his place with an elbow, exchanged a fleck of boisterous Smoke with a half-drunk apprentice mailing a letter to his mam. Thomas asks for two pencils and five large sheets of drafting paper. The clerk grumbles but fetches them, the paper already lightly stained. While he is gone, Thomas's gaze falls on four printed posters, nailed to the wall next to the man's chair. Each holds the drawing of a face. Charlie is well-rendered, looking young and a little fatter in the cheek. Livia is unrecognisable, eyes lowered and shrinking into the shadow of a bonnet. He himself looks fierce, the jaw jutting, a thunder of brows. It's Julius who is oddest, hung separately, and staring pale and startled from under a floppy fringe. The clerk notices Thomas's stare; turns to follow his gaze, then rests his eyes on Thomas.

'Well then,' he mutters into Thomas's sudden terror and takes some coins straight out of his palm. '"Missing. No Reward." It's not like I give a shit.'

He hands over the folded-in-half sheaves then chases Thomas with a wave of his hand. 'Get, boy. Next.'

A man has elbowed past before Thomas has recovered enough to step aside.

Φ

Outside, Thomas sprints a good half mile then stops for breath. The rain has turned to drizzle but even so the paper he purchased is already damp. He folds the sheets, shoves them down the waistband of his trousers, then stands breathing, elated by his escape. A beggar, his back propped up against a house front, sits watching him, one leg a calfless stump.

'You're looking like the cat that made off with the cake,' he calls. 'Spare some pennies, friend?'

Thomas laughs and strolls over to him.

'Anybody ever give you any?'

'Sure they do. The good people of London!'

'Really?' Thomas pictures it, this city of ruffians, doling out charity. 'Why?'

The man shrugs. 'They just do. Sentimental, I suppose. Got themselves a heart.'

Thomas accepts this answer and puts some pennies into the man's cup. He crouches down so he and the beggar can speak face-to-face.

'If you could,' he asks, his mind wandering back to the twin queues at the post office, 'if someone gave you the power, would you magic away the Smoke? Stop it, I mean. Make it disappear.'

The beggar eyes him, greedy for another coin.

'Sure,' he shouts. 'Stop it, I say! To hell with Smoke.'

'Really? You wouldn't miss it?'

'Then don't,' the man backtracks. 'Keep it how it is. Nuttin' wrong with it. Only yer undies chafe a little on yer privates.'

'And what do you think of rich folk?'

'The rich?' Reckless now, enjoying their game. 'Hang 'em! Hang 'em high.'

'And the Queen?'

'Oh, I like 'er! Hang 'em but save the Queen!'

'How about love, then? Can it exist? Real love, here in the meanness of the city?'

'Sure it does. Got a baby girl. Clutch her to my chest so hard each morn, we smoulder like embers.'

'Here,' says Thomas, and gives him all his remaining coins. 'You earned it. You may be the wisest man in the whole of London.'

'Sure I am. And in the whole Empire besides.'

Φ

Thomas returns late-morning. A nod and a look is enough to draw Charlie out of his melancholy. The moment is as good as any: Mrs Grendel is out bartering for food, Sebastian is building his sewer and Grendel has gone to tell the priest he shan't be coming to work for a few days.

Livia watches them assume their roles: the burglar and his assistant. A confidence man is what the newspapers would call him: someone who can charm the petticoats off a schoolma'am. The beauty about Charlie is that he does not even realise his own gift.

And indeed it proves easy. Charlie simply enters the kitchen, sits down on the side of the table that will ensure her mother's face is turned away from the hallway and the door to her own room. It must be, Livia finds herself thinking, that her mother is bored. It cannot be easy being stuck here, waiting, surrounded by her stroppy daughter and her friends. She could do with a bath, a walk, a horse ride around the estate. But Lady Naylor is a gaoler now.

A gaoler cannot leave his gaol.

'You know about Grendel,' Charlie begins, frank and guileless in his guile. 'Sebastian said he told you last night.'

'Yes, he did. I should have noticed it earlier, I suppose, but my mind was elsewhere.'

'Aren't you shocked?'

'Oh, but I was! Who could have dreamed it? Though it is not entirely unprecedented.' She purses her lips, leans forward, closer to him. 'Have you ever been to an asylum, Mr Cooper? A hospital for the insane. I toured one some years ago, after my husband fell ill. These days they are constructed according to the Pentonville model. Individual cells, spread out along long, spoke-like corridors, so the inmates don't infect each other with their Smoke. Once a week the orderlies go into each cell and scrape off the Soot, to sell it to the manufacturers of cigarettes. On the sly, of course, though the proprietors know and receive a cut. As for the inmates, some are like my husband. Others have nothing wrong with their intellectual faculties at all. They are criminals, or libertines, gentlemen who have flaunted their vice. And others yet – well, for a long time now there has existed a rumour. A whisper amongst scholars; a footnote in an article by an Oxford don. That there was a man, an inmate, down in the cellars of New Bethlem Hospital, who was just like your friend here. A freak of nature! He must have died in his cell.'

'But why was he locked away?'

'Don't let's be naïve, Mr Cooper. He was that which mustn't exist. A virtuous man without pedigree. Monstrous, impossible, a threat to the realm.'

Livia listens to all this, hovering in the corridor outside, a relay station between the two boys. She gives Thomas a nod. He saunters across, into her mother's room, quietly but without haste; leaves the door open so she can warn him if need be. Charlie, receiving Livia's nod, hastens to carry on.

'There is something I don't understand, Lady Naylor. You see,

Grendel used to smoke. He told Livia and Thomas: that he smoked as a child. So what happened to him?'

'Impossible to say with certainty. Some kind of metabolic corruption, I suppose. A disease, one that attacks not just the Smoke glands but the whole of the affective system. It must have destroyed large parts of it. The part that governs behaviour we call sin.'

'Then isn't that the answer? A disease that will make us good.'

Livia hears her mother grow agitated at this.

'It would not work, Mr Cooper. The disease is clearly non-infectious. But even if we could bottle it somehow, and pass it on at will . . .' She pauses, composes herself, leans forward towards Charlie. 'Let me ask you this. Do you admire Mr Grendel?'

'No. I pity him.'

'Why?'

Charlie answers at once. 'He has no choice about being good.'

'Precisely. Imagine if a man like Grendel fell into the hands of Renfrew. How long before he'd start dreaming of a race of men just like him? It's what he wants after all. A nation of choirboys. Of automata. And he's a good scientist, your Dr Renfrew. God knows what he might cook up in his laboratory.'

'Renfrew's dead.'

'Dead? No, he isn't. I asked Sebastian to make inquiries. Gravely injured, it is said. Stabbed and mauled by an intruder. There are rumours that it took "Continental medicine" to save him.'

'I am glad he's alive.'

Charlie says it slowly, after much thought, a note of wonder in his voice. Livia hears it and feels a pang of pride constrict her chest.

Then she turns away from him and watches Thomas search her mother's room.

Φ

The room is small and stuffy with spent air. Other than the heavy-framed bed, it holds a wardrobe, a washbowl and a chair. Thomas stands still for a minute, lets his eyes wander. The wardrobe's door is broken and stands open; it holds nothing but clothes, Lady Naylor's hanging from hooks, the Grendels' displaced onto the wardrobe floor. The bed is made; when Thomas runs his hand under the sheet he finds a negligee. A silver hairbrush is tucked beneath the pillow. Underneath the bed stands milady's travelling valise, holding

343

underclothes and a collection of French poetry. Its frontispiece shows a naked woman in the embrace of a swan.

The sewer maps are hidden between mattress and bed-base. Thomas unfolds them, one next to the other, slips the drafting paper out of his trousers. It is thin enough for the print to shimmer through. Copying it all would take hours. But he does not need all. He finds a line marking the river, works up from there, copying the main thoroughfares first of the 'Ashton' plan, then traces the turn-offs marked only on the plan entitled 'Aschenstedt'. Back and forth he works, quickly, his hands sure, listening with half an ear to the conversation outside. When he is satisfied with his copy and has re-placed the plans, he looks over at Livia, sees her urging him to leave. But he isn't done yet. Something else has caught his eye, a box, quite large but shoved to the corner of the bed frame in such a manner that its form merges with the bulk of the oaken leg. Thomas drops down onto his stomach and pictures Lady Naylor do the same, to deposit it there. The box is heavy as he slides it out; varnished wood reinforced in metal at the corners. The latches are not locked, open on a flask sunk in a satin-lined depression that precisely matches its proportions. He pulls it out, notices its weight: a squat, short-necked bottle made of tinted glass, holding perhaps as much as half a gallon. The stopper is buried with care but is mounted with a brass ring to aid its removal; the glass of the bottleneck seems inordinately thick. Thomas raises the jar, feels a viscous liquid shift inside. Livia gestures, but he won't be hurried, casts around and finds a cup Lady Naylor has brought here from the kitchen, its bottom encrusted with a smudge of tea. It takes both hands to pour. The liquid moves sluggishly, then leaps out in a sudden gulp of purest black. Thomas holds it far from him, watches it cling to the cup, receiving his hand's shudder and transmuting it into the ponderous slide of molten lead.

Quickly now, putting down the cup for a moment, he returns the bottle to its satin-cushioned, bottle-shaped hole, and the box to the back of the bed. At just this moment, the conversation outside hits a lull. Livia's eyes warn him, swivel back to Charlie.

Thomas freezes and stands waiting, in his fist a liquid distillation of all the darkness in this world.

Φ

Lady Naylor makes to rise. She mustn't. And so Charlie detains her, with words, of course, some truth he has been working towards, Livia can see it in the hot-eared earnestness of his face. It's an answer to Renfrew perhaps, to that which he did to him, in the name of good morals and the future of the realm.

It may work on her mother just as well.

'The most difficult thing,' Charlie says, his voice rising half an octave, a boy nervous, confessing his soul, 'the most difficult thing is to compromise. To sit in between, not leaning too far one way nor the other, not taking things to their conclusion. To be sensible. Boring.'

Livia's mother scoffs at his words. But she resettles in her chair.

'Can it be that you are a coward, Mr Cooper?'

Livia watches Charlie flush at this, swallow his Smoke. He is speaking to her, Livia, now, only to her, his words low and precise.

'Perhaps I am. A coward.'

'Oh, Charlie! It appears I have made you angry.'

'That's why it is so hard to stand in the middle. Someone will always point their finger at you and mock.'

Her mother shrugs as though to concede the point, then props her chin up on her hands. 'The problem is this, Mr Cooper. Your *compromise* is nothing other than the status quo. It's sitting on your hands and being decent. It will never change the world. But then, your parents would like that.'

'What do you mean?'

'Don't play stupid now, Mr Cooper. You come from one of England's great families, wouldn't you say? By pedigree. But also by wealth. Of course, much of this wealth isn't as ancient as all that. Two generations, no more. But wealth is like a spinster: it is impolite to inquire about its age. The truth is your family's fortune has grown tenfold in less than thirty years, and along with it, its influence, its standing. It begs the question: how?'

All at once, Charlie's face turns pale.

'That's what Renfrew said to me,' he whispers. '"Ask yourself where all the money comes from."'

'And, Mr Cooper, have you?'

He hesitates. 'I don't know.'

'Hazard a guess then.'

345

Again he hesitates. Then – eyes rising, committed to the truth – the word tumbles out of him: 'Sweets.'

'B&S. Quite. Shares in the factory, up until recently. A royal licence to import the raw ingredients. Colonial holdings. Import licences. The Spencers bought up the monopoly of manufacture, of course, but the business as a whole is far too lucrative to leave to one family alone. Did you know your father was in Parliament yesterday, introducing a new bill? A grief-stricken father: he thinks you dead and blames some Irish migrants who were found with Julius's gun. The Tory papers call it the New Isolationism. A return to purity, both moral and ethnic. Kick out all foreigners, all nonconformists. Chase off the Catholics and Jews. Limit trade to what we import ourselves from our colonies. No more foreign sin! A high-minded bill. And incidentally rather lucrative for those who hold an import licence. Your father can avenge you and line his pockets all in one quick swoop.'

She pauses just long enough for Charlie to put his head in his hands.

'Oh, don't berate yourself, Mr Cooper. All the grand families are involved. In sweets and, with the more adventurous families, cigarettes. It's a system, a network, the weave of the land. Compromise won't change it.' She rises. 'It has been a pleasure talking to you, young man, but it is getting late. Mrs Grendel will be back any moment and will want her kitchen.'

In response to Livia's gesture, Thomas emerges from Lady Naylor's room. He is just in time to cross the hallway, brush past Livia, and disappear unseen.

Φ

Dinner is toad-in-the-hole and mash, lies heavy in the stomach. Sebastian comes and leaves again, surprises them with sticky pastries that Charlie has no heart to eat. He remains morose and restless, spends an hour staring through the keyhole at the child. Grendel has found some toys for him, and the little boy sits on the ground, spinning a spindle, before picking it up and smashing it against a wall. It is eerie, watching his anger, with no Smoke rising from his pores.

Later yet, they sit together, Charlie, Thomas and Livia, blocking the door to the boys' bedroom with their backs. A teacup stands in front of them, not far from their feet, and a sheet of paper lies spread out on their laps. It is, thinks Charlie, like they are preparing a walking trip into the hills. For the third time now, he bends to study the crude map and for the third time fails to wrest meaning from it, seeing only its surface pattern, nothing else. Line scrawls on a dirty page; turn-offs marked; crossings circled. A map to the underworld. Legible only to the dead.

And to Thomas.

'I think it must be this.' He points, tapping his finger on a row of rectangles, a finger long. 'It's the only place that's *different*; and they are in an area quite separate from the rest. And look here, this is the same place drawn in cross section. The rectangles look like they've been let into the floor.'

'They might be pools,' Livia suggests, thinking perhaps of the wet docks that played harbour to Mowgli's ship. 'A series of pools.'

'Could be.' Thomas points at another section of the map. 'This here is the river. And this here must be an entrance. Tomorrow I will go and find it. If I can match the shape of the riverbed to the map, I should be able to locate the street.'

'What about this, then?' Livia asks, pointing her chin at the cup.

'You know what it is,' Thomas mutters. 'Soot. Murderers' Soot. The kind your mother was collecting when I first saw her. The laboratory was full of it.'

He leans towards it, reluctant to touch it, then dips a pinkie in, retrieves it, holds it close to the lamp. They put their heads together, stare at its darkness. As she did the previous day, Livia pulls out the stub of a cigarette, undoes the paper, picks through its contents. It's like comparing road grit with purest tar. There is no easy way of telling whether this Soot is quickened or remains inert.

'How will your mother save the world with this?' Thomas wipes his finger on the floor, then rubs the spot with a heel, unable to erase the mark.

'We could ask her. Press her on the point.'

'No, Charlie. No more questions, no more lies, no more oaths "on her husband's life". The only thing worth knowing is what we learn for ourselves.'

Neither Livia nor Charlie sees fit to disagree. Instead, Livia asks Thomas, 'Are we holding on to it?'

'You do it. I cannot stand to look at it.'

'Then we need a container with a lid. I will ask Grendel for a mustard jar.'

'He is spending time with your mother, Grendel is. I saw them talking just now. She talks. He listens.'

Charlie says it flatly, without insinuation, but immediately Livia is in a temper.

'He is helping Mowgli!' She makes to say more, but then jumps up and storms out, hands deep in her pockets like the urchin as whom she is dressed.

Φ

They remain alone in silence, Thomas and Charlie, legs sprawled in front of them across the floor. It is like it was at school; a mouldy wall where bathroom tiles should have cooled their backs. It's good this, Charlie thinks, feeling his friend's weight against his shoulder. Familial; familiar. He is sitting by Thomas's good ear. It would feel less of a comfort, perhaps, whispering into the wound.

'I have been thinking,' he says, 'about what Lady Naylor said. She must have a hand in cigarette manufacture. There is no other way she would know: about the fact that asylums sell the manufacturers their Soot.'

'Do you think she owns the factory?'

'No. She would not need to borrow money if she did.'

'The Spencers then.'

'Them, and a few others. Cigarettes and sweets. The bedrock of Empire.' Charlie spits, feels his breath grow dark. 'Funny thing about greed,' he continues. 'It doesn't generate Smoke. I imagine it's quite a problem for our theologians.'

Thomas turns to him, puts an arm around his shoulder.

'Don't be bitter, Charlie. It does not become you.'

Charlie tries not to be. It is difficult, he finds. He had no cause before to feel ashamed for being a Cooper.

Φ

As they settle down to sleep, Thomas asks him one more question. He asks it gently, into the two-foot gap that separates their bedding.

'Have you talked to Livia?' he asks.

'Not yet.'

'You should.' Then: 'She misses you.'

'Don't, Thomas. I thank you. But don't.'

Thomas's response carries the notes of genuine wonder.

'Christ, Charlie, can't you smell her Smoke? Can't you smell what she feels?'

Φ

The next morning Sebastian calls before dawn. He is in a rush, will barely come in, won't take off his coat. All he wants is to talk. When Charlie, sleep-creased, alerted by his urgent whisper, arrives in the front hallway he is unsurprised to find Grendel to be part of the conversation. Or rather: Grendel is being spoken to, Sebastian's hand on his wrists. The tones of instruction; too quiet to carry. Lady Naylor is there, too, holding Sebastian's doctor's bag. It's heavy enough to give a list to her tall frame. In the kitchen doorway Mrs Grendel stands. She, too, is out of earshot, at five feet's remove. Their gazes meet, hers and Charlie's. A moment later she beckons to him.

'What's going on?' he asks once he has followed her into the kitchen. Her back is turned, her hand reaching into a clay pot on the sideboard.

'Lady Naylor sent me out for this,' she replies. 'Yesterday. Had me walk for miles, going somewheres where they wouldn't know me. So it won't attract attention, me growing rich one day to the next.'

She takes hold of Charlie's palm and deposits a brown, sticky lump in it. Sugar.

'Go on,' she says, 'you need fattening, you do.'

He puts it in his mouth, speaks past the shock of its flavour, sickly and moist.

'What is Sebastian saying? Something go wrong?'

'Don't know,' she answers, sneaking some sugar herself. 'Trust in Grendel.'

But as her tongue picks through her teeth, hunting sweetness, Charlie wonders whether he can.

Φ

Sebastian leaves soon after that. A minute later, Livia is at the front door. She slips out so quickly, Charlie has no time to think. A glance his way before the door closes. An unspoken question. The suggestion of a shrug.

Then she is gone.

By the time Charlie has his shoes on, there is no sign of her, the street outside choking with strangers, refuse, drifting fog. Back in their room Thomas is still sleeping, twitchy in his dreams.

Φ

Livia returns just before lunch. Thomas has woken and left, in search of the sewer entrance. Charlie offered to come, but they did not want to let Lady Naylor out of their sight. It is better this way: it affords Charlie time to gather his courage. All he needs now is for Livia to return before his friend.

Charlie hears her footsteps in the stairwell. He has been waiting for their sound and slips out onto the tiny landing to catch her there. It has been raining and she is wet, her hair clinging to her head and face. It makes the ears look large, their rims delicate and pale, like fine bone china. The miner's jacket is big around her shoulders, weighted down by water and dirt. Charlie looks and looks. He wants to tell her that all is forgiven; that he does not want to stand in her and Thomas's way; that things are not her fault and, anyway, there are bigger things afoot. He wants to touch her, hold her hand – like a friend, a brother – rest his forehead on her shoulder.

'You followed Sebastian,' he says.

'Yes. I found out where he lives. A hotel, not far from here. I thought it might be useful to know.'

'Good idea.'

She steps up to the landing, makes to round him. But then she stops, inches away. The cock of her head is that strangest of mixtures. Modesty and strength. City grime dusting the fine down of her cheeks.

A pencil line of Smoke rises from Charlie, light and grey. He is glad for it. It will tell her what he feels.

She looks at it without flinching; opens her mouth, tasting it, tasting him; reaches out and laces her fingers into his.

'Whom do you love?'

He says it and sees Livia smile over the phrase. What would Thomas have said? But that's just it: Thomas wouldn't have asked.

'You,' she says. 'Him. Both.'

'Yes. But you love him like a bride. And me like a sis—'

She interrupts, cheeks flushing, displeased at being told what she feels.

'It isn't as simple as that.' She snorts, steps up, kisses him. 'There! I've been learning to smoke.'

It's a peck or rather a bite: his lips between hers, tugged and held for the length of a breath; a passing of Smoke, of emotion – hunger, confusion, triumph, fear – from skin to skin and lung to lung. Then Livia rounds him and opens the door.

Behind it, Grendel stands, looking flustered, Mowgli's porridge on a tray.

Φ

Charlie watches the feeding. The boy won't handle the spoon himself but he will sit there, mouth open, and allow Grendel to deposit a spoonful; will chew it slowly and sigh, world-weary, his eyes screwed up and cold. When the bowl is nearly finished the boy holds a dollop on his tongue then suddenly bends forward and spits it at Grendel's feet. It is deliberate, a test: the small brown face insolent, the body tense, ready to bolt. Grendel kneels, cleans it up, offers another spoonful from the bowl. But the child has moved away and wrapped himself in blankets. All this Charlie sees from the keyhole. When Grendel turns to leave, the boy looks after him. A curious look. Suspicion mingled with the dawning of trust. Charlie rises just before Grendel pushes open the door.

'Can I go to him?' he asks, but Grendel shakes his head.

'Mr Sebastian does not wish it.'

'Why do you follow his orders?'

'The boy is scared,' Grendel says. 'You are kind, but you will scare him. With me, he knows I won't smoke. Even when he bites. He can sense that I'm harmless. Down to my bones.'

Charlie understands what he means. Grendel radiates something. Holiness; an absence. A man estranged from sin.

'Then Livia is right. You are an angel.'

Grendel hesitates. 'I fear I am one of those who stood at the edge of heaven, looking down. Dreaming about their Fall.'

Φ

Thomas returns late. Finding the sewer entrance proved harder than he thought, his hand-drawn map of the underground and the city's streets impossible to match. In the end he chanced upon an Ashton engineer in a company cab and ran behind it until it led him to a

351

work site. Thomas sneaked into the sewer for several hundred yards before being thrown out by a foreman. What he saw was a maze of tunnels and a mechanical pump the size of a house, pumping water down a giant bore. He got nowhere near those giant pools marked in pale rectangles upon his map.

'We are running out of time,' he keeps saying. 'It's been forty-eight hours since they infected Mowgli. Another day and he'll start changing. We must find out what she is planning before then.'

'Then we will go tonight,' Charlie suggests. 'We must take him along. In case we don't want to return.'

Thomas and Livia are quick to agree. They are all fed up with waiting. One might start a revolution, it comes to Charlie, or thwart it, just from this, a hunger for movement, for action.

'Mowgli is locked in,' Livia reminds them. 'But Grendel has the key. I will talk to him.'

They see her speaking to Grendel later. It is easy that evening to catch him alone: Lady Naylor has been much preoccupied and has kept to her room. It is a whispered conversation, private, at the end of the corridor; Livia holding her holy man's hand. His face is so kindly, so prone to blushes and nervous smiles that it is only by the tilt of Livia's chin they can guess at the urgency of their talk.

'Will he help us?' Thomas asks her bluntly when she returns.

'Of course he will!'

'And he won't—'

'He gave his word,' she barks, storming off, leaving both Thomas and Charlie in the wake of her Smoke. They sniff it like the lovelorn pups they are.

'Pissy,' Thomas decides.

'But she's pretty when she is.'

And for a moment they forget, almost, that they are to fight a duel for the favours of her heart.

Φ

They decide on leaving early that night, but deep in the flat they can hear Lady Naylor stir and move about, so they wait until the moon is gone and the night made blacker by rain. The plan is a compromise of sorts, between Livia's trust and the boys' suspicion. Thomas will sneak into the room in which the Grendels sleep and see whether he can find the key to the child's cell. If not, Livia will wake their host and remind him of his promise.

'He will help us without fail.'

But in the end there is no need to wake Grendel. When they step into the hallway, they see his wife's shadow, sitting alone in the kitchen, the faint glow of embers in the stove behind her back. Not for the first time Charlie notes their ignorance of her Christian name. She remains, to them, a stranger. They start, crowd around her, assault her with whispers.

'Quiet,' they hiss. 'Don't be alarmed.'

And: 'We need to speak to Grendel. He must unlock the child's door.'

The angel's wife is stony-faced. She seeks out Livia's form amongst them, shorter than the boys' and framed by pale hair.

'I know. He told me you had asked him. He told me everything.' The woman rises, pushes through them, pulls something out the pocket of her skirt. 'There is no need to wake him. I have the key.'

The door squeaks when she swings it open for them. Charlie winces, but nothing stirs in Lady Naylor's room across.

'Quick now,' says Thomas. 'The child must not call out.'

They rush forward, into darkness, find the blankets, the bunk. Behind them, the door falls back into its frame, the lock snaps.

'I'm sorry,' says Mrs Grendel. Her voice is dull, muffled by wood, by distance. 'He said you mustn't follow. They'll be back before long.'

Around them the room is empty, the child long gone.

Caesar

They capture Nótt. This happens before Mother but after Sebastian. I'm having trouble with words, with time. I'm different now, transformed. A buzzard climbing the updrafts of Smoke. My bones hollow, my body a husk: reinhabited. I, the dark twin of my former self, flesh of my own liver. I am my own father and mother; Renfrew my midwife; the mask my baptism and my last rites. Children cower when I pass them in the streets.

They take Nótt away. A man with a billy club, breaking her legs. They tie a rope around her neck and drag her; her jaws snapping, a whine in her throat, not a bark. I watch them do it, and I do nothing. It is of no consequence. Nótt is the past, my boyhood, my becoming. I trained her nose for Smoke. My own nose is better now, better than hers. I can smell your needs across the chill of a city square, can sort their flavours, weigh each urge: taxonomise. What I like, though, is to get close, inhale you like a flower. Dogs with their noses up each other's arses. I understand it now. The bouquet of vice. Bottle it and you'll be rich.

But, of course: I am already rich.

London is an ocean of Smoke. People float on it like scum: waterlogged, helpless, half aware of others circling in the depths. I came to it and plunged, handed myself over to its rhythms; its storms and tides; its eddies and swells. Cold, rich, salty. I plunged and I gorged. Not on food, mind. I don't remember what I ate. Refuse, wild things scuttling in the alley; scoops of old, encrusted Soot. My head is light these days, my stomach a knot. My clothes hang from me like rags.

Here is how I pass the hours. I walk the streets. Stand in the thoroughfares, open-mouthed, imbibing every current, belching it back into the air. Smoke flowing through the filter of my body. Irritation turning to anger; drunken joy to mischief; boisterousness to wounded pride: behind me a dark wake, dragging others off their paths. Whirlpools of corruption. I am Smoke's slave and also its master; drift like flotsam yet command its tides. *Dialectics*. A Fritz philosopher called Hegel. I am *Aufhebung*: my own cancellation; a new, a higher version of myself. I am the end of history. I played dice with a gang of child thieves in Hampstead; wrestled a beggar in a ditch by Covent Garden and bit off his nose; danced the polka with a lunatic from Palestine, loused his hair and broke his face. I am a leech, a dog, a sparrow. I am a moraine eel. I am, I am, I am. I'm having trouble with words, with time, with order.

Order!

First. First I came to London. Trailing him: Charlie Cooper. Nótt and I, sharing the road: on my knees, half the time, my nose to her snout, palms in the dirt, sniffing for his trace. We lost it, both of us. He smokes too little, that one, and there were too many others, covering up. Siren songs all over the city, calling to me, moth to the flame. A boarding house in Clapham. An opium den in Limehouse. A mother clutching her stillborn, all alone under a bridge. Distractions. I am he: a boy in a sweetshop, blindfolded, sniffing for a single ginger nut.

Then: a trace. No, not of the one I followed. The *other one*. My cousin, my double. But how different his Smoke smells to me now. Where once I sensed rivalry, I now taste promise; where I saw hatred, I now divine kinship. But how weak it seems, this shred of Smoke, leeched by doubt and temperance; how distant from the moment we stood in the ring and beat paths to one another's souls. I want to find him, wake him to his nature. Taste him, own him, crawl into his skin. Ingestion, osmosis. Cannibalism. Flesh of my flesh, Smoke of my Smoke. In pain and rage we shall become one.

Order though, order! The world of man has sequence. Cause and effect. The world of Smoke is different. Noumenon: the thing-in-itself. Kant? Cunt! I am Smoke's avatar. I am its prophet, its priest, its monk. I am—

Order!

First. First I come to London. Then comes the trace. Too faint to follow. Chasing it, losing it. A church, the river, distractions.

Then – Sebastian. I remember where he lives. It is like floating up from the dark of the ocean: relearning the skills of men. Planning. Remembering. Thinking in sentences, in words. All against my newfound nature: my mouth level with the waterline, heart, lungs and liver in the waves. Leviathan circling at my feet. The Regency. A hotel for gentlemen; porters by the door. Licensed sweets in their mouths. Uniforms speckled with London's Soot. Room 14. Sebastian, Ashton, Aschenstedt. Smoke, Soot and Ash.

There is no light in his room, no movement behind the window. No matter; I wait. Darkness falls. Sebastian returns. *His* Smoke has touched him, has seeped into his clothes. The faintest of traces. I could stop him at the entrance, make him talk. But it is better to wait, let him lead me to *him*. Sebastian goes upstairs and turns on the light. One can see it from the square. That's when I learn there are other watchers. First two, then more, chins raised to his window. Men in long overcoats, truncheons clipped to their belts. One at each entrance to the square. They spot us soon after I have spotted them. Perhaps they have a description: Renfrew's killer, wanted by magistrates. A gentleman and his hound. It's Nótt they capture: they see me too but hesitate; allow me to slip away. Fear. I catch its smell and scuttle off; watch across the shoulder of the throng.

Nótt makes it easy for them. A sick dog, she is, ever since Renfrew. My smell has changed, she sniffs me with suspicion, no longer sure of her own master. Keeps her distance, always six steps behind. A cast-off shadow, chasing the memory of love. Head down, tail tucked, forlorn. I should have gotten rid of her before. But it is hard to kill old habits.

It takes four of them, converging on her, arms spread out like wrestlers. A crowd gathers at once, eager to see. It separates me from the action. I watch from afar. There is a flavour to the one with the club. He need not have broken her legs but he does so anyway, Smoke rising from his shaven cheeks like a blush that catches fire. He is fair-haired and slight, but in the cast of his mouth he has something of Mr Price. A man with potential; sergeant to this platoon of thugs. They drag Nótt into a waiting cab. One of the men goes along, the rest resume their watching. Patient, expectant, eyes glued to his window, two floors up. I remain out of sight, cower in the mouth of an alley.

We wait.

Sebastian leaves before dawn. They all fall in line with him, strung out across the length of a street. I make up the rear. Already I know he has spotted them: a thread of Smoke following him, of fear and defiance, too weak to be visible, a beacon to my nose. How simply he gives us all the slip. He walks to work, a satchel in one fist. The sewers. I paid for them, studied the plans. A guard hutch outside a hole in the wall. It swallows him. The watchman turns the pursuers away.

There are other ways in. It takes me a while to find one that is free of guards, my mind tracing the memory of neatly drawn lines. Down below, I find what he's been building. Iron bars stop me, I give them the slip. Mother lied to me. An investment opportunity, she said, a vineyard of sorts, ripe for the harvest. A mine, an oil well. A pit of dirt. Another lie. Another betrayal.

How many have there been?

Rage takes hold of me, breeds madness. I step beyond words. Daniel and Stephen from Donegal are walking with me, Renfrew in their midst. Mr Price holds a lamp. Green tiling, Caracalla. A room beyond the laws of physics. Light holds no flame here; past turns to present. I bathe, I feed. My stomach bulges but my limbs are weak.

Order!

He pulls me back. I catch his scent, it carries on a ventilation draught, recalls me to the world of thought. *He* is here. Not close, not in this chamber, but in some tunnel far away, where the sewer meets the city above. It lures me back; a long ascent. My cousin, my mirror, my bride. Blood wedding; together we'll be twice myself.

I leave the sewers on all fours. Dark outside, the sun long set, beggars jeering at me, then covering their faces when I pass. The trail is fresh; is sweet with courage, with desire, with doubt. His destination: a house half burnt. Soot mixing with soot. I look up the stairs. *He* is inside.

But so is Mother.

Her Smoke has a scent all its own, sweet and treacly like a sick man's piss. The baron's doing. He cut her deep, Mother showed me the scar. My fingers down her bodice. Seduction: a way of reminding me that I came from her womb. She has betrayed me, used me, given me life. I hate her, I love her. Commonplaces: every mother's son. I am reborn, remade, a thing of her dark dreams. I am my own becoming. I am the alpha and the omega. I am . . . I am not ready for her yet.

I wait. The house draws me, repels me in turn. I squat in the gateway down below. They are all inside. *He.* Charlie. Livia. Half-sister, empress for a day. *He* wants her. She wants—

Mother.

I'm afraid of her.

357

But I shot Mr Price. Father figure; hole for a heart. I could kill her at a hundred yards. A twitch of the finger, no need to look her in the eye. One hundred yards. But the Irish kept the gun.

I squat in the gateway, watch a tart serve clients in the mouth of the alley across. The men smoke. She does not. Only with the last one does she finally catch, converting his lust to her anger, pale silvery green. Alchemy. Like a goose eating grass and shitting gold. She pulls down her skirts and bolts. The moon rises then is lost in cloud. It rains. I stick my tongue out, each drop seeded with Soot. Sand corns in oysters. Pearls for a swine.

Time.

I am no good with time. Half the night gone in the blink of an eye. Then the door opens above and I hide. Mother crosses the yard. Behind her a man, an abomination, carrying a boy, a cripple, a blank. Two rents in the fabric of Smoke. My blood puckers. Puckers, I say: not the skin, the blood, a scrotum dunked in ice. They are in a hurry, Mother and man, walk quickly into the rain. I know where they are heading. Mother. I shot Mr Price. If only I had kept the gun.

But first: inside. To *him*. Smoke wells up, consumes me. Rage. Yearning. Time. I am no good with time. A minute, an hour, just to take the first step. Put a leash on my Smoke. A game, let's make a game of it. Savour it. Sommelier. Wine is bitter under the tongue.

At the top of the stairs: a seam of *his* Smoke. Old, caked in, stuck to the brick. I put my lips to it. Feeding or kissing? A bloom of mould growing up the wall underneath. Mould and Soot. London's flowers. They should put them on its crest. Ahead, the door is locked. I stand there sniffing. Time? I am no good with time.

Order!

Who am I? Lord Spencer? Julius? Caesar. *Et tu.* Before (before Nótt, after London; *before*) I entered a church. *He* had been there: a trace of him on the steps by the gate. The man inside crossed himself. High Anglican: a confession box like a coffin, the priest slumping on its stool. The haste of drunk fingers. Forehead, belly, both sides of the chest. It made me chuckle. The devil, then? The devil is a schoolboy. I stare at my hands. My skin has turned grey, like ash.

A fist of ash.

It knocks gently on the door.

Part Five

Above and Below

Imagine that you yourself are building the edifice of human destiny with the object of making people happy . . . of giving them peace and rest at last, but for that you must inevitably and unavoidably torture just one tiny creature . . . and raise your edifice on the foundation of her unrequited tears – would you agree to be the architect on such conditions? Tell me the truth.

Fyodor Dostoevsky, *The Brothers Karamazov* (1880),
translated by Richard Pevear and Larissa Volokhonsky

No man is a hero to his valet . . . Not because the hero is no hero, but because the valet is a valet.

Georg Wilhelm Friedrich Hegel,
Lectures on the Philosophy of History (1837)

Demons

'Please, Mrs Grendel! You must let us out at once. You have no right. And it is very important that we catch up with them. The little boy is in danger. Please. We insist.'

Livia listens to her own words and frowns.

We are speaking to Mrs Grendel as though she is stupid.

Mrs Grendel is not stupid. In fact her account of the situation is remarkably lucid. She tells them that the previous evening, as he returned to his hotel, Sebastian noticed a man in the foyer who, while pretending to read, studied Sebastian's ascent up the stairs with uncommon interest. When Sebastian returned to the front desk some hours later, under the pretext of asking for his mail, the man was still there, reading the same paper. Sebastian concluded that he had been discovered and placed under surveillance. Indeed he was followed when he left his lodgings early that morning, but, using the sewer as a shortcut, he managed to lose his pursuers. He came, informed Lady Naylor, considered 'going into hiding', but resolved to return to his rooms instead. As long as he was under surveillance, he argued, the authorities' energies were tied up and they would not dare to make too obvious a search of the sewer system. Lady Naylor was left in charge of what he playfully – in Mrs Grendel's opinion childishly – called 'the operation'. The lady, in turn, decided not to delay any further and had left an hour previously, taking Grendel along. All this her husband told Mrs Grendel that very evening just as she is now relaying it to them. Mr Grendel did not, it appears, invite Mrs Grendel's own thoughts on the matter.

'But where did she take Mowgli?' Charlie mutters. 'It's too early. Lady Naylor said seventy-two hours. It hasn't been much more than fifty.'

The voice beyond the door is unmoved by his reasoning.

'I don't know about that. Perhaps she lied. People do.'

Throughout the exchange, Livia is conscious that Thomas is only half listening. Unlike Charlie and her, he has no faith in words.

361

Instead he is busy searching the room. He finds a candle first of all, high up on a shelf; a box of matches. Next, working by candlelight now, he examines the window, finds it expertly barred. An engineer, Sebastian Aschenstedt: thorough. On the floor, not far from the bed, lies his doctor's bag. Livia remembers his handing it over to her mother when he visited last. The bag has been ransacked, its few remaining contents spilled across the floor. Syringes and little glass vials sealed with tinfoil. The small round tin Sebastian used to infect the child, looking for all the world like a tin of shoe polish, a needle hole at its centre. Thomas unscrews it and finds it encrusted with oily crumbs of brownish Soot. Not far from him, head-high, Mowgli's mask hangs off a nail like a forgotten face. That's all, Thomas's inventory complete. There is nothing in the room that would help them escape.

Livia returns her attention to the door.

'You are doing it for money,' she shouts, spite tinting her breath. 'You are a greedy dried-up woman who cares only about herself.'

A silence follows the words. But Mrs Grendel is still there. Livia can see the shadow of her feet through the crack at the foot of the door.

'You've never been poor, duck,' she says, reasonably. 'And Tobias *asked* me. He never asked a thing of me, not once, in all these years. Until tonight. "Keep 'em here," he said. "The lady wishes it. Lock them in if you must. They are still only children," he said. "Keep them safe."'

'It was Grendel's idea?' There is no masking the hurt in Livia's voice. 'I don't believe you! Grendel acted under duress. Mother forced him to come.'

Again the answer is devastatingly reasonable.

'Lady Naylor needs him to keep the child quiet. The boy trusts him, you see. No Smoke, the little mite, but a cheeky bugger all the same.'

A note of hope swings in this last phrase. What did Grendel say to Livia? *We were not blessed ourselves.*

'He struck a bargain.' Livia realises at last. 'For Mowgli. But it's impossible. Grendel promised he would help me. And Grendel can't lie.'

'Can't he?' Mrs Grendel snorts. 'Lies are but words, and he can speak just fine. It's hate he can't. That, and there are limits to his love.'

A moment after she says it, Thomas tries to run down the door. He tries it with a kick first, near the lock. Then an angry charge, a fine mist of Smoke growing darker when it fails. Next Thomas and Charlie try it together. The door does not budge. On the far side, they hear Mrs Grendel walk away with fast, disgusted steps.

Φ

They sit defeated, both boys rubbing their shoulders. Livia looks from one to the other, Charlie's lean, honest runner's face; Thomas bolder, more intense, ugly in his anger. She pictures herself walking over to them, wedging herself there, in the half-foot gap between their hips. A step from them the respirator leers from its nail on the wall, its saucer eyes reflecting a twinned her.

Then: a knock on the front door. Five little raps, so soft Livia barely hears them. A friend calling. Steps answer, coming from the kitchen.

'See! Here they are, back already.'

Mrs Grendel's voice sounds pleased with the development. It is their first hint that she is not comfortable with the situation.

They hear her open the door. The next instant there is the opening syllable of surprise, or perhaps it is a question, cut short before it shapes itself into words. It is followed by the sound of two pairs of footsteps, very close together, as of two people dancing, eerie in their tidiness. The steps stop outside the door and a new sound finds them, an animal sniffing, head-high. Through the gap underneath the door a haze invades the room, dark and tentacular, leaving tracks on the floorboards. It's Charlie who reacts first, scrambling to his feet, drawing Thomas and Livia away from the door.

'It's Julius.'

The steps resume, still locked in dance. As they retreat into the kitchen, there sounds a scream, the pure notes of panic, a voice so divorced from its normal usage that it takes Livia a heartbeat to ascribe it to Mrs Grendel. The next moment, Thomas has once again thrown himself against the door. He hammers on it. It does not drown out the second scream. Neither does his shouting.

'Julius!' he shouts. 'Julius Spencer. What are you doing to her?'

Beside him Charlie stands, face drained of colour.

'Julius is not what he used to be,' he says.

He has used these words before, precisely these words, talking about the events at Renfrew's. It is only now that Livia begins to understand what he means.

Then the presence returns to the door. A voice: Julius's, not Julius's. Speaking not to them as a group but only to Thomas. As though Julius knows he is there, inches away, right behind the door.

'Are you listening, cousin? How weak you smell. Naked, are you? Come now, don your rage. Here, I'll help: bait the badger. First the old lady. Livia next. It'll bring out your plumage. Then we wed.'

'Don't,' Thomas pleads.

Julius does not appear to hear.

'Locked you in. Thick door! Good of her. A helping hand. Or is it luck? *Fortuna* is a woman. I am her husband, I am her child. I am the darkness behind her eyelids. I am . . .'

He trails off. Then his steps move away again, back to the kitchen. The silence that follows is worse than the earlier screaming. Thomas kicks at the door. The door will not break.

Φ

Livia is not sure what gives him the idea. He acts as though he has rehearsed it, quickly, efficiently, without hesitation. Dips a hand into her jacket pocket; pulls out their mustard jar of purest black; unscrews the tin of Soot from Sebastian's bag and replenishes its contents. Then Thomas takes the mask off the nail and stretches its rubber over his head and face until his dark eyes are ringed by its glass goggles. The limp tube dangles from his mouth like a length of fireman's hose. The tin screws smoothly on its copper spout. Sebastian again. Precision work. Only when Thomas tries to insert the needle of one of the spare syringes into one of the glass vials does he slow down. Wearing the goggles, his sense of depth appears to be compromised. He misses twice, breaking off the needle on the floor; labours to attach another. Then Charlie is there, trying to stop him.

'What are you doing, Thomas?'

'You heard! He is coming for us. He is killing Mrs Grendel and then he is coming for us. For Livia. I am too weak. I can't even break down the door.' Thomas wraps a hand around the tin dangling at the bottom of his rubber snout. 'I need strength. The strength of madness. This is murderer's Soot. Black as black. From your mother's secret stash. And this here' – he stabs down with the needle, misses the little ampulla – 'will quicken it.'

364

'You will get lost,' Charlie says. 'Lost in the Smoke.'

All the same he kneels down and attempts to help Thomas draw the liquid into the syringe. But his hands, too, are shaking. It's up to Livia then. She threads the needle through the thick wrapping of foil that seals the little bottle, draws its inch of liquid into the cylindrical glass chamber.

'Good! Now release it into the tin.'

She hesitates, her eyes on Charlie, then Thomas.

'What will happen to you?' she asks.

'Do it!'

'What if—'

'Do it!'

Thomas cups her hands in his. She leans forward. His face is rubber. The goggles are easiest to kiss. A smudge on their glass, his eyelid fluttering underneath. Already he is smoking, green and yellow, an aggressive kind of fear.

'I love you.'

He says it to Charlie as much as to her. Livia injects the liquid into the tin, hears him inhale. The eyeglasses ink over, darkness in the mask. A spasm, followed by the wheeze of respiration. Then Thomas pushes her aside and charges, all his weight thrown against the door. Again and again he batters the wood, heedless of injury, until his left arm hangs like a flipper broken at his side. The noise brings Julius running; when the lock finally breaks, he has to jump aside not to be showered in splinters. Livia only sees him indistinctly: there is too much Smoke. In the room, but also in her blood, infected as it is by Thomas's rage. An emaciated figure, ash-grey, the whites of his eyes dyed and curdled, purple-black. His hands are up, boxing style. The voice surprisingly light. Taunting.

'There,' Julius says. 'The gloves are off. And you found a mask. Second face. It grows into you. After a while, you can't tell if it's on or off.'

Then he and Thomas disappear in an explosion of Smoke.

Φ

It is ugly, and also happens at a distance, inscrutable, hidden from view. It's like a hole has opened up in the centre of the hallway, a window to another place, far away. The darkness of a well in winter. You can throw the bucket down into the dark. You will hear it hit, but what it finds down there is beyond the realm of the senses. The water you draw is black.

Livia would like to go and help Thomas. But even at a distance the Smoke that reaches out to them in thin dense tendrils frightens her blood. Infects it, yes, but also chases her away, to the front door where she cowers, consumed by baseness, hate and fear. Not far from her, she can see Charlie in his own battle against the Smoke, leaning into it as though into a storm. Beyond, there is the wild flailing of limbs, accompanied by sounds, dull, spongy thuds, meat beaten soft by a butcher. Shouts in between, yelps, something like laughter. After what seems like an age, a hand reaches for her, Charlie's. They lace fingers, so hard she can feel his bones pressing on hers. His hair and face is black with muck.

Together, she and Charlie finally work their way closer, aware that the fighting has slowed, that it is just one figure beating the other now; that the Smoke is dying down. The Soot that coats the floor is slick like axle grease and they find themselves skidding, then falling gracelessly alongside the prone figures. Thomas is on top. What is on the bottom is motionless and running red with blood.

And still Thomas is beating him, one fist rising into the space above his head and coming down on chest, head, neck, like a toddler in a strop, hammering the floor. She bends down to him, tries to reach him, the mask on his face. He feels her tug at him, turns, goggles black and bulbous. Then he pins her, puts a hand around her throat, throws his weight on her. His fingers are slick with blood, move from her throat, to her face, her hair, tear at her clothing; his body heavy and hot. It's Thomas, she reminds herself, struggling; *Thomas*. She manages to hook a hand around the rubber tube that juts from his jaws and yank it up, dislodge the mask; something dark rising in her worse than fear. Then Charlie is there, riding his friend's back, pushing him down beside her. They hold him wedged between their bodies.

She watches the change: his mouth snarling, threatening her skin, the very teeth turned black with Soot. Then, like a child emerging from a tunnel, something else starts surfacing in Thomas's eyes. Intelligence. Recognition. It is followed by such an intense burst of shame that she wants to turn away from him, not to burden him with her witnessing. And still his weight lies heavy on her, on her chest, her thighs. She scrambles away, bumps into the lump of flesh that is Julius, the mouth a cavity of tooth stumps, hair ripped out in clumps.

Φ

'He was starved, weak. Skin and bones. Nothing but rage. He did not stand a chance.'

That's the first thing Thomas says. His left shoulder is dislocated, his hands swollen to twice their size, his shirt ripped to shreds. 'Renfrew was right all along. I'm a killer.'

'You were not yourself.'

'Wasn't I, Charlie?'

He is crouching in a corner, chin curled into his chest. Thomas has yet to look at Livia. She wants to make it easier for him, but it's hard, past the memory of his body forcing its weight on hers. Her face and shirt are covered with both cousins' blood.

'It's over now,' is all she manages.

At this, his eyes rise. No tears. That same unblinking stare. Never flinching from the facts.

Not even now.

'Yes, over. My nature is out.' He rises, takes a step towards Mrs Grendel, then stops. 'You do it. See whether she is all right.'

Mrs Grendel has yet to move. She is sitting on a stool in a corner of the kitchen, huddled into herself. One of her eyes is swelling shut. Other than that she is not visibly hurt. Livia crouches in front of her, tries to talk to her. But the woman stares right through her. It is not that she is unconscious and does not see. Her eyes look beyond, at Julius. On her large, ruddy, working woman's hands, the veins crisscross like parcel string.

'We must go,' Charlie whispers behind her. 'Find Mowgli.'

'Yes.' Livia stands up, looks down herself. The miner's shirt is ripped and stained, the blood already half dried. She thinks she can smell it. 'I must get changed.'

'There is no time. And you have no other clothes.'

'I must get changed,' she repeats, brusquely, then rushes into her mother's room.

When she emerges Livia is wearing one of the dresses Sebastian brought for her mother. It is too large for her and feels alien after days spent in men's clothing. It is as though she has stepped back into another life. She raises the hem as she steps over Julius.

The boys stare at her when she enters the kitchen, even Thomas, beaten, miserable Thomas. She has scrubbed her face and hands with lye soap and a boar-bristle brush. Her body underneath the dress remains as filthy as ever. There just wasn't the time.

'Hurry,' she says, needlessly. The two boys rush past her at once, each eager not to touch her, now that she is once again a lady. There is a bulk to the petticoat that gives new width to her hips.

Before leaving, Livia returns to Mrs Grendel one more time.

'Are you all right?' she asks and then, when the woman does not respond: 'What is your name, Mrs Grendel? Your Christian name?'

The delay in the answer is such that Livia has already turned and walked three steps before she hears it.

'Berta,' the beaten woman says. 'Berta Grendel.'

They do not say, 'Goodbye, Berta.' They simply leave.

Φ

Thomas leads. He is spent, broken, hollow-eyed with fear. And yet he leads them, towards the sewer entrance he discovered. Livia and Charlie follow, hand in hand. Her fine dress elicits comments, cat-calls, caps doffed in mock homage. London, a city of louts; sleepless, even in the middle of the night, a steady stream of figures peopling its streets. She trades pallid Smoke with her hecklers, stains grey the ruffles of her sleeves. There is, in her Smoke, a tiny whiff of her own thrill at being noticed.

It isn't long before they reach their destination. An unmarked building, its gateway leading to a courtyard; and there, set into the courtyard's wall, the brick-rimmed entrance to a stairwell, leading underground. A squalid place, anonymous, the site of an old cess-pool now pumped empty. The courtyard is littered with construction materials. A chalkboard screwed into a wall marks the rota of work shifts. Thomas told them that when he found it earlier that day, the entrance had been guarded by a foreman with a ledger, ticking off names against a list. There is no foreman now, nor any workers, no one to tell them that they must not enter at their leisure. There is only one hitch, a problem so simple it has eluded their plans. The entire gateway is blocked by an iron gate.

When he sees it, Thomas covers his face with his hands.

Φ

They try the handle, rattle the doors, study the hinges. The lock is complex and made of steel; the bars sturdy and firm. There are no more than a few inches between the top of the gate and the top of the gateway; less space at the bottom. A cat could squeeze through; a rat. No doubt a thousand have.

Charlie articulates it first. 'There we are. After all we have been through. Defeated by a lock.'

His bitterness is fed by Thomas, who continues to stand passively, smokelessly by his side. Livia watches him in his impotence and despair; lets drop again the hand she has raised to touch him. At another time, another hour, they would sit and talk to Thomas, help him mourn. But this is no time for funerals, not even to bury your best friend's soul.

For five, ten minutes they simply stand there, wallowing in their defeat. Then Livia gathers her skirts in front of her and marches off. The boys follow.

'Where are we going?'

She only answers Charlie when the hotel comes into sight. Two porters stand outside its front steps, each flanked by a lamppost. The rest of the Regency lies in darkness, save for a window on the upper floor. Aschenstedt's window. She remembers following him to this square; remembers his opening the shutters and looking out.

'We need to find Mother. And there is only one person in the whole world who can tell us where she is.'

'It won't work. Sebastian has no interest in showing us the way. Besides, you heard what Mrs Grendel said. He's being watched.'

Charlie is merely being reasonable. Nonetheless she grows angry at once.

'What else do you want to do? Wait and do nothing?'

They watch the square. Despite the late hour there are quite a few people there, some drinking, some talking, some merely passing through. The longer they watch, the more they are aware of a number of men who do none of these things but simply stand there, in thick overcoats, their eyes on the hotel.

'Three, I think,' Thomas says. And then (weary, resentful, mustering the last of his will): 'I'll go.'

Charlie stops him before he can take a step. 'You can't. You are covered in blood. You'll never make it past the doormen.' He hesitates, continues. 'I will go. I can talk them into letting me through.'

Thomas sinks his fingers into Charlie's sleeve. One sticks up funny. Hurt and fear constrict his voice.

'The last time you went off by yourself, Charlie, a man tied you to his bed and whispered about virtue. If anyone goes, I—'

'Neither of you can go,' Livia interrupts him. 'It is a good hotel. A place for gentlefolk. And you both look like vagrants.'

They do not listen, caught up in their struggle over who can be trusted to risk his freedom. By the time they understand what she is saying she is halfway across the square. She turns once, to shake her head and forbid pursuit. It is Charlie who holds back Thomas. Rational, principled, disciplined Charlie. Trusting her. Treating her as his equal.

She is grateful and disgruntled all at once.

Φ

The doormen never try to stop her. She raises the hem of her skirts and pushes past them, ignoring the tipping of their hats. From the corner of her eye she sees one of the watchers stir. She wonders whether there will be another one, lurking in the semi-darkness of the reception hall. A concierge mans the high wooden desk. She waves him close, so she can avoid being overheard. *Coquettish.* And wonders did she learn it from Mother or from one of the girls in school; or is it simply in her blood?

'I am here to see Mr Ashton,' she confides. 'A surprise visit.'

The young man takes in her filthy hair and splendid dress.

'I am a family friend,' she adds.

The concierge appears reassured by this. Not the words, she realises, but the accent. The tones of the nobly born. The smell of a sweet is on his breath.

'It is very late, miss.'

'Indeed. But his light is burning. I saw it from my trap.' She pauses, moves her face closer to his. 'He will be most grateful that you let me through.'

The concierge shifts his sweet from one cheek to the other; locates a timbre at once flirtatious and shy.

'In that case, miss, go right on up.'

The man does not provide her with a room number, assuming perhaps that she has been there before and knows the way. But the hotel's layout is easy enough to understand. She ascends to the

370

second floor and then matches the door to the light they saw from down below. Room 14. Her knock is soft. Part of Mother's outfit was a new pair of deerskin gloves.

Sebastian does not open the door at once. She can hear him shift inside, approach. A long hesitation, his breath curiously laboured. When he finally opens up and sees her, his face floods with relief.

'Miss Naylor!'

He pokes his head around the doorframe, squints down the corridor to see if she is hiding other callers, then yanks her in by the wrist. No sooner has he locked the door than he releases her, staggers, drops his weight into an armchair. Sebastian is wearing a paisley-patterned smoking jacket. Each of its pockets is bulging with a bottle.

'And here I thought they had finally grown sick of waiting and had come to take me away! *Die Stunde der Wahrheit*, ha! The pliers and the rack. But instead it's you, wearing a dress!' He laughs, slips a hand onto one bottle, uncorks it, and takes a long swig.

'Dr Aschenstedt. You are drunk!'

'Yes,' he beams. 'Plum brandy, from Poland. And this here is laudanum. For later, you see. One cannot question a sleeping man.' He jumps up from his chair once more, strides over to her, confides. 'You see, I am a revolutionary, Miss Naylor. A Robespierre! (Only better than Robespierre, because what a blockhead he turned out to be!) But alas, my dear – I am also a coward. Positively a coward. Lily-livered! It is almost shameful.' He giggles, stamps his feet. 'But sit, my dear, sit. Here, why don't you drink a little glass?'

It's a two-room suite, fashionably furnished. The door to his bedroom stands open, the bedding is unmade. Its presence only feeds Livia's feeling of disorientation. Not long ago this would have been unthinkable: standing in a hotel room with a man, a drunk, alone in the night. Even the week in the mine seems licit by comparison. That was an adventure. This is the stuff of dormitory whispers and banned French novels. It is, for girls of her station, the very centre of the Smoke. She picks her way through the books and papers that litter the floor and cautiously takes a seat. The fireplace is burning. Black husks of charts, letters and notes are floating in the hot air above the flames.

Sebastian follows her gaze, jumps over to his desk, takes up a sheaf of papers and is about to feed them into the fire when something distracts him and he starts reading them instead. He catches himself, flushes, drops the papers on the floor.

'You see I have been busy. Hiding evidence! In case . . . but of course, what does it matter now? Still, you never know . . .' He stoops, picks up the papers once more but again fails to place them on the fire. 'The trouble is, these records are precious. Letters, articles, drafts of learned essays. The next frontier of science! Besides, they've already searched the room. The hotel porter let them in, the swine. No man's a hero to his valet, eh?'

He mutters to himself, totters, then looks over at her with sudden interest. 'What about you though, Miss Naylor? What in the devil's name are you doing here?'

Livia has her lie prepared; practised it on the way up the stairs and readied it for the moment he opened the door. Then Sebastian scattered it with his drunken antics. Now the words come haltingly and are belied by a blush.

'I'm afraid things have gone wrong, Dr Aschenstedt. Mother has been arrested and you are being watched. We have Mowgli. You must tell me where to take him. It is our only chance.'

He blinks, suppresses a burp, dismisses her words with a flap of his hand.

'You are lying, of course. Your mother left with Mowgli and you are trying to follow her.' He drops back into the armchair, happy as a clam, leans over to her, grows avuncular, then sentimental, all in the space of three breaths. 'But there is something else, is there? You look aggrieved. *Wie ein Häufchen Elend.* "Like a little pile of gloom." Come now, you must tell me.'

'Julius,' Livia finds herself saying. 'He found us. There was a fight.'

Before she knows it, she has given Sebastian an account, her voice raw with the horror over the thing Julius had become. Sebastian listens intently, his hands wrapped around one of his bottles, pale and fretting now. When she is done, he shakes himself like a man wishing to shake off his doubt.

'A dark angel, you say,' he mutters even though Livia used no such phrase. 'Indeed! He's been imbibing our Soot! And did you know he stole it from us, the rogue? But then, we were all of us rogues. Your mother and I tricked him out of his money. And he ran off with half our precious harvest. Poetic justice, yes?' Without waiting for a response, Sebastian carries on, cryptically, incoherently. 'What do you think, though – would you and I have taken to darkness as readily as that? You see, despite it all, I hold with Monsieur Rousseau, not dour Master Hobbes. We are born for the herd, not the jungle, eh?'

He sighs, kicks his slippers off like a schoolboy on vacation, and, content to have settled the point, slouches forward towards the fire in order to warm his stockinged feet.

Φ

She pleads with him. 'Explain it to me,' she pleads. 'You owe us that much. What is Mother doing with the child?' When Sebastian does not answer Livia adds: 'You lied to us! You said it would be three days before the infection took hold.'

This last bit rouses the slouching man, wakes his inner pedant. Sebastian sits up.

'Oh no, it wasn't a lie. It takes between fifty and eighty hours. These things are never precise. It varies with the dose, you see, and how strong the child's defences are. In Mowgli's case' – Sebastian pulls out a pocket watch, sits squinting at its hands – 'well, he might already be there! There is a test, in any case, a simple test.' He beams, reaches over, tugs at her sleeve. 'Those fools outside, eh? Even while they are standing there, freezing, your mother is changing the world. Ha! They are so sure that it must be I who lights the fuse! They don't expect a woman to have this much pluck.' He giggles, settles back into his chair, drink-flushed and happy. 'But hush now, Miss Naylor! I mustn't say any more. The less you know the better. In case . . . You see, it might be another twelve hours. And they may catch you yet and place you under duress.'

He takes another swig, raising the laudanum bottle by accident, then checks himself just in time and guzzles brandy. By the time he has put it down, she has dug the mustard jar out of her pocket. A smear of Soot remains in it. It sits at the bottom like a liquid piece of night.

'What is this for, Sebastian?'

He squints, takes the jar from her, flushes with excitement.

'From your mother's bottle, yes?' He holds it close to the fire, watches the light be swallowed by its contents.

'Best to destroy it, I suppose,' he mumbles with a strange reluctance. Then a thought occurs to him, something clever, it scrunches up his face like a prune.

'You want to see it?' he mutters. 'After all, what is the harm? And I can't be there, can I? Stuck here like bait in a mousetrap, while history is being made.'

He jumps up, opens a drawer on the desk, and sorts through its contents to retrieve a small glass vial.

'Here. Another something I did not dare to destroy! Foolish. So, let's make amends.'

Quietly, hardly daring to breathe lest it change his mood, Livia watches him drop to his knees and roll back a corner of carpet to expose the wooden floor underneath.

'Come, look,' he calls to her. 'An experiment. A demonstration!'

He waits until she has knelt beside him, then unscrews the mustard jar and shapes a tiny island of Soot onto the floor.

'Observe,' he whispers, handing her the vial he retrieved from the desk. 'What do you see?'

The vial is smooth-bodied and cylindrical, narrowing to a thin neck at the top. It takes her a moment to understand it has no opening, no stopper. A liquid fills it, heavy as treacle, but water-clear. At the heart of this substance sits a single red drop.

'What is it?' She matches his whisper. 'Dye?'

'Blood! Our very last drop. Vacuum sealed. Oh, how much did we waste until I found a way of preserving it!'

'Whose blood? Mowgli's?'

But Sebastian only shakes his head, jumps up and runs to his bed in the other room, from which he retrieves a pipette that appears to be one of many instruments strewn amongst its blankets. Without pausing for breath, he resumes his position on the floor, takes the vial from her hands, and breaks off the whole of its neck; plunges the pipette into the gelatinous liquid within; and pulls up the scarlet drop into the pipette's glass shaft. Then he ceases all movement and bows his head, as though in prayer. Beneath their knees the floorboards are dark with decades of old sin, long absorbed into their grain. On top, like a canker, sits the abomination her mother scraped off the skin of dying murderers, looking as though it is seeping its evil into the surrounding wood.

'What is Soot?' Sebastian begins to question her, like a catechist checking her lessons, his chin still resting on his chest. His left hand has, quite naturally, sought out her knee and is petting it distractedly.

'Spent Smoke,' she answers.

374

'Is it live?'

'No. Inert.'

'Can it be quickened?'

'Yes.'

'How?'

'You showed us how. Some chemical substance, mixed into the Soot.'

'Herbal, my dear, not chemical. Precipitating a weak reaction! Only the blackest Soot, only briefly, and at tremendous cost. A field of flowers for a dozen cigarettes. And then? Three short puffs, and half an hour of borrowed emotion!'

'Flowers? What flowers?' she interjects, confused, but Sebastian is too absorbed in his thoughts to answer.

'Now then. Do you want to do the honours?' He looks up, smiles expectantly, then immediately discards the idea. 'No, it'll be better if I! Shall we? Only get ready to jump! On three: one, two . . .'

He places the pipette into the little mound of Soot, releases the blood. The next moment he has pulled her up with him, and leapt two paces back.

'Wait for it!' he mutters.

Nothing stirs. Then, his elbow prodding hers with excitement, the Soot combusts, belches a violent jet of Smoke into the air, from which they flee into the corner of the room. Chest-high, the Smoke reverts to Soot; snows down in ashen flakes onto the floor only to reignite as though by magic, leaping up in jerky puffs, like kernels of corn thrown on a sizzling pan. Each little explosion carries with it a spray of lighter Smoke, the Soot of the floorboards whispered into pale life. It is as though the very room is exhaling its sin. Two, three times the cycle repeats. Then it ceases, quietly and suddenly. Nothing is left of the inky scoop they emptied on the floor. Sebastian runs over to it, crouches, runs his fingers over the patch of floorboard that lies pale and naked as though bleached.

Livia stands breathless, her voice brittle with fear. 'What just happened, Sebastian?'

'A dress rehearsal. For the Great Quickening! But hush, now, hush.'

'But that Soot you used. It's evil!'

'Oh yes, evil, pure as pure!'

'And the blood. It was infected, wasn't it?'

'Infected, yes, but still fighting the infection. Neither one nor the other. The body rejecting its new state. A narrow window!'

'So that's what you want from Mowgli.' She raises her hands in front of her, fingers spread wide, as though trying to take hold of something floating in the air. 'The Great Quickening! Tell me, how can that bring justice?'

Sebastian does not answer, flips from his knees over to his bottom, sits there, hugging his knees, excited and happy. For a moment he has something of Charlie, full of the joy of being alive, here and now, partaking in things. The next moment his thoughts veer to dead children. His expression remains just the same. All she does is ask another question.

'Whose blood was that in the vial?' she asks.

This time he answers.

'We called her Lilith. After Adam's first wife. A feisty little mite! Cantankerous.' He smiles with the memory, fingers his bottle. 'How we scoured the world for them, in the years after we learned of their existence. All the best scientists of Europe: mounting expeditions to the furthest corners of the world. A new age of exploration. And how naïvely, how clumsily did we proceed. Walking into igloos with nothing but a scarf wrapped around our mouths, infecting whole tribes in the process. They died in droves. You see, most adults could not survive the anatomical adjustments initiated by the infection. Children though! There was our hope. And little Lilith: a lovely girl, pretty as a picture. She caught a cold, in the end, an ordinary cold! Your butler buried her, out in the woods. Your mother was heartbroken.'

The Smoke jumps out of her in a cloud of rage, is immediately smothered by some other part in her, cooler and more calculating, in need of further answers. Lilith is dead. Mowgli may still be alive. It is his blood her mother wants.

'How much do you need?' she finds herself asking.

He does not appear to have heard, sits on the ground and plays with Soot.

'Ah, there's the rub,' he mutters at length, letting some flakes rain from his fingertips. 'Two thousand two hundred cubic centimetres. It seemed little enough on the chalkboard, when I did the maths.'

Again she finds her mind reeling, starts walking abruptly, in demented circles, as though searching for sense through the geometry of movement. Her steps displace fresh motes of Soot that swirl around the hem of her dress, half harbingers, half retinue, as unsettled as she.

'We saw a row of rectangles,' she says into their dance, still pacing, not looking at him, no longer able to bear the sight of his hale face. 'On your secret map of the sewers. Pools, we think. What's in those pools?'

'Oh, it's very clever, Miss Livia, very clever, if I say so myself. At first glance, a simple problem of filtration. Water, dirt, Soot. But the devil's in the details!'

She pictures it; imagines an aquarium as dark as her mustard jar, and a child's open vein fertilising its mucoid tar. 'The Great Quickening – you are making Juliuses!' she whispers, as though infected by Sebastian's incoherence. Then – that part of her mind quite separate from her anger – she notices something in the fireplace: quite literally a scrap of hope. She drops to her knees, heat flushing her face.

'I just cannot fathom it,' she says, no longer hopeful for an answer, wishing only to distract him, her fingers sorting through hot embers. 'All along I thought you would end the Smoke. Why this? Release more darkness into the world? The streets will run with blood.'

He takes a swig from his bottle before answering and emerges in a new stage of drunkenness: sadder, sentimental, sleepy.

'Blood?' he repeats as though suddenly unfamiliar with the word, nods off, eyes slowly closing, a baby after his feed; then jerks upright with a thought: 'And did you know that in France, at the height of the Terror, they built a temple to Reason and a new type of clock designed to tame the irrationality of time?'

Drunkenly, dreamily, he begins lecturing her on the beauty of the decimal system and the division of the earth's daily revolution into tenths. But Livia is no longer listening. She rises, stills the madness of her pulse.

'You won't help me find Mother.' She speaks into his flow of slurry eloquence. 'Then I must leave.'

She says it simply, despair replaced by purpose. A shred of paper is burning in her fist.

Φ

377

Sebastian helps her, unexpectedly. Gathers himself up from the floor, the plum brandy finished, fetches his hat but not his coat, and offers to lead off the watchers to ensure her escape.

'A perambulation! *Ein Spaziergang.* Why shouldn't a man go for a midnight walk? If they pounce,' he continues, 'I have this,' patting the bottle of laudanum poking out of his smoking jacket.

'*Auf Wiedersehen,*' he announces, opening the door and pressing his coin purse on her as though in thanks for an illicit assignation. 'In a newborn world!

'Black rain,' he confides, half shivering. 'I have been dreaming of black rain. The wind blows northerly tonight. In from the sea!'

She stands by the hallway window of the second floor and watches him emerge from the hotel's front doors. He surveys the square, slowly and theatrically, then starts walking in a mincing, unsteady gait. Five yards on a giggle shakes his frame, and he darts to the left down the shadows of an alley. For a heartbeat nobody reacts. Then the men posted in the square all fling themselves into pursuit. Four men, rather than the three Thomas counted: one of the vagrants leaps up from his dirty blanket and joins the chase. A fifth man bursts from the hotel. Their departure is so conspicuous that it raises a cheer and laughter from the drunks, beggars and ragamuffins that still populate the square. Livia takes it as her signal to leave. The stairwell is empty, the night porters standing in a huddle on the steps outside, wondering at the noise. Within a minute she stands breathless in the shadowy corner where she left Charlie and Thomas. They don't see her at once, are absorbed in discussion, Charlie talking intently, soothingly at his friend. Thomas's shoulders are hunched, his good arm raised in front of him, warding Charlie off. His hand is so swollen it looks like a mitt.

They catch sight of her in the same instant. For all their differences their faces show the same expression. Concern. Relief. Love. She smiles despite herself and they each smile back; even Thomas, past his hurt. A moment's happiness in the chaos of their lives. Then Livia does what has to be done.

She spoils it.

'I know what they are up to,' she says. And: 'I have an address.' She unfolds the fist she made ten minutes ago. 'He burnt this. Of all the papers he was reluctant to burn, he made sure to burn this!'

They stare at the scrap of paper like it will provide salvation. It is ripped in half and scorched black, had floated up on the chimney's hot draft and then got stuck upon the brickwork of the fireplace's outer lip, the paper's edge still fire-red and smouldering when she snatched it. Together they read the few legible words. A company name and a street address. 'Ryman's Fine Tobacco Products. Manufactory and Wholesale.' The opening line promises a detailed report on the progress made on the construction work performed within the factory cellars. The next line has been eaten by the flame.

A *cigarette* factory. *Construction* in its cellar.

A gateway to the sewers.

'How will we find it?' asks Charlie.

'Sebastian gave me money,' Livia answers, displaying the purse. 'So I could ride home in a cab. We must hurry,' she adds. 'Two thousand two hundred cubic centimetres. How much blood does a human child hold?'

Berta

'It's a dead end, sir. This one's had it and that one won't talk. And just look at the dog. It's his scent she followed. And now she's grieving over him.'

'He's not dead.'

They came in without knocking, or at least I did not hear them. Suddenly they were there. Gentlemen in suits. And a crippled dog dragging its hindquarters on a little two-wheeled cart. It has been strapped to it with a belt. A fat man holds the leash.

'He's not dead,' I say again and this time my lips move with the words. I don't want them to leave me alone again. Not while he – *it* – is still in the room.

The fat man hears me. He walks over to the water jug and pours me a glass. While he watches me drink he orders one of his men to hold a mirror to *its* mouth.

'I can hear 'im breathing,' I say. 'He's broken. But I can hear 'im breathing all the same.'

The fat man nods as though he understands, pulls up a chair and sits next to me.

'Tell me what happened here. We already know the half of it. Lady Naylor was here, and perhaps also her daughter. And a man came to visit, I should wager, a bookish man with a foreign accent.'

She nods.

'Do you live here alone?'

'My 'usband is away.'

'What about that boy over there?'

I do not look where he is pointing.

'He came here. I don't know why. He hit me. But mostly he just held me. Held me close. His Smoke—' I break off. 'He isn't human.'

The fat man nods, pats my hand, and asks me gently worded questions. I answer a surprising number. Somehow, it is good to talk.

I do not tell them about my husband. Not about his condition, nor that he went along with her. Nor do I put into words what it has been like, sitting there, listening to *it* breathe, so faintly that half the time I convinced myself *it* was already dead. Sitting there, alone in the dark, listening, trying to pluck up the courage to cut *its* throat. I could have left, I suppose. It's like it was when I was living with Father, yearning for escape. I could have left. Even before Tobias. But you never do, do you? You sit in the dark and endure.

They revive him. It does not take much. They stand over him, pouring water on his face, shout at him, get angry, wreath him in faint Smoke. The next moment he sits up. Like a jack-in-the-box.

The fat man bends down to him, asks question after question. It's like his gut is filled with them. The one on the ground has no face any more, just a swollen mess, the tongue disturbingly bright within its blackness. But he speaks clearly enough.

'I know where she is,' he says. '*He* will be heading there.' Then, with intense purpose: 'Mother. She betrayed me. I can take you to her.'

'Can you walk?' the fat man asks.

The thing that was once a young man rises, stands slope-shouldered as though hanging from a nail.

'I can take you to her,' he says again. 'To Mother. And to him. You and I, Trout. Just us two. Only make sure to bring a gun.'

The Smoke that spreads from him is almost liquid. It gathers in a film around his fancy boots.

The fat man considers the offer. But it is obvious he will agree. What else is he going to do – beat the truth out of this thing?

'I'll need one of my men, Mr Spencer. Just one. Any one of them will do. You can take your pick.'

It does not hesitate, raises one twisted arm and points to a man with a slight, wiry frame.

'That one. He broke Nótt's legs, didn't he? Bring him. And remember the gun.'

The fat man nods and orders another of the men to pass over the shotgun to their colleague. He is about to say more but *it* is already moving, heading for the door with surprising speed. The walk is like a marionette's. The body is broken, but some other thing moves *it* along. *It* makes no sound as *it* scuttles down the stairs.

The man with the gun and the fat man follow, leaving the rest of his men behind. There are three of them, standing in my kitchen, at a loss. They have not received any orders. It takes them a full minute to even frame the problem in words; one man rifling through the cupboards, looking, he says, 'for a bite to eat'. Then they begin to argue. One maintains that they must take me into custody; another declares that they are 'duty-bound to return to our post'. The third man insists that they must follow the chief, 'quickly, on the sly' and that they have 'wasted too much time already'. They argue as though they are playing cards, each placing his argument neatly before his mates, at once friendly and competitive. In the end they have waited too long to follow anyone and are too lazy or too principled to arrest an old, beaten woman. They leave me without a word and forget to close the front door behind themselves.

They leave the dog, too, half lying, half sitting on its cart, its maw tied shut with a strap.

When I am sure they are gone, I slide off my chair and crouch down beside it. It growls, then whimpers, dangles drool from its jowls. We sit there, side by side, the broken-legged dog and me with my swollen eye. When the fear rises up in me again, hot like a fever, I drench us both in Smoke.

Factory

Livia cannot stop speaking. It's an open cab, and she has to yell over the noise of wheels and hooves on cobbles, lean forward and halfway across Charlie's lap to make herself heard. Up on his box, the coachman is making haste; sends his nag flying into corners and keeps craning his neck, too, listening in, or perhaps just staring at her, this gentlewoman with the stringy hair and her two filthy companions. His bowler is rain-dark; it has played feast to many tribes of moth.

'It was as though he had poured petroleum over the floor!' Livia shouts again. 'An explosion: *contagious*. As though it would never stop.'

She raises her chin into the wind, stabs her hands into the air, cutting off some question Charlie has been trying to voice.

'"A problem of filtration," Sebastian said. Separating sin from muck and water. That's what he has been doing down in the sewers. Creating a giant sieve and collecting London's Soot! Dredging every cesspool for it, the bottom of the river, two and a half centuries' worth of crimes. They want to quicken it!'

Throughout her monologue, Thomas sits quietly, only half listening, lost in himself. The urgency of his horror has abated and left behind something duller, slow in its wits. He has been watching his hand, the right one. It has swollen to the size of a club, the fingers so thick they feel fused, all but the pinkie which rides up, crooked, above the others. The blood on the knuckles might be his own or it might be Julius's. Most likely it is both of theirs, mingled. Blood brothers. As a child he read a book about that, two boys whittling open their palms with a blunt penknife. The coach veers, pushes him into Charlie. His thoughts veer with it. He is conscious that he needs to pee.

Killer. It is a funny word. Not an act: a mode of being. A profession. Some trades, you pass them on from father to son. They say his father killed *his* man in a rage. One of his tenants. There was slander involved, drink, a tavern. A pewter mug scooped up where it had fallen on the ground. A pewter mug. Smart. His father knew how to protect his hand.

Back home, Thomas used to call those who spoke of it liars. Liars! – turning his eyes on them, Smoke on his lips. They stopped speaking of it in his presence. He wonders now: did he sit there, his father, *afterwards*, on a stool at the bar, nursing his wrist, his bladder nagging at him like a bad joke? Thomas does not know. The only letter his father sent from prison was a will, stipulating that his son was to inherit his leather hunting breeches and his good lamb's wool coat. Thomas has never grown sufficiently to fit into either.

So, Thomas now says to himself, *I have come into my patrimony. All I needed was a bit of priming. Then I took to it like a boar to his rut.*

But the ease of his corruption, it isn't really the worst of it. He has known he is susceptible all his life. *A boy with a temper*; rage, like a pet, always faithful by his side.

The worst of it is that it was *fun*. Being consumed by the Smoke. Letting go of all restraint. Stripping naked as the day you were born and becoming a creature of pure want. For Thomas discovered something. At the heart of the Smoke he found waiting for him the unselfconsciousness of childhood, of those years before speech. How perfect, how natural it felt to live there, in a place that knew no consequence. His fists swollen, the heat of Livia's body pinned under his weight.

Just as he is thinking this, squirming in his seat with the power of the thought, Livia turns to him, her head thrown forward so she can see him across Charlie. Thomas looks away. The coach veers, his bladder strains. He wants to talk to her, explain himself. He wonders where to pee so she won't notice.

He is, in short, confused.

Then they arrive: a dank street without lighting.

The coach races off as soon as Livia has paid the driver.

Φ

It might be Ratcliff or Southwark: Thomas did not pay attention to the way. All he knows of London are a dozen or so streets and a score of names he has overheard. Lambeth, Hammersmith, Wapping. Limehouse. Shoreditch (always mentioned in a hush). They remain close to the river in any case; he can smell its stink. A great grey slab

384

of a building rises before them, looking more like a fortress than a factory. Initially Thomas thinks that it is here they are headed. But it is the smaller, red-brick building growing out of its flank that wears the name of Ryman's Fine Tobacco. There is no fence at the front, just a sturdy green door at the top of a short flight of steps. For the third time that night they try a door handle and find it does not move. The knocker rings through the building beyond but fails to summon either a doorman or a guard. They are alone.

This time, though, there is an alley running down the flank of the building, and a side door. In the mud outside, footprints are visible, amongst them, unmistakable, the heel of a woman's boot. The door is closed but not locked. It is a carelessness that speaks of haste, of having one's hands full. Beyond, a gaslight has been left burning. A corridor connects a string of offices, shabby-looking despite their once-decent carpets. It is a place of business, not of reception. Before they venture further, Thomas turns on his heel and returns to the alley to relieve himself against the factory wall. It is a moment's bliss in the middle of a nightmare.

Inside again, he finds Charlie and Livia have run ahead. The main floor holds the facilities associated with the sale and manufacture of ordinary tobacco. A front desk, an orders department; a workshop floor for packaging; and across the cobbled inner courtyard, a warehouse smelling like a giant pipe.

It is in the basement that the other factory is located. To enter one has to negotiate another, sturdier door, also left unlocked, and descend two revolutions of a carpeted spiral staircase. At its bottom a cavernous storehouse opens, suffused in a smell at once floral and rotting, emanating from a row of giant copper vats that loom like pillars in an old cathedral. Slender copper pipes emerge from these vats and move in coils towards a separate tank, minute by comparison, and holding the results of some long process of distillation. A cloying, wet heat stands in the room. Charlie has climbed the brass rungs riveted into one of the vats to get to its open top, has stuck a hand beyond the rim and is scooping up a palmful of its contents. Not far from him, Livia is examining a glass cabinet that holds a series of pharmaceutical bottles, each carefully labelled with dates.

'Flowers,' Charlie calls surprised, holding aloft a delicate stem crowned by a papery bloom, not unlike a poppy but of veined purple-grey. 'The vat is filled to the rim with some kind of flower, submerged in warm liquid. There must be a million flowers here. And the smell . . .' He sniffs his hand. 'Like cigarettes, but faint.'

Livia, five steps from him, has uncorked one of the bottles and sniffed its contents.

'Sebastian mentioned flowers. He said: "A field of flowers for a dozen cigarettes." It must be how they produce the solvent: that which quickens Soot.' She lets her gaze wander between the giant vats and the small glass bottles with their labels, clearly struck by the misproportion. Almost reverently she accepts the flower Charlie holds out to her.

'Can you picture the size of the plantations, Charlie? Half of the Empire must be kept busy growing these.'

'In the full knowledge of the authorities, no doubt. And all part of the Cooper business empire. Your mother said we hold special import licences. One day I shall be very rich.'

Charlie's eyes offer Thomas a share of his dark-cheeked indignation, but Thomas will have none of it. He is not interested in the Coopers' stake in horticulture; stands unmoved, or *re*moved rather, still separated by the fog of his own thoughts.

Killer, he thinks. *Blood brother.*

The proverb's right: the apple does not fall far.

Apples, falling. Isaac Newton: built a bridge without nails. Now they bring Germans over to build our sewers, Sebastian said. Ash-Town. Taylor, Ashton and some made-up Sons.

Father.

That piss was good, Thomas thinks. And you are a coward, a coward, wallowing in pity. He moves back into the staircase doorway, hooks his left arm into its frame, and wrenches his shoulder back into its socket.

Φ

There is a room that leads off one end of the distillation chamber. A smaller room, boxlike and mould-walled, where a row of work-benches stand bolted to the floor. It is here that Thomas walks his sense of isolation; stands and studies it with self-absorbed patience.

Three workbenches, each with two work places. Each place marked by an oak stool and a little machine, screwed into the table's wood, combining the features of a sewing machine and a pencil sharpener. Six stools in total, plus a chair for the supervisor, at three yards' remove and upholstered in bottle-green leather. On the wall, like so many hats or umbrellas, hang six respirators from numbered metal hooks. Tan, well-worn rubber, each snout ending in a chunky, perforated filter, smeared with Soot. Thomas stares at these then sits down at a work place; turns the little wheel of one machine and works out its purpose. Around him, at the wall, stand small kegs of Soot each labelled with a quality sign, ranging from *Alpha*++ to *Gamma*–. At the centre of the workbench stands a box full of little squares of cigarette papers; next to it a similar box, somewhat larger, holds a supply of ordinary tobacco. A pipette completes the sets of tools and materials provided for each worker.

Mechanically, holding at bay both thought and emotion, Thomas threads a piece of paper into the machine, fetches a pinch of Soot from one of the barrels, mixes it with tobacco and begins to roll a cigarette. Halfway through the process he takes up the pipette; looks back through the doorway to the rack of solvents Livia has discovered; pictures spreading the sticky liquid into the mix of tobacco and Soot to make it ready for consumption.

'They are wearing the respirators,' he says out loud though he is speaking to himself, not his friends, 'so they don't imbibe any of the quickened Soot. It protects them, and also keeps them docile; and it ensures that not a precious gram is lost.' He gets up, fetches a respirator, spreads it out before him, goggles at the top. 'And so they sit. Six slaves, masked, and strangers to one another. And the foreman, he will have a club.'

He hears Livia walking up behind him, listening to his words; continues with his numb recital of the facts.

'And that door over there with the heavy lock will lead next door. Did you notice it when we drove up? A big house like a fortress. Barred windows: a gaol. Of course, whoever works down here must never be released – otherwise they would go into the world and spread the news about cigarettes far and wide. No, they are stuck here for life. I wonder what crime warrants that? Something temperate, I should think. Forgery, counterfeiting, or some clever kind of theft. You wouldn't want murderers near such Soot. They might get ideas.' He looks over at the kegs by the side of the wall. 'What a paltry harvest! Dark Soot is a rare commodity. Until now. Pools, you say, a filtration system. Sebastian has been dredging the sewers to distil three hundred years of crime. No wonder Julius put up the money!

Your mother must have told him it was to expand operations. The profits would have been astronomical. I doubt she told him it was all to go up in Smoke.'

He falls silent as Livia takes the stool next to him; watches her study his face.

'Does all this not make you angry, Thomas?'

He could say: *I can't afford my anger. It is too much fun.*

Or: *We have seen what my anger leads to.*

Or: *Back there, pressed hip to hip, my trousers wet with Julius's blood, I could feel your pulse beat in your upper thigh.*

But he merely shrugs his shoulders and watches her nostrils dilate around a stringy slug of Smoke.

Φ

Charlie joins them. He has raced from room to room and wall to wall, inspected each shelf, each alcove and each tool. Now he drops his weight onto a third stool.

'There is no sign of Lady Naylor. And no exit. Just that one' – he points over to the bolted door near them – 'and you say it leads to the gaol. Which means we have lost her. We have lost Mowgli.'

When neither Thomas nor Livia responds, he jumps up, races around the rooms once more, frantically searching the walls for a clue. On his return he is too restless to sit; walks up and down in front of them, his face open, flushed and worried.

'We know that she's been here. The door was open and her footprint was outside. And Sebastian's letter spoke of construction works. Down here, in the basement. There must be a doorway, then, a passage; something to connect one of these rooms to the sewers. But I looked at all the walls and can't see evidence of any construction.' He mutters to himself, walks another thirty yards in four-step paces. 'Let's think it out. Only quick now, quick. What do we know? She has been collecting Soot. Black Soot, the darkest she can find, has scraped it off murderers, spent millions to build this sewer to get more. Well then, for what purpose? To quicken it, you say. No, not just quicken it but make it explosive. Self-perpetuating. *Contagious.* And not by the usual method, using the solvent produced in this factory, which is weak and does not last, but with Mowgli's blood, two thousand two hundred cubic centimetres – four pints! – of his blood. Do I have this right? Yes? All right! The sewers will steam with rage. A black cloud like nothing anyone has seen, rising out of the ground and infecting the city. But then what? I don't understand.'

'He kept talking about the French Revolution,' Livia answers. 'Robespierre. Decimal time. The Terror.'

Charlie stops mid-step. It nearly costs him his balance.

'Is that what she's planning? An uprising! An age of anger. Nobody working, the factories idle, the docks closed. An army of Juliuses, infecting one another, looking for food beyond the city. Marching on the manor houses.' He stands, head cocked, appalled and baffled. 'But why would your mother want such a thing?'

'She's evil.'

Charlie won't have it. 'Even evil needs reasons,' he says. 'You don't destroy the world *just so*.'

'Mad, then. Mother's gone mad. Just like Father. She hates Discipline. It broke him. She thinks she's avenging him.'

'Mad?' says Charlie. 'I don't know. When is the last time you saw your mother smoke?'

Φ

They sit perplexed and passive, minutes trickling away. Thomas is aware that both Livia and Charlie are looking at him, waiting for him.

Lead us, these looks appear to say. *You always have.*

But Thomas is afraid to lead.

It is a weak sort of fear, cowering and smokeless, at a remove from life. His shoulders rounded, his chin tucked in Grendel's abject stoop. The respirator remains spread out on the table in front of him, built to filter Smoke from the infectious air and wall in its wearer within the safety of his private self. Thomas is conscious of Livia watching him as he turns the mask within his hands; once, twice; disappointment cleaving her face. Then she bends to him, leans into him, lip to lip, and shouts her anger into his face – 'Help us, God damn you!' – each word a sulphurous taunt summoning his manhood, in that strange language of Smoke in which love and derision can be as one.

It is enough and not enough; sends him to his feet and away from the table, half in obedience to her call to arms, half in flight from her challenge. Like Charlie before him, he storms around the room housing the fermentation vats. It is not the walls he inspects but the floors; and seeing nothing, no fresh seams nor any irregularities in the dark tiling, his courage already abating, he grabs a wrench from a toolbox in one corner, and systematically, hurting his wrist and damaged hand, hammers away at a copper pipe emerging from one of the hulking vats like a spout, until it gives way and a sickly floral liquid pours in a thousand gallons across the floor. Then he stands, watching the room fill inch-deep with flowers and liquid, eyes peeled, head cocked, like a man on the hunt.

'Why did you—' Charlie begins but Thomas hushes him, hears then sees the pop of bubbles in one corner, where the liquid is drawn to some flaw within the flooring and is rushing to a pocket of air trapped underneath. As the liquid's level slowly begins to fall, the flowers floating within it arrange themselves into a rough and soggy square, marking the outline of a well-masked trapdoor underneath their feet.

Φ

They have to wait until the weight of the liquid has shifted from the door, then kick aside the pulpy mass of drenched and half-fermented flowers. The trapdoor itself has a tiny keyhole and is locked. This time it is Charlie who acts: he fetches a giant steel ladle from the same box of tools that supplied the wrench, manages to wedge it into the minute gap between trapdoor and floor, and throws his weight against it. Soon Thomas too is pushing at this lever. Together, they break the lock and bend the ladle, open the trapdoor to a rough-hewn wooden staircase leading down.

They descend. The staircase is new, wet and strewn with dead flowers; the air rising out of the stairwell thick with the smells of excrement and offal. At the bottom, a light burns. They walk towards it and come to a landing and an arched gateway, much older than the stairs. Beyond lie the sewers: a dark canal of stagnant water, flanked by slime-spattered walkways on each side. But their eyes are riveted elsewhere. Dangling from the ceiling, suspended by a rubber string, hangs a bulb of murky, unwavering light. No flame flickers within. It is like an ailing, miniature sun, fetched down from the sky and nailed here by a hangman. When Thomas touches it, it burns his fingertip, then quivers and dances like a hooked fish.

'How will we ever stop her?' Charlie whispers, faced with this new magic.

Livia's answer is curt. 'We must try.'

Thomas is aware of a mixture of shame and relief when he sees her take the lead; of a flare of timid anger when she reaches back and takes hold of Charlie's hand. Charlie, in turn, stretches his free palm behind himself, looking for his friend's. Thomas ignores the gesture.

He follows warily, at two steps' remove.

Φ

It isn't far. A hundred yards of sewer, thrice stripped of its murk by a bulb holding the same mysterious, unflickering light; then an archway opens to a room so long it too feels like a corridor, though it measures a good ten yards in width. The room is built from dark brick, ancient and porous, the mortar worn like a petrified sponge. The ceiling is low above their heads and supported by steel girders, much newer than the brick. A garland of lamps, interconnected by a black line of rubber cable, marks the central axis, from the archway through which they enter, to the far end, hundreds of feet ahead. Beneath these lamps, filling three-quarters of the room and only leaving a narrow strip of walking space at either side, lies a series of interconnected pools, tiled in shiny, almost fluorescent green. Each pool is separated from the next by a permeable membrane made of some waxy cloth. Only the top foot of the tiles is visible. The water that stands heavy in the pools beneath is mirror-dark. It is as though a communal baths has been pumped full of ink. All this Thomas sees in passing, following his friends on the long march to the other end. Lady Naylor is there; and Grendel; and Mowgli, tied with belts to a heavy wooden chair.

She notices them within ten steps. There is no cover, just the open narrow passage between wall and poolside. They are walking slowly on the wet, uneven ground, sunk and cracked in places, smeared with sewage muck. Thomas sees Lady Naylor squint; sees her hand flicker for something, raise it up before her chest, then drop it to her lap upon recognition. Each step reveals a new detail. Lady Naylor has made herself cosy amongst the dirt; she is sitting in an armchair, a wineglass and a bottle on a coffee table by her side. It's a wonder she has not brought her slippers. By her other elbow, a worktable, made presentable by means of a starched tablecloth and laden with various instruments. The dark shape of her Soot bottle rises amongst them. At the other end of the table, Grendel stoops over the boy,

391

assiduously wiping his brow. Halfway across the length of the room, Thomas begins to make out Mowgli's face, sweaty and feverish, and the spasmodic shivers that pit his little body against the restraints. He thinks of Renfrew's dentist chair; of Renfrew's niece as described by Charlie; and wonders darkly whether there exists a world in which children are not bent to purpose by a strap. Something – a needle? – grows like a mechanical tumour out of the boy's naked flank, at the height of the liver. Grendel is fussing with it: solicitous, chin curled into chest, as though bowing to the child.

It's another ten steps before Livia starts speaking. She has to shout: the spongy walls soak up all sound. It is Grendel she is addressing, not her mother. Thomas, behind her, walks through her anger as through morning mist.

'You lied to me, Grendel!' she shouts and they watch him flinch with a second's delay. 'But what is worse, you lied to Mowgli. He trusted you. Now look at him. Why are you hurting him?'

Grendel stares across the forty, fifty steps still separating them, flaps one hand, unchanged in the mildness of his gestures.

'He has a fever, you see. Lady Naylor says his organs are changing. But not to worry, it will be over soon.'

'She wants to bleed him, Grendel. Bleed him dry. And you are helping her.' Then bitterly, Livia's Smoke coming thick now and settling in frothy billows on the uneven floor: 'They were right about you all along. You are a monster, Grendel. You were supposed to love him.'

He looks back at her, crestfallen, baffled. Perhaps there is to his sloping neck a hint of doubt, of regret. Across the distance, in this eerie light, it is possible to imagine all manner of things into a face, a posture. Grendel bends down to the needle growing out the child's emaciated torso, opens some kind of valve and releases a thin flow of blood into the glass chamber at its top. If Lady Naylor has been impassive through the exchange, she rises from her chair now, something heavy and metallic dangling from one fist.

'Oh how melodramatic, Livia. But come, leave Mr Grendel alone. It's me you are angry with.' She moves forward a step as though to hasten their approach, opens her arms in welcome. 'You will have to tell me how you found me here. But really, I am glad. The dawn of a new world. We shall welcome it together.'

Twenty more yards. Thomas sees it all clearly now. The tiny, short-snubbed, two-barrelled gun that burdens Lady Naylor's gesture of welcome, tilts it sideways to the right; the bottle of black Soot standing on the table as though ready for decanting for their final supper; Grendel testing the drops of blood within the vial with a strip of yellow paper that, upon contact, instantly turns blue. And above all he sees Mowgli, Mowgli's face, looking up at his tormenter with an awful expression of hope and appeal, of trust misplaced, the eyes swollen and glossy with his fever.

'The paper. It turned blue!' Grendel calls to Lady Naylor. 'It is as you said. Mowgli's blood, it's *active*. May I undo his straps?'

Lady Naylor answers without turning. 'Soon. First open the valve as I have shown you.'

And just like that – at the mention of a valve, as though a child were a keg, or a steam engine, ripe for the draining – something returns to Thomas, a sense of urgency misplaced amongst self-pity and doubt, and the next thing he knows he has shouldered aside his friends and is running, then stumbling, falling across the age-eaten floor, scrambling back up to his feet.

He is not aware of the words Lady Naylor is shouting at him, nor does he know whether his friends follow; is charging towards her tall figure, his head and shoulders lowered for a rugby tackle, and a fine trail of Smoke fluttering behind like the tails of a coat.

He gets to within six or seven steps. Then his toe catches, and a shot sounds. In the dull, dead air of the chamber it is like the clap of two wet hands. Ahead: a shout, a spray of blood, or perhaps of Soot; the chandelier tinkle of broken glass; then the tidal surge of darkness, as one after the other, with a fraction's delay, the bulbs above the pools give out, each with the dull plop of a cork plugged from its bottleneck.

The ground ploughs into Thomas and empties his lungs of all their air.

Witchfinder General

Julius leads us to a sewer entrance not ten minutes' walk from the flat. It's an unmarked stone slab covering a manhole in the corner of a dirty yard. The slab must weigh forty pounds but Julius, broken-limbed, listing, labours it aside without asking for help. Underneath, a shaft leads straight down, its circumference roughly equal to my girth. An iron ladder is screwed into the brick. I am winded from the pace Julius has set, crablike, scuttling sideways down the streets, and gesture for him to wait. He does but spurns repose; paces the alley from wall to wall. Watching him – his jerky movements, the way he twists his neck too far around the anchor of his trunk; remembering that this was once my student, a boy placed in my care – makes me sick to my fat stomach. My man, Boswell, appears immune to such queasiness. He kept both lamp and gun trained on our guide as we followed him and now descends the shaft first, so as to cover Julius from the bottom while he climbs. Myself, I carry my Colt stuck in its holster on my belt. The thought of drawing it fills me with dread.

The shaft is perhaps fifteen feet deep. At its bottom lie the sewers. For the past few days, I have been sending men down here. Spies. Ever since I learned that Ashton was Aschenstedt; that Parliament, in its infinite wisdom, had given a terrorist the mandate to clean up the former capital. I imagined the sewers to be an orderly thing: a system of tunnels, with waste running down their centre. What they reported was a web, a maze. Old tunnels and new, lying at different depths in the earth, cross-connected by vertical shafts and silo-like chambers. Neighbourhood cesspools five storeys deep, tapped and drained by Aschenstedt's men. Steam-powered drills; sluices and locks; water pumps the size of grain silos sitting in purpose-built chambers; exhaust pipes leading to air vents above. It would take a team of engineers a month to make sense of it all. My lads are many things, but engineers they are not.

Now that we reach the bottom of the shaft, however, I see none of this complexity. A slimy tunnel smelling of the privy, that's all. Within ten steps we roust a nest of rats. Julius leads the way as before, hurtling ahead, straining against the edge of Boswell's lamplight like a hound on a leash. I am not sure whether he is following a trail or already knows our destination. At times he pauses at intersections and stands sniffing the foul air. Once, he leans against the wall and darts his tongue across its mould. Then he is off again, always with the same jerky, marionette movements and attended by the cape of his Smoke. My watch has stopped, won't be wound. We have stepped beyond time.

I ask Julius where he is leading us.

'Ahead,' he says without modulation, the broken jaw flapping with the word.

Ahead. So be it: in the name of the state. Like me, Julius has now become its servant. The state is not choosy; enlists whatever tool is fit to its purpose; cares not for the tool's own motivations, or rather enlists those too, weaving them into the fabric of its needs. For what *does* he want, this broken, nightmare boy? Why does he lead us with such haste? Revenge on Thomas, I suppose; matricide. Whenever I mention Mr Argyle or Lady Naylor, a darkness spills out of him that I try my best not to inhale. My man, Boswell, catches it once or twice: the whites of his eyes are turning dun. Julius, I realise, is not mad. He is that thing from which madness is knit.

We arrive at last. Or rather, we get close. Then a barrier stops us, a grate of wrist-thick, vertical bars set wide enough apart to admit an arm and shoulder but little more than that. A bright light, oddly flat and lifeless, throws the grate's shadow across our approaching forms. I gesture to Boswell to set our lamp down on the ground, then squeeze my stomach against the bars; lean my cheek on their rusty cold. Our position is such that I can see but a small part of the space before us: a cavern, a worktable, the slender neck and pinned-up hair of Lady Naylor. Her torso and legs are hidden by the backrest of her armchair and even her head is more than half obscured by a steel girder that supports the ceiling midway between her and us. The table next to her is laden with instruments and beakers, most prominently the bulbous form of a glass jug heavy with tar. At the far end of the table, in a clear line of sight, is the hunched form of a man tending to a child. The man is nondescript: a greengrocer with a sloping neck; the cheeks fleshy and florid. The child is foreign, brown-skinned, strapped to its chair. Only the head is visible, rises above the tabletop to the base of the neck. Captain van Huysmans's demon is looking poorly; his mouth wide open, tufts of hair coming loose above the ear. It is as though he is moulting, a new boy being born out of his sweat and pain.

Φ

We do not even attempt to break down the grating. Its ends are cemented straight into ceiling and floor. It would take an hour and a pickaxe to get us through. Thus there is only one thing to be done. Boswell knows it too. When I turn to look at him he has already cocked his rifle.

'Where do I shoot?' he asks. He is speaking softly but there is in his voice a note of expectation.

'Mother,' the marionette-boy says. 'Punish Mother.'

He sounds like a child wheedling for a sweet; points with a finger broken at the knuckle, bending sideways where a finger must not bend.

'Mother. *Mama*. Now, now, now!'

His tongue in Boswell's ear.

But Boswell hesitates. 'Difficult shot,' he says at last. 'Girder's in the way.' And, after a pause: 'How about the child?'

And God help me, I know in my gut he is right. If we want to stop this (whatever *this* is), put an end to this infernal plot, it is by far the safest option. The child is the key. Aschenstedt and Lady Naylor paid a fortune to have him smuggled into the country. Even now she is looking to the boy, waiting for something, some revelation or event. Once he is eliminated, we can arrest her at our leisure. She is a lady of the peerage, she has the right to a trial. Not so the child. And after all, it is our duty. For Queen and country; for the good of the state. It wills it. We must obey.

Boswell is looking to me with his Smoke-curdled eyes. An impatient look. He is awaiting the order from his commanding officer. I look straight back. Beyond the bars, in a part of the room we cannot see, a voice calls out, the words swallowed by distance. Lady Naylor rises and answers; her hand discloses a snub-nosed gun. She steps, gestures, commands. A patrician voice.

Her son's Smoke is filling our lungs.

Boswell tastes it, licks it, decides. His finger curls around the

396

trigger. My hand slaps the barrel when the bullet is already racing along inside: I feel the hot quiver of its passage. It is treason then and nothing less, the deliberate betrayal of my mission. Borne of what? Of decency, I suppose, a distaste for death. It appears the witchfinder in me has lost his callous love of justice. I have been a headmaster for far too long.

The shot is deafening. The bullet hits the table, an explosion of glass. Then everything happens very fast. Boswell is working the bolt for a second shot when Julius takes the gun away from him. He does not wrestle it free or even wrench it: he simply takes it into his broken hands. Takes it, turns it, swings it, and buries it inch-deep in Boswell's face. The man is dead before he hits the ground. A black cloud leaps out of him and straight up Julius's chest like a dog changing masters. Then Julius turns the gun on me.

He gives me time to draw my Colt. God only knows what thought is running through him now: in his face not hatred but sulky petulance at not having had his way. I fumble for the holster, tear free the revolver but cannot thread my finger through the hole. In the end I let it drop. It falls and spins between my toes.

Julius shoots me. He shoots me in my fat gut, just where my belt runs across the navel. I fall almost as an afterthought and watch him stand over me, his mouth wide open and the lips curled back across his toothless gums, savouring the Smoke that is rising from my wound like steam out of a heating pipe. Where it passes through his body, it changes colour and doubles in intensity; unfurls behind him like a flag. Julius stands and drinks me and works the lever for a second shot.

Then something steps up behind him. He wears the bluff features of a greengrocer. I know at once he is not human. He does not smoke. He stands on the far side of the metal bars, not a foot away from Julius; stands in the boy's Smoke, the very thick of his Smoke, and adds no Smoke of his own. A kind face, seen up close: fleshy, balding, ruddy. The grocer threads his arm through the bars. Milady's gun is in his hands: a Beretta, double-barrelled, decorations beaten into the steel of its short snout. Its tip touches Julius's neck.

There is a pause, a moment of conspiracy, a wish asked and granted, as boy and grocer share a look. Two monsters from adjacent pits; one smokeless, one dripping with raw need. Then the shot rings out. As he falls, I notice something in Julius's Smoke, something so essential to it, so all-pervasive, that I did not notice it before. It is the very solvent in which all his evil is suspended. Self-loathing, a hunger for his own destruction; a desperate desire to find rest. Julius drops forward, into the bars; kneels before the grocer. The man turns to me. The gun turns with him. It points calmly at my bulk.

He will shoot me too. I can see it in his face. He'll do it calmly, benignly, without passion or ego, not for himself, not from anger, not from triumph or because he is possessed by a truth; simply because I can do harm to him and his while alive, and none dead.

Then he sees I am already dead and turns away. I look after him with dread and admiration. Perhaps his kind are the future. It might please the state.

The grocer will make it a good servant.

Fuse

And so they are made to watch Julius die a second time. It is a sort of shadow play, something a favourite uncle would project upon a bedroom wall to amuse the children with the clever shapes of his hands; happens off-centre, backlit by the weak light of a gas lamp, turned low and placed on the ground somewhere behind the players' bulk. Grendel's shot that closes the play rips the half-light like a fork of lightning. As though in answer, first one, then several of the lamps above their heads flutter back to intermittent life, oscillating between a bromide darkness and flashes of dull yellow.

Within Charlie's arms, Livia is writhing, fighting his embrace. He does not remember grabbing hold of her, pulling her head into the flimsy safety of his chest. She wants to run over to where her mother lies lifeless in the dirt. A few steps ahead of them, Thomas is picking himself off the ground. Further ahead, Grendel places the pistol on the table – a tool discarded – and bends to free Mowgli from his straps. He removes the needle from his body and, along with it, a small beaker now filled with the boy's lifeblood; stoppers the beaker and places it carefully upon the table, inches from the gun, before strapping the feverish child into a cloth sling that he fastens across his chest and hip.

It is only when Grendel steps away from table and gun that Charlie releases Livia, all the time conscious of the confusion in her Smoke. She darts away from him, catches up with Thomas who himself has started moving. For two steps they run abreast, touching elbows for comfort. Then their paths separate. Livia is heading to her mother, Thomas to the dead schoolmate of theirs who hangs tangled in iron bars like a fish within its netting: down on his knees, his ashen head stuck through the grating, arms thrown outward at a messianic angle. Beyond Julius lies a man with a beaten-in face and a fleshy mound that was Headmaster Trout.

Charlie himself starts moving. As he draws closer he comes to understand his destination. Mowgli. Grendel. The gun. Even so, his eyes are locked onto Livia and Thomas. The former has fallen to her knees by Lady Naylor's side; is untangling her mother's face from the mass of undone hair and soon finds her hands bloodied. As for the latter: for a moment Charlie thinks that it is fear that drives Thomas to such haste. He killed Julius earlier that night; broke him, not one breath rising out of the wreckage of his body. And yet *he* rose, a dark Christ. Who is to say he will not rise again; jerk up and scuttle off into the dark? But then Charlie sees Thomas tug at Julius, pull his emaciated arms halfway through the bars. Thomas is not checking for movement. He is trying to shake Julius awake. *Let him rise*, his action seems to be saying. *Let him scuttle*. It would acquit Thomas of something at least.

And on Charlie walks, steadily, mechanically, as though in a dream. He passes Livia; sees that Lady Naylor is alive, sees her daughter trying to revive her first with words then with frightened little slaps, to the good cheek, the other mangled by lacerations and welts. Livia's eyes plead for his help but Charlie has a more urgent destination. Here, near the table, the ground is covered in glass shards. They crunch at his every step. He reaches the table, the gun; pockets it and feels some tension fall from him. Next to it a beaker of blood rests calmly on the table; two steps away, Grendel is rocking his charge, fingers spread along Mowgli's back. From this angle, it looks as though two heads are rising from his trunk, one old and kindly, the other childish, mottled by fever but mirroring the other in its boundless calm. It is this calm that thrusts the Smoke back into Charlie's lungs and colours his breath with the plume of disgust.

'You shot him,' he says needlessly, the words drifting over to Grendel and the boy in a sulphur haze and moving through them without a ripple. 'We argued about it once. Whether it is possible to kill a man righteously, without Smoke.' Then Charlie adds, quietly, angrily: 'I did not think then that it would be so horrible.'

But when Grendel turns to look at Charlie, the angel's face is as placid as ever, untouched by doubt or self-reproach.

'Hush now,' he says. 'You will frighten the child.'

Charlie looks at him and cannot bear it. He turns away, back to his friends. For a second there is a sort of lull. Everything that has urged them here is resolved. The boy is alive, Grendel disarmed, Sebastian's plot defeated. Their triumph is mocked by a sound, a quiet mewing. It takes Charlie some moments to realise it issues from Lady Naylor; to interpret it as the sound of acute distress.

Φ

'What's wrong with her? Is she shot?'

'I don't think so.'

'And the blood?'

'Cuts on her face and arms. The gun hit the bottle, I think. The big bottle of Soot standing on the table. There is a cut near her left eye, but it isn't very deep.'

'Then why is she like this?'

In truth Lady Naylor is irrational with pain. She is lying on her belly and is crawling through the shard-spiked mud of the floor. Initially Charlie thinks she is heading towards her son; that it is his death that has deranged her so. But her gaze never strays to where Thomas continues to minister to the dead. It is riveted instead on the ground, her hands picking up glass shards and clawing at little pools of Soot. The left side of her face hangs in shreds, a flap of skin literally cut loose above the cheekbone and bleeding freely, the rest swelling fast. Charlie steps over to her, arrests the movement of her arms by taking hold of her wrists.

'Are you injured?'

'All lost,' she whispers in response. Her lips are pale, the same colour as her teeth. It makes it hard for Charlie to concentrate on her words. 'Scattered. No good. We barely had enough as it was.'

Charlie ignores her words, tries to pull her up, hears her emit a yelp of intense pain. He lowers her down again, lies her on her back, her head in his lap.

'Your leg?' he asks, studying the focused stillness of her limbs. 'Were you shot in the leg?'

Lady Naylor shakes her head. 'Got a fright. Slipped. Broken hip. Or maybe the femur.'

Charlie nods, points behind himself. 'It was Headmaster Trout and his man. Julius was with them. Your son is dead, Lady Naylor. I am very sorry.'

She does not appear to have heard, starts shivering, then mumbling to herself.

'All lost,' she says again. 'An imperial gallon! But Julius stole half. Half! Barely enough. Now scattered, useless; lost, lost, lost.'

Charlie looks down at her, trying to make sense of her gibberish. Livia kneels by his side and transfers the weight of Lady Naylor's head to her own lap. She has fetched the bottle and glass that have survived unscathed on their perch by the armchair and has poured out a measure of port. Her mother drinks the sugary liquid in greedy little sips, while Charlie disentangles himself, stands up, and studies the table and room, alive to a new thought.

Φ

The bullet must have hit the bottle right at the centre. Or perhaps it was buckshot rather than a bullet, a dozen lead pellets ripping into its thick glass. All that remains of it atop the table is the sphere of its base, finger-thick. Around it, the tablecloth is filthy with Soot, but much must have flown beyond it, in a spray of deepest black, and has been absorbed into the spongy, muck-slick ground. Beyond the table, the pellets have peppered a large metal box from whose innards emerges the cable that feeds the lamps above. Other than that the table is virtually undisturbed, especially at its far end, where stands the chair into which Mowgli was strapped. A tin bucket with clear water sits next to this chair, a wet flannel folded over its rim. It must have been used to manage the child's fever. Still wrestling with his thought, Charlie picks up this bucket, offers Livia the flannel, then pours the water carelessly onto the ground before walking to the side of the filtration pool closest to them.

The pool is filled to within inches of its rim. Scooping up a bucketful proves easy. Frustrated by the flickering light, Charlie carries it to the glow of Trout's gas lamp that shines from beyond the iron bars; has to wrestle with nausea before plunging his hand into its darkness; feels the particles of Soot, like silt suspended in a murky pond; scoops up a palmful and studies it. A shadow leans over him, Thomas bending to see what he has found. Soot quivers in the up-turned cup of Charlie's hand. It is very dark.

But it is not black.

They exchange a glance: of confusion on Charlie's side; of mournful anger on Thomas's.

Next Charlie knows, Thomas has turned his back on him and is marching to the prone figure of Lady Naylor.

Charlie follows hard on his heels.

Φ

Charlie has watched Thomas take on many roles the past few days. First bloodhound, relentless in his search for clues; then martyr and demon, descending into the darkness of his being; repentant killer, suspended between self-hatred and apathy. Now Thomas turns inquisitor. He has rediscovered the sharp edge of his anger, or perhaps just turned it outward, like a knife he's found stuck between his ribs. He walks it to the table first, this anger; collects the little beaker of blood, crouches down before Lady Naylor. Livia has thrown back her mother's skirts, exposing the undergarments. Lady Naylor's leg, beneath her hose, is so swollen it looks like a football has been strapped to her outer thigh. Neither Charlie nor Thomas looks away as Livia continues her examination. Thomas bends over milady, trying to see into her face, then gestures to Charlie to prop her up, no matter what pain it may cause her. She is pale and conscious; the right side of her face handsome, the left risen like dough. Thomas holds the beaker to the eye that has not swollen shut.

'Mowgli's blood,' he begins. 'Fifty to eighty hours into infection. Sebastian told Livia it took two thousand two hundred cubic centimetres. Four pints or thereabouts. But this is less than half a glass.'

Lady Naylor watches him and almost smiles: ashen gums, one corner of her mouth tucked deep into the swelling.

'Fifty millimetres. Five thimblefuls.' A cough that stands in for a laugh. 'Did you think I was a vampire, Thomas?'

'We thought you devoid of scruples, milady.'

She accepts this, closes her good eye, opens it again with a flash of pride. 'It is true. I have none.'

'Two thousand two hundred cubic centimetres,' Thomas continues, unmoved. 'Livia misunderstood. Sebastian meant Soot not blood. And you have been crying over a bottle. Your son is dead and you are mourning dirt. Worse than dirt: bygone murders, harvested with the scrape of your razor. In the armpits. Under the tongue.' Thomas gags, spits a pearl of phlegm onto the ground, watches it steam as though the floor is a griddle. 'What's so special about that Soot, Lady Naylor? You built a whole sewer system to gather vice. You must have a hundred thousand gallons right there.'

When Lady Naylor, shaken by a spasm of pain, does not answer at once, Charlie does so for her, looking down at the murky mess he scooped out of the pool.

'The Soot in the sewers is not dark enough. Even now that it is filtered! For whatever it is you are planning, only murderers' Soot will do.'

Lady Naylor shivers, masters herself. 'Not just murderers' Soot, Charlie. It's much purer than that: the darkest passions of the heart, with all humanity removed. I had to pick through my harvests grain by grain. Not ten per cent was usable. It's the blackest Soot ever assembled. In bulk it becomes liquid.'

Charlie watches Thomas reel at this, form fists. 'You gathered an imperial gallon. You said that just now. But the bottle was not much more than half that. Julius took the rest?'

She nods, holds Thomas's gaze. It is his turn to shiver.

'It explains what he has become. And I.'

Thomas says it and sighs, his anger exhausted, leaving him younger and tired. It's Charlie who presses on.

'I still don't understand, Lady Naylor. Why? What were you planning? Why build these pools? None of it makes sense.'

She slumps, seems to drift into her pain, then jerks out of it with sudden animation.

'I can show you, Charlie. Give me Mowgli's blood. Just a drop. You will see for yourself.'

Φ

It's a trick. It must be, for Lady Naylor is evil, wants to drown the world in bloody revolution.

Or is she? Looking at her – pale, beat-up, courageous – Charlie finds it hard to believe that her ambitions were so crude, and so prosaic. That, and there is the matter of her sadness. 'I have already failed,' she keeps saying into their hesitation. 'Nothing can change that. So please. One drop. I just want to see.'

They look to one another, Thomas, Charlie and Livia, weighing their distrust. At long last Livia takes the beaker out of Thomas's hand. She turns to her mother, her face savage.

'Tell me what to do,' she whispers. And: 'Don't you dare lie to me, Mother. Not this time.'

Lady Naylor nods, revived by expectation.

'The bucket first,' she instructs her daughter. 'Just one drop.'

'I know what will happen. Sebastian showed me.'

All the same Livia kneels down next to the bucket, unstoppers the glass, and cautiously pours a single drop over its lip. It drops from sight, into the dark of the bucket. The next moment Livia scrambles away. They wait, one breath, two breaths, five.

Nothing happens.

'Soot is slow to quicken. The lighter it is, the harder it is. Sebastian filtered it, the city's vice, the darkest Soot here, getting lighter pool by pool. Decades upon decades of London's anger and plight. If we carried down the vats of solvent from the factory above we might be able to quicken some fraction of it. But with Mowgli's blood, it takes a purer sort of Soot to initiate the reaction.'

Lady Naylor tries to sit up, winces, points at an ink-black stain three feet from her hip, still clinging to a shard of glass like honey to a spoon. It is so very dark it looks like a hole cut in the ground.

'Now try it there, Livia. Please.'

Again Livia stares at her with great ferocity; again she finds herself compelled by curiosity to walk to the smear and tilt the beaker. Charlie walks over with her, steadies her hand.

'I need to know,' Livia says as though in apology, 'what she was up to. Whether she is telling the truth.'

Charlie nods, catches Thomas's eye, watches the drop fall into the Soot as though into a void.

What happens next is hard to make sense of. Livia tried describing it to them, but it is one thing to hear of a firework and quite another to see it. For a moment all is still. Then the Soot ignites in a plume of vile black. They recoil, watch it spread like a miniature bushfire, setting alight minuscule deposits of Soot long grown into the ground: threads of Smoke scurrying like beetles across the floor, no longer just black but many hued; clambering up the legs of the table, diving into the gaps between the worn brick; jumping into the bucket to raise a rainbow-coloured flag of Smoke. Here and there other droplets of pure Soot ignite, each setting off chain reactions of their own, volatile, then dead within a yard. They stand amongst this crazed resurrection, imbibing its flavours, soon answering with their own native Smokes, joy, anger, fear and pangs of desire tangling them up within their webs. It is like a hushed conversation conducted by their bodies: shameless, honest, intimate, bypassing both brains and tongues. It is a conversation not free of anger and want; but also rich, immediate, generous: a brazen sharing of the self. In the midst of all this, unmoved, unmovable, stands Grendel, comforting the child strapped to his chest. Never before has Charlie been struck by his isolation as much as now. For just a moment, still smoking, he pities the man with all his heart.

Φ

It takes several minutes for the last of the Smoke to die down. Two or three times they think it dead, when a step from them a new plume – pink, yellow, brown – rises and sets off another network of threads. The Smoke runs out of energy, subsides, then jumps back to life ten inches hither; makes a half-yard's gain only to burn itself out. In the end all Smoke is gone, and Soot rains down on them under the flickering light of the bulbs. When Charlie turns to Lady Naylor he sees that she is crying.

'There,' she says. 'The end of our dreams. It took me three years to collect that Soot; many months to refine it. Mowgli's blood will soon lose its properties. If we had been able to access my lab, we could have preserved it in its present state. But here – we don't have the tools. We could find another child, I suppose, another innocent. But there may be none left.' She speaks to Charlie then, who is standing closest and has bent to listen; speaks confidentially and sadly, eloquent in her defeat. 'So it will be your father's world, Charlie, or else Renfrew's. Either the smug hypocrisy of the rich or the pitiless straitjacket of self-surveillance. Which one will you choose?'

But Charlie only looks at her blankly.

'What dream exactly, Lady Naylor? What in the hell have you been cooking up down here?'

Φ

But in truth Charlie already knows, or at any rate he has guessed it. He looks to Livia as he begins putting it in words; looks to Thomas, each of them chewing the same thought.

'Most Soot is slow to quicken. It's like wet fire logs, impossible to light. Only dark Soot will catch. So you collected the darkest Soot that you could find. A full gallon of it, just to be safe.' He gestures to where the bottle of Soot stood on the table, waits until he has registered Lady Naylor's nod of confirmation. 'But the point is not merely to quicken black Soot. It's to change it, make it volatile.

406

That's where Mowgli's blood comes in. It does something special, something the stuff used in cigarettes does not do. It starts a chain reaction. The Quickening spreading like ripples around a dropped pebble. Self-perpetuating, on and on: the Soot in the bottle acting as *kindling*, setting alight the Soot in the darkest pool, which in turn will set alight the pool further down, and on and on, until even the weakest Soot has caught and carries the spark. But where will it go, all the Smoke in this chamber? There are no chimneys after all, nothing to connect it to the city.' He pauses, pictures again the map Thomas drew, the intricate web of lines, all connected, all leading in one final direction. 'It's not just a filtration system, is it, Lady Naylor? It's a fuse! The pools lead back to the sewers. And the sewers lead back to the river.' Charlie swallows, thinks it through. 'So the Thames would have caught; it is filthy with Soot. As are its tributaries; the groundwater and wells. Perhaps the ocean itself would have started smoking.'

'Black rain,' whispers Livia into his sudden silence. 'Sebastian said he's been dreaming of black rain. It's monstrous, Mother.'

Lady Naylor stares back at her daughter and refuses to hang her head in shame.

Φ

It's Thomas who picks up the thread. A practical mind, his. He is not interested in fuses and chain reactions; the physics of Smoke. He wants to know what it would have done to the world. And to himself.

'An age of darkness, then, Lady Naylor. Britain drowning in self-perpetuating Smoke. Chaos; murder; villainy. I should have done well in this world, only I would have grown skinny like your son over there, too mad to remember eating. Perhaps there will be many of us, stumbling about, muttering gibberish, violence in our wakes. The Last Judgement, eh?' He stops, squats in front of Lady Naylor, stares into her disfigured face. 'You must be very disappointed with the world to punish it thus.'

But milady simply shakes her head. 'It wouldn't have to be like that, Thomas. You misunderstand Smoke. No monsters. Just a people receiving passion, in all its many shades. A month of carnivals. The death of Discipline. The reinvention of God.'

Thomas scoffs, looks at the darkness of the pools behind him.

'No monsters? Not even one?'

Lady Naylor does something unexpected then. She cups Thomas's face in the palm of her hand. He winces but does not recoil.

'Don't live your life afraid of yourself, Thomas. You are a fine boy.'

'A fine boy? I killed your son, Lady Naylor. With my bare hands! Oh, he rose again, but I killed him all the same.' He swallows, shakes off her hand, straightens. 'You don't understand evil, milady. It runs in certain families. My father—'

Now it is her time to scoff. 'Oh, enough! Sons and their fathers. How silly it all is! Forget your father. What was he? An irritable drunk. It's your mother you take after. How little you think of her. She was one of us. A nonconformist. If not for her cancer she would have been standing here, giving me a hand.'

Φ

They make preparations to leave. There is nothing else to be done. Lady Naylor is bleeding on the inside, her leg swelling to grotesque proportions, and a temperature now colouring her cheeks. It gives her an odd liveliness, both prophetic and diseased. Charlie casts around for something they can use as a stretcher, but the tabletop proves too heavy to lift and the chair too awkward. In the end he turns to Grendel, crooked-necked Grendel, Mowgli's chin half buried in that crook. From the side, watching his little arms slung around Grendel's shoulders, it looks like the boy is comforting him. But Grendel, Charlie reminds himself, requires no comfort: all this while he has been watching, impassive, untouched by events, like a butler awaiting orders. Now that Charlie waves to him, he rushes over without hesitation. Charlie has trouble looking at him, has noticed that Livia shares his revulsion, while Thomas stares at him with open disgust. Charlie keeps his eyes on the boy instead, but finds him illegible, beyond his understanding: a scrunched-up face, ugly and sallow, softening only for the stunted man who wishes to be his father. When Charlie finally speaks, he finds himself addressing the floor.

'We need your help, Grendel. Lady Naylor needs a doctor. We must carry her. Thomas has hurt his shoulder and we cannot lift her without help.' But before Grendel can respond or even nod, Charlie carries on, incoherently and haltingly, moved by his horror of this man. 'I don't understand it, Grendel. Why did you help her? Was it

408

to win custody over a child you don't know how to love? Or did she sell you her dream of a future that you cannot hope to share?'

Grendel considers this, his crooked neck tilting further, his hand stroking the child's back, gently and mechanically.

'I have a strange fate, Mr Cooper. I stand apart. All my life I have wondered why. She told me there was a purpose in it, a way of giving it meaning.' He dares a shy smile. 'It was naughty, wasn't it, Mr Cooper? Almost a sin.'

'Naughty?' Charlie echoes, no longer speaking to him but only to himself, picking through thoughts that, in tangled ways, connect Grendel to his father. 'So that's what it was. An angel playing at vice. But really you are on Renfrew's side. The side of reason. He too would have shot Julius. And the other side? The other side would have bought off the witnesses and hushed up his crime.'

Grendel nods, uncomprehending, walks past him, adjusts the boy to ride on his back, and crouches down to gather Lady Naylor in his arms.

Φ

Livia intervenes, won't let him, is in no rush to release her mother from her pain. Instead she kneels, interposing her body between Grendel's and Lady Naylor's, daring him to interfere. Her hands take hold of her mother, not from solicitude, Charlie thinks, but to make sure of her attention.

'Before we go,' she begins, 'while we are still in this cave of your dreams: explain it to me, Mother. "A month of carnivals". "The re-invention of God". Pardon me, Mother, but it's gibberish. Explain it to me, your vision. You won't have another chance.' A twist of Smoke darts from her breath as she speaks. Charlie stands close enough to take it into his blood. All at once it is clear what she is asking. Livia wants to know whether it is possible to forgive her mother; whether there are grounds for appeal. Charlie imagines a similar situation: his asking his father for an accounting. But he would merely frown and send Charlie to his room.

Not so Lady Naylor. She answers willingly, eagerly even, buoyed by her rising fever. It is as though she is speaking at her own tribunal, or on the executioner's platform; as though the words are long prepared, different versions of the same speech, pouring out now all at once.

'The Smoke was never a problem,' she begins, haltingly yet, waiting for Charlie to fill her glass with wine. 'It is simply who we are. What connects us, a thousand subtle threads of want and need. But for centuries now, we have been living a lie. The whole world has been living it, but we most especially, here on our little island, where we have made a devil of our Smoke. It shapes us, this lie: our relations, woman to woman, man to man; orders our polity; divorces us from any possibility of change.

'Power,' whispers Lady Naylor, 'is underwritten by morality. Those who rule, rule because they are better people than their subjects. It's written on our linen. It cannot be denied. Oh, you will say that it's because we have sweets. That we are faking our virtue. But the lie goes deeper than that. We spend a lifetime training ourselves against Smoke. We go to school, are punished, learn to watch our words, our actions, our very thoughts. It turns us into nuns. Miserable, cold-blooded nuns. Trapped in our Discipline; capable of meanness, of judgement, of greed. But not of love.

'As for the "people", those we presume to rule because of the commonness of their sins, they are in awe of us. Oh, of course they make jokes about our manners, our fussiness, our mincing ways. There may even be small pockets of resistance. But who can watch the Smoke and deny it; see one person clean and the other mired in their messy desires; one regal and enjoying God's good favour, rewarded for his goodness by his power and his wealth, and the other toiling and miserable, underfed, poor, his very skin scorched by diseases of bad hygiene – who can see all this and not feel the superiority of one and the inferiority of the other? It is as though two races walk our land, one blessed, the other cursed.

'And so it has served us to perjure Smoke, misrepresent it. Cigarettes and sweets, vice and virtue, black and white: what a crude vision of our lives! And yet, how powerful it has proven, how deeply it has grown into our souls so that we routinely reject what we apprehend with our senses, and defend our crude fiction even against our own interests if need be.

'No, our problem is not Smoke, it's what we have grown to believe it means. We need to remake our sense of good and evil; learn to apprehend Smoke anew. But how? We need a sign. From the land itself. From the very heavens! A storm; a cauterising fire. Sweeping away the high and mighty; curing us of our self-told lies. We dreamed of a world where people would argue and make love without fearing they are making God mad.

'Oh, it would have burnt out soon enough. A few weeks, a month or two at most. Enough for a new beginning. Tabula rasa. A second childhood for mankind. We grew up stunted the first time around.

'So again, Thomas: no monsters. We did not plan to release the black of cigarettes, that manufactured vice scraped off prison cells and the bodies of the mad. It's a Puritan's version of sin. My bottle, the pools here, they were to be mere "kindling", as Charlie put it so well: a spark that flares out the moment it has ignited the real flame. Out in the world, Soot lies weak, human, dormant. It lies in the water and the soil, in every brick that's ever been baked. We wished to free it, quicken it; allow it to fill the air, communicate. Let men know one another. We wanted to fight the lie that we are filthy creatures; that all loss of control leads to murder, all passion to rape. *Passion*: flexible, complex, ever-changing passion, not dividing but uniting the land.

'For what after all is Smoke? Yearning. Courage. Anger. The type of fear that coils itself into a fist. Defiance. Triumph. Hope. It's the animal part of us that will not serve. That won't do the homework. That won't take orders. I dreamed of a world where people will not serve.

'Tell me, Livia, tell me honestly. Was it not a beautiful dream?'

It takes Livia some moments to answer. Her face is very dark. It is as though she has caught her mother's fever.

'You wanted to make a world where nobody turns the other cheek,' she says at last.

'Perhaps, my child. But who does it serve, all this cheek-turning of yours, who counts its profits? And after all, perhaps some would turn the cheek all the same. There is love in Smoke. And none in Discipline. I had hoped you would have discovered this by now.'

Φ

Thomas listens, grim in his scepticism; Charlie thoughtfully, stirred despite himself. As for Livia, she is not content with the answer, seems suspicious of its very eloquence, the facility with which it leaves her mother's lips. Again Grendel stoops to gather Lady Naylor in his arms, again Livia intervenes, stops him, watches him cringe before her angry gaze.

'I don't believe you, Mother. I want to, you see, but it just doesn't fit. You talk of change and a new Eden. But I know you too well. Deep down, you don't give a fig about revolution, or power, and about the common people least of all. Then why, Mother, why? Just because Father went mad? You will remake the world because he took Discipline too far?'

Her mother winces, looks up, cold fury in her one good eye.

'You were too young to see it, Livia. How he changed. A happy, healthy man. Fond of his food.' She coughs, swallows. 'He forbade the cook to put any salt in his food, lest it warmed his thoughts. He wouldn't sleep, because the Smoke might come in his dreams. He even grew afraid to laugh. And he stopped coming to my bed.' She pauses, her tongue chasing for spit. 'He cut me, Livia! Cut me open. Me, the woman he loved. And he did not smoke. Do you want to live in a world such as that?'

Livia looks at her mother with an expression that fuses disparate emotions.

Incredulity.

Terror.

Pride.

Her mother studies it calmly.

'I can see that you don't understand,' she whispers. 'You have never really been in love.'

Φ

For a third time Grendel stoops to gather her; for a third time Livia interposes her body and pushes him out the way.

'Say it was noble,' she mutters. 'Your revolution. Your dream. It does not justify it, Mother. The things you did to Mowgli. And to others. Sebastian told me about Lilith. It was wrong, Mother. Reprehensible.'

Her mother shivers, holds Livia's gaze.

'I know, my dear. But I did it anyway.'

Livia nods, bends forward suddenly, as though afraid her courage will leave her, kisses her mother full on her mouth. Smoke comes pouring out of her, Smoke of grief, of love. And slowly, painfully, something in her mother answers, a Smoke strangely damaged and shy, like a widow long shut out from the ways of the living, daring a peek past her front door. It lasts a minute, maybe two. When it ends, Lady Naylor is in tears.

412

'Thank you, my dear.'

'I cannot forgive you, Mother.'

'I know. I read it in your Smoke.'

Livia lets go of her mother.

A moment later Grendel has carried her away.

Φ

They watch him take the lead, Mowgli on his back, Lady Naylor cradled to his front, a three-headed beast, lumbering across the uneven floor. They should help him, perhaps, but for once Charlie fails to summon his good nature, is sunk in thought. All the same he starts to follow, Thomas by his side. It's Livia who holds them back; places a hand on each of their shoulders and arrests them in their steps. They watch Grendel go, never once stumbling under the weight. At the hall's far end, by the entrance to the sewers, Grendel turns and sees they are not coming. He does not call to them and they offer no explanation; and within a heartbeat he has turned again and continued on his way.

When Grendel is out of sight, Livia takes both boys' hands and walks over to where Julius's body hangs entangled within iron bars.

Grendel

I get her home, first carrying her by myself as far as I can manage, then hiring a man to help. I pay him with the money she thrust at me that very night, for services rendered. We are in luck: he is a kindly man, if drunk, and once he sees that she's injured he carries her gently. Me the head, him the feet, trying not to dunk her bottom in the dirt. Throughout milady is faint, mutters to herself, not always in English. Mowgli watches her from over my shoulder; from the corner of my eye I can see his frown.

I dismiss my helper on a street corner not far from the house. The staircase is hard work, the door bolted. Berta opens only when I call her by name. I ask her where her bruises come from, and the blood that stains her sleeves, but when she sees my load, the surgeon's daughter takes over and she becomes deaf to all questions.

'Put her in bed,' she commands. 'Mowgli too, he has a fever.' Then: 'Bring water.'

In the kitchen a dog lies dead, dragged into one corner. Its hind legs are strapped to a cart. Its skull appears crushed. I call out, but again Berta ignores me; she rushes between her patients, barks at me to boil more water, to find a clean cloth and cut it into strips.

It keeps my hands busy and my mind free. I watch as Berta applies a cold flannel to Mowgli's head and sings to calm him; then crouches over Lady Naylor and cleans up her face. She sends me out when it comes to undressing her and examining her hip. Lady Naylor is conscious, watching me retreat across the length of the room.

I stand outside and weigh that look.

Why exactly did I do it? Agree to help her when she asked? When I knocked on her door late that night I came only to plead for Mowgli. Berta had sent me. We thought he might be as I am, blighted, incapable of Smoke. I explained my condition and watched milady start in shock and recognition. She gave me more that night than the promise of a child. 'I have use for you,' she said. 'You cannot smoke.

But you can be Smoke's shepherd.' She did not pressure or cajole; did not see fit to explain her thoughts or confide the details of her plans. A noblewoman talking to a commoner: she never pretended we were equals. But she shook my hand when I left, long-fingered and firm. It was then I knew I would assist her.

Can a man such as I be seduced by a courtesy?

And so I lied to Livia. It made sense, ensured that she and the boys were safe from reproach. The lie came easily. What frightened me was how small was my capacity for shame.

Φ

Berta emerges. She is shaking her head.

'It's the top of her thighbone. I cannot set it. She needs a surgeon. If it infects—'

'There is a dog in the kitchen.'

'It went mad,' she answers, obscurely, as though that explains its presence. 'I smoked and it went mad. Angry, snapping at me. But it was sad too. A mad dog with a broken heart.' She grimaces, shudders. 'It seemed a mercy, Tobias.'

'I will get rid of it.'

'Leave it by the street corner. Someone will take it for its meat. It's January. A hungry month.'

When I return, I look in on Lady Naylor. She remains awake, tucked under sheet and blanket, her dress draped over the backboard flaring its skirts.

Her eyes are wet with tears.

'My son is dead,' she whispers when I draw closer. 'But my daughter loves me.'

I watch a shiver ripple through her frame, bend down to her mangled, bandaged face.

'Your Smoke,' I tell her. 'When you said goodbye to your daughter. It looked different.' I search for the right word, cannot find it. 'Weak. Thin. Reluctant.'

She nods, pulls away the blanket and displays her naked flank without shame. The scar is an ugly thing, rises mottled from her skin.

'He damaged me. When he cut me. I am almost as broken as you.

'It would be best if we both were dead,' she carries on. 'We will give people ideas. Renfrew's ilk.'

415

Then Berta is there, walks over to the bed and pulls the blanket back to cover her.

'You go on, die,' she tells Lady Naylor. 'My son needs a father.'

Φ

We spend the rest of the night at Mowgli's bedside. The boy drifts in and out of sleep. His face is serious. At times he cries with some internal pain, quietly, not wiping the tears. I do it for him. He does not flinch at my touch.

In the periods when he sleeps, Berta and I talk. I try to describe to her what happened. Berta is not interested.

'I shot a man today,' I tell her. 'I shot milady's son.'

'What does it matter now? It's over and done with. Mowgli's here.'

'Miss Livia called me a monster. And then she would not look at me, not once.'

'She is young,' Berta says. 'She has a narrow view of life.'

I nod, unconvinced.

'It'll be dawn soon. We should get some sleep.'

But we stay. Mowgli wakes when light starts filling the room. His temperature is down, he is alert. Berta bends to him slowly, afraid she will startle him. His arm comes up, cautiously, his little hand grabbing at her face, her nose. It withdraws and displays between his index and middle fingers the little wedge of his thumb. Berta raises her hand to her face as though looking for her nose; mimes finding nothing there, only a blank; stares in mock terror at the boy's raised-up thumb. He does something miraculous then. He giggles. And grabs for her nose once again.

Emotion pours out of Berta. It pours out as a sob, as pale, hazy Smoke. The child sees the Smoke, waves at it, finds he can dance shapes into it with the movement of his fingers.

And I?

I sit there abject, smiling, yearning to feel as they do; contented and removed.

Baptism

'He looks like a statue.'

'Like a saint. At prayer. Only, you know. Crucified.'

'And evil.'

But even as Charlie says it he realises it is not true. Julius is kneeling, arms out, his mangled face drooping halfway through the bars. It isn't just that Thomas's fists have cut loose his features. The Soot has come off where his temples and ears have slipped through the bars, along with something more substantial than skin. Livia is right then. Julius looks like a saint: whittled from a block of charcoal, or black burnt wood. Brittle to the touch.

Not that they have touched him yet. They are in awe of his death. He looks impossibly thin; the hands ready to snap off at the wrists, the shoulders sharp and angular. Only his stomach is oddly distended, half spherical, as though ready to burst with undigested Soot. Charlie watches Livia study him. She lifts her hand once, as though to rearrange him, then lets it drop again.

'He could have stepped through,' she says at last. 'If his head fits, the rest would have, too. I wonder whether he realised.'

She frowns, steps forward suddenly, and takes hold of one arm and shoulder. A shifting of the weight, a twist, and Julius's right shoulder and chest slide through the bars; the arm splayed out ahead of him, hand spread, the skin oddly white underneath the fingernails. His movement leaves a trail of tar along the iron of the bar.

They crouch down to him, Charlie and Livia. Thomas is behind them, a shadow watching from afar. Charlie wonders whether Livia wants to transport and bury her half-brother; wonders, too, at the two other men lying beyond the barrier, out of reach. What she does, however, is unbutton Julius's shirt. Charcoal skin, flaking off him; Soot and flesh fused. Charlie watches her touch Julius's chest, recoil; pokes his own finger at the ribs, and feels it sink in to the knuckle.

'It's like he is made of sin,' she mutters. Then: 'You would have thought Mother would have noticed it. But she wouldn't look at him.

417

And she was in pain, in shock. It's funny, I suppose. Crying over her failure. The means to reverse it a dozen steps behind her back.'

All at once, Charlie knows what she is thinking. It sends a shiver through him, gut-deep, of fear, of excitement; the burden of choice.

Revolution.

What young man has never dreamed of being its cause?

Φ

Charlie stands, breathes. What is happening within him cannot be called thought. It has no words, for one thing, and knows no maths; does not calculate, but is simply the slow ascent of a decision already made, up from his centre to that sluggish organ that is his brain. He does not know how long it takes. His mouth, he notices, is full of Smoke.

Then he acts. Bends down to Julius, takes hold of his armpits, feels the brittle flesh move under his grip. Twists and pulls, trying to line up the shoulders, then the stomach and hips; that potbelly sticking, like a wine bladder pert with mud. Livia does not help him with his labour. Neither does Thomas; stands watching behind. Only when Julius's thighs (emaciated; sticks of bone and black, the trousers torn beneath both knees) come sliding through, does Thomas step close. He pulls Charlie out of his crouch, looks him hard in the eye.

'What are you doing with him, Charlie?'

'You know what.'

Thomas stares at him, sniffs his breath.

'It's catching then,' he decides. 'You said it to Grendel. "An angel playing at vice." Charlie Cooper is going to change the world.' Thomas puckers his lips as though to spit, swallows it instead. 'Are you going to scrape it off him, or just sink him in the pool?'

And Charlie stands there, listening to him, already connected to Thomas by fine tendrils of Smoke, chest to chest and hip to hip, his blood alive to a single truth. *This is it, our duel. Who would have thought it would be like this? Me, kind, goodly Mr Cooper, standing here, lighting the fuse. And he, the dark one, standing in my way. In another moment we will go at each other with our fists.*

A duel.

Or else Livia will decide.

'You are afraid,' Charlie taunts Thomas. 'We can make a difference,

418

and you are shaking in your boots. I can smell it in your every breath.'

They are standing close now, have stepped into each other's heat and exhalations, too close even to throw a punch.

'Tell him, Livia,' Thomas says without turning. 'Tell him it is dangerous; madness. He *loves* you. He will listen to you.'

They both start when she closes the gap and puts a hand on each of their arms.

Φ

Oh, how well she understands them both. Everything is written in their Smoke.

Their friendship is in there. Charlie's doubt and Thomas's secret longing for the Smoke. She is there, too, flesh and blood, the things each wants to do with her; their focused wonder at that body beneath her dress. It is as though they have all shed their clothes.

'Tell him,' Thomas says again, exhaling the words into Charlie's face.

Then he appears to remember that it was she, Livia, who led them back to Julius's corpse. The thought diminishes him, slumps his shoulders, pulls down his chin.

'You too, then?'

He does not wait for her nod.

'How eager you both are,' he goes on, spiteful now, all alone, 'to dance to milady's tune. She blew you a kiss, Livia, and taunted Charlie about his father. And here you are ready to do her bidding. In the name of the people! Do you think the people want it, the chaos you'll be starting for them here?'

Before Livia can answer, Charlie does.

'*I* want it,' he says, half in anger, half in wonder at himself. 'I need it. Otherwise, Father will . . .' He trails off, catches himself, a hint of amusement lightening his Smoke. 'That's awfully selfish, isn't it?'

Thomas frowns and smokes and walks away.

Φ

He does not go far. Two steps. The no-man's-land between Julius's haggard body and the rim of the closest pool. Livia follows as he must have known she would, until she stands as close as she did before. It's a choreography of sorts: some birds, her mother once told her, dance before they mate. Thomas is calmer away from Charlie, sadder.

419

'We don't know a thing about it, Livia. How long will it last? A few weeks, a month, your mother said, but how can she know? Not rape, she promised, not murder. Everyday sins. A fever of passion. All urges laid bare, all secrets shared.' He grimaces, winces when she takes his hand. 'Even if your mother is right – if her dark fuse burns itself out in the lighting of a gentler fire; if the world does not choke on its store of anger; if we all bare our souls to one another and are not appalled by what we find . . . imagine it, Livia. A whole world letting go of reason. Chaos; confusion. Nobody working the fields.'

'It's winter, Thomas. The fields don't need working.'

'Still. A volatile world. Don't underestimate its darkness. Every argument that draws a knife, every man beaten, every woman forced: it'll all be our fault.'

'Yes. And if we don't: every child sewn into some apparatus; every prisoner made to roll cigarettes; every lie told from dawn till dusk; every year that passes without change or hope. That too will be our fault.

'But it's more than that,' Livia continues. 'She loves me, you see. Mother. She watched me trying to become holy, all the while afraid I would go mad like Father.' She smiles, crooked, tender; a hint of flirtation in her words. 'I'm angry with her. But it's hard to resist love. Don't you think?'

Thomas winces, makes fists.

'Charlie is right,' he says at last. 'I am afraid.' He studies her, fiercely, like an enemy. 'What if I get lost in all the Smoke? What if *I* go mad and turn into a beast?'

She returns his gaze, at a loss how to answer.

Then Charlie is there. He is smoking; repeats her mother's gesture, cups Thomas's face.

'Then we will drink you and go mad together.'

'Will you?' Thomas asks, more out of despair than doubt. 'What ever happened to compromise, Charlie?'

Φ

Julius's body floats gently on the water. Thomas expected it to sink. He was surprisingly heavy to carry, each withered limb a deadweight swinging on its joint. Once they lower him, however, the Soot is as though magnetised by him, dresses and shrouds him, like a sodden sheet, so that the whole pool becomes one with his lean figure. They leave Thomas to fetch the blood. Charlie is sitting on the pool's edge, his hands and feet in the water, holding on to Julius and supporting his head as though it is important that he does not drown. Livia, in turn, has her hands on Charlie's shoulders, to reassure him and help him up, when the time comes. And so Thomas goes to retrieve the blood in its little beaker, swishes it around like wine in a glass. How easy it would be even now to hurl it across the room, let it shatter in a dirty corner; or stumble, fall, as though by accident, and crush it under his weight.

They assemble at the pool's edge. Charlie sitting, Livia hunched, Thomas upright. It would make a good picture, Thomas thinks; the black of the pool, the dull, pulsing light of the lamps overhead. Charlie's expression has changed in the past few minutes. The fierceness is gone; there has been time to think. *He has opened some door inside himself*, it flashes through Thomas, *and doubt has crept in*. Perhaps, then, he will recant. Thomas is surprised to find he is disappointed as well as relieved.

Charlie looks up at him, too honest to mask his doubt.

'We can't have it, can we? Just a little Smoke. Enough to make us human?' He pauses, frowns, corrects himself. 'But that's just it, isn't it? How much is enough?'

He moves his hand through the dun liquid, scoops some up, holds it next to Julius's charcoal cheek. Thomas thinks he understands what troubles Charlie. It is wrong, somehow, that evil should be a question of proportion; that *this* much Smoke should be the weave of life, and *that* much produce murder; and that no Smoke at all should produce a cruelty of a different sort. Charlie has a tidy mind: he must feel there should be more system to life. All at once Thomas wants to comfort the friend he was ready to fight before.

'Two, three weeks during which Smoke takes over the world,' he muses. 'Maybe longer. A carnival of passions. Black rain and all that. Do you think, Charlie, this means we won't have to go back to school?'

Φ

The smoking starts halfway through their giggles. It rises easily, naturally, articulates their tension, their fears, the feeling of standing on a precipice, toes in the void.

We don't know what we are starting.

No. But we do know how things are at present.

And after? When the Quickening has burnt itself out. What will the world be like then?

But it is not like that, the Smoke, it has no use for words. It speaks in images instead, in feelings referencing memories that, recounted later, across a pillow in the dark, will appear both familiar and strange. In this wordless realm these whispers are not *something* yet, are but the possibility of thought; like a joy neither voiced nor performed, shapeless and real. And all the while the Smoke surrounds them, humming their melodies, sneaking its tendrils across the borders of their individual selves.

Thomas's Smoke is the darkest, raw and confused. It sings his fear – of Julius; of becoming like him; of being abandoned for his crimes – and the bliss of self-forgetting. His father is in his Smoke, cradling a pewter mug. Livia, too, her shirt wet and clinging to her chest. Charlie: befriending him on that first day of school. His mother dying; a bullet slamming into his head. A nurse's kiss; a boxing bout; bones breaking under knuckles. Gypsy vagrants fighting, rutting in the dirt. A church floor, littered and noble; a drunken priest. Hope.

Charlie's Smoke is different, more marshalled and orderly, a procession of people sketched in white, tan and grey. There is the woman in the woods, dressed in her shift and smoking as naturally as she is breathing. There are Renfrew and Eleanor, sewn into her harness of leather and steel. Thomas, Livia, flushed and beckoning; bare shoulders entangled under a linen sheet. His parents, stiff-backed, sitting in their ill-begotten house and wondering whatever happened to their son. A room of coachmen, huddled together on the floor against the cold. The tattoo of a mermaid, her bosom blinking with each movement of the coachman's thumb.

And threaded into their Smokes, unpredictable, at turns more controlled and more volatile than either's, is Livia's, in violet and green. Her mother, crying, in front of the cell she had built to make prisoners of little boys and girls. Her father strapped to his attic bed, staring up at her with fearful eyes. Francis the miner walks in, tugging a pony on bandy legs. Grendel, her killer angel, brandishing a snub-nosed gun; Mowgli hiccupping his first billow of Smoke. Thomas, half naked, holding out to her the black of the mask. Charlie, in darkness, tongue to her tongue.

'Yes?' she asks into the Smoke, her eyes closed, a hand on each of the boys.

'Yes,' says Charlie.

'Yes,' says Thomas. He removes the stopper, tilts the beaker, and washes Julius's head in blood. The next moment Charlie pushes Julius's body to the centre of the pool; the Soot shifting with him, his bridal train, his burial shroud.

Then they step back, Livia, Thomas and Charlie.

And run like hell.

Part Six

Cloud

If thou art displeas'd with Lawes Divine, and Civil,
I know not what will fit thee, but the Devil.
— 'The Anabaptists'

Then wonder not at them so black in skin
But at your selves so foul, so black by sin.
— 'The Blackamores'

The liver doth contain unwholesome blood,
And Melancholick, which is never good.
Of this disease if you the Symptomes heed,
The fundamental veins break forth and bleed.
— 'The Hemerrhoides'

Rowland Watkyns, *Flamma Sine Fumo*
(*Smoke Without Flame*, 1662)

Thomas

How do you start a revolution?
  You baptise a corpse.
That's what we will say when they ask us, years down the road. Oh, they will tell us that we did it for the wrong reasons. Charlie because he is ashamed of his privilege, and Livia because she wants to impress her mother. And I because I love them more than I fear myself. And because I could not stomach the thought of returning to school.

Does anyone ever do anything for reasons better than these?

We wait for the Smoke by the banks of the Thames. We are not alone. Crowds have gathered, are staring downriver at the storm front moving in. Others are fleeing the city. They are walking so fast they will be deep in the home counties before nightfall. A steady stream of vagrants, trampling on good folks' lawns. Harbingers of change.

We did not see very much before we left the sewers. No explosions; no fireworks. Something moved in the pools behind us, a shadow spreading in the water. That's all. Out on the street all was quiet; a prisoner singing in the gaol adjoining the tobacco factory, a forlorn tenor, straining against the limits of his range. Charlie asked Livia whether she wanted to go to Grendel's and find out how her mother was, but she only shook her head. Livia wants her mother's love; is worried sick about her leg. But she is angry with her, too. So we kept to the streets.

Dawn came slowly, us walking around, trying to stay warm. Without meaning to, we drew to our church just as the sun came up. The gates remained barred, the windows broken, but the cross on top caught the weak light. Brass. It is a miracle nobody has bothered to steal it.

As dawn turned into morning, we started to get restless.

'Maybe,' Charlie said, 'maybe it did not work.' An odd note to his voice as though he did not know how to feel.

'Maybe.'

By ten o'clock we could see the river start to boil.

It happened very quickly, deep under the surface, a darkness spreading, like a school of black herring hurtling upriver, forswearing the salt of the sea. The speed of a dark thought. On the surface, hovering an inch or two above the water, Smoke formed, shaping a second river, following its bend.

The real change, though, happened far from us. Somewhere there, in the east of London, where the river widens and begins its journey into the sea, something blew up. I have no better way of saying it. A column of Smoke reaching up into the sky, its borders clean, defined near the ground then fraying into a thousand threads and dispersing into the clouds. God only knows what caused it. Perhaps that's where Sebastian engineered the sewers to release the flood. Perhaps Julius drifted there, borne along by strange currents, and only there released the full brunt of his pyre. Or else the Quickening found a repository of Soot so rich as to make Sebastian's pools look like puddles. Spit in the ocean. Out of the cloud, rain is forming. We are too far away to know whether it's black.

Charlie turns to me. At some point during the night he managed to smear Soot over his lip in precisely such a way that it looks like a moustache. It suits him. Soots him. I almost smile. His hands too remain stained from where he pushed Julius under the waterline. The devil, washed of his sins in infected blood.

Charlie was his baptist.

'We should run for the hills,' he says now. 'Get above the cloud level. Wait out the worst of it.'

I know he wants to protect me, that he is worried what might happen to me and my volatile blood. But I shake my head.

'Above the cloud level? In England? No, Charlie, we made a choice. Pandora's box. We opened it. Now we have to brave it out.'

I take his hand again into my aching right one, take Livia's into my left. We have been walking like this most of the morning. A storm is gathering. I may be headed for madness, the world for the abyss.

I have never been happier in my whole life.

Charlie, too, looks happy.

'Do you know what theatre is?' he whispers, not really asking, musing aloud. 'A boy at school told me about it. Grown people acting out a story. Love, revenge, the fall of kings. For more than two hundred years now, it has been banned.' He smiles, almost shyly. 'Do you think there'll be theatre again, after the Smoke?'

And then he goes on, still smiling, but sadder now, thoughtful: 'It won't work, you know. It cannot work. Us three.'

'Why?'

I see him struggle to put it in words.

'We are more than friends. We love one another. And when people love one another, there is Smoke involved. Here –' he raises the hand that joins him to Livia – 'but also here' – he raises the hand that joins him to me. 'Livia can't marry both of us,' he adds shyly then is surprised when she stops him and tells him off.

'Why not, Charlie Cooper? It's a new world. Who can tell us now what we can or cannot do?'

And she kisses him and she kisses me, and a chimney sweep standing next to us in his dirty suit cheers and offers us dusty applause.

The last word goes to me.

'Shall we?' I ask.

Together, hand in hand, we walk into the shadow of the cloud.

We thank the Smoke.

Afterword

Like most texts purporting to be about the past, this is a book about the present. The past is to it both canvas and foil: a shadow-thing that makes thinking about ourselves more interesting, less fettered to good sense. The novel may be political but it has no thesis: novel-writing is interesting to me in so far as it is an open-ended process – a search, a jazz solo – rather than the skilful realisation of a pre-existing blueprint or the rehearsal of a subtly constructed argument. The best relationship of an author to his or her novel, I believe, is that of a reader; for to the reader belongs that greatest act of creation where stories are concerned, the transformation of words and sentences into tentative meaning, forever on the move.

This particular novel found me more than I searched for it. It grew out of a chance encounter with the Dickens quote that opens the book and reconnected me to a childhood feeling of being ambushed by narrative, a feeling both luxurious and urgent. For this I am deeply grateful; and grateful too to those people who encouraged me to surrender to this feeling wholesale (for it takes courage, sometimes, to indulge oneself). These are Simon Lipskar, my agent, who threatened me with violence and perdition were I not to pursue this project; my editors, Bill Thomas, Kirsty Dunseath and Jennifer Lambert, whose insight and kindness enabled me to give the book its final shape; and James Boyd White and Andrew Herbert Merrills, who read early drafts and offered sage advice. My greatest thanks goes to my wife, Chantal, who read each chapter with me hovering in the background pacing to and fro asking, *Are you finished yet*? For your patience as much as your encouragement, my love, I thank you from the bottom of my heart.

ACKNOWLEDGEMENTS

It takes a lot of people to make a book.

Huge thanks to my agent, Zoe Waldie, whose blend of frankness, insight and tenacity is invaluable. I am ever grateful for her shrewd advice and fulsome support.

At Hutchinson, my editor Emma Mitchell has championed this book from the start. She has been a delight to work with, and I have benefited greatly from her keen instinct for the drama of a scene.

I was fortunate to have the talented and unflappable Anna-Sophia Watts as my spirit guide throughout the latter stages. I value her contribution immensely.

Thank you to Jocasta Hamilton, Najma Finlay and the entire Hutchinson and Cornerstone teams for their warm welcome and superb professionalism.

Gifted writer friends—Anne Aylor, Vicky Grut, and Elise Valmorbida—provided detailed comments on various drafts. Their forensic approach made Siren an infinitely better book.

I am grateful to the ZenAzzurri writers past and present—Roger, Anne, Elise, Gavin, Jude, Oana, Richard, Nick, Sally, Aimee, Fra, Steve, Anita, Marg, Susan and many others—for candour, friendship, and Tuesday night critiques. Sincere thanks, also, to Clare, Piya, Sue and Vicky for our indispensable Friday sessions.

The following people made all the difference. Thanks to each one of them: Gillian Stern for a crucial boost at just the right moment; Lexie Hamblin for her energy and enthusiasm throughout the early stages; Julie Stevenson, for her generous encouragement at a rocky time; Rory Meade, for being my plot consultant extraordinaire.

Writers need grit but they also need hope. Those who run the many competitions and journals supporting emerging writers are the hope merchants. Without the precious milestones of publications and prizes, my road would have been a much lonelier one. In particular, thanks to the organizers of the Bridport Prize, who published the 'seed' story for Siren some years back, and to that year's judge, Ali Smith, whose comments made me realize that it wasn't really a story at all but the jumping-off point for a novel.

Writers also need peace and quiet (and food!). I'm grateful for time spent at the Tyrone Guthrie Centre at Annaghmakerrig. Sincere thanks to Robbie, Mary, Lavina, Ingrid and the rest of that wonderful team for everything they do so very well.

I would simply not have the time and space to write, were it not for the support of my family. Biggest thanks of all to my wonderful husband, Mike, and to our lovely sons—Patrick, Conor and Rory—for absolutely everything.

ANNEMARIE NEARY

The Orphans

In 1992 on a Goa beach, eight-year old Jess and her little brother Sparrow are playing at the water's edge when their parents vanish. For hours, the children hold hands and wait for their mother and father to come back. But one sleep goes by, then two, then twenty-two, right until the end of numbers. And nobody came back.

In present-day London Jess has become a mother and a locker of doors, determined to protect the life she has built around her. But her brother Ro has never been able to leave that Goa beach. He has grown unpredictable, obsessive, his life devoted to chasing every spurious sighting of his mother around the world.

When new evidence suggests that their mother might indeed have lived on after Goa, Ro re-enters Jess's life. Convinced that his sister knows more than she claims, he is intent on answers.

And then bad things start to happen.

COMING SOON

Available to pre-order now